Praise for the novels of Debbie Macomber

"Macomber is a skilled storyteller."

—*Publishers Weekly*

"Readers won't be able to get enough of Macomber's gentle storytelling."

—*RT Book Reviews*

"Whether [Debbie Macomber] is writing lighthearted romps or more serious relationship books, her novels are always engaging stories that accurately capture the foibles of real-life men and women with warmth and humor."

—*Milwaukee Journal Sentinel*

"Debbie Macomber tells women's stories in a way no one else does."

—*BookPage*

"Macomber...is no stranger to the *New York Times* bestseller list. She knows how to please her audience."

—*Oregon Statesman Journal*

"Popular romance writer Debbie Macomber has a gift for evoking the emotions that are at the heart of the genre's popularity."

—*Publishers Weekly*

"Debbie Macomber is one of the most reliable, versatile romance writers around."

—*Milwaukee Journal Sentinel*

"Bestselling Macomber...sure has a way of pleasing readers."

—*Booklist*

"No one writes better women's contemporary fiction."

—*RT Book Reviews*

DEBBIE MACOMBER

Navy Brides

mira

mira

ISBN-13: 978-0-7783-3121-6

Navy Brides

Copyright © 2018 by Harlequin Books S.A.

The publisher acknowledges the copyright holder of the individual works as follows:

Navy Wife
Copyright © 2003 by Debbie Macomber

Navy Blues
Copyright © 2003 by Debbie Macomber

Recycling programs for this product may not exist in your area.

For questions and comments about the quality of this book, please contact us at CustomerService@Harlequin.com.

Harlequin.com

Printed in U.S.A.

CONTENTS

NAVY WIFE

One

After walking over to the window in her brother's empty apartment, Lindy Kyle paused and let her tired gaze rest on the view of downtown Seattle. Dusk was settling over the steel jungle, and giant shadows from the skyscrapers fell into the maze of concrete across the picturesque waterfront. In another mood Lindy would have been struck by the intricate beauty of what lay before her, but not now.

Seattle, as Steve had claimed, really was a lovely city. When she'd arrived, she'd been so preoccupied with trying to find the address of the apartment and the appropriate parking space for her Volkswagen Rabbit in the lot behind the building that she hadn't taken the time to notice anything around her.

Now she sighed at the panorama that lay before her. "I'm actually here," she said, mainly to hear herself speak. She'd come to expect a lot from one western city. She felt as an immigrant might have years ago, sailing into New York Harbor, seeking a new way of life and freedom from the shackles of the past. Lindy had been bound, too, in the chains of grief and unhappiness.

Dramatically she posed, pretending to be the Statue of Liberty, her right hand held high as if gripping a lighted torch, her left firmly clasping imaginary stone tablets. "Okay, Seattle, give me your tired, your poor, your huddled masses yearning to breathe free." Lindy sucked in a shaky breath and battled back tears. "Seattle, calm my fears. Clear my head." She dropped her arms and swallowed at the growing knot in her throat. "Heal my heart," she added in a broken whisper. "Please, heal my heart…"

Exhaling raggedly, she dropped her arm and admitted it was too much to expect—even from a place that had once been honored as the most livable city in the United States. Far too much to ask.

Suddenly exhausted, Lindy picked up her suitcase and headed down the narrow hallway toward the two bedrooms. She opened the first door and stood in the doorway examining the room. The closet, which was partly open, displayed an organized row of civilian clothes hanging inside, crisp and neat. A framed picture or two rested on the dresser, but Lindy didn't pay attention to those. This had to be the bedroom of Rush Callaghan, her brother's roommate. Currently both men were at sea serving six-month tours of duty. Steve was an officer aboard the submarine *Atlantis*, somewhere in the Pacific upholding God, country and the American flag. Lindy had no idea where Rush was and didn't particularly care. Men weren't exactly her favorite subject at the moment.

She closed the bedroom door and moved on to the next room. A dresser drawer hung open, mismatched socks draped over its edge. Bulky-knit sweaters were carelessly tossed on the ledge above the closet and shoes were heaped in a pile on the floor.

"Home, sweet home," Lindy said with a soft smile. She really was fond of her brother, and although he was nearly ten years older, her childhood had been marked with memories of his wit and warmth. She laid her suitcase across the unmade bed, opened it and reached for Steve's letter. "Come to Seattle," he'd written in his lazy, uneven scrawl. "Forget the past and make a new life for yourself." Steve had had firsthand experience with pain, Lindy knew, and she respected his judgment. He'd survived the emotional trauma of divorce and seemed to have come out of it with a new maturity.

"You'll know which bedroom is mine," Steve's letter continued. "I can't remember the last time I changed the sheets so you might want to do that before you crash."

Crashing certainly sounded inviting, Lindy mused, sinking with a sigh onto the edge of the unmade bed.

Although she'd nearly memorized Steve's words, Lindy read completely through the letter once more. Clean sheets were in the hall closet, he explained, and she decided to tackle making the bed as soon as she'd unpacked her things. The washer and dryer were in a small laundry room off the kitchen, the letter went on to say.

When she finished reading, Lindy placed Steve's instructions on top of the dresser. She stripped off the sheets, carried the bedding into the laundry room and started the washing machine.

When the phone rang it caught her off guard, and she widened her eyes and placed her hand over her heart as shock waves washed over her.

It rang one more time before she decided to answer it.

"Hello?"

"Lindy, it's your mother."

"Oh, hi, Mom." Lindy smiled at her parents' habit of identifying themselves. She'd been able to recognize her own family's voices since she was a child.

"I take it you've arrived safely. Honey, you should have phoned—your father and I've been worried."

Lindy sighed. "Mom, I just walked in the door not more than ten minutes ago. I was planning to phone after I fixed myself something to eat."

"Did your car give you any problems?"

"None."

"Good." Her mother sounded relieved.

"Everything's fine—just the way I said it would be," Lindy added.

"What about money?"

"Mom, I'm doing great." A slight exaggeration, but Lindy wasn't desperate—at least she wouldn't be if she found a job reasonably soon. The unemployment problem was one she hoped to correct first thing in the morning.

"I talked to your Uncle Henry in Kansas City and he said you should think about applying at Boeing…that airplane company. He claims they're always looking for someone with a degree in computer science."

"I'll do that right away," Lindy answered in an effort to appease her mother.

"You'll let us know when you've found something?"

"Yes, Mom. I promise."

"And don't be shy about asking for money. Your father and I—"

"Mom, please don't worry about me. I'm going to be just great."

Her mother expelled her breath in a long, anxious sigh. "I do worry about you, sweetie. You've been so terribly unhappy. I can't tell you how disappointed your father and I are in that young man of yours."

"Paul isn't mine anymore." Lindy's voice trembled a little, but she needed to say it out loud every now and then just to remind herself of the fact. For four years she'd linked all thoughts of her future with Paul; being without him felt as though a large part of herself was missing.

"I saw his mother the other day, and I'll have you know I took a great deal of pleasure in looking the other way," Grace Kyle continued, with more than a hint of righteous indignation.

"What happened between Paul and me isn't Mrs. Abram's fault."

"No. But she obviously didn't raise her son right—not if he could do something this underhanded and despicable to you."

"Mom, do you mind if we don't talk about Paul anymore? Ever?" Even the mention of his name brought with it a sharp pain, yet part of her was still hungering for news of him. Someday, Lindy vowed, she'd look back on these awful months and smile at the memory. Someday, maybe. But not now.

"Lindy, of course I won't talk about Paul if you don't want me to. I was being insensitive—forgive me, sweetie."

"It's all right, Mom."

A short, throbbing silence followed. "You'll keep in touch, won't you?"

"Yes," Lindy answered and nodded. "I promise."

After a few more minutes of filling her parents in

on the news of her trip, Lindy replaced the receiver. The washing machine went into the spin cycle behind her, and she tossed a glance over her shoulder. That was the way her world felt lately, as if she were being put through a churning wash. The only question that remained to be answered was if she'd come out of this drip-dry and wrinkle free.

Rush Callaghan stood on the bridge of the USS *Mitchell*, a pair of binoculars gripped tightly in his hands. He paused to suck in a deep breath of tangy salt air and sighed his appreciation for the clear, clean scent of it. Being on the open seas stirred his blood back to life after three long months of shore duty. He relaxed, home at last, as the huge 1,092-foot-long aircraft carrier cut a wide path out of Puget Sound and into the dark green waters of the north Pacific. Rush was more than glad. He had recognized from the time he was a boy that his destiny lay on the swirling waters of the world's oceans. He'd been born on the sea and he'd known ever since that this was where he belonged, where he felt truly alive.

Rush had dedicated his life to the sea, and in turn she had become his mistress. She was often demanding and unreasonable, but Rush wouldn't have had it any other way. A gentle breeze carried with it a cool, soothing mist. The spray came at him like the gentle, caressing fingers of a woman riffling through his hair and pressing her body against his own. Rush grinned at the picturesque image, knowing his lover well. She was gently welcoming him back into her arms, but Rush wasn't easily fooled. His mistress was fickle. Another time, possibly soon, she would lash out at him and harshly slap his face with cold, biting wind and rain. Her icy fingers would sting him with outrage. It was little wonder, Rush thought, that he'd come to think of the sea as his lover, since she often played the role.

When the *Mitchell* had pulled out of the Bremerton shipyard eighteen hours earlier, Rush had left nothing to tie him to the shore. No wife, no sweetheart, nothing except a Seattle apartment where he stored his worldly goods. He wasn't looking to build any bridges that would link him to the mainland. He'd learned early in his career that a wife and family weren't meant for him. If the waters of the world were his mistress, then the navy would be his wife. There'd been a time when he'd hoped to divide his life, but no more.

A quick exchange of angry words followed by an outburst of disgust from his fellow officer, Jeff Dwyer, caught Rush's attention and he lowered his binoculars.

"Problems?" he asked when Jeff joined him on the bridge.

Jeff's mouth tightened and he nodded. "The captain's just ordered us back."

"What the hell?" Rush felt a hot surge of anger pulse through him. "Why?"

"There's something wrong with the catapults. Apparently maintenance doesn't have the necessary parts to repair the problem."

Rush swore under his breath. The catapults were used to launch the Hawkeyes, Intruders, Tomcats and other aircraft from the carrier runway. They were vital equipment for any assignment at sea.

Fortunately the squadrons flying in from two navy airfields on the West Coast—a hundred planes were scheduled to rendezvous with the *Mitchell*—had yet to arrive. As chief navigator it was Rush's job to guide the carrier through the waters; now it was up to him to head the *Mitchell* back to the shipyard.

"I've already sent out word to the airfields," Jeff informed him. "They've turned the planes back."

Frustration built up in Rush like a tidal wave. After three months shore duty and a mere eighteen hours at sea they had to bring the *Mitchell* home to port with her tail between her legs.

"How long?" Rush asked between clenched teeth.

"Maintenance doesn't have a figure yet, but if it's as bad as it looks, we could be sitting on our butts for at least a week."

Rush spat a four-letter word.

"My sentiments exactly," Jeff answered.

Rush let himself into the dark apartment and set his seabag just inside the door. The way things were working out he could be here awhile. The realization angered him every time he thought about it. He moved into the kitchen and set the six-pack of cold beer on the counter. He rarely indulged himself this way, but tonight he was in the mood to get good and drunk.

Not bothering to turn on any of the lights, Rush took one chilled aluminum can and carried it with him into the living room, pulling off the tab as he went. Standing in front of the wide picture window, he offered a silent toast to the glittering lights of the waterfront several blocks below. He took a large swig of beer. Tonight something cold and alcoholic suited his temperament.

He took another long drink, sat on the sofa and propped his feet on the coffee table. What he needed was a woman. One sexy as hell, with big breasts and wide hips to bury himself in—one who would relieve his angry frustration. Rush frowned. The crude thought wasn't like him. He rarely allowed his mind to indulge in such primitive fantasies. But tonight, after watching weeks of planning and months of hard work go down the drain, Rush wasn't in the mood for niceties.

Against his will, Rush remembered the look in his friend Jeff's eyes when he'd stepped off the gangplank. Jeff had been hurrying to get home to his wife, Susan. Rush didn't need much of an imagination to know what Jeff was doing about now—and it wasn't drinking cold beer in a dark living room. He allowed himself to grin. Jeff and Susan. Now that was one marriage Rush wouldn't have bet good money on. But Susan Dwyer had pleasantly surprised him. When Jeff had left Bremerton earlier in the week, there'd been no tears in her eyes, only smiles. She'd been a good wife to Jeff from the first. Susan wasn't a clinger or a complainer; the only bonds she'd wrapped around her husband had been in his heart.

Rush had seen subtle changes in his friend since his marriage. He'd been looking for major ones. Over the years Rush had witnessed the power a woman could wield over a sailor's life often enough to recognize the symptoms. But Susan Dwyer hadn't been like some of the others, and Rush had silently admired her—and envied Jeff. His friend had gotten damn lucky to find a woman like Susan. Luckier than Rush… But then Rush had given up trying.

The sound of someone moving behind him jerked Rush into action and he vaulted off the sofa. The bathroom door closed and he heard the rush of running water. What the hell! Someone was in the apartment.

It had to be Steve. He moved down the hallway, looked inside his roomate's bedroom and cocked his eyebrows in astonishment. A silk robe was draped across the end of the bed and the room was littered with female paraphernalia.

Rush released a slow, exasperated breath. He'd been afraid something like this might happen. Steve was still working his way through the pain of his divorce and it had left him vulnerable. Rush was all too familiar with the seductive wiles a woman could use to cloud a man's better judgment. And now it appeared that some schemer was taking advantage of his friend's generous nature, planting herself in their apartment. Apparently Steve was still susceptible to being tricked and used. Well, Rush wouldn't stand for it. A surge of anger at the thought of someone taking advantage of his friend's kind heart made him clench his fists.

He'd gladly handle this situation, he decided. He'd get rid of her, and if Steve asked for an explanation later, Rush had the perfect excuse. After all they had an agreement about this place and it didn't include inviting women to move in. His mouth tightened into a narrow line. From what little he could see, this one had made herself right at home. Well, no more.

With beer in hand, he leaned against the wall, crossed his legs and waited. Within a couple of minutes the bathroom door opened and the woman stepped out. Her dark eyes rounded before she let out a soft gasp.

Obviously startled half out of her wits, the woman's hand flew to her heart, gripping the lacy edge of her pajamas. "Who are you?"

Dear God, wouldn't you know it, Rush groaned inwardly. This wasn't just any woman, but one as sexy as the one he'd been fantasizing about, with nice, round breasts and long, inviting legs. One look and Rush could understand why his friend had set her up in this cozy arrangement. Lord knew she was tempting enough. Her sheer baby-doll pajamas revealed peekaboo nipples, firm hips and shapely legs. It took him a full second to realize her hair was dark and nothing like that of the blondes that usually appealed to his friend.

She continued to stare at him, eyes as round as golf balls, her hands pressed flat against the wall behind her. She opened her mouth and stammered, "Wh-what are you doing here?"

Other than the small gasp, Rush noted, she revealed no real fear. "Isn't that supposed to be my question?" he taunted, and his mouth twisted into a cool, appraising smile. She didn't make an effort to cover herself, but perhaps she wasn't aware of how the muted moonlight played over her pajamas, giving him tantalizing glimpses of her full breasts. Then again, maybe she was.

"You must be Rush."

"So Steve mentioned me?" That surprised him.

"Yes...of course." The woman worked her way past him and retrieved her robe from the foot of the bed, quickly donning it. She made an effort to disguise her uneasiness, but Rush noted that she was trembling. Even from where he was standing he could see that her heart was pounding like a jackhammer. She glanced his way once, silently appealing to him with those huge brown eyes of hers, but Rush was unmoved. If she thought to practice her charms on him, then she could think again. Steve Kyle was his friend and he wasn't about to let his buddy be used by this woman or anyone else.

As nonchalantly as possible Rush followed her into

the bedroom, ignoring the soft scent of jasmine. "How long have you been here?" Her clothes hung in the closet and her things were lined atop the dresser. He lifted the sleeve of a blouse and let the smooth feel of silk run through his fingers. From the look of things, she'd settled right in as though she owned the place. Perhaps she assumed she did; but she'd learn soon enough.

The woman didn't answer him right away. Instead, she moved out of the bedroom and into the kitchen and turned on the lights. "Only a couple of days."

"You didn't waste any time, did you?"

She looked at him as though she hadn't understood his question. "No."

He snickered. "I thought not."

Her gaze left his and rested on the partially empty six-pack of beer. The sight of that seemed to make her all the more nervous and she rubbed the palms of her hands together as though to ward off an unexpected chill. "You've been drinking." Her words sounded like an accusation. The woman's judgmental attitude only served to amuse Rush. He had to give her credit, though; under like circumstances he didn't know if he could have exercised such an impudent spirit.

In response to her statement he reached for another beer. His mouth twisted into a sardonic smile. "Care to join me?" he asked, gesturing toward the four remaining cans.

"No thanks." She tightened the cinch on her robe and squared her shoulders.

"Somehow I didn't think you would." Rush tossed his empty can into the garbage and reached for another. More to irritate her than anything, he took a long, slow drink, letting the cold liquid slide down his throat.

She watched him and braced her hands against the back of the counter. "How long will you be…staying?"

She had one hell of a nerve. "I think I should be the one asking questions, don't you?"

"I—I suppose."

She continued to stare at him with those wide, appealing eyes, and Rush struggled to ignore the false innocence of her silent entreaty.

"I take it Steve didn't let you know I was coming."

"No, he forgot to mention you." It was apparent to Rush that his roommate probably had no intention of letting him know. It would have been easy enough to let the matter slide since Steve would be returning from sea duty before Rush was due back into port.

"I'm Lindy."

He didn't acknowledge her greeting.

As though to cover her embarrassment, she opened the refrigerator and took out a carton of milk.

Rush watched her actions carefully and noted that the inside of the fridge was well stocked. The observation only served to irritate him more. Knowing how generous Steve was, Rush didn't doubt that he'd given her the money to get set up in the apartment.

Lindy poured herself a glass and replaced the milk. "This does make things a bit awkward, doesn't it?"

Again Rush ignored her. Instead of answering her question he pulled out the chair opposite her and sat down, nursing his beer. As hard as he tried, he couldn't take his eyes off her. She was more than just pretty. Delicate, he decided, with a soft injured look about her. Damn, he fathomed better than he would have liked what must have led Steve to invite this woman to move in. In addition to the fragile beauty, she was soft and feminine—the kind of woman a lonely sailor imagines sleeping in his bed, waiting for him. Rush understood all too well, but he didn't like the idea of some woman using his friend. Not when Steve was ripe for pain.

She took a quick swallow of the cold milk, her soft, dark eyes hardly leaving his. Rush was growing more uncomfortable by the minute. He didn't want her here, didn't want her anywhere near this apartment. As far as he was concerned she was trouble with a capital *T*. She must have sensed this because he noticed her fingers tighten around the glass. Obviously she didn't plan to make this easy.

"It would help if we could reach some kind of agreement to share the place—at least until you leave again," she said, looking both embarrassed and uneasy.

His slow answering smile was as cool as Rush could manage. He wasn't about to let a woman sway him out of doing what he must, unpleasant as the task seemed. "Listen, honey," he said brusquely, "the only one of us who's going to be leaving is you. And the sooner the better. So pack your bags; I want you gone before morning."

Two

So Rush Callaghan was kicking her out of the apartment, Lindy mused. Terrific. What else could go wrong? The answer to that was something she didn't want to find out. Oh Lord. She'd known Steve's invitation was too good to be true. Nothing was ever going to be right for her again—she'd been sabotaged by fate while still in her prime...

A quick calculation of her limited funds suggested that she could possibly last two weeks if she rented a cheap hotel room and ate sparingly. Two weeks and she'd be forced to return to Minneapolis a failure. The thought wasn't a comforting one. Her parents would gladly take her in, but their excessive concern right now was more suffocating than she could bear.

With deliberate calm Lindy drank the last of her milk, carried the glass to the sink and rinsed it out. All the while her thoughts were a churning mass of wary doubts.

She would leave, she decided, because Rush Callaghan had decreed that she must. But she could see no reason to hurry. Simply because he was an officer used to giving orders and having them followed didn't mean she had to jump at his every command.

"Did you hear me?" Rush asked, his narrowed gaze following her deliberate movements.

"I'll be out before morning," was the only answer she would give him, and she forced those words to come out as stiffly as starched sheets.

It gave Lindy fleeting satisfaction to witness the surprise in Rush's eyes. He stared at her almost as if he'd been looking forward to an argument, to sharpening his wits on hers. Apparently he'd thought she would stand up and issue some kind of challenge. Well, Lindy just wasn't in the mood to put up much of a fight. If he wanted her out, then fine, she'd pack her bags and leave.

Wordlessly she opened the dishwasher and set the glass inside. His eyes followed her suspiciously, apparently disliking her cool compliance. For the first time he looked unsettled, as though it was on the tip of his tongue to suggest that she could stay until morning. But if the thought crossed his mind, that was as far as it went. He said nothing. Lindy supposed he was right. She could see no reason to prolong the inevitable. But damn it all, she'd never felt so helpless and lost in her life. A condemned man walking to the hangman's noose had as many options as she seemed to have at the moment.

Lindy turned and left the kitchen. She tried to walk away proudly, but her shoulders sagged with abject defeat. She heard the kitchen chair scrape against the floor as Rush stood and followed her.

Standing in the doorway to her bedroom, Rush glanced at his watch. Lindy pulled out her suitcase from under the bed and looked in the direction of her clock radio, noting the late hour.

As though it went against his better judgment, Rush stuck his hand in his uniform pocket and murmured, "Listen, tomorrow morning is soon enough."

"Not for me, it isn't."

"What do you mean?"

"Never mind," Lindy said with a righteous sigh.

"Lord, how like a woman," Rush murmured to the ceiling, the words tight and controlled. "She tosses a dart at me and then refuses to acknowledge it. What she really wants me to know is that she couldn't bear to be in the same room with me. Well, honeybunch, the feeling is mutual!"

Some of Lindy's control slipped at his taunt, and she angrily jerked a blouse off a hanger. "I don't suppose you stopped to think that I didn't move in here without an invitation. Steve invited me. I have his letter right here to prove it if you'd take the time to read—"

"Unfortunately Steve didn't clear this cozy little arrangement with me," he interrupted, "and I have no intention of sharing this place with you or any other female."

"You men think you're really something, don't you?" Lindy cried, jerking yet another blouse from a hanger. "You like being in control, dictating whatever you wish on nothing more than a whim."

He looked surprised that she'd revealed any emotion. Good heavens, just what did he expect from her? Lindy didn't know, and at this point she simply didn't care. When she'd finished emptying her closet, she whirled around to face him.

"All along Steve's been telling me what a great friend you are, a terrific guy. You should meet him, Lindy. I know you'd like him," she said sarcastically, mimicking her brother's praise. She cast Rush a disparaging look. "Some roommate you turned out to be. I'll tell you one thing, mister…"

"Spare me, would you?"

"No." Lindy slammed the lid of her suitcase closed. "You're all alike. Every last one of you is just like Paul."

"Paul?"

Her index finger flew at his chest and she heaved back in indignation. "Don't you dare mention his name to me. Ever!"

"Lady, you brought him up, I didn't!"

"That was a mistake. But then I seem to be making a lot of those lately."

"Your biggest one was moving in here."

"Tell me about it," she returned with a sneer. "Well, you needn't worry. I'll be out of your way in a few minutes." She yanked the suitcase off the bed and reached for her coat, preparing to leave. Boldly she paused and raised her eyes to meet his. With her lips curved upward, she regarded him with open disdain. "Steve is really going to be upset about this."

"I'll deal with him later." The look he was giving her said that if anyone had a right to be angry, it was him. As though Steve had been the one to let *him* down.

With a carefully manufactured calm, Lindy stopped at the front door, set down her suitcase and slipped the key to the apartment off her chain.

Rush held out his hand and she pressed it into his waiting palm. Once again he looked as if he wanted to say that she could stay until morning. She didn't know what stopped him—probably his pride. Men had to have their pride. No doubt he was aware that she'd take delight in throwing the invitation back in his face.

Lindy watched as Rush's dark eyes narrowed, then she sadly shook her head. For years she'd been hearing Rush's name exalted. According to Steve, Rush Callaghan was both an officer and a gentleman. In the space of fifteen minutes, Lindy had quickly discovered he was neither.

"Bad judgment must run in the family," she said, more for her own ears than his. "If Steve thinks you're so wonderful, then my mistake about Paul seems like a minor miscalculation of character." With that she picked up her lone suitcase and pulled open the front door.

Rush's hand reached out and gripped her shoulder, stopping her. "Family? What exactly do you mean by that?"

"Steve Kyle, my brother. You know, the man who pays half the rent for this place? The one who wrote and claimed I was welcome to live here until I found a job?"

His fingers closed painfully over her shoulder and his eyes simmered with impatient anger. "Why the hell didn't you say you were Steve's sister?" He reached for her suitcase, stripped it from her hands and jerked her back inside the apartment. Rush slammed the door shut after her and studied her as though seeing her for the first time.

"Don't tell me you didn't know!" she shouted back. "Just who the hell did you think I was?" The answer to that was all too obvious and a heated flash of bright color invaded her neck and cheeks. "Oh, honestly, that's…disgusting."

Rush raked his fingers through his hair in an agitated movement and walked a few steps past her before turning around to confront her once more. "Listen, I didn't know. Honest."

"Does this mean I'm welcome to spend the night in my own brother's apartment?"

He let that taunt pass. "Yes, of course."

"How generous of you."

Rush picked up the suitcase and carried it back into Steve's bedroom, his jerky movements revealing both his chagrin and his anger. Lindy followed him, no longer sure what to make of this man. She knew Steve's invitation had been a spur of the moment thing. The two men easily could have gotten their wires crossed. From experience Lindy knew how letters could get held up in the military, and it was likely that Rush hadn't known she was planning on moving in. Still that didn't excuse his arrogant attitude toward her.

Lindy was two steps behind the man who Steve claimed was his best friend. Rush set the suitcase back on top of the mattress and hesitated before turning around to face her once more.

"I apologize. Okay?"

She answered him with an abrupt nod. His apology was followed by a short, uneasy silence. Lindy didn't know what to say. After a tense moment, she murmured, "I think the entire incident is best forgotten."

"Good." Rush buried his hands in his pockets, looking as uncomfortable as Lindy felt. "Of course you're welcome to stay in the apartment as long as you like. I'm hoping to be out of here by the end of the week."

"I thought you'd already left. I mean…"

Apparently he knew what she meant. "I had, but there were some mechanical difficulties and the *Mitchell* is back in the shipyard for repairs."

"For a week?" After nearly drowning in love and concern from her parents, Lindy had been looking forward to living alone. Well, so much for that—at least for now.

"Possibly longer, but don't worry about it. You're welcome to stay," Rush murmured, still looking uncomfortable.

Lindy guessed that he didn't often make apologies. "Thanks, but I have no intention of burdening you any longer than necessary. As soon as I've found a job, I'll be on my way."

"'Night," Rush said abruptly, taking a step in retreat.

"Good night," Lindy returned with a weak, dispirited smile.

Rush walked out of the room and Lindy closed it in his wake and leaned against the frame. Her mind was whirling. She knew even before she climbed between the sheets that she wasn't likely to sleep any time soon. Rest, like contentment, had been a fleeting commodity these past few weeks.

Rush smelled fresh coffee when he woke the next morning. With some reluctance, he climbed out of bed and dressed. He'd made a heel of himself and he wasn't eager to face Steve's sister with his head throbbing and his mouth tasting like something floating in a skid-row gutter. After he'd left Lindy the night before, he'd tried to sleep, given up an hour later and gone back to drink the rest of the six-pack of beer and watch television. Now he was suffering the consequences of his folly.

He sat for a moment on the edge of his bed, his head in his hands. For years he'd heard stories about his friend's younger sister. How intelligent she was, how clever, how pretty. Steve was more than fond of his sister. He adored her and now Rush had gone and insulted her, and in the process maligned his best friend. He should have realized that Steve wasn't fool enough to set a woman up in their apartment. Hell, Steve was still so much in love with his ex-wife that he couldn't see straight.

Damn it all, Rush mused, irritated with himself. He shouldn't have downed those first two beers. If his head had been clearer, he might have recognized her name.

Rush frowned. He vaguely recalled Steve telling him about some fancy job with a large insurance company that was supposed to be waiting for Lindy once she graduated from college. Come to think of it, he thought Steve had said she was engaged to be married this summer, as well. He wondered what she was doing in Seattle, but after their poor beginning he wasn't about to drill her about her job or problems with her fiancé.

Lindy sat at the kitchen table with the morning newspaper spread out in front of her. She chose to ignore Rush. As far as she was concerned the man had all the sensitivity of a woman-hating Neanderthal. Okay, so they were going to be sharing the apartment for a while. A week, he'd said. She could last that long if he could.

Rush walked over to the coffeepot, poured himself a cup, then muttered something that sounded faintly like a growl. Lindy supposed that was his own prehistoric version of "good morning." She responded in kind.

"What was that?" he demanded.

"What?"

"That disgusting little noise you just made."

"I was just wishing you a good morning."

"I'll bet," he muttered, lifting the steaming mug to his lips. He took a sip, then grimaced as if he'd scalded his tongue. He paused to glare at Lindy as though to blame her for his troubles.

Swallowing a chuckle, Lindy stood, deposited her coffee cup in the kitchen sink and left the table, taking the morning paper with her. It wasn't until she was in her bedroom that she realized she was smiling—something she hadn't felt like doing in a long while. Maybe having a man around to thwart and frustrate wasn't such a bad idea. With few exceptions, she'd recently come to view the opposite sex as both demanding and unreasonable. Rush Callaghan certainly fit the mold.

Gathering her clothes and a few personal items, Lindy headed for the bathroom. She'd discarded her robe and had just leaned over the tub to start her bathwater, when Rush strolled in.

"Are you planning to—" He stopped abruptly, his jaw slack.

Reluctantly Lindy straightened, gripping the front of her gaping pajama top with one hand. Color mounted in her cheeks like a red flag rising as she realized that her bent position over the tub had probably granted Rush a bird's-eye view of her rounded derriere. The flimsy baby-doll top no doubt gave him an equally revealing study of her breasts through the thin material. Incensed with herself as much as at Rush, she jerked a towel off the rack and wrapped it around her middle.

"Sorry," he muttered and quickly moved out of the room. He stood just across the threshold, watching her as though he couldn't jerk his gaze away. He swallowed hard once before stiffly stepping away.

Lindy walked over and purposefully closed the door. To be on the safe side she locked it.

"Just how long are you planning to be in there?"

Rush shouted, apparently not feeling the necessity to disguise his bad mood.

Lindy reached for her Timex. She looked at the watch and gave herself fifteen minutes. "I'll be out before eight." She expected an argument, but if Rush had any objection he didn't voice it.

Once Lindy was soaking in the hot bathwater, she found herself grinning once more. It was obvious that Rush Callaghan wasn't accustomed to having a woman around. The thought pleased her, but it didn't surprise her. The man was a grouch and dictatorial to boot, acting as though it were a woman's duty to humbly submit to his every command. There weren't many females who would be willing to put up with that kind of chauvinistic attitude. Lindy certainly wouldn't.

Nor had she been oblivious to his admiring appraisal. Just the memory of his slow, hungry look was enough to lift her mood considerably. After Paul, it did her ego a world of good to realize another man found her appealing. Plenty of doubts had surfaced over the past few weeks regarding her feminine charms, and it gave Lindy a cozy feeling deep down to realize she possessed enough allure to tempt a man.

Now that she had time to think about it, Lindy admitted that Rush wasn't so bad-looking himself in a fundamental sort of way. Until a woman recognized his condescending ways, Rush would undoubtedly fascinate her. He was well over six feet tall, with a muscled, whipcord leanness that spoke of discipline and control. His broad shoulders tapered to narrow hips and long legs. Without much effort, Lindy could picture him standing at attention in full-dress uniform, surveying all that was before him with an arrogant tilt of his square jaw. Lindy was surprised at the sudden strong charge of pleasure the thought gave her. Her mind conjured him standing tall and immovably proud, shoulders squared, gaze focused straight ahead. With the thought, some of the pique she'd been feeling toward him vanished.

But what intrigued her most about Rush Callaghan, she decided, were his eyes. Although he hadn't said more than a handful of words to her this morning, his dark blue gaze was highly expressive and more than able to telegraph his sour mood. She'd gained a good deal of pleasure in provoking him and then watching his brows crowd his eyes, narrowing them into slits of cool, assessing color. Later when he'd confronted her in the bathroom, those same clear blue eyes had revealed much more.

As her mind continued to play with the thoughts, Lindy scooted down into the hot water, raised a washcloth and idly drizzled the water over her smooth, flat stomach.

In the hallway outside the bathroom door, Rush paced like a stalking, caged tiger. He'd checked his watch every damn minute for the past five. Just how long did it take a woman to bathe, for God's sake? Too damn long, for his tastes.

Finally accepting the fact that pacing wasn't going to hurry her any, he retreated into his bedroom and sat on the edge of the mattress. In an effort to be honest with himself Rush admitted that it wasn't the fact that Lindy was hogging the one facility in the apartment that irritated him so much. It was the tantalizing figure she'd presented to him when he'd inadvertently walked in on her.

Her firm young body had all but taken his breath away, and when he checked his hands he found he was still trembling with the effects of the brief encounter. He hadn't a clue as to why she would wear that silly piece of lace. The silky see-through fabric didn't hide a damn thing.

Like an innocent, he'd moved into the bathroom only to be confronted by the sweet curve of her buttocks and the milky white skin of her long, shapely legs. Rush could swear the woman's legs went all the way up to her neck.

If that sight hadn't been enough to hammer the breath from his lungs, having her turn around and confront him had. Her full pink breasts had darkened at the tips as she struggled to hold the front of her pajamas together. Not that her efforts had done much good. Her nipples had hardened and pointed straight at him as though begging to be kissed. Even now the image had the power to tighten his groin and make his breath come in harsh, uneven gulps.

A week. Oh Lord. He wondered if he could last that long. He inhaled deeply and closed his eyes. He hoped the *Mitchell* would be ready to sail by then because he didn't know how much longer he could contain himself around Lindy. He knew he had to avoid a relationship with her at all costs. In addition to being his best friend's sister, Lindy was hurting, Rush realized. Something had happened—he didn't know what, didn't need to know—but he'd recognized the heavy shadow of pain and grief that hung over her head like a dark thundercloud. Something had knocked her world off kilter. And Rush wasn't in a position to right it. He wasn't anyone's savior. In the meantime, the best thing that could happen was for him to keep his eyes and ears to himself and pray the *Mitchell* left ahead of schedule.

Lindy found Rush was in the kitchen when she returned from job hunting late that afternoon. Her day had gone amazingly well and she felt greatly encouraged. After filling out dozens of forms and passing a series of tests, she was scheduled for an interview at the Boeing Renton plant for the following Monday. The salary was more than she'd hoped for and the benefits substantial. She held high hopes for the interview. Perhaps the worm had finally turned and her luck was going to change. She certainly hoped so. But in the meantime she felt obligated to keep job hunting in case something else turned up between now and then. Besides she didn't relish lingering around the apartment, bumping into Rush every time she turned around.

"Hi," Lindy greeted Rush cheerfully, draping the strap of her purse over the back of the kitchen chair. She was in the mood to be generous with her reluctant roommate. After her fruitful day of job hunting, she was actually beginning to feel a little like her old self.

It was obvious, however, from the vicious way Rush was scrubbing away at the dishes that his earlier dark mood hadn't improved.

He grumbled a reply, but didn't turn around. "Listen, I've got a schedule posted outside the bathroom so there won't be a recurrence of what happened this morning."

A schedule for the bathroom? He had to be joking! "Okay," she answered, having difficulty disguising her amusement. She opened the refrigerator and took out a cold can of soda, closed the door and momentarily leaned against it. It struck her then that she was hungry. She'd eaten lunch hours before, but with her limited funds she couldn't afford a fancy restaurant meal and had opted, instead, for a fast-food chicken salad. She had started to search through the cupboards when Rush turned around and nearly collided with her.

"Excuse me," he said stiffly.

"No problem." She pressed herself against the counter as he moved past.

From the way he skirted around her, one would think she was a carrier of bubonic plague.

Without another word, Rush wiped his hands dry, rehung the dish towel and moved into the living room to turn on the television.

Since he didn't appear to be the least bit communicative, she wasn't about to ask him if he'd eaten or if he was hungry. Far be it from her to appear anxious to share a meal with Rush when he obviously wanted to ignore her. They weren't on a Sunday-school picnic here, they were merely polite strangers whose presence had been forced on each other.

Sorting through the cupboards, Lindy brought out spaghetti noodles and a bottle of spicy Italian sauce. After weeks of a skimpy appetite, it felt good to think about cooking something substantial.

The sausage was frying up nicely and the faint scent of fennel and sage wafted through the kitchen. Lindy brought out an onion and had begun dicing it to add to the meat when the knife slipped and neatly sliced into her index finger.

The sight of blood squirting over the cutting board shocked more than hurt her. She cried out in a moment of panic and rushed to the sink, holding her hand.

"Lindy, are you all right?"

She ignored the question. The cut hurt now. Badly. Closing her eyes, she held her finger under the running water.

"What happened?" Rush demanded, joining her at the sink.

"Nothing." Already the stainless steel was splashed with blotches of blood.

"You cut yourself!"

He sounded angry, as though she'd purposely injured herself in a futile attempt to gain his sympathy. "Are you always this brilliant or is this show of intelligence for my benefit?" she asked through clenched teeth. He looked stunned for a minute as though he didn't understand a word of what she was saying. "Any idiot could see I've cut myself," she cried, her voice raised and laced with a healthy dose of fright.

"Let me take a look at it."

She shook her head forcefully, wishing he'd go away so she could assess the damage herself. The terrible stinging had been replaced by an aching throb. She couldn't keep herself from bouncing, as if the action would lessen the pain.

"Give me your hand," he demanded, reaching for it.

"Stop shouting at me," she yelled, and jerked away from him. "As far as I'm concerned this is all your fault."

"My fault?" His expressive blue eyes widened.

"Any fool knows better than to keep sharp knives around." Lindy knew she wasn't making sense, but she couldn't seem to help herself.

"For God's sake, stop hopping around and let me get a good look at it."

Using his upper body, he trapped her against the counter. She really didn't have any choice but to let him examine the cut. Biting unmercifully into her bottom lip, she unfolded her fist, while gripping her wrist tightly with her free hand.

His touch was surprisingly gentle and she watched as his brow folded together in a tight frown of concern.

"It doesn't look like you're going to need stitches."

Lindy expelled a sigh of relief. With no health insurance, a simple call to the hospital emergency room would quickly deplete her limited funds. And although her parents were willing, Lindy didn't want to ask them for money.

"Here." With a tenderness she hadn't expected from Rush, he reached for a clean towel and carefully wrapped it around her hand. "It looks like the bleeding has stopped. Wait here and I'll get a bandage."

It was all Lindy could do to nod. She felt incredibly silly now, placing the blame on him for having a sharp knife. He left her and returned a couple of minutes later with some gauze and tape.

"I didn't mean what I said about this being your fault," she told him, raising her eyes to meet his.

His eyes widened momentarily, and then a smile flickered in their blue depths. "I know," was all he said.

Although she was willing to credit her loss of blood with the stunning effect of his smile, there was no discounting the way her heart and head reacted. The simple action left Lindy warmed in its afterglow long after her finger was bandaged.

Three days passed and Rush and Lindy became a little more comfortable with each other. There were still a few awkward moments, but Lindy discovered that they could at least sit across the table from each other and carry on a decent conversation without risking an argument.

Rush tended to stay out of her way—and she, his—but there were certain times of the day when meeting was inevitable. In the mornings when they were both hurrying to get ready to leave the apartment, for instance. Twice Rush had gone out in the evening, leaving abruptly without a word. Lindy hadn't asked where he went and he didn't volunteer the information, but Lindy had the impression that he was simply avoiding being at close quarters with her.

Since it seemed silly for them to cook separate meals, they'd reached an agreement that Lindy would prepare the meals and Rush would do the dishes.

Rush was sitting in the living room when Lindy let herself into the apartment on Friday afternoon. She tossed her purse aside and slumped down on the opposite end of the sofa away from him.

"Any luck?" he asked in a conversational way, watching her.

Lindy noted that he looked tired and frustrated. "No, but I'm hoping everything will come together at the interview on Monday."

He stood, rammed his hands into his pockets and looked away from her, staring out the window. "I'm not exactly filled with good news myself."

"Oh?" She studied him closely, wondering at his strange mood.

"Without going into a lot of detail," he said, his voice tight, "the problem holding up the *Mitchell* isn't going to be easily fixed."

Lindy nodded and drew in a ragged breath, not sure what was coming next.

"It's going to take as long as a month to have the parts flown in," he continued.

"I see." She straightened and brushed aside a crease in her blue skirt, her fingers lingering over the material. "I suppose this means you want me to leave then, doesn't it?"

Three

"Leave?" Rush echoed, looking both surprised and angry.

Lindy bounded to her feet, her hands clenched at her sides in tight fists. "It's a perfectly logical question, so don't snap at me."

"I'm not snapping."

"A turtle couldn't do it better."

"Are you always this prickly or is it something about me?" He was glaring at her, demanding a response, the look in his eyes hot enough to boil water.

Although his voice was deliberately expressionless and quiet, Lindy knew by the tight set of his jaw that he was getting madder by the minute. Not that she cared. The man drove her absolutely loony. She'd never known anyone who could control his emotions the way Rush did. Oh sure, he laughed, he smiled, he talked, he argued, but in the entire four days that she'd been living in the apartment with him, he'd revealed as much sentiment as a marble statue. Even when she'd cut her finger and hopped around the kitchen like a crazed kangaroo, he'd been as calm and collected as though he handled hurting, frightened women every day of his life. Nothing seemed to faze Rush. Nothing.

"Well, you needn't worry. I'll go," she announced with a proud tilt of her chin. "It won't be necessary for you to ask twice." She bent down and reached for the strap of her purse, her heart pounding like a charging locomotive. Moving was something she should have done the minute she realized she wasn't going to have the apartment to herself.

"Damn it, Lindy. I didn't say you had to leave."

She blinked. "You didn't?"

"No. You jumped to conclusions."

"Oh." Now she felt like a bloody idiot. It was on the tip of her tongue to apologize. She'd had a rough day; the heel had broken off her shoe and the job she'd gone to apply for wasn't the least bit as it had been advertised. Although they'd offered it to her, she'd decided against it. Good grief. She wouldn't have been anything more than a glorified desk clerk. Maybe she shouldn't be so particular, but after four years of college she wanted so much more than to file papers and answer a telephone.

Maybe she was feeling a little guilty because she'd told Rush she hadn't had any luck when she'd actually gotten a job offer. And refused it.

They stood not more than five feet apart and his piercing gaze locked with hers, burning straight through her proud resolve.

When Lindy spoke her voice was husky with emotion, and her heart began a heavy muted pounding against her rib cage. "I lied."

Rush's eyes clouded, then hardened, and Lindy felt the dread crowd its way into her throat. Rush wasn't the type of man who would take something like this lightly.

"What did you lie about?"

"I got offered a job today. I turned it down." With her long tapered nails biting into the flesh of her palms, she explained the circumstances. "I thought you should know because...well, because I plan to rent my own place as soon as I can after I find something. But it looks like I could be around awhile."

A smile flickered over his lips and he appeared to relax a little. "I can stand it if you can."

"That's debatable."

They were both grinning then, and Lindy felt the uneasy tension seep from her limbs. Now that she'd explained things to Rush she felt much better. In fact, possibly for the first time, she was completely at ease with him. It wasn't that he intimidated her so much as he challenged her. She felt as if she had to be constantly on her guard with him. Watch her step, keep the peace— that sort of thing.

"You must be hungry." she said, turning toward the kitchen. "I'll get dinner going."

"Lindy."

She twisted around, her eyes questioning.

"Since it's Friday and we've both had a trying week, how about going out for a pizza?"

The minute Rush issued the invitation, he was convinced he'd done the wrong thing. His biggest concern was that he was giving Lindy the wrong impression. When the repairs on the *Mitchell* were finished he'd be leaving, and he didn't want to give his best friend's sister the idea that there could ever be anything romantic between them. The circumstances in which they were living were tempting enough, and here he was adding to the tension by deepening the relationship to something beyond their polite but strained friendship.

Hell, he wasn't even sure why he'd suggested they go out. The last couple of nights he'd purposely left the apartment and sat in a bar on the waterfront, nursing a drink or two. The best way to deal with this awkward situation, he'd decided, was to stay away from Lindy as much as possible. Remove himself from temptation, so to speak. Because, damn it all, Lindy Kyle was one hell of a tempting morsel. Her young, firm body was ripe and it had been too long since he'd had a woman. Every time he was in the same room with her, he felt the charge of electricity arc between them. Until today, he'd been able to deal with it, and now he was purposely exposing them to God only knew what.

He wanted to be angry with her—needed it to dilute the effect she had on him. When she'd admitted she'd lied, he'd felt a reassuring irritation surging up inside him, rough and heated. As far as he was concerned, women weren't exactly known for their integrity. Although disappointed in her, he'd made a conscious effort to control his ire, knowing it wouldn't do any good to blow up at her.

And then she'd told him about turning down the job, her clear brown eyes soft and filled with contrition for having misled him. Her eager, young face had been as readable as a first-grade primer. She'd stood before him, so forthright and honest, and he'd felt something deep and fundamental move inside him. Before he'd even known what was happening, he'd offered to take her to dinner.

It was more than that, too. Steve's letter had finally caught up with him, explaining what had happened to

Lindy. The poor kid had been through a lot. Apparently she'd been deeply in love with this Paul Abrams, and she'd been crushed when he'd broken the engagement. Rush had been crippled by emotional pain once himself. He knew from personal experience how devastating letting go of a loved one could be.

After reading his friend's long letter, Rush's opinion of Lindy had altered. Not that he'd made any dyed-in-the-wool assumptions about her before the letter's arrival. The fact was, he chose to think of her as little as possible. But after reading what Steve had written, he'd discovered that he admired Lindy for picking up the pieces of her life and forging ahead despite rejection and defeat.

Something else Steve had mentioned had strongly affected Rush. Throughout everything, Lindy hadn't shed a tear. Her entire family continued to worry about her because she was taking everything far too calmly, holding up much too well. It wasn't natural, Steve had claimed, sounding very much like the concerned older brother he was. Almost grudgingly, Rush found himself appreciating Lindy's courage and unsinkable pride. Not so long ago he'd been left to deal with the trauma of a lost love. He could still remember the pitying looks sent his way after Cheryl. The effort and control it had demanded on his part to pretend nothing was wrong, that losing Cheryl didn't really matter, had drained him. When all the while, every breath he drew had been a reminder that he'd been a fool to ever have trusted the woman. And worse, to have loved her.

Rush could identify with Lindy's attitude all too well. He would have walked over hot coals before he'd show his pain to anyone, friend or foe. Apparently she felt the same way. Maybe that was the reason he found himself wanting to spend more time with her, looking for a way to be her friend.

A Michael Jackson song blared loudly from the pizza parlor's jukebox and, much to her surprise, Lindy found herself tapping her foot to the music and wanting to snap her fingers. Rush sat across the booth from her, looking more relaxed and at ease than she could ever remember seeing him. A tall, frosty pitcher of beer rested in the middle of the table.

Lindy had already downed two thick mugs of ale and was feeling the dizzying, warm effects of the alcohol. Rarely had she tasted better pizza, and she'd pigged down three enormous slices, astonishing them both. Now she felt content and happy, two states of mind that had been sadly lacking in her life recently.

"If there was a big enough floor space, I'd want to dance," she told Rush, who instantly looked relieved—no doubt because he'd chosen a restaurant without one. Lindy giggled.

"What's so funny?"

"You!"

"I'm glad you find me so amusing."

"Don't take it personally. It's just that it feels so good to sit back and relax like this."

"That amuses you?"

"Yes, because you look like you've just been granted a pardon from the governor because you don't have to dance. And something else."

His dark brows shot up. "There's more?"

"Oh yes. For the first time since we met, I don't feel I have to keep my wits sharpened around you." She said it with a smile, hoping her good mood would cut any sting from her words. "In case you didn't know it, Rush Callaghan, you can be one hell of an arrogant jerk. Imagine posting a schedule to use the bathroom!"

His eyes narrowed, his jaw clenched in mock consternation, and still he looked every inch the sturdy, capable naval officer she knew him to be.

"There are a few truths about yourself I could enlighten you with as well, Lindy Kyle."

"Perhaps," she conceded.

He was teasing her and Lindy found herself warming to him. When he chose to, Rush could freeze out an Eskimo with one piercing glare. She hated to think of the men on the *Mitchell* facing his wrath because, although she hadn't seen it in full force, she'd witnessed enough to know his anger would be formidable. Discovering this gentler, fun-loving side of his nature had been an unexpected surprise.

Still smiling, Rush stood and threw a couple of dollars onto the table. "Come on, let's get out of here before someone pushes aside a few tables and starts up a band."

Lindy laughed and reached for her sweater and purse. Rush's hand lightly touched the small of her back as he guided her out of the restaurant. "So you really aren't going to take me dancing?" she asked, once they were outside in the cool June air.

"Not on your life."

Lindy released a slow, expressive sigh and glanced up into the dark warmth of his gaze. A small taste of excitement filled her, and some of the heavy feeling that had weighted her heart for so many interminable weeks lifted.

"Would the lady consider a walk instead?" Rush said,

his voice oddly tender, indulgent. He lifted his hand and rested it against her shoulder, his touch amazingly light.

Lindy had the impression that he'd rather not have his hand where it was, but that he couldn't help himself, and she waded through a surge of elation. It was marvelous to feel like a woman again, and she was highly aware of her power, however fleeting.

They strolled toward the busy Seattle waterfront, weaving in and out of the crowds that lingered on the sidewalk. The air was clean and fresh, smelling of tangy salt and seaweed, and although the sun had set, the gentle breeze carried with it a pleasing warmth.

Rush bought them coffee from a seafood bar and they silently walked along the pier, staring at the lights from the ferryboat as it glided across the murky green waters of Puget Sound.

"Can I see the *Mitchell* from here?" Lindy asked.

"No. It's in the shipyard in Bremerton, which is all the way across the Sound."

"You really love the sea, don't you?"

Rush's fingers momentarily tightened their grip on her shoulder. "Yes, I do. Did Steve ever tell you I was born on a ferryboat?"

"No."

"I think my destiny was cast then. My mother named me Rush because they were hurrying to get her to the hospital in time. Unfortunately, or fortunately, depending on how one chooses to look at it, I was born on the water."

"And have been at home there ever since," she added in a soft whisper.

He nodded and their eyes met in a brief exchange of rare understanding. Rush continued talking, telling her a little of his youth and his early days at Annapolis. He made a striking figure, leaning against the edge of the pier, Lindy noted. He paused and smiled down at her. His eyes narrowed briefly with appreciation and it was as if they had become two different people for this one special night.

Rush looked younger, Lindy mused, more open. For the first time since she'd arrived in Seattle, she felt that she was beginning to appreciate this complex man. Maybe because he was really talking to her, sharing a small part of himself with her. There was no pretense between them tonight. Somehow Lindy realized how rare it was for Rush to expose this amiable, sensitive part of himself, to let down his guard and throw caution to the wind. She felt as though she'd been granted a rare gift, one that she would look back on years from now and treasure.

They left the pier a few minutes later, discarded their Styrofoam cups and continued strolling down the busy sidewalk until they reached Waterfront Park. Lindy braced her foot against the bottom stair, which led to an observation deck and a museum on the second level.

"It's a beautiful night," Rush commented, staring into the sky.

Lindy had the feeling he was about to suggest they head back to the apartment. She didn't want the evening to end. Everything was too perfect for them to leave so soon.

"Come on. I'll race you up the stairs," she called, letting the breeze carry her challenge. Not waiting to see if he was going to follow her, she grabbed for the railing and hurled herself up the concrete steps, taking two at a time.

The wind, which had recently picked up, whipped her hair from her face as she made a mad dash up the stairway, doing her best to swallow her laughter.

"Lindy."

Rush's exasperated voice was directly behind her, and not wishing to be outdistanced, she lurched forward.

He beat her easily and was waiting for her, blocking her way when she breathlessly reached the top.

"You little fool."

Still panting and laughing, she tried to leap around him but almost lost her balance. A look of horror crowded his face as he reached out to grab her, but Lindy quickly darted in the opposite direction. Rush tried to block her there, as well, and she shrieked with the sheer joy of the moment and scooted sideways from him.

"Lindy, stop."

She dodged to her left and when he followed her, she darted to her right, then triumphantly stumbled past him, running to the railing, her eyes wild with joy.

"I won," she declared triumphantly, swinging around to face him.

Rush collapsed on the park bench, barely winded. "You cheated."

"Oh, honestly. Can't you admit it when a woman outsmarts you?"

"I'd admit it if it was true."

"My foot, you would." Lindy slumped down on the bench beside him, her breath coming in uneven, shallow gasps. Good Lord, she was out of shape. She let her head fall back so her hair rushed away from her face, granting her a feeling of complete freedom.

Lindy exhaled, dragging the oxygen through her lungs. "Oh, Paul, I can't remember a night when I've had more fun." The instant the name slipped through her lips, Lindy tensed. "I meant… Rush."

The excitement that had galloped through her blood just seconds before felt like a deadweight pressing against her chest. For one crazy moment she was paralyzed. She had trouble breathing, trouble moving, trouble thinking. Scalding tears burned in her eyes, and the huge lump in her throat felt as if it were monumental.

Moisture rolled down the side of her face, burning her skin like acid, and she sucked in a trembling sob.

"Lindy, are you all right?"

Rush brushed away a tear and his finger felt incredibly warm against her icy cold cheek.

"Something must have gotten into my eye," she lied, turning away so he wouldn't be able to see the extent of her emotion.

"Here."

He pressed a white handkerchief into her numb fingers, and she made a quick job of wiping her face dry. "I think we should be heading back. Don't you?"

"Anything you say."

He sounded so concerned when it was the last thing she wanted. Suddenly Rush was the last person in the world she yearned to be with. Escape seemed of paramount importance. Somehow she found her way to her feet, although the cement seemed to buckle beneath her shoes. With some effort she managed to keep her balance and rush away from the bench.

It would have been too much to hope that Rush would let her go. But oddly enough he seemed to appreciate her mood, remaining silent as he matched his quick steps to hers. Side by side they started up the hill toward First Avenue.

The climb was steep and Lindy was winded by the time they'd gone only a few blocks.

"I'll get a taxi," Rush said.

"No. Don't, please." She wanted to walk—needed to wear herself out physically so she could collapse in her bed exhausted. It was the only way she could guarantee she would sleep. The simple act of putting one foot in front of the other, climbing up one street and then the next one, seemed to help her contain her emotions.

By the time they reached the apartment building, Lindy's lungs ached and her calf muscles violently protested the strenuous exercise. She waited impatiently while Rush unlocked the front door.

He held it open for her, and in that moment she detested him for the small display of manners. Paul had impeccable manners and look what he'd done to her. Look what he'd reduced her to.

Without even glancing in Rush's direction she paused just inside the living room and said, her voice weak and faltering, "Thank you for dinner."

He didn't answer her for what seemed an eternity, and she had the impression he was willing her to turn around and face him. But she knew she couldn't without dissolving into wretched emotion.

"Anytime, Lindy." His words were low and as smooth as velvet.

"Good night." The sooner she got away from Rush the better.

"'Night." Again his voice was so gentle, so tender.

She made it all the way to the bathroom door before her gaze blurred so badly with tears that she had to stop and wipe the moisture from her eyes. Drawing in several steadying breaths between clenched teeth gave her some relief. She'd be damned before she'd cry over Paul Abrams.

Damned. Damned. Damned.

Without being aware of how it happened, Lindy found that she had stopped and braced a shoulder against the wall, using it to keep her upright, needing its support. She pinched her nose with her thumb and index fingers, willing back the release of torrential tears.

"Lindy, you need to cry."

The words seemed to come from a far distance, echoing around her in a canyon of despair. She dropped her hand and looked up to find Rush standing beside her.

"No," she said forcefully. "I won't."

"Don't let him do this to you."

She tried to push Rush away, but her effort was puny and weak. "You don't know anything," she cried. "How could you?"

"I know what it is to hurt."

"Not like this." No one could ever hurt this much. No one.

"Listen to me," he said, and his hands gripped her shoulders. But even his fingers were gentle when she wanted them to be hard and punishing. "Cry. Let it out before the grief strangles you."

"No." Still she resisted, wildly shaking her head. "No. I hate him. I hate him."

"I know, honey. I know."

The dam broke then, and the tears that had been pent up inside her soul, shoved down and ignored for so long, bled from her eyes. A low, mewing sound slid from the back of her throat, nearly choking her. Sobs overtook her, huge, oxygen-robbing sobs that shook her shoulders and made her breast heave.

Rush didn't try to hold her and she was grateful because she couldn't have borne being restrained. Unable to remain upright, she braced her back against the wall and slumped to the floor. She gently rocked back and forth, weeping bitterly for the innocence she had lost, and wailing for the love she had given so freely to a man who didn't deserve it. She cried until there was nothing left inside her.

Lindy started to retch when her tears were spent, and she knew she was about to lose her dinner. Rush's hand under her elbow helped her to an upright position and into the bathroom. He stood behind her as she leaned over the toilet. She thought she felt his hand on her back, but she couldn't be sure.

When she was finished he handed her a damp washcloth. She held it to her face, letting the coolness soak away some of the terrible red heat. Her eyes burned like fire, her throat felt gritty and coarse, and her hands shook.

"Here." Rush handed her a glass of water.

She felt an abundance of shame at having allowed him to see her like this, and worse, that he should be the one to take care of her. She sank to the edge of the tub, afraid her shaky legs could no longer support her.

"You're going to be all right now," Rush told her confidently. "It's over."

She couldn't look at him but nodded because it seemed the right thing to do. Rush had no way of knowing what Paul had done to her. No way of knowing that the man she'd loved and planned to share her life with had married another woman while Lindy proudly wore his engagement ring. Rush Callaghan didn't know a damn whit about shattered dreams or the pain of a broken heart. He would never allow himself to be hurt this way.

"Come on," he said. "I'll take you into your room."

She stood with his help, and he tucked his arm around her waist as he led her into her darkened bedroom. Gently he brushed the wet strands of hair from her face and lowered her onto the mattress in a sitting position.

"I trust you don't need anyone to undress you."

"No, I'm fine."

"It's a damn good thing," he said, and there was more than a trace of a smile in his words.

He started to walk away from her but paused just before he reached the door, turning back to her. "You're a beautiful woman, Lindy Kyle, and someday there'll be a man who will love you the way you deserve to be loved."

Her mother had said almost those identical words to her. At the time, Lindy hadn't been ready to accept them; she wasn't sure she could now. All through college there'd only been Paul. Every thought of the future had been linked with him. Every dream. Every ambition. She felt as if fate had sent her tumbling into oblivion, uncaring what ill fortune befell her.

But it wasn't in her to argue with Rush. Instead she brought her feet up onto the bed and pressed her head against the feather pillow. Her eyes ached unmercifully and she closed them.

"Did you hear me?" Rush demanded softly.

She wanted to shake her head that she hadn't, but there wasn't enough spirit left in her to challenge him. "I'm too selfish to pine away for Paul Abrams," she said, her soft voice trembling. "I'm not willing to be miserable any more."

Her words seemed to please him. "You're one hell of a woman, Lindy, and don't you forget it."

"Right." She couldn't contain the sarcasm. Although she kept her eyes closed, Lindy knew it was a long time before Rush left the doorway. His presence all but filled the room. Only when he'd slipped away did she feel comfortable enough to relax and sleep.

Lindy woke around two, her throat dry and scratchy. Her temples throbbed, and her eyes were red and swollen. She didn't turn on any lights as she made her way into the kitchen, preferring the shield of darkness.

The drapes were open and the city lights flickered in the distance. Taking the cold glass of water and the aspirin with her, Lindy stood at the window and expelled her breath in a long sigh. She'd made such an idiot of herself in front of Rush. The thought of facing him in the morning was almost more than she could bear.

Fresh tears dampened her face at the memory of the humiliating way she'd sobbed and moaned and rocked with grief. She exhaled a quivering breath and brushed her cheeks free of moisture.

"It's over, Lindy, there's no need to cry anymore."

She whirled around to discover Rush sitting in the darkened room, watching her.

"I'll cry if I damn well please," she hissed.

"There's no need to now."

Lord, she hated it when men thought they were so wonderfully logical. Everything seemed to be so cut-and-dried for them.

"Who made you king of the universe?"

He chuckled at that.

"I don't find that the least bit amusing. I honestly want to know what makes you think you know so damn much about human nature that you can decree when enough tears have been shed?"

"I know."

Lindy slapped her hand against her side in an action meant to reveal her disgust. "So the big lieutenant commander has spoken." She whirled around and placed the water glass down with such force that the liquid sloshed over the sides.

"How could you possibly know about loving someone and then losing them? You can't imagine what it's like to have your heart ripped from your chest and be left with a gaping wound that refuses to heal." She was yelling at him now, but not because she was angry. The memory of the way she'd broken down in front of him was more than embarrassing. Heated words were her only defense.

Rush was out of the chair so fast that it shocked her. He loomed at her side like a dragon, his jaw as tight and contorted as she'd ever seen it.

"I know more than I ever cared to." Each word dripped with ice, his message clear.

They stood, their gazes locked in the moonlight, glaring at each other, refusing to look away. She saw his pain then, as raw and jagged as her own. His guard was down. He'd lowered it for her tonight when she'd spilled out her heart, leaving himself exposed and trapped in pain-filled memories.

"Rush," she whispered, "I'm sorry. I didn't know." Slowly, she lifted her hand and touched his shoulder, wanting to offer him comfort the way he had helped her. "I didn't know."

He reached for her then, crushing her in his arms, burying his face in the curve of her neck. He didn't fill in the details. He didn't need to.

Four

Lindy slept on the davenport across from Rush, but the sweet luxury of oblivion escaped him. Even now, hours later, he couldn't forget the unselfconscious way she'd wrapped her arms around him and held him, her tears soaking through his shirt. Rush wasn't sure who she was crying for anymore: him or her. It didn't matter.

Her body felt unbelievably good against his own, and her warmth had chased away the arctic chill that had seemed to cut all the way through to the marrow of his bones. He didn't like to think about Cheryl and rarely did these days. But somehow being a witness to Lindy's anguish had brought the memory of his own bobbing uncontrollably to the surface of his mind. Like a cork, the remembrance of his love and foolishness had refused to sink, and he'd been left to deal with the pain that had suddenly seemed as fresh and real as it had been eight years ago.

The memory of Cheryl had weighed on him like a steel cloak, tormenting his heart and mind. He'd loved her with a love that was pure and innocent. A love so rare that he never hoped to feel such deep, heart-

wrenching emotion again. Leaving her to go to sea had
been the most difficult thing he'd ever done. Every day
of the tour he'd written to her, spilling out his heart. On
payday he'd sent her every penny he could, living on a
bare minimum himself because it was important to him
that she have the things she needed.

When he'd reached home port, he couldn't get off
the aircraft carrier fast enough. After six months at sea,
he was dying to hold her again, dying to love her. But
she hadn't been at the dock. Bitterly disappointed, the
only thing Rush could reason was that she was ill. Well,
he'd been partially right. Only her sickness was of the
nine-month variety. From what he'd learned later, sweet
innocent Cheryl had shacked up with another sailor a
week after he'd left San Diego. She'd apparently hoped
to pass the baby off as Rush's. Rush, however, hadn't
needed a degree in math to calculate the dates.

It might have made things easier for him if they'd
fought. He might have been able to release some of the
bitter anguish he'd experienced over her infidelity. But
instead he'd simply told her goodbye and walked away,
the diamond engagement ring he'd intended to give her
seeming to sear a hole through his palm.

In the weeks and months that followed, his mind
played crazy tricks on him. He tried to convince himself the baby was his, although God knows it was impossible. He heard from a friend that Cheryl married
some poor schmuck fresh out of officer training within
a month after Rush had left her.

A couple of years later he'd run into her in a bar.
Her big blue eyes had clouded with tears as she'd told
him they'd let something good slip away. With a wedding band on her finger, she'd placed her hand high on

his thigh and suggested they get together for old times' sake. Rush had thought he was going to vomit, she repulsed him so completely.

He never saw her again, never wanted to. Cheryl had taught him valuable lessons, ones destined to last a lifetime. She'd destroyed a part of him that could never be resurrected.

The first faint light of dawn seeped into the sky, extinguishing the stars one by one, and still Rush couldn't sleep. But the even meter of Lindy's breathing as she lay sleeping on the sofa was a soothing balm and gradually he felt the rigid tension leave his limbs.

They'd sat for hours, his arm around her, her head nestled over his heart. Neither had spoken—or wanted to. It was a time to remember. A time to forget. When she'd fallen into an exhausted sleep, he'd gently slipped free of her hold and lowered her head onto the sofa.

She was going to be all right now.

So was he.

Lindy squinted as the sun flooded the living room and seemed to rest, full force, on her face, disturbing her deep sleep. Her neck ached, and it was then that she realized that her only pillow had been the small flat decorative one from the couch. She felt disoriented until the memory of what had happened between her and Rush gushed through her mind like melting snow rushing down a mountainside during a spring thaw. She groaned and covered her face with her hands, embarrassed anew.

Slowly, almost against her will, she sat up and opened her eyes. She felt empty inside, depleted. Shaky.

A quick survey of the room told her Rush wasn't anywhere in the immediate vicinity, and she sighed with relief.

Coming to her feet, she brushed the mussed dark hair away from her face and stumbled into the kitchen. The coffee was made and a note propped against the base of the machine. Lindy reached for the slip of paper and blinked several times in an effort to clear her vision. Rush had duty and wouldn't be home until late afternoon.

Thank God.

She wasn't up to confronting him. Not now, anyway. What could she possibly say to him after she'd stripped herself emotionally naked and exposed her soul? Lord, she didn't know, but she'd figure it out later. Right now she wanted a hot bath and some breakfast, in that order.

By five that afternoon, she'd washed windows, baked a fresh apple pie and scrubbed the shower. Occupying herself with a dozen domestic tasks until she was forced into the inevitable confrontation with Rush.

She was frying pork chops for dinner when she heard the front door open, and she tensed, instantly filled with dread.

An awkward silence ensued when he stepped into the kitchen. Since she wasn't sure how to begin, she glanced around nervously and offered him a falsely cheerful smile.

Rush was frowning and she watched as his gaze bounced around the apartment, growing darker and more irritated with each passing moment.

Despite her best efforts, Lindy felt completely unstrung, and still Rush just stood there, looking straight through her with those impassive blue eyes of his.

"I baked a pie." It was an absurd thing to say, but

Lindy was quickly losing a grip on her determination to be cheerful and pleasant.

"That's not what I smell."

Lindy saw him wrinkle up his nose a couple of times, sniffing. "What are you?" she asked, forcing a light laugh. "A bloodhound?"

Obstinately Rush refused to respond to her attempt at good humor. If anything, his face grew more marred by dark shadows and anger kindled in his eyes. "It smells like pine needles in here."

"Oh." Why, oh why, couldn't he play her game? He had to know how difficult all this was for her. "I scrubbed down the cupboards. I think I was supposed to dilute the cleaner more than I did."

Her back was braced against the counter, her fingers gripping the edge. She could feel a pulse come alive in her temple. She'd had all day to make up her mind what she was going to say to Rush, how she was going to act, but her conclusions had been vague and fearful. That was when she'd decided she wouldn't utter a word about what had happened, praying he wouldn't, either. She should have realized Rush wouldn't let her forget it.

"You've been busy."

She nodded eagerly. "Yeah, I decided to spruce up the place a bit."

Her efforts didn't appear to please him. Damn, but she wished he'd say or do something to help her. He had to know what she was going through.

"You said something about pork chops being your favorite dinner," she offered next, almost desperate. All the while, her eyes pleaded with him. She'd just found her footing with this man, and now she was floundering again, her feet slipping out from under her every which way she turned.

"That was thoughtful." Still he frowned, his brow crowding his eyes, darkening them all the more.

Lindy rushed to the stove and used a cooking fork to turn the sizzling meat. She dared not look at him, and when she spoke the words strangled her. "I wanted to thank you, I guess."

"For what?"

Obviously Rush wasn't going to exert the least bit of energy to help her. The stoic look of the marble statue was properly in place once more and she wanted to hate him for his ability to disguise his emotions so effortlessly.

"Lindy."

She ignored him, flipping the frying meat when it was totally unnecessary.

"Lindy, turn around and look at me."

She shook her head.

"Those pork chops are going to turn into rubber if you cook them much longer."

Forcefully she turned off the burner and slapped the cooking fork on the stove top. "I could hate you for this," she muttered between clenched teeth.

"Well don't, because it isn't any easier for me."

Her chest was heaving with indignation when she slowly turned so that they faced each other once more. Nothing about him said he was the least bit uncomfortable. They could have been discussing the weather for all the reaction Rush revealed.

"Well?" she demanded, not having a single clue as to what he was thinking. He wore the hard mask of disciplined self-control, and she longed to slap it from his face.

"I'm embarrassed, too," he admitted finally.

"You? Whatever for? I was the one who made a complete idiot of myself. I was the one who was wailing like a banshee." She whipped the hair from her face. "What could you possibly have to be embarrassed about?"

He looked as if he were going to answer her, but Lindy wasn't about to let him. An entire day of worry and frustration was banked against her fragile control.

"Why couldn't you have let it drop?" she continued. "Trust me, I was willing to forget the entire incident. But, oh no, Mister Know-It-All has to rub my nose in it."

The muscle in his clenched jaw leaped so hard his temple quivered, and a strange light flared in his eyes. "I didn't want any pretense between us."

Defiance and pride filled Lindy's breast and her long nails threatened to snap as she continued to grip the countertop behind her. "I don't, either," she whispered after a moment, willing now to release her resentment and accept the wisdom of his words.

"I'd like us to be friends."

She nodded, dropping her gaze to the freshly waxed kitchen floor. "Lord knows, I could use one."

He smiled at that, and when she glanced up she noted that his eyes had softened perceptibly.

"How did you know apple pie is my favorite?"

Relaxing, Lindy returned his smile. "A fine naval officer like you should know the answer to that. Apple pie has to rank right up there with hot dogs and the American flag."

They both laughed aloud then, but not because she'd been especially clever. The matter had been settled between them and they were on an even keel once more. They could be friends.

"Well, how do I look?" Lindy asked Rush Monday morning. She stood beside the kitchen table, where he sat reading the paper and drinking coffee. Her interview wasn't scheduled until noon, but she'd been dressed and ready since eight, pacing the living room. Lord, he swore she'd straightened the same stack of magazines ten times.

"You're going to do great."

"You didn't even look at me," she accused, her hands clenched together in front of her. She was a picture of efficiency in her dark blue business suit, white blouse and navy pumps. If it were up to him, he would hire her on the spot.

"You look wonderful," he said, meaning it. Too damn good for his own peace of mind, if the truth be known.

She checked her wristwatch and nibbled nervously on the corner of her bottom lip. "I think I'll leave now."

"Good idea." To be truthful, he'd be glad to have her out of the apartment. But not because she was making a nuisance of herself. Oh sure, her pacing was beginning to get on his nerves, but far more profound than that— Lindy was beginning to get to him. Bad.

She reached for her purse. "I'll see you later."

"Break a leg, kid."

"Thanks."

Her quick smile ate like a sweet-tasting acid all the way through him. He'd been a fool to think their non-relationship would fall neatly back into place after Friday night. He'd been a first-class idiot to believe they could just be friends. Oh, they were that all right, but God knew he hungered for more. Much more.

Rush's breath escaped on a long, disgusted sigh as he pushed his coffee cup aside. Every time he looked at Lindy his body started to throb. It wasn't even funny. In fact it was downright embarrassing.

He leaned back in the chair and folded his arms over his chest, trying to reason matters out. Lindy was years younger than he. Ten, at least. And she'd been hurt, the pain much too fresh for her to trust her feelings. To further complicate the situation, she was Steve Kyle's little sister. Rush might be able to overlook the first stickler, but not the second or the third. Lindy was too vulnerable now, too susceptible. And Steve Kyle was much too good a friend to lose because Rush couldn't maintain his self-control.

Lord, he wished she'd get that damn job and move out of the apartment. And out of his life. Once she'd cleared out, maybe things would go back to normal and he could concentrate on matters that were important to him.

That wasn't true, Rush admitted even as he thought it. He liked having Lindy around, liked her being there when he came in after a frustrating day aboard the *Mitchell*. Liked talking to her in the evenings. That was the problem in a nutshell. He liked every damn thing there was about Lindy Kyle.

Rush was mature enough, disciplined enough, to ignore the physical attraction, although God knows it was difficult. A thousand times he'd cursed the memory of that morning when he had found her in the bathroom, and seen her all soft and feminine. His mental picture of the way her breasts had peeped out at him, firm and round and proud, had the power, even now, to eat a hole straight through his mind. For his own sense of well-being he couldn't allow his thoughts to dwell on how good she'd felt in his arms, or how she'd fallen asleep with her head resting securely over his heart. Nor did he choose to think about how he'd sat and stroked her hair, drinking in her softness, marveling in her gentleness.

Lindy's allure, however, was much more profound than the physical. In the space of one week she'd managed to reach into his heart, dragging the emotion out of him like hidden scarves from the sleeves of a clown. Each one more colorful than the last. Each one a surprise. Lindy made him feel vulnerable, threatening him in ways he'd never expected to experience again.

He wanted to stay away from her, avoid her as he had in the beginning. But Lindy was like a magnetic field that drew everything to itself. He couldn't be anywhere near her and not want her. Physically. Emotionally. Every damn way there was to want a woman.

He stood then, determined not to think about her anymore. A cold shower was what he needed to wake him up to a few fundamental facts. He wasn't an inexperienced youth, unable to control himself. Rush had been around the block more times than he cared to count.

With a fresh set of clothes, he stepped into the bathroom and shut the door. He hesitated, closed his eyes and slumped against the side of the sink. Inhaling the faint flower scent of Lindy's perfume, he released a groan that came from deep within his chest. The fragrance wove its way around him like an early morning mist, tempting him, enticing him, reminding him of everything he swore he was going to forget.

With his jaw knotted so tight his teeth hurt, Rush reached for the shower dial and turned it on full force.

Grimly he wondered how much cold water it would take to distract him from the ache in his groin.

"Rush." Lindy threw open the front door of the apartment. "I got the job." Filled with joyous excitement, she tossed her purse aside and whirled around the living room like a ballerina, her arms clenched tightly over her breasts.

She was so dizzy she nearly stumbled, but she didn't care. Breathless and laughing, she stopped and braced her hand along the back of the sofa. "Oh, come on, Rush, you've got to be home!"

A quick check of the rooms told her he wasn't. The minute she'd been free, Lindy had hurried out of the Boeing offices, dying to tell Rush that the job was hers. The money was great. More than great. Wonderful. Health insurance, paid vacations, sick leave. And ten days off at Christmas. The whole nine yards—or was that ten? She didn't know. What she did know was that this wonderful, fabulous job was hers.

She couldn't have asked for a better position. The woman who would be her supervisor had taken Lindy around to meet her co-workers and everyone had been so nice, so friendly. Lindy had known almost immediately that she was going to fit right in.

"Rush," she called out again, in case she'd missed him somehow.

His name fell emptily into the silence. Oh well, he'd hear her good news soon enough. She went into her bedroom and changed into jeans and a soft pink ten-button Henley shirt, pushing the three-quarter length sleeves up past her elbows. She reached for her purse and as an afterthought scribbled Rush a note that said she was going out to buy thick T-bones, and when she got back they would celebrate.

By the time Lindy returned from the Pike Place Market, Rush was on the lanai and the barbecue was smoking.

"Hi," she called out, and set the grocery bag on the counter. "I got the job."

"I didn't doubt for a minute that you would."

Rush looked wonderfully relaxed in casual slacks and a light blue sweater that set off the color of his eyes to a clear cornflower blue. The sun glinted through his dark hair, and when he turned to smile at her, his face fairly danced with happy mischief, as if he'd known all along she'd do well and was as pleased as she that she had gotten the job. And exceedingly proud.

"Well, you might have shared some of that confidence with me," Lindy told him with mock disgust. "In case you didn't notice, I was a wreck this morning. Imagine leaving two hours before an interview." She could chide herself about it now, but she'd felt as if an army of red ants had decided to use her stomach as a place to dig their farm.

"I was confident enough to buy a bottle of champagne to celebrate," he informed her, moving into the kitchen and opening the fridge. He brought out the bottle and set it on the counter with all the ceremony and flair of a wine steward.

"Oh Rush, we can't drink this," she whispered, reverently examining the bottle. This wasn't the normal cheap champagne Lindy was used to drinking at Christmastime, but an expensive French variety, decorated with a gold seal and a fancy blue ribbon.

"Why not?" His brows shot up.

"It's too good... I mean, I can't even pronounce the name of it." She tried, her tongue stumbling over the French vowels. In high school she'd taken a couple of years of the language, but she could never be considered fluent.

"You can't say champagne?" His voice dipped with sarcasm while tiny pinpricks of light shimmered in the depths of his eyes.

"Oh stop. You're being deliberately obtuse."

Already he'd peeled away the decorative top foil. "If anyone has reason to celebrate, it's you."

Lindy sighed and nodded, utterly content. "I can't tell you how pleased I am."

"You don't need to," he teased. "Anyone within a five-block radius could feel your happiness." His gaze held hers briefly before he dragged it away and started working to remove the cork.

Lindy felt strangely breathless and dizzy with joy. She was truly happy, when only a few weeks before she'd doubted that she'd ever experience elation or excitement again. Now she felt as though destiny had finally caught up with her again, and she was riding the crest of a wave, surging ahead, grabbing at every good thing that came her way. And lately, since she'd met Rush, there seemed to be so much to feel good about.

The sound of the cork popping and the bubbly liquid spraying into the sink caused Lindy to gasp, then giggle.

"Here, here," she cried, handing Rush one of the tall narrow glasses he'd set out. She didn't want any of this precious liquid to be wasted. God only knew how much Rush had paid for the bottle.

"A toast," Rush said, handing her a glass and taking his own. Tiny golden bubbles popped to the surface as if to add their own congratulations. "To Lindy Kyle, computer expert," Rush murmured, completely serious.

"I'm not really an expert."

"Are you always this argumentative, woman?"

"All right, all right," she laughed and licked the moisture from her fingertips. "IBM owes everything to me. Mr. Wang himself calls me his friend." Her eyes were laughing, her joy and enthusiasm exuding with every breath, because it was impossible to contain them.

"Mr. Wang?" Rush asked her. "What about Mr. Callaghan? Is he your friend?"

"Oh most assuredly. The very best kind there is."

"Good."

Lindy thought his voice sounded slightly husky, pleased, but before she had time to analyze it or study him further, Rush poised his glass next to hers. Gently they tapped the delicate rims together and Lindy tasted a sample. The smooth liquid was wonderfully light and mellow and so delicious that she closed her eyes to properly savor it.

"This is marvelous stuff," she said, taking another sip.

"I thought you'd like it."

"I bought us steaks," she said, suddenly remembering the sack. "And enough vegetables to open our own fifty-item salad bar."

Rush chuckled. "You get the salad together and I'll manage the steaks."

"That sounds like a workable plan."

"Good grief," he chided, unwrapping the thick T-bones from the white butcher paper. "You're already using office lingo."

Lindy resisted the urge to swat his backside as he returned to the lanai, and turned her attention to the variety of fresh vegetables for the salad.

She finished before Rush did, and taking her champagne glass with her, joined him outside. It had rained for part of the week, but the sun was out this afternoon and the breeze was fresh and clean.

"The coals aren't quite hot enough yet," he told her, leaning against the wrought-iron railing, looking at ease with himself and his world.

Perhaps it was the champagne or the fact she'd stood too long in the sun. Lindy wasn't sure which to blame. But standing beside Rush she suddenly felt the overwhelming need to have him kiss her, the overpowering desire to glide her moist lips back and forth over his and taste the champagne on his tongue.

"Lindy?" He was frowning at her, and for a moment she was sure he'd read her thoughts. "What is it?"

"Nothing." She shook her head for emphasis, pushing down the impulse. It was insane, stupid, wrong. And yet something kept driving her. Something primitive and completely unmanageable. Before she could change her mind, she took both their wineglasses and set them aside, her hands shaking.

Rush watched her like a man in a trance.

She leaned forward and planted her hands on his shoulders, her intense gaze holding his.

At her touch, she felt a quiver work its way through his lean, hard body. He stiffened, his shoulders at attention as though a visiting admiral were passing by for inspection. But still he didn't try to stop her, didn't gently push her away as she thought he might. His hands bunched into tight fists at his sides.

Filled with purpose, and more determined than she

had been about anything in a long time, Lindy stood on
tiptoe and briefly touched her lips to his.

It was better than she'd thought, better than she'd
dreamed. She cocked her head so their noses wouldn't
present a barrier and kissed him again. Lightly. Tentatively. Shyly.

Rush stood stiff and motionless, but a low moan
slipped from deep within his throat. His dark eyebrows
cramped his piercing blue eyes, and he glared at her. If
he hoped to intimidate her with a look, he failed. Lindy
felt incredibly brave, ready to take on a fully armed
armada if need be. Surely managing one weary sailor
wouldn't be so difficult.

Rush closed his eyes then opened them, searching
her face, his look tormented. He seemed to be telling
Lindy to stop. Begging her to move away from him because he hadn't the will to move himself. But Lindy had
no intention of following his silent demand. None. Instead she smiled boldly up at him, her heart in her eyes.

Rush claimed her lips then, and groaned anew as if
holding her were the last thing in the world he wanted
to do. His mouth clung to hers, warm and demanding
as his tongue plundered the dark, sweet secret of her
mouth, taking all that she offered.

His hands pulled her tight against him and he continued to kiss her again and again until she was flushed
and trembling and her blood felt as if it could boil.

"Oh God, Lindy. No. No. This isn't right." His voice
was tortured and barely audible. But still he didn't release her.

Five

Rush's face was hard. Harder than at any time Lindy could remember. His eyebrows were pulled down over his eyes, which were busily searching her face, seeking answers she couldn't give him.

Gently, his hands at her waist, he broke her hold on him and turned away, but not too far, because she was able to view his profile in the afternoon sunlight. He sucked in a giant breath and savagely jerked his fingers through his hair, his face dark and ravaged with what looked like guilt and regret.

"Rush," she whispered. "Listen…"

"No, you listen…"

The same mindless force that had driven her to kiss him led her now, and she moved behind him, wrapping her arms around his torso and fiercely hugging his back. She could feel the coiled resistance in him, but refused to release him.

"Lindy, damn it, you're not making this easy." His hands moved to break her hold and release himself from the trap of her arms.

At least Lindy thought that was his intent. But instead his fingers closed over her knuckles, squeezing her hands together with such force she nearly gasped with pain. But when his hand touched hers something seemed to snap inside him and he relaxed, causing her to melt all the more intimately against him.

She was shocked by how good Rush's body felt. He was tall and lean and hard and he stirred some inherent need in her.

An eternity passed before either moved. They hardly seemed to breathe. Lindy would have held on to Rush until the Second Coming if he hadn't broken free of her clasp and moved away from her. His breath was choppy then, as though it had cost him a great deal to leave her arms. His intense blue eyes stubbornly avoided hers.

"I think it would be best if we forget that ever happened," he said gruffly, and seemed to be engrossed in placing the steaks on the barbecue.

"I'm not going to forget it." Lindy didn't know why she felt she had to argue with him, but she did. "I thought you were the one who was so keen on us being honest with each other."

"This is different." He shook enough salt over the meat to preserve it into the next generation. Pepper and garlic powder followed, so thick they practically obliterated the juicy T-bones.

"You said it was important there be no pretense between us," she pressed. "And you're right."

"Damn it, Lindy. Just what the hell do you want from me?" He remained hunched over the barbecue, refusing to meet her eyes. "Do you want me to tell you I find you attractive? Fine. You turn me on. I hope to hell you're satisfied now."

She couldn't have stopped the spontaneous smile that

joyously sprang over her face had their lives depended on it. Just knowing Rush was attracted to her gave Lindy a giddy sense of power.

"I find you appealing, too," she admitted, having trouble keeping the elation out of her voice. Actually that was a gross understatement. She was drawn to Rush the way a thirsty flower is to rain.

"Well, you shouldn't, because..." he paused and forcefully exhaled a breath, looking both angry and confused.

Lindy's heart thudded expectantly. "Why not? Is it so wrong?"

Rush rose slowly to his feet then, faced her and placed his hands on her shoulders in a brotherly fashion, his eyes clear. Determined.

"Lindy, listen to me. You've been badly hurt recently. Devastated by a man you loved and trusted, and now everything seems to have turned around. You've got a reason to be happy, to celebrate. But my being here is much too convenient. It's only natural that you feel attracted to me, living at close quarters the way we do. You're a young, passionate woman, filled with the love of life and...you're excited now. I don't blame you, especially after everything you've been through. Your pride suffered a major setback not so long ago, and here I am like a savior, the means of salvaging it all."

"Rush...no."

"But Lindy," he continued, unwilling to let her cut him off, "you're too vulnerable right now. The attraction you feel toward me is only natural under the circumstances. But you've got to understand something important here. Given the same situation, you'd experience these identical emotions toward any healthy, red-blooded male. It's not really me who appeals to you, it's the thought of another close relationship."

"You can't honestly believe that. Why, that's ridiculous, Rush Callaghan."

"No, it isn't. Think about it, Lindy. Think hard. You want a man tonight." His voice was rough with intensity. "I can understand your feelings, sympathize with what's happened to you, but making love wouldn't be right. I'm not the one for this, and I refuse to take advantage of you. Find someone else to build your ego."

"I find that insulting," she told him earnestly, but without anger. She had thought he might try to avoid her by starting an argument, and she refused to swallow the bait, no matter how much he irritated her.

"I'm not saying this to offend you. You're the one who insisted upon honesty. You got it." He returned to the steaks, as calmly as if they'd been discussing something as mundane as stock prices or the outcome of a baseball game.

"You're making this difficult," she said next.

"I plan to make it impossible."

"Honestly, Rush. Would you stop handling me with kid gloves? I'm a woman."

"Honey, that's one thing you won't find me arguing about." His words were followed by a harsh chuckle. "Now, come on. Be a good little girl and eat your steak."

The dishwasher was whirling softly in the background when Lindy reached for the telephone a couple of hours later. As soon as their meal had been completed, Rush had left her without so much as a word to tell her where he was going or when he intended to come back. The bloody coward!

"Hi, Mom," Lindy said when her mother picked up the receiver on the third ring.

"Lindy, sweetheart, is everything all right?"

"It's wonderful. I got a job with Boeing and start first thing in the morning."

"That's terrific."

Lindy could hear the relief in her mother's voice, and smiled, remembering again how great she'd felt when the personnel director had offered her the job.

"Sweetheart, I couldn't be more pleased. I knew everything would work out, given time."

"I have more good news."

"More?" her mother said, and laughed softly.

"I've met someone."

"You have?" The question was followed by a brief, strained silence. "Isn't this rather sudden?"

Lindy could all but hear the excitement drain out of Grace Kyle's voice to be replaced by weary doubt. "Now, before you say anything, let me tell you something about him. He's wonderful, Mom, really wonderful. He's helped me so much, I can't even begin to tell you everything he's done for me. He's a good, kind person. Honorable."

"Oh, Lindy," her mother said with a sigh, "do be careful."

"I will, Mom. I promise." The comedy of the situation struck her then, and she started to giggle.

"What's so funny?" Her mother obviously hadn't stopped to think things through.

"Mom, I'm twenty-two years old and when I told you that I'd met someone, you said I should be careful, like I was seven years old again and about to cross a busy street alone for the first time."

"But, Lindy, you're hardly over—" Grace paused and exhaled a disgusted, uneven breath. "I refuse to even mention his name."

"Paul." Lindy said it for her. "He can't hurt me anymore. I refuse to let him."

"That's nice, sweetheart. Now tell me—where did you meet this young man you think so highly of?"

Lindy gnawed on her lower lip. Explaining her living arrangements to her mother would surely be cause for concern, but Lindy wasn't in the habit of lying. "I met him a few days after I arrived in Seattle."

"Oh. And what's his family like?"

"Mom, we've only known each other a little while. I haven't met his family."

"But I think you should find out about them, don't you?"

"I suppose. In time. Listen, Mom, I just wanted to call and let you know that everything is going terrific. I've got a good job and I couldn't be happier. Really."

"I'm so pleased for you."

"I know. I feel good about everything, and I don't want you to worry about me anymore because nothing's going to hold me down again."

"I knew you'd find your footing, given time."

"I have, Mom."

"Goodbye, sweetheart."

"'Bye, Mom. Give my love to Dad."

"I will."

Lindy thought she heard a trace of tears in her mother's soft voice when she replaced the receiver. She was surprised to note there was a hint in her own.

With Rush gone, the apartment felt like an empty tomb and the evening dragged by. Lindy watched television for a while, worked a crossword puzzle and added an extra coat of pink polish to her nails. By eleven she was tired and ready to give up her vigil. Rush had been determined to get away from her, to leave her alone to recognize the foolishness of her actions. She knew what he was thinking as clearly as if he'd announced his intentions. Only it hadn't worked. If anything, Lindy was more determined than ever to get him to face the truth of what was happening between them.

Discouraged, she undressed and climbed between the cool sheets. But sleep wouldn't come. Instead all she could think about was how good it had felt to be in Rush's arms. How good and how remarkably right.

She recognized there was some validity to what he'd claimed. But he was wrong to think she was using him. The feelings she had for Rush had absolutely nothing to do with what had happened with Paul. The attraction she felt for Rush was because of who he was. She'd meant every word she'd said to her mother. Rush Callaghan was an honorable man, and there seemed to be few enough of them left.

Rush had given her a priceless gift. Her freedom. His patience and tenderness had released her from the shackles of pain and remorse. He'd held her hand and shown her the way out of the dark shadows. He'd led her gently into the warm healing glow of a summer sun.

If he were with her now, discussing matters the way he should be, Lindy knew exactly what he'd say to her. He'd tell her she was grateful. She was, but it was far more than gratitude she felt toward Rush. He'd taken her wounded heart and breathed new life into it. He'd let her feel again when her every nerve ending had been numb, and her very existence had seemed pointless.

She couldn't stop thinking about how perfect she'd felt in his arms, her breasts flattened against his broad chest, her nipples hard and erect. Just the memory was enough to stir her senses back to life. That brief time with Rush had produced an incredible range of new awarenesses. His kiss had been warm and tender, his lips lingering over hers as though this moment and place were out of time and meant for them alone.

His tender touch had brought with it the sweetest, most terrible yearning to be loved by him. Completely. Totally. Lindy didn't need anyone to tell her that when Rush Callaghan gave his heart to a woman, she would be the most incredibly fortunate female alive.

Lindy had just begun to scratch the surface of his multifaceted personality. Over the years, Rush had built several thick protective layers around himself, and Lindy had only managed to peel away the top few, to gain a peek inside. But she believed with all her heart that underneath he was sensitive and strong, daring and bold, and yet in some ways almost shy.

In time, Rush would realize she knew her own mind—and her own heart. In no way was she rebounding from Paul. Her former fiancé had actually done her a big favor, although it had been difficult to recognize it at the time. Paul was weak. Blinded by her love, she hadn't seen it before. Paul didn't possess the principles Rush did, either. Rush, on the other hand, was noble, reliable and completely trustworthy. Lindy would stake her life on it. Her judgment had been poor once, but she'd learned something from Paul, and although the lesson had been bitterly painful, she'd been an apt student. She knew an honorable man when she saw one. And Rush Callaghan fit her definition to a T.

Still awake at midnight, Lindy bunched her pillow in half and rolled onto her stomach. She might as well climb out of bed and wait for him as toss and turn all night. She'd no sooner made the decision to get up when she heard the front door open.

Relieved, Lindy smiled and eagerly threw aside the blankets. She slipped her arms into the sleeves of her robe and headed out her bedroom door, impatient to talk to him.

Rush was just coming down the hallway.

"You're home," she greeted, not even trying to disguise her pleasure. It wasn't one of her most brilliant statements, but she didn't care.

He grumbled something that she couldn't make sense of.

"You didn't need to leave, you know."

"Yes, I did." He kept as far away from her as space would allow.

"Rush, we need to talk."

"Not now."

"Yes, now," she insisted.

"You have to go to work in the morning. Remember?" he argued, and rubbed his hand wearily over the back of his neck. "And for that matter so do I."

Lindy took a step toward him, and stopped. The cloying scents of cheap perfume and cigarette smoke clung to him like the stench of an infection. Shocked, Lindy tensed and braced herself against the wall to avoid getting any closer to him than necessary. She felt as though he'd driven a stake through her heart, so violent was the rush of pain. Rush had left her arms, scoffed at her timid efforts at lovemaking and gone to another. Someone with far more experience than she.

She glared at him through wide, angry eyes. "You're disgusting." She spat the words vengefully with all the vehemence her heart could muster. Then she whirled around and returned to her room, slamming the door with such force that the picture of her family on the dresser tumbled to the carpet.

Rush didn't bother to follow her and Lindy was glad.

She was trembling uncontrollably when she sank onto the edge of her mattress. The honorable man she'd been so willing to place on a pedestal possessed clay feet. Clay feet and a clay heart.

Lindy may have slept at some time during the long night that followed, but she doubted it. She was so furious she couldn't allow herself to relax enough to sleep. She had no hold on Rush, she realized. There was no commitment between them. A few kisses were all they'd ever shared, and yet she wanted to throttle him.

Apparently she wasn't as apt a student as she'd thought, and she didn't know which had disappointed her more—Rush's behavior or her own inability to judge men.

Rush heard Lindy tossing and turning in her room long after he'd retired to his own room. He knew what she believed and had purposely let her go on thinking it, hoping she'd forget this silly notion about letting a romance develop between them. That had been his original intention. But when he'd seen the flash of pain in her eyes, he knew he couldn't go through with it. Unfortunately Lindy wasn't in any mood to carry on a levelheaded conversation, he'd decided. He'd explain things in the morning.

Rush had gotten out of the apartment as soon as he could following dinner, afraid of what might happen if he stayed. The truth of the matter was that it had taken every damn bit of restraint he'd possessed to walk away from Lindy. The cold beer he had nursed in a sleazy waterfront bar was small compensation for his considerable sacrifice.

His biggest problem was that he believed every word he'd said to Lindy. She was vulnerable right now. Vulnerable and trusting. A lethal combination as far as Rush was concerned. If he loved her the way she wanted, she'd wake in the morning filled with regrets. Rush couldn't do that to her. Hell, if he was honest, he couldn't do it to himself. He wasn't so much a fool not to recognize that loving Lindy once would never be enough. A sample would only create the need for more. Much more.

The simple act of kissing and holding her had nearly defeated him. When she'd leaned up and brushed her lips over his, his body had fired to life with a heat that had threatened to consume him. It had demanded every part of his considerable self-control not to lift her into his arms and carry her into his bedroom.

The sweet little witch must have known it, too. She'd pressed her softness against him, fully conscious of what the intimacy was doing to him. And then she'd paused and looked up at him, her eyes wide and trusting and filled with such delectable love that it was more than a mere man could resist. He'd kissed her until he'd felt her weak and trembling in his arms. He had no idea what had stopped him then, but whatever it was, he was grateful.

Escape had been his only alternative, and he'd left the apartment when he could. He didn't want to be in the bar, but after a brisk walk there hadn't been anyplace else he knew to go. A woman who often loitered there had strolled up to his table, sat down without an invitation and tried to start a conversation. Rush had glared at her and told her he wasn't in the mood for company. Apparently she'd taken his words as a challenge and before he could stop her, her arms were all over him.

Rush didn't realize the scent of her sickeningly sweet perfume had stayed with him until he saw Lindy's look of complete disgust.

He was going to settle that matter first thing in the morning.

It was with a sense of righteousness that Lindy snapped a rock-music tape into her cassette player and turned it up full blast. Tapping her foot to the loud music, she wove the hot curling iron through her hair and waited. Within a couple of minutes, Rush staggered into the bathroom, apparently having just awakened, looking as if he intended to hurl her portable stereo out the living room window.

"Is that really necessary?" he shouted.

With deliberately slow movements Lindy turned down the volume. She regarded him with wide, innocent eyes. "What did you say?"

"Is that god-awful music necessary?"

It gave her a good deal of pleasure to smile sweetly back at him and ask, "Did I wake you? I'm so sorry, Rush."

"I'll bet," he grumbled and turned to stumble back to his room.

Lindy loved it.

Her sense of timing couldn't have been more perfect some time later when they met again in the kitchen. He grumbled something that sounded faintly like a plea for coffee. He had just gotten down a mug and started to pour himself a cup when she switched on the blender full blast. Hot coffee splattered over the counter and Rush jumped back, cursing savagely.

He whirled around to face her and once more Lindy gave him her brightest smile. She finished her task and asked, "Would you like some orange juice?"

"No," he grumbled.

She swallowed a laugh and with a good deal of ceremony, poured herself a glass.

Rush was studying her with a tight frown. "Now I know what they mean when they say 'hell hath no fury like a woman scorned.'"

Lindy gave him a vague look. "I'm sure I don't know what you mean."

"Like hell," he exploded. "Exactly how long is it going to take you to properly mete out justice?"

"Rush, I think you got out of the wrong side of bed this morning. You seem to be imagining all sorts of things. What could I possibly be angry about?" Already she was feeling better. Okay, so maybe her revenge was a tad childish, but Rush deserved everything he got—in triplicate.

"Damn it, Lindy. You've got the wrong idea here."

"Wrong idea about what?" She batted her thick lashes a couple of times for effect and had the satisfaction of seeing him clench his jaw. From experience Lindy knew mornings had never been Rush's favorite time of day. He looked disoriented, out of sorts and more than a little lost in knowing how to deal with her. As far as Lindy was concerned, Rush's confusion was poetic justice.

"While I'm still alive and breathing," he managed,

"I think you'd better know there's been a minor misunderstanding here."

"I haven't the slightest idea what you're talking about," she returned, her look as earnest as she could make it and still hold back her amusement.

His hand slammed against the counter. "And I'm sure you know exactly what I'm talking about," he countered, unable to restrain his fury. "You've tried and convicted me without knowing the details."

The particulars were the last thing Lindy wanted to hear.

"Spare me, please," she told him, the amusement of her game vanishing. "You can sleep with a harem for all I care." It astonished her how easily the lie slipped from her lips. Rarely had she been more bitterly disappointed in anyone than she had been in Rush.

"Lindy…"

She cut him off with a quick shake of her head. "I wish I had more time to sort this out," she lied again, but not as smoothly this time. "But in case you've forgotten, I've got a job to go to."

She walked away from him and was already in the living room when she paused to add, "You were right about one thing, though. I'm not ready for another relationship." She turned to face him then. "You don't need to worry about trying to clear the air. I understand, Rush, far better than you know."

His eyes held hers and a strong current of energy passed between them. As always she could read little in his impassive expression. But he must have agreed with her because he said nothing, and she hurriedly walked away, eager to escape.

It was while she was brushing her teeth that a sheen

of tears brightened her eyes. After everything that had happened to her, it was a surprise. She'd assumed she had more control of her emotions than this; she blamed the tears on lack of sleep.

With her purse in her hand she headed for the front door. She'd learned several lessons in the past few months, but they didn't seem to be getting any easier.

Walking down the hallway, she was forced to pass Rush, who was sitting on the sofa in the living room. She forced a smile and squared her shoulders, prepared to move past him with her head high.

Just as she reached him, Rush's arm reached out, grabbed her hand and stopped her cold. His eyes held her more tightly than any vise.

"I won't have you face your first day on the job with doubts. There was no one last night, Lindy. No one but you."

She blinked back the surprise and uncertainty, not sure what to believe. The evidence had reeked from him.

Rush tugged at her arm, bringing her closer. When she was within easy reach, he wrapped his arm around her waist and brought her down onto his lap. She landed there with a plop. His hands found their way to her face and he turned her head so her unwilling gaze was forced to meet his.

"I can't let you go on thinking I could've touched another woman after kissing you." His eyes filled with an emotion so powerful that Lindy couldn't speak. Gone was the mask—lowered or destroyed, she didn't know which—and what she saw in his wonderful eyes gave flight to her heart. His look was innocent, youthful almost. Seeking. He needed her to believe him, was pleading with her in a way she knew was foreign to this proud man.

Tears pooled in her eyes, and she nodded, silently telling him that she trusted his word.

The pad of his thumb wiped the moisture from the high arch of her cheek.

"Damn it, Lindy. We're in one fine mess here," he said, his voice gruff with emotion. "I want you like hell. What are we going to do?" His warm mouth, only inches from hers, brushed lightly over her parted lips.

Lindy just managed to stifle a groan and kissed him back softly, her mouth lingering over his own, needing his warmth.

By this time he'd wrapped her in his embrace. As though they had all the time in the world, Rush brought her lips down to his own with an agonizing slowness. The kiss was filled with such aching tenderness, such sweet torment that the fresh tears rolled unheeded down the side of her face.

"I should have trusted you," she told him brokenly. "I should have known."

"Lindy...don't cry, please. It's all right. It doesn't matter." He pulled her more completely into his embrace and held her tightly.

The memory of his look when he'd stumbled into the bathroom caused her to laugh and cry at the same time.

"Honey...please. I can't bear the thought that I've made you cry. You are crying, aren't you?"

Lindy laughed aloud, then sobbed. She reached for his hand to kiss his knuckles. "Did you burn yourself when you spilled the coffee?"

He looked at her as though they should give serious

consideration to having her committed to a mental facility. "No," he said tightly.

"I'm so sorry," she told him, spreading kisses over the edge of his jaw. "Oh, Rush, I thought horrible things of you. I thought—"

"I can guess," he muttered, cutting her off.

"But you're good and honorable and I was so wrong."

He chuckled and shook his head. "If you had a hint of what I was thinking of doing right now, you'd amend the honorable portion."

It was difficult to read his expression, but what she saw there caused her to wrap her arms around his neck and kiss him with a hunger that left them both shaking.

"Shall I tell you what I'm thinking, Rush Callaghan?"

Six

"Rush, guess what?" Breathless with excitement, Lindy let herself into the apartment and stopped abruptly, swallowing the remainder of her good news. Another man was standing next to Rush, and it looked as though the two had been arguing, or at least heatedly discussing something.

For the first time in recent memory, Rush didn't look pleased to see her. Apparently she'd arrived at the worst possible time. Her dark eyes met his and she offered a silent apology. His brief smile both reassured and warmed her.

After an awkward moment, Rush stepped forward. "Lindy, this is Jeff Dwyer. Jeff, this is Lindy Kyle, Steve Kyle's little sister."

Jeff resembled a fat cat who had just been presented with a pitcher of rich cream. The corners of his mouth twitched with the effort to suppress a smile, and his eyes fairly danced with mischief and delight. "I can't tell you how pleased I am to meet you, Lindy."

"Thank you." Her gaze moved from Rush to Jeff and then back to Rush, who gave her a fleeting smile that revealed his chagrin. He wasn't overly pleased about something, but he wasn't angry, either.

"Since Rush didn't bother to explain, I will," Jeff went on to say. "We're both officers aboard the *Mitchell*. Rush and I've worked together for the past four years." He hesitated and rubbed the side of his jaw. "Until recently I thought I knew everything there was about my fellow officer, but I guess I was wrong."

Rush placed his hands in his pants pockets, ignoring the comment. "Jeff and his wife Susan are visiting downtown Seattle this afternoon."

Jeff couldn't have looked more pleased. Lindy didn't know what was happening between the two men, but she'd apparently loused things up for Rush.

"Sue's having the twins' pictures taken at one of those fancy studios," Jeff continued. "She didn't seem to need me, so I thought I'd stop off and see my good buddy Rush."

Lindy nodded, not knowing how else to respond.

"How long have you—ah, been living here?" Jeff asked.

Unsure, Lindy's gaze sought Rush's.

"It's not what you're implying, Jeff." Rush's frown was fierce as he glared at his friend. "In case you didn't hear me the first time, I'll say it once more. Lindy is Steve Kyle's little sister."

Again the edges of the other man's mouth moved spastically. Jeff looked to be exerting a good deal of effort to hold back his amusement. The more pleased the other man's look became, the darker Rush's frown grew.

"I heard you," Jeff said.

"Isn't it about time for you to pick up Susan and the

kids?" Rush asked in an emotionless tone that was devoid of humor.

Jeff made a show of looking at his wristwatch. "I suppose," he admitted reluctantly. His gaze drifted to Lindy. "It was a pleasure to meet you. A real pleasure. Next time, I'll bring Sue along."

"I'd like that."

Rush was already standing next to the front door when Jeff left her. Lindy could vaguely hear the two exchange farewells followed by a couple of heated whispers.

"What was that all about?" she asked, once Rush had returned.

"Nothing."

"Don't give me that, Rush Callaghan. I know better."

He lapsed into silence for a moment. "Jeff came over to investigate a suspicion."

"Oh?"

"How did your day go?"

His effort to change the subject wasn't subtle, but Lindy could tell pressuring him to explain what had been going on between him and Jeff Dwyer wouldn't do her any good.

"Oh," she said, her eyes rounding with excitement. "I nearly forgot." Her hands eagerly started digging through her purse, tossing aside her compact and eel-skin wallet in her rush. Triumphantly she held up two tickets. "I got box seats for the Mariners' game tonight." When Rush just stood there staring at her, she blinked back her disappointment. She'd hoped he'd be as enthusiastic about attending the game as she was. "You do like baseball, don't you?"

His nod was decidedly absent. "Box seats?"

"On the one-hundred level. A girl I work with got them through the office. She can't go tonight, and asked if I could use them." Lindy had been so eager she could hardly make it back to the apartment fast enough, convinced Rush would want to see the Mariners play as much as she did. But looking at him now, she wasn't sure what to think. "Why are you looking at me like that?" she demanded, a little piqued.

"Like what?"

"Like that… Just now."

He shrugged. "I was just thinking about something Jeff said. I'm sorry. Did you say something I missed?"

Slowly Lindy shook her head. He hadn't told her any part of his conversation with his friend, and Lindy knew it would be useless to even try to get him to discuss the details with her.

"Do you want to go to the game or would you rather skip the whole thing?" She tried to sound nonchalant, but she was really hoping Rush would want to attend the game.

"The game, of course. Don't you think you'd better change clothes? Starting time is in another forty-five minutes."

"Right." Still confused, Lindy moved down the hallway to her bedroom. She didn't know what to make of Rush today. They'd been getting along so well lately, spending as much time together as possible, cramming all they could into the days and nights before the *Mitchell* left.

In three days they'd done something together every night. Tuesday he'd taken her to the Woodland Park Zoo, and they'd fed peanuts to the elephants and been splashed while watching the playful antics of the seals.

Wednesday they'd gone on a picnic on the shores of Lake Washington, where Rush had lain on the sweet-scented lawn, resting his head on her thigh while he nibbled on a long blade of grass. Thursday they'd eaten fish and chips on the waterfront and strolled hand in hand in and out of the tourist shops that dotted the wharf. Each night they'd laughed and joked and talked freely. And each night Rush had kissed her. Once. And only once. As though anything more would be too much temptation for him to handle. Rush treated her with kid gloves, touching her as if he were handling live ammunition. His kiss was always gentle, always controlled—too controlled to suit Lindy. If she hadn't felt the soul-wrenching reluctance and regret in every part of him when he gently left her arms, she would have been deeply discouraged.

Lindy knew that Rush was having problems dealing with the emotions she aroused in him. He didn't trust their attraction. Didn't trust her, believing she couldn't possibly know her own heart so soon after Paul. And perhaps, Lindy realized, Rush didn't trust himself. He'd certainly gone out of his way to behave like an endearing older brother—except when he lowered his guard just a little each night to kiss her. He wanted her. He'd told her as much, and she wanted him. But the time for them wasn't right.

As fast as she could Lindy changed out of her work clothes and rejoined Rush in the kitchen, prepared to hurry to the baseball game. He took one look at her and burst out laughing.

"What's so funny?"

"You. I thought you said we were going to watch the game. You look like you plan to participate in it."

She'd chosen faded jeans, a Mariner T-shirt and Steve's old baseball cap. "Have you got a problem with this, fellow?" she asked him, her eyes sparkling with fun and laughter.

Still grinning, Rush shook his head. "Come on, Babe Ruth, we've got a game to see."

They were settled in their box seats with foot-long hot dogs, a bag of peanuts and cold drinks by the time the first pitch was tossed. Rush had never been much into baseball. Football was his game, but he couldn't have refused Lindy anything. Her energy and enthusiasm for life were like a breath of fresh tangy air after a storm at sea. Being with her stirred his senses to vibrant life and made him glad for who and what he was. There were odd moments, now and then, when he resisted the magnetic pull he felt toward her and recounted the arguments—that she was too young, too vulnerable and his best friend's sister. But each day the echoes from his conscience came back weaker and his arguments sounded flatter. He was losing the battle, convinced he was being swept away in the whirlpool with little control over what was happening to either of them. For the most part Rush had given up the struggle and was living one day at a time, spending time with Lindy, savoring the moments they were together. But he couldn't, wouldn't allow the fickle Fates to carry him where they would, knowing full well they'd place him with Lindy, warm and willing, in his bed.

Jeff Dwyer knew him well enough to have guessed something had changed Rush's life. The day before, Jeff had confronted Rush and suggested that he revealed all the symptoms of a man in love. Rush had denied that, probably a lot more forcefully than he should have, because Jeff had gone on to enumerate the changes he'd seen in Rush since the *Mitchell*'s arrival back in Bremerton.

Not willing to drop the matter, Jeff had shown up at the apartment. He seemed to take delight in informing Rush that he'd been watching him closely of late. Jeff had noticed how quickly Rush left work the minute his shift was over, as if he couldn't wait to get back to his apartment. It used to be that Rush hung around awhile to shoot the bull with the other guys. No more. Rush was out of the shipyard like greased lightning. And furthermore, Jeff had claimed, Rush walked around with a cocky half smile, as though he found something highly amusing. As far as Jeff was concerned, these telltale symptoms added up to one thing: a woman.

Rush hadn't argued with his friend. He'd simply refused to discuss the subject. A lot of good it had done him. Just when he'd thought he was making headway and Jeff was about to drop the entire matter, Lindy had come bursting in the front door. Her eyes had glowed and sparkled as they sought him, confirming everything Jeff had been saying ten times over.

At his side, Lindy roared to her feet cheering. Lost in his thoughts, Rush hadn't been watching the game and now he saw that the Mariners had just scored. He joined Lindy and shouted once for effect.

Lindy laughed gleefully, turned to him and hugged his waist, her eyes alive with joy. With hardly a pause, she sat back down and reached for the bag of peanuts. Rush took his seat as well, but his mind was whirling. He wanted to kiss Lindy at that moment, and the need was so strong in him that it demanded all his restraint not to haul her into his arms right then and there. He reached for the peanuts himself and noted grimly that his hands were trembling with the need to touch her.

The game must have gotten good, because several times during the next few innings Lindy scooted to the edge of her seat and shouted advice to both player and umpire. As far as Rush could tell, he'd responded appropriately throughout the game. He'd cheered and hissed a couple of times, applauded and booed when Lindy did, but he hadn't a clue what was going on in the field. Dealing with what was happening to his own emotions was all he could handle for now. He was plowing through mine-infested waters with Lindy, and he was gradually losing his grip on his control with each minute he spent in her company.

Following the baseball game they walked from the Kingdome back to the apartment, a healthy two miles. Personally he would have preferred a taxi, but Lindy was in a mood to walk. She chatted as they strolled along, hand in hand. She was pleased that the home team had won and soon Rush felt himself caught up in her good mood.

Lindy didn't know what was wrong with Rush, but he hadn't been himself all evening. He'd hardly spoken during the entire game, and although he seemed to be paying attention, she could have sworn he hadn't noticed a blasted thing.

For her part, Lindy felt great. More than great. She felt wonderful! And so much of this newly discovered inner peace was due to loving Rush. She even knew the precise minute she'd recognized the truth about her feelings for her brother's friend. It had been the morning of her first day at Boeing, when he'd told her he couldn't let her think he'd touched another woman after kissing her. Even now, the memory of his words had the power to bring tears to her eyes. For days she'd yearned to tell him how her life had changed since she'd met him. But her words would only embarrass him, so she'd kept them locked inside her heart until she was convinced she'd choke on them.

When they reached the apartment, Rush held open the door for her to precede him inside. Lindy stepped into the living room, but didn't turn on any lights. The view of the Seattle skyline from the window drew Lindy there.

"Isn't it lovely?" she said, looking out over the glimmering lights of the waterfront. All seventy-five floors of the Columbia Center were lit, as was the Smith Tower.

Rush stood behind her, but said nothing.

Lindy turned and slipped her arms around his middle, pressing her ear to his broad chest, hugging him, savoring the peace of the moment, knowing he wouldn't allow it to last long.

His lips brushed the top of her head and she smiled. From experience Lindy knew that he tensed before he kissed her, as though gathering together his reserve of self-control. True to form, he stiffened and she smiled because she was beginning to know him so well. Eager now, she raised her head and tilted it to one side to receive his kiss. As it had been on previous nights, his mouth was warm and moist as it glided smoothly over hers. In welcome she parted her lips and slipped her arms up his chest to lazily loop them around his neck.

His kiss was light. Petal soft. Controlled.

Already his hands were braced on her shoulders, cupping them as he prepared to ease himself out of her arms. Lindy felt as though she were starving and a delectable feast was within easy reach, and yet Rush wouldn't allow her more than a sample.

"No," she objected in a tight whisper. She raised her hands to touch his face, her fingertips gliding over his features, hoping to memorize each one, burn it into her heart so that when he left her she could bear the parting.

"Lindy, don't," he groaned, and squeezed his eyes closed. He gripped her wrists and brought her fingers to his lips, kissing the tips.

"Hold me for just a little while longer." She thought for a moment that he was going to argue with her, but he didn't. With her arms draped around his neck, she pressed her cheek over his and felt him relax ever so slightly. But it wasn't nearly enough to satisfy her, and unable to resist, she turned her head and nuzzled his ear with her nose. Her mouth grazed his clenched jaw. Her lips worked their way across his brow, over his eyes and down the side of his nose to nibble on his lower lip. She hesitated, then ran the moist tip of her tongue over the seam of his lips.

Rush's arms tightened around her and he whispered her name on the tail end of a plea for her to stop.

He wanted her. She could feel the evidence boldly pressing against her thigh, and the knowledge of his desire gave her a heady sense of power. Led by instinct, she edged as close as possible to him and rotated her hips once, biting back a cry at the pleasure the action gave her even as it created a need for more. So much more.

"Oh God," he moaned through clenched teeth. "Lindy, don't do that."

"All I want you to do is hold me for a few minutes more. Is that so much to ask?"

"Yes," he returned, and his breath came in hot, quick gasps.

If he had planned on arguing with her, he didn't follow through—apparently having decided it was a losing battle. His hands, which until that moment had been on either side of her waist, moved slowly upward as though drawn there by a force stronger than his will.

Lindy's breasts strained against the fabric of her T-shirt with the need to experience his touch. Slowly his palms encircled her breasts, cupping them, weighing her ripe fullness.

Her soft moans echoed his.

"Lindy, no," he breathed, and the words seemed to stagger from his lips, low and reluctant. "Tell me to stop. Remind me what a good friend your brother is." His thumbs rotated around her nipples, which beaded into hard pebbles and stood proudly at attention. Rush groaned once more.

He kissed her then, hard, thrusting his tongue deep into her mouth as if to punish her for making him want her so desperately. She used her hands to hold his head as her eager tongue met his and they dueled and stroked against each other.

He broke away from her and sucked in deep, uneven breaths. "This has got to stop," he whispered fervently into her hair. "Now."

Lindy found she could say nothing. She searched his handsome face for some sign, anything that would explain why it was so urgent for them to stop kissing when she felt so right in his arms. Her heart was pounding in a hard, fast rhythm that made her feel breathless and weak.

Yet at the same time she was filled with an awesome sense of power. Standing on tiptoe, she slanted her mouth over his and used her tongue to torment him, probing his mouth with swift, gentle thrusts.

"Oh God, Lindy." He kissed her then, firmly, leaving her in no doubt that he was the one in control, not she.

Without Lindy being sure how he'd managed it, Rush had her T-shirt off and her bra unfastened and discarded. The next thing Lindy knew, they were both on the sofa, she in a reclining position, Rush above her. He kissed her face, her forehead, her eyes and lips, again and again, until she lost count. Then his mouth worked its way down the delicate line of her jaw to her neck. She sucked in a wobbly breath when his moist, hot lips found one of her nipples and drew it into his mouth for his tongue to torment. When he'd finished with it he moved to the other nipple, licking it until it ached and throbbed, taut and firm.

He kissed her lips repeatedly, and waves of erotic sensation lapped over her like water pounding relentlessly against the shore.

Lindy was throbbing everywhere. Her mouth, her tongue, her breasts, her belly and the area between her thighs. Her fingers wove their way through his hair.

"Rush." She whispered his name in a tormented whisper. "I love you so much."

He stilled, and after a torturous moment he raised his head. Poised as he was above her, his eyes feasted on her, studying her for what seemed an eternity. Then he shook himself as though coming out of a mindless fog. "You don't mean that. You don't know what you're saying."

"I know exactly what I'm saying." She held his head with her hands and said it again. "I love you." She punctuated each word with a swift kiss on his lips.

Rush's brow folded into a dark, brooding frown. "You can't possibly mean that. Lindy, for God's sake, you barely know me!"

"I know everything I need to." She smiled up at him, not willing to listen to any more of his arguments.

As though he wasn't sure how to respond, Rush slowly disentangled their limbs one by one, the whole time looking as if he didn't have a clue how they'd ended up that way. When he'd finished, he sat on the edge of the sofa and wiped a hand back and forth over his face.

"Lindy, listen."

"No. I'm not going to because you're going to argue with me, and I won't let you." She sat upright, their thighs so close they touched.

"It's only natural…"

Lindy slid off the sofa and pressed one knee to the floor so she could look him in the eye, but his gaze stubbornly refused to meet hers.

"I know exactly what you're going to say."

His face was tight with what looked like embarrassment as he reached for her T-shirt and handed it to her. Lindy smiled and slipped it over her head.

"I love you," she repeated, feeling more sure of herself every time she said it.

"Lindy…"

"I'm not too young to know my own mind." When his gaze shot to her, she knew she'd stumbled over one of his objections. "I'm twenty-two years old, for heaven's sake. I'm not a child."

He opened his mouth to argue with her, but she pressed her finger over his lips to silence him. "Now this is the biggie. You're worried about what happened with Paul and you think all this emotion I feel for you has to do with him. I can understand your concern, and in the beginning you might have been right. But not now. I was mulling this over the other night. Thinking about how low I was when I moved to Seattle and how I was convinced nothing good would ever happen to me again. Then I met you, and, Rush…" she stopped, biting into her bottom lip as the emotion filled her eyes.

"There's no need…"

"Yes, there is." Her hands cupped his face, her gaze delving into his, showing him all the love that came shining through from her heart. "When I think about everything that led me to move to Seattle I haven't a single regret. Not one. All the pain, all the disillusionment was worth it. In fact, I'll always be grateful to Paul because it was through him that I found you."

"Lindy, stop. Don't say any more."

"But I have to. Don't you see?"

Rush closed his eyes and pressed his cheek next to her tear-stained one. His breathing was as labored as her own, but otherwise he didn't move.

"It took what happened with Paul for me to find you, appreciate you, understand you. I love you so much… I can't keep it inside anymore."

"Oh, Lord, don't say that."

Once more, she pressed her finger over his lips. "I don't want anything from you. Nothing. You didn't ask for this, and I've probably embarrassed the hell out of you by blurting it out. I apologize, but Rush—my noble, honorable Rush—I do love you."

She stood then, her legs a little shaky. "Having gotten that off my chest, I'm going to leave you."

"Lindy?" His gruff voice stopped her.

"Yes?"

He had the look of a man who'd been pulled apart on a torture rack. He rubbed a hand down over his face and then shook his head. "Nothing."

The following morning Lindy woke to hear Rush rummaging around the kitchen, albeit quietly, no doubt hoping to escape without having to confront her. She climbed out of bed and greeted him with a warm smile.

"'Morning."

He grumbled something in return.

"Did you sleep well?"

He gave her a look that told her he hadn't. "I've got watch today."

"Yes, I know."

"It's Saturday. How come you aren't sleeping in?"

She dropped her eyes. "I wanted to be sure of something."

"What?"

"That you believe what I told you last night."

His gaze found hers and Lindy could tell he was struggling within himself. The stern look he wore so often in the morning softened somewhat, but when he spoke his voice remained gruff. "Listen, I'm not much of a conversationalist at this time of day, and now probably isn't the best place to discuss this." He paused as though to compose his thoughts, sighed and then continued. "I want you to know, I'm truly flattered that you think you love me."

"But—"

"But," he cut in, "you can't trust what you're feeling right now. So let's leave it at that. Okay?"

"Leave it?" she flared. "Rush, no…"

"I'll be your friend, Lindy, but that's all I ever intend to be."

"My friend?"

"And that's it, so don't argue." He downed the last of his coffee and set the cup in the sink with as much force as if he intended to shove it down the drain. "I'll see you later."

"Okay. If that's the way you want it."

"I do."

"Then I'd be honored to have you for a friend, Rush Callaghan."

He paused, his back to her. "No more kissing, Lindy. I mean that."

"No kissing," she echoed.

"We're going to live as brother and sister from here on out."

"Brother and sister." Lindy knew that would last until about lunchtime tomorrow, if that long.

"And if it proves too difficult for us, then I'll make arrangements to live aboard the *Mitchell*."

"If you think it's for the best," she agreed, doing her best to swallow her amusement. Rush's reaction was exactly as she'd guessed it would be. "If that's what you honestly want."

His hand slammed against the counter. "You know it isn't," he said, and whirled around to face her. "Damn it all to hell. Have you the slightest notion of how close we came to making love last night?"

She nodded.

"I've never known a woman who could tie me into knots the way you do. I promised myself I wasn't going to touch you again, and here it is seven-thirty in the morning and I want you so damn much I hurt."

Silently she stepped to his side and looked up at him, her eyes wide and innocent.

"Damn it, Lindy," he groaned. "Why do you have to be so beautiful?" He slipped his arms around her waist and exhaled sharply. "Now kiss me before I go. I'll be back as soon as I can."

Obediently she twined her arms around his neck and raised her lips to his. "Anything you say, big brother."

Seven

Freshly ground hamburger squished between Lindy's long fingers as she meshed the meat and spices together to form patties for the barbecue grill. It was a lovely summer afternoon in a week that had begun with such marvelous promise.

The front door opened and Rush let himself in to the apartment.

"Hi," Lindy called out, pleased to see him. He was fifteen minutes later than usual, and she'd hoped he hadn't missed the ferry, which ran hourly. "How do barbecued hamburgers sound for dinner?"

"Fine."

The word was clipped and impatient, as though what she served for their evening meal was the least of his concerns. Surprised at his gruff tone, Lindy turned around to find him standing in the doorway, his brow furrowed in a frown so tight it darkened his face.

"Did you have a bad day?"

"No."

Something was obviously troubling him, but from the hard set of his mouth, she knew it wouldn't do her any good to ask. In an effort to ignore his surly mood, she hurried to tell him her good news. "I got word from Steve. The *Atlantis* is due in as early as next week."

Rush acknowledged the information with a curt nod.

"There's cold pop in the fridge if that interests you."

Apparently it didn't because Rush left her and moved into the living room to turn on the television. Lindy finished her task, washed the hamburger goop from her fingers and joined him there, sitting on the arm of the sofa. She rested her elbow gently on Rush's shoulder while Susan Hutchinson from Channel 7 relayed the latest news-making incident from the Persian Gulf.

When Rush pulled out of Bremerton, Lindy knew the *Mitchell* would be headed for those same trouble-infested waters. Her heart thudded heavily in her chest as she battled to control her anxiety. She hated to think of Rush in any danger and wished the *Mitchell* was headed for the South Pacific or somewhere equally pleasant.

Rush must have sensed her fears because he wrapped his arm around her and gently squeezed her waist. Her hand slid over his shoulder and she kissed the top of his head, loving him more each minute of every day.

"Lindy?"

"Hmm?"

The tension in his shoulders was so severe, she wondered how he could hold himself stiff for so long and still breathe.

"When I leave, I don't want you clinging to me."

She blinked, not sure she understood what he was saying. He seemed to be implying she would make a scene on the dock, weeping and gnashing her teeth because the man she loved was heading out to sea. That he would even imagine such a thing was an insult. The other implication was even more offensive.

"Are you suggesting that once you leave I should start dating other men?"

A week seemed to pass before he answered. "Yes. I think that would be a good idea."

Lindy was slow to react to what he was suggesting. Her emotions went from surprise to mild irritation, then quickly broadened to out-and-out fury. She jerked her arm off his shoulder and leaped to her feet. "Well, thank you very much."

"For what?"

If it hadn't been so tragic, so painfully sad, Lindy might have laughed. She'd never felt as close to any man as she had to Rush these past two weeks. When she'd declared her love, she hadn't been looking for white lace and promises. The words had been seared against her tender heart and she hadn't been able to hold them inside a minute longer. She hadn't asked anything of him, but she certainly hadn't expected this intolerable pat on the hand, telling her she was too young, too immature or too stupid to know her own mind.

"For God's sake, think about it, will you?"

"What?" she returned in like voice. "That I'm still a baby and certainly incapable of sound judgment? How about the fact that I'm looking to prove myself after Paul? What I feel for you is obviously some rebounding thing to soothe my injured ego. Right? Is that what you want me to think about, Rush? Unfortunately I can't come up with a single reason I should, since you've already shoved those things in my face at every opportunity."

His jaw was clenched so hard that his temple went white. "You're fresh out of college…"

"And still tied to Mama's apron strings. Is that what you mean to imply?"

"No."

Oh, the gall of the man. Rather than continue arguing, Lindy returned to the kitchen. She was so furious that she clenched her hands into hard fists and exhaled several times to gain control of her simmering rage. She gritted her teeth as she went about fixing their meal. If Rush was so keen for her to start dating someone, then Lindy could see no reason why she should wait until the *Mitchell* left Puget Sound. A small sense of satisfaction lifted the corner of her mouth in a soft sneer as she thought about having men come to the apartment to pick her up and the pleasure she'd derive from introducing them to Rush. Oh, he'd really love that. She might even stay the night with a friend from work and let Rush stew, thinking she was with another man. Then she'd see exactly how eager he was to have her meet someone else.

Lindy braced her hands against the counter and hung her head in abject defeat. Behaving that way was childish and immature and impossibly stupid. Sure, she'd make Rush suffer, but *she* would end up being the one with a broken heart and myriad regrets.

Rush seemed to be telling her something more. Yes, he hungered for her physically. The circumstances in which they were living were rife with sexual tension. Each day it became more difficult to ignore the fire between them, and more than once they'd gotten close enough to the flames to singe their self-control.

The realization hit Lindy then, the impact as strong as if Rush had slugged his fist into her stomach. In some ways it would have been easier if he had. Rush didn't love her. He pitied her after what had happened with Paul. All his tenderness, all his concern, everything he'd done had been born of pity. She'd mistaken his touch, his soul-wrenching kisses for passion when, from the beginning, all he'd really felt was compassion for her.

"Where's my book?"

Rush's question came at her as if from outer space. She turned to discover he stood not more than five feet away, looking irritated and impatient. She hadn't a clue what he was talking about.

"My book?" he repeated. "The one that was in the living room last night. What did you do with it?"

Still numb, she raised her hand and pointed toward his bedroom. "I set it on your dresser."

Since there was so little time in the morning, Lindy had gotten into the habit of straightening up the apartment before she went to bed. The night before Rush had been at a meeting, and she'd retired early, tired from a long day, before he'd gotten home.

"I'd appreciate it if you left my things alone," Rush said in a low growl. "Move whatever you want of yours, but kindly keep your hands off mine."

Answering him with anything more than a shake of her head would have been impossible. Lindy didn't know what had gone wrong, but in the space of fifteen minutes her world had been badly shaken. First Rush had told her he wanted her to start seeing other men and then he'd jumped all over her for putting his book away. Nothing seemed to make sense anymore.

The insight came to her then—it seemed to be the night for them—Rush wanted her out of the apartment. When she'd gotten the job with Boeing, it had been understood she'd need to wait for a couple of paychecks before she could afford to rent her own place. They hadn't actually discussed it, and at the time Lindy had let the subject drop because she'd wanted to spend as much time as she could with Rush. He hadn't asked her about it, and she'd assumed that he wanted her with him just as much. Once more, she'd been wrong.

Quickly calculating her limited funds, she realized that with what remained of her savings and her first check, which was due on Friday, she could possibly afford a studio apartment. If she asked around at the office, there might even be someone there who was looking for a roommate.

The muscles in her throat constricted as she fought down the regret. She'd been such a fool.

Rush noted that Lindy left the apartment as soon as she'd finished preparing their dinner, not bothering to eat anything herself. For that matter he didn't have much of an appetite either, but he sat down at the table, propped his book open in front of him and pretended an interest in both the book and the dinner.

It had been on the tip of his tongue to ask Lindy where she was going, but he'd swallowed the question, realizing how stupid it would sound after the way he'd laid into her earlier. He hadn't meant to start a fight, hadn't even been looking for one. It had just happened, and he was as shocked by his insensitive demands as Lindy had been. He hadn't meant a thing he'd said. The hurt in her expressive dark eyes returned to haunt him now. When he'd asked her about the book, she'd stood looking at him in confusion, the violet smudges that appeared beneath her eyes a silent testimony to the trauma his words had inflicted.

As for the suggestion she see other men, that was downright idiotic. Talk about inflicting self-torture! He wanted to see Lindy with another man about as much as he desired a bladder infection.

The problem, Rush knew, was that he loved Lindy Kyle. She was stubborn, headstrong, proud...warm and vibrant. She might as well have branded his heart, because he belonged to her.

Rush pushed his plate aside and wearily wiped a palm across his eyes. Hell, this was the last thing he'd planned would happen. He was thirty-two years old, for God's sake. Mature enough to recognize when he was headed for trouble. He'd known what was going to happen with Lindy from the first night he'd seen her standing, all soft and feminine, in the hallway outside Steve's bedroom. He'd known the morning she'd blasted the rock music loud enough to hurl him out of bed because she was hurt and angry. He'd known when she'd held his head between her hands and stared into his soul and whispered so sweetly that she loved him.

Rush stood and walked out onto the lanai, hands buried in his pants pockets. The dark green waters of Puget Sound were visible and Rush snickered softly. So much for not seeking a bridge to tie him to the mainland. He was trapped on shore now and he dreaded leaving. He used to think of the navy as the only wife he'd ever need. But recently, when he crawled into bed at night, it was Lindy he longed to wrap his arms around. Lindy he longed to love. He wanted her to be a permanent part of his life. She was laughter and sunshine. She'd made him feel again, laugh again, love again. He couldn't bear to think of what the future would be like without her. Two weeks. He'd only been with Lindy for two weeks. Before that she'd been a name, the sister of a good friend. He couldn't ask her to share his life based on a two-week acquaintance. It was crazy. No, he'd be patient with her, force himself to wait. The six-month separation would do them both good. Time would test the strength of their love. Time would reveal the truth.

It was only a little after eight-thirty when Lindy returned to the apartment. She would have preferred to stay away much longer, but after reading through the evening newspaper for apartment rentals and wasting money on a horrible movie she didn't know where else to go or what else to do. Eventually she'd need to return anyway, and knowing Rush, he'd probably left the apartment, as well.

He wasn't in the living room or kitchen, and she didn't bother to check any of the other rooms, not wanting a recurrence of their earlier argument. It was obvious he wasn't in the mood for company.

Sitting at the table, Lindy spread out the classified section and read the apartment-for-rent advertisements once more.

Quite by accident she found a section she hadn't thought to look at before: roommates wanted. She read a couple of those and decided to phone the one that looked the most promising.

"Hello," she said brightly when the woman answered. "I'm calling about your ad in the paper."

Rush walked into the kitchen, hesitated when he saw her and opened the refrigerator to take out a cold can of pop. Lindy strove to ignore him as much as possible.

Her fingers gripped the pen unnecessarily hard as she doodled while the woman on the other end of the line explained a few of the details regarding her ad.

"It says here that you're looking for a nonsmoker. I... I don't smoke and I've recently moved into the area and need a place to live. I...have a job."

"Lindy."

Rush called her name, but she pretended she hadn't heard him. Besides she was already involved in one conversation and if he chose to be rude that was his problem.

Undeterred, Rush waved his hand in front of her face. "Get off the phone."

"Excuse me a minute please." Lindy spoke to the woman, enunciating each word as she held her temper by a fragile thread. She pressed the receiver to her shoulder blade and glared up at Rush. "Just what do you think you're doing?" she hissed between clenched teeth.

"There's no need for you to find an apartment," he told her, returning her heated stare.

"I beg your pardon, Rush Callaghan, but this is my life, and if I choose to leave this apartment, I'll do so with or without your permission."

Rush cursed beneath his breath and walked away from her.

"I'm sorry to keep you waiting," Lindy said sweetly into the telephone receiver. "Perhaps it would be best if we met?"

"Damn it, Lindy," Rush shouted, twisting around to face her once more. "Will you kindly get off the phone so we can talk?"

He might as well have been speaking to a stone wall

for all the attention Lindy paid him. "Yes, Tuesday afternoon would be fine."

Rush's returning glare was hot enough to peel thirty-year-old wallpaper off a wall, but still Lindy ignored him.

"You won't be meeting whoever that is," he told her sternly, looming over her. "You're only wasting time."

"Kindly excuse me again, would you?" Lindy asked softly, deliberately calm. She turned to Rush then and half rose from her chair. "Would you shut up? I can't hear a word she's saying."

"Good."

He was making Lindy more furious by the minute, and she tried to tell him as much and still keep control of her temper. "I'm sorry to keep interrupting our conversation," she said to the woman on the phone.

Rush walked around the table a couple of times, looking like a man trapped in a small space—or a shark circling its kill. Finally he stopped, standing directly across from her. He closed his eyes and rubbed a hand along the back of his neck as though to relieve an ache there, then paused and looked at her. "Lindy, I'm leaving."

The words were nearly shouted. She hesitated and prayed for patience, and when that didn't work, she counted to ten. Flippantly she raised her hand and waved goodbye. Still, he didn't move.

"I'm twenty-two," Lindy answered the woman's question. "No…no you needn't worry about that sort of thing. There isn't anyone important in my life at the moment." She swallowed tightly at the lie.

She exchanged a look with Rush and feared he was going to explode. "I thought you were leaving," she whispered heatedly, cupping her hand over the mouth-piece. "Don't let me stop you."

"Not the apartment," he raged, staring at her as though she were completely dense. "The *Mitchell* is sailing out."

"I know... In two weeks."

"The catapults are being tested tomorrow and possibly Wednesday. If everything works out we'll be gone by the beginning of next week."

"The beginning of next week," she echoed, hanging up the phone. She kept her hand on the receiver feeling numb with shock, numb with fear. "But you said it would be at least a month."

"As I recall, I told you it could be as long as a month. As it happens, it's only two, possibly three weeks."

"Oh, Rush." She turned to him, her eyes wide with a hundred emotions she didn't know how to define. She'd accepted long ago that their time together was limited. But she'd counted on every minute of these remaining weeks. Needed them. Needed Rush.

"It shouldn't come as any great surprise," he told her, and pulled out a chair to sit across from her.

"It isn't... It's just that... I don't know." Her stomach twisted into hard knots and for a painful moment she couldn't breathe. She was stunned, and she felt Rush's eyes slowly search her face. With everything in her, she met his gaze, determined to appear cool and composed. Her heart might be quivering with apprehension, but she'd die smiling before she'd allow him to know it. He'd already told her once that he didn't want her clinging to him when he left. And she wouldn't. She'd stand on the dock with a smile on her lips and a tear in her eye, and wave until her arm dropped off, but she'd never let him know it was killing her.

"About tonight," he started again. "I didn't mean any of what I said."

He dropped his gaze, but not before Lindy saw a strange mixture of regret, desire and remorse. In the two weeks they'd been together, Lindy had thought she'd witnessed all Rush's moods. She'd seen him at his cynical best, when he'd been purposely aloof and brash. She'd experienced his comfort, his tenderness as he held her in his arms while she sobbed against his chest. And she'd heard the music of his laughter, stood transfixed by his sometimes warm-hearted, playful moods. Oh Lord, she was going to miss him. Miss everything about him.

"Lindy, I'm sorry for what I said."

His hand reached for hers, rubbing warmth back into her chilled fingers. She shook her head, hoping that would suffice as acceptance of his apology.

They were silent for a moment, caught in the surging tide of their individual thoughts.

"I don't have any right to ask you to wait six months for me."

"I'll wait," she offered quietly. Lindy had no other choice.

"If you meet someone else..."

"Is that what you want?"

"No." Anger flared briefly in his eyes. Then his expression changed to that cool, watchful look he wore so often. "No," he repeated softly.

"That isn't what you said earlier." She tried to laugh, but the sound of her pain was carried in the mirth.

"I didn't mean it. Not a word."

"You don't believe that I love you, do you?"

He waited a long time before he answered. "I don't know. I think it's too soon after Paul for you to know what you're feeling."

Lindy closed her eyes in an effort to control the urge to argue with him. She did love him, and never more than now. She'd just learned he'd be sailing out of her life for half a year, and her only thought was how she would manage without him.

She watched as a small pulse started in his temple. "I don't want to leave you, Lindy."

Her gaze shot to his, and her eyes widened with astonishment. Rush loved the sea. The navy was more than his career. It was his life, the very reason he got out of bed every morning. She'd listened for hours while he described for her the warm sensations that went through him when he was on the open seas. She'd felt his pride and exhilaration when he spoke of standing alone against the force of a fierce storm. He loved everything about navy life. It was his dream, just as the oceans of the world were his destiny.

And he didn't want to leave her. What he felt for her was stronger than the lure of the sea.

Tears shimmered in her eyes and she bit hard on her lower lip to hold them at bay. Rush wouldn't tell her he loved her—not with words. It would have been more than she could expect. But by admitting that he didn't want to leave her, he said everything.

When Lindy had composed herself enough to look up at Rush again, she felt the tension in every line of his lovingly familiar face.

"I want you to stay at the apartment," he said, and his hand continued to rub hers, holding her fingers in a grip that was almost painfully tight. "Steve will be back soon, but he'll only be here a few weeks, if that long."

Lindy nodded.

"Then the place will be empty for months."

Again she acknowledged his words with an abrupt movement of her head.

"It would be better if there was someone living here. As it is now, an empty apartment is an invitation to burglars. You'd actually be doing Steve and me a favor if you agree to say."

"I'll… I'll want to start contributing toward the rent."

"Fine. Whatever you want. When Steve arrives the two of you can work it out."

"What about when Steve is here?" Lindy asked. "Where will I sleep?"

"He can have my room."

"But what about when you're both here?"

Rush frowned, and then a strange, almost humorous light entered his eyes and a soft smile crowded his face. "Let's cross that bridge when we get to it. Okay?"

"Okay."

"Anything else?" he asked.

She dropped her gaze to his hand, which was holding hers. "I love you, Rush, and I'm going to miss you like hell."

He raised her hand to his lips, closed his eyes and kissed it gently.

The coffee was ready by the time Rush met Lindy in the kitchen the following morning. Although she'd been physically and mentally exhausted, she'd hardly slept, managing three, maybe four hours of rest at the most. Now her eyes burned and she felt on the verge of tears.

Rush joined her at the table. He wordlessly reached for the morning newspaper and buried his face in it, not speaking to her—apparently pretending she wasn't there. Lindy stood it as long as she could.

"Would you like some breakfast?" she asked.

He shook his head. The stupid newspaper still presented a thin barrier between them.

Whereas Lindy had felt loved and reassured after their talk the night before, this morning she felt lonely and bereft. Rush hadn't sailed away yet, but he might as well have for all the companionship he offered.

"I think I'll get dressed now," she whispered, hoping that would gain his attention.

"Fine."

"Stop it, Rush."

That worked, and he lowered the paper, peering at her over the top of the page, his face clean of expression. "Stop what?"

"That!" She pointed an accusing finger at the newspaper. "I hate it when you do this."

"What hideous crime am I guilty of now?"

"You haven't left yet… I'd think you'd want to spend every minute you could with me… Instead you're hiding behind the *Post-Intelligencer* so you won't have to look at me."

"You're being ridiculous."

"I'm not. It's almost as if you can hardly wait to get away from me."

With deliberately slow movements he folded the newspaper and set it aside. "Is it because I didn't want any breakfast? Is that what's upset you so much? You know I seldom eat this early."

"No…of course that's not it."

"What is it then?"

"I…don't know." Lindy felt like such a fool. She didn't know why she was acting like this, but she couldn't stand it when Rush treated her this way. She could deal with his anger far more easily than this intolerable patience.

"What exactly do you want from me, Lindy?"

"I want some emotion," she cried.

"What?" he barked, clearly not understanding her.

"Not tears. I want you to…oh, never mind. Go back to reading your precious paper with that same stoic expression you always wear in the morning. I humbly apologize for having interrupted your reading time."

Lindy couldn't get to her bedroom fast enough. She took small pleasure in slamming her door. Her intention had been to dress as quickly as she could and leave the apartment. Instead she found herself sitting on the edge of her bed, trembling and teary eyed, confused and suddenly feeling utterly, desperately alone.

When her bedroom door flew open, Lindy gasped. Rush's gaze pinned her to the bed as he silently stalked across the room.

"Damn it, Lindy." The words were ground out through his teeth before he sank onto the bed beside her. His arms tightened around her trembling body, pressing her down against the mattress. His hands found and cupped her breasts as he buried his face in her hair, spreading a wildfire of kisses along her cheeks and face, but avoiding her lips.

All Rush had to do was touch her and the desire curled in her belly like an anchor rope ready to plunge her into dark, inviting depths of passion.

His fingers tightened on her shoulders as he raised

his head and stared down at her. He looked as though he were trying to stop himself but couldn't. Then his mouth closed hungrily over hers, rubbing back and forth, his tongue probing hers.

Lindy's arms found his back and she arched her spine, grinding her hips against him, needing him so desperately she could barely breathe. The longer Rush kissed her, the deeper she sank into the turbulent waters of desire. She felt like she was drowning, oblivious to everything except the primitive need to be loved by Rush.

"Oh, Lindy…" The words came out softly as he lifted his head from hers. He paused and dragged in a heavy breath, held it a moment then expelled it. "Well," he whispered, "is that enough emotion for you?"

Eight

Lindy liked Susan Dwyer the minute the two met. Susan's reddish-brown hair was naturally curly, and although it was styled fashionably short, it managed to fall in an unruly array surrounding her pert face. She possessed the largest, liveliest brown eyes that Lindy could ever remember seeing on anyone. They sparkled with intelligence and vitality, glinting with warmth and curiosity as they studied Lindy.

"Jeff has talked of little else since he met you the other day," Susan confessed.

"It was certainly nice of you to invite Rush and me over for dinner," Lindy returned. Twin boys, about eighteen months of age with reddish caps of curly hair like their mother's stood at the edge of their playpen, silently regarding the two women through large, doleful brown eyes. They'd recently awakened from a late-afternoon nap and looked mournfully toward Susan in the hope that she'd abandon her dinner guests and play with them.

"A meal is a small price to pay to meet you."

Lindy smiled at that. "I take it Rush hasn't said much about me?"

"Are you kidding? He's been so tight-mouthed one would think you were top-secret information."

"That sounds like Rush." Lindy's gaze sought him out and found him and Jeff on the back patio, lighting up the barbecue grill. Just watching him gave her a solid, warm feeling deep inside her breast. She'd found him attractive before, but now, set against this low-key social background, dressed casually in jeans and a striped shirt, looking relaxed and at ease, she found she loved him all the more.

"Rush and Jeff have been friends a lot of years," Susan went on to say. She opened the refrigerator, brought out a large bowl of potato salad and set it on the kitchen counter. "Jeff knew the first day after the *Mitchell* returned that something had happened to Rush. He mentioned it to me right away, but it wasn't until last week that he knew that Rush had found a special woman."

"Rush is the one who's special." Lindy continued to study him, trying to put the knowledge that he'd be leaving out of her mind long enough to enjoy this one evening with his friends.

Susan turned around and her gaze followed Lindy's. "He's happier now than I can ever remember seeing him. More serene. You've been good for him, Lindy—really good. I didn't used to like Rush... Actually I was only reciprocating what he felt toward me. I think I may have reminded him of someone he knew a long time ago. Although Jeff's never told me this, I believe Rush may have tried to talk him out of marrying me."

"I've never known a man who can frown the way he does," Lindy said with a soft sigh. "I swear one of those famous looks of his could curdle milk a block away."

Susan hooted. "I know exactly the look you mean."

"How long have you and Jeff been married?" From everything Rush had told Lindy about Susan, and he'd spoken of little else on the hour-long ferry ride to Bremerton, Rush held his friend's wife in the highest regard. She was surprised to hear he'd once felt differently.

"We've been married about two and a half years now."

Jeff said something that caused Rush to chuckle. The low, modulated laugh seemed to shoot into the sky. Then they both laughed.

Surprised, Lindy and Susan turned around.

"I don't think I've ever really heard Rush laugh quite like that... So free," Susan murmured, as she gazed at the two men. "He's always been so cynical, so stoic. I never really knew what he was thinking. When we first met he terrified me."

"I know what you felt," Lindy said slowly. "The first couple of days after I met Rush, I found myself wanting to thwart him. He can be such an arrogant bastard."

"And at the same time there's something so appealing about him," Susan answered thoughtfully. "And I'm not talking about how good-looking he is, either, although God knows he's handsome enough. But even when he openly disapproved of me, I couldn't help admiring and respecting him. It took time to earn his trust, and despite everything I was glad he was Jeff's friend. There's something inherently strong about Rush. Strong and intensely loyal. I've always known Rush would look out for Jeff no matter what the circumstances. It helped when Jeff had to leave... Knowing he would be with Rush."

"He's the Rock of Gibraltar, I know," Lindy answered

softly, loving him so much her heart ached. "Loyal and constant." She tried not to think about the huge aircraft carrier sailing out of Bremerton, taking Rush thousands of miles away from her. She attempted to push away all thoughts of how empty her life would be after the *Mitchell* left.

"What's it like?" Lindy whispered, hardly aware the words had slipped from her mouth.

Intuitively, it seemed, Susan knew what she was asking. "I don't sleep for the first week. No matter how many times Jeff leaves, it's always the same. For seven days I lie in bed and stare at the ceiling, my stomach in knots. As much as I try I can't seem to stop fretting and worrying. Finally I'm so exhausted my body takes over, and I'm able to sleep."

"Rush told me you are one of the strongest women he knows… The best kind of navy wife."

Susan's countenance softened and her cheeks flushed to a fetching shade of rose pink. She dipped her head a little and murmured, "How sweet of him to say so."

"What does Jeff say about your sleeping problems?" Lindy asked.

Susan shrugged. "He doesn't know."

"But…"

"He has enough worries and responsibilities aboard the *Mitchell* without me burdening him with more. As much as possible I send him off with a smile and handle anything that arises as best I can while he's gone."

"I'm afraid," Lindy admitted reluctantly. "Not because Rush is leaving. I… I can accept that. But I worry about them sailing in the Persian Gulf." Every night, it seemed, the news was filled with reports of violence in the troubled waters of the Middle East. Before they'd

left the apartment she'd heard reports about gunboats
that had attempted to attack the U.S. Naval forces that
very afternoon. Lindy hadn't mentioned to Rush what
she was feeling, knowing he'd brush off her concern.
She wanted to be strong, wanted to be brave for both
their sakes.

Susan's dark eyes clouded and her chin trembled just
a little. "After what happened to the *Stark*, we're all concerned. You aren't alone. But if any of us wives were
to dwell on the danger, we'd soon be basket cases. I try
to put it out of my mind as much as I can. I believe in
Jeff, too. He's damn good at what he does and he's part
of the most advanced naval fleet in the world. My security rests in the fact that he can take care of himself
and his men. Rush can, too."

"I haven't told Rush how afraid I am."

"Good." Susan's gentle smile was encouraging.

"I…love Rush." The words came out hoarse and broken. She didn't have the security Susan and the other
navy wives had. Rush had done nothing more than
ask her to wait for him. At most, she could be considered his girlfriend, his sweetheart. "I don't want to
lose him." She dropped her gaze and rubbed her open
hands down the front of her jeans, more fearful than
ever over what the future could hold. "I've only known
him two weeks… I can't believe I feel this strongly."

"It was like that with Jeff and me. We married within
a month after we met, and he left for six months in
the South Pacific almost immediately afterward. Talk
about worry!"

"But I thought that area was relatively peaceful."

Susan cast an affectionate look toward her husband.

"It wasn't that. I... I was more concerned about how attractive Jeff would find those lovely Polynesian girls."

"Oh." Lindy hadn't thought of that.

Susan blushed a little. "I was pregnant at the time, feeling completely miserable and about as sexy as a tuna casserole. Naturally we didn't know it was twins and I was desperately sick every morning. The highlight of each day was when the mail was delivered. I'd wait all morning and pray there'd be a letter from Jeff. When one finally did arrive, Jeff wrote in detail, telling me about this erotic show he and Rush had managed to see while on shore leave on a small island whose name I can't even pronounce. Topless dancers and the whole bit. I was so upset I cried for days, convinced he didn't love me anymore, and if he did that he'd never want to make love to me again." She pressed her hands over her small breasts. "In case you haven't noticed, I'm not exactly richly endowed in that area."

"I'm not exactly Dolly Parton myself."

They laughed together in an easy camaraderie, as if they'd known each other for a long time instead of just a few short hours.

"Anyway, I didn't write back. Every time I thought about him gawking at those other women and their gorgeous boobs, I got all the more furious. Here I was, heaving my guts out every morning and my loyal, true-blue husband was living it up on shore leave on some exotic island and writing home about how randy he was."

"I don't blame you for not writing back. I'm not sure I would have, either."

"Oh, Lindy," Susan said, pressing her hand on Lindy's forearm, her eyes wide and serious. "It was a terrible thing to do. Jeff about went crazy. He didn't know what had happened to me, and I think it nearly broke him mentally. I got the most soul-wrenching, tormented letter from him, begging me to let him know what had happened. His mind had worked everything into such a terrible state that he was convinced I'd lost the baby—we didn't know it was *babies* then—or even that I might have left him for another man. When I finally wrote and told him how unhappy I was that he'd gone to a stupid topless show he made me promise never, ever to do anything like that to him again."

"Was Jeff here when Timmy and Tommy were born?"

Hearing their names mentioned, the twins cooed and stamped their feet, wanting out of their playpen prison. Susan was busy putting the finishing touches on the relish plate, so Lindy lifted first one and then the other, balancing them on her hips. The two were an armful, but Lindy managed, briefly wondering how Susan coped with them twenty-four hours a day.

"It worked out that Jeff was home for the birth, but we were lucky because he was scheduled for sea trials on my due date. The boys obliged us by arriving ten days early."

Timmy wound his fingers through Lindy's hair while Tommy took pleasure in playing with the spaghetti strap of her summer top.

"Rush is the boys' godfather," Susan explained. "The only times I've ever seen him let down his guard were with them—and then tonight with you. He'd make a wonderful father someday."

"I think he would, too," Lindy said, kissing the chubby cheek of each twin. The boys laughed and Timmy tried to lean over and grab a pickle from his mother's hands.

"Just a minute, son," Susan told him. "Dinner's almost ready."

To keep the pair entertained until their mother dished up their dinner plates, Lindy bounced them up and down on her hips in a jaunty, trotting step around the kitchen. She was laughing, her face flushed and happy, when she looked up to discover Rush standing on the other side of the sliding glass door, watching her.

His deep blue eyes were so intense that her breath caught in her throat. Lindy thought for a moment that she might have done something to anger him. His gaze had narrowed, but there was a light shining from it that didn't speak of anger, but of something else, something far stronger that she couldn't define. A muscle worked in his cheek, and he seemed to be taking in every detail of her as she bounced the chubby cherubs on her hips.

Jeff must have called him because Rush turned abruptly and left without saying a word.

"Here, I'll take one of the boys," Susan offered, lifting Tommy from Lindy's hip. She carried the squirming child outside where two high chairs were positioned side by side next to the round picnic table.

Lindy followed her onto the patio and slipped Timmy into his seat.

"I learned a long time ago that it's best to feed the boys before Jeff and I even try to eat."

Lindy noted Susan had dished up foods her young sons could eat with their hands: chicken legs, finger-Jell-O, pickles and potato chips made up the twins' meal.

"They're getting so independent. They make a terrible fuss if I try to spoon-feed them anymore."

"Can they feed themselves?"

"For the most part." Susan was busy strapping in each toddler. "Believe me, it's a test of patience because more food lands on the floor and wall than ever makes it into their mouths. Afterward it's easier to squirt them down than to try to wash their hands and faces."

Lindy laughed at the visual image of Susan holding the boys while Jeff brought around the garden hose.

Rush's friend strolled to his wife's side and slipped his arm around her slim waist. Susan was a full head shorter than her husband and fit neatly into his embrace. "Are you ready for me to put the steaks on the grill?"

Susan nodded and leaned her supple form against her husband. She went up on tiptoe and brushed a kiss over his cheek. She paused then and smiled up at him. "Anytime you want."

Lindy watched, fascinated by the tender exchange between husband and wife. From what little Susan had told her she knew the couple had gotten off to a rocky start. They'd worked hard to find happiness together and it showed. Jeff and Susan didn't require words to communicate. A shared look, a soft sigh would often be all that was required. How Lindy envied them. How she wished everything was settled between her and Rush. But it wasn't. And he'd be leaving her in just a few, intolerably short days.

They caught the nine o'clock ferry back to Seattle. Jeff dropped them off at the terminal and after Susan and Lindy had shared hugs and Lindy had kissed the boys goodbye, Lindy and Rush walked onto the waiting boat.

Although he shouldn't have been, Rush was astonished at the way Lindy and Susan had become such fast friends. The two had talked and laughed as if they'd known each other since childhood. Now that he thought about it, the two women were quite a bit alike. Both were intelligent, sensitive and personable. And both were in love with navy men. It took a special breed of woman to fit into the military life-style, to accept the long separations, brief reunions and the fact that family must always come second in their husbands' lives.

Both Lindy and he had come away from the evening refreshed. Jeff had given definition to the unknown emotions Rush had been dealing with the past two days. Rush had asked his friend how he managed to leave Susan and the twins and not look back—and had witnessed the instant flash of regret that shot into his friend's eyes. Jeff had explained that the last days before he sailed were always the worst. He didn't want to leave Susan, didn't want to think of not being able to love her for months on end. Nor did he like to think about all that he was missing in his children's lives. He'd been at sea when their first teeth had come in, and on sea trials when they'd taken their first steps. Now he'd be leaving them again, and his mind was crowded with everything he wasn't going to be there to experience.

Then Jeff had asked Rush if he'd had a fight with Lindy recently. Rush's astonishment must have shown because Jeff had laughed and said the same thing happened to him and Susan every time he found out when he'd be sailing. Like clockwork. His fault, usually. But he and Susan had made a promise to each other long ago. No matter what they fought about, they never left anything unsettled between them.

"I'm going to stand outside," Lindy said, cutting into Rush's thoughts. The ferry had been underway for about twenty minutes. She stood and buttoned her sweater before heading for the weather deck.

"Sure. Go ahead," Rush answered. He didn't mind the long ride to and from the shipyard each day. Most of the navy personnel lived in Kitsap County, across Puget Sound from Seattle. But Rush preferred the cultural advantages of living in a big city.

Rush watched as Lindy moved outside the passenger area and stood against the stern, her hands on the rail. The wind whipped the hair from her face and plastered her thin sweater against her soft curves.

Just watching Lindy, Rush felt his heart constrict. When she'd been holding Timmy and Tommy, laughing with them, bouncing the twins on her hips, Rush hadn't been able to tear his gaze away from her. The earth could have opened up and swallowed him whole and he swore he wouldn't have been aware of it.

Seeing her with those two babies had been the most powerful, most emotional moment of his life. The sudden overwhelming physical desire for her was like a knife slicing into his skin and scraping against a bone—it had gone that deep. Not once, not even with Cheryl had he thought about children. He enjoyed Jeff's sons. They were cute little rascals, but seeing Lindy with those babies had created a need so strong in him he doubted that his life would ever be the same again. He wanted a child. Son or daughter, he didn't care. What did matter was that Lindy be their mother.

Even now, hours later, his eyes couldn't get enough of her as she stood, braced against the wind. He thought about her belly swollen with his seed, her breasts full and heavy, and the desire that stabbed through him was like hot needles. The sensation curled into a tight ball in the center of his abdomen. He'd longed for her physically before now. The thought of making love to her had dominated his thoughts from the first morning he'd stumbled upon her in the bathroom wearing those sexy see-through baby-doll pajamas.

But the physical desire he was experiencing now far exceeded anything he'd previously known. And it was different in ways he couldn't even begin to explain.

Unable to stay parted from her a minute longer, Rush left his seat and stepped outside, joining her at the railing.

Wordlessly he slipped his arm over her shoulder. Lindy looked up at him, and her eyes were unusually dark and solemn. The effort it cost her to smile was revealed in the feeble movement of her mouth.

"Lindy?"

She pressed her index finger across his lips the way she did when she didn't want there to be questions between them. Although she strove valiantly to prevent them, tears filled her sweet, adoring gaze. Inhaling a wobbly breath, she pressed her forehead against his chest in a vain attempt to compose herself.

Rush wrapped his arms around her, needing to comfort her, feeling strangely lost as to what to say or do, and not completely understanding what was wrong. Her lithe frame molded against him and he reveled in the feel of her softness pressed to him. "Honey, what is it?"

She shook her head. "Susan said…"

"She offend you?" Rush couldn't imagine it, and yet the anger rose in him instantly.

Lindy swiftly jerked her head from side to side. "No…no, of course not." Her arms were around his middle now, her eyes as dry as she could make them. But her chin quivered with the effort.

She lifted a hand and touched the side of his face, her eyes full of such tenderness that it was all Rush could do to meet her gaze.

"Do you remember the night we met?"

He grinned. "I'm not likely to forget it. I nearly tossed you into the street."

"You were perfectly horrible. So uncompromising... so unreadable."

"So arrogant," he added, regretting every harsh word he'd ever said to her.

The corner of her mouth quirked with a swift smile. "A good dose of healthy arrogance to put me in my place as I recall."

He brushed the hair from her face and nodded, resisting kissing her, although it was difficult.

"I disliked you so much... I actually looked forward to thwarting you. I could hardly wait for you to leave. And now...now I dread it. I wish I could be more like Susan. She's so brave."

"She's had far more experience at this than you." Rush searched her face, and under his scrutiny the normally cool, composed features began to quiver with unspoken anguish. He understood then. She was afraid, almost desperately so, and bravely holding it all inside. Pierced to the quick by his own thoughtlessness, he tightened his grip on her and breathed in the sweet flowery fragrance of her silky dark hair.

"Honey, nothing's going to happen to me."

"But...the gunboats...the missiles."

"I'm coming back to you, Lindy."

She brushed her hands down her cheeks to wipe away

the sheen of tears. "You think I'm being silly and emotional, don't you? This isn't wartime, and nothing is likely to happen, but I can't help thinking…"

He took her by the shoulders then, gripping her tightly. "No," he said sternly, his heart filling with a mixture of concern, tenderness and understanding. His mind groped for the words to comfort her. "You're not overreacting. It is going to be dangerous. I'm not trying to whitewash our assignment. But, Lindy, my sweet Lindy, I've never had anything more to live for than I do right this minute."

"You'd better come back to me, Rush Callaghan." She said it as though it were a fierce threat and the consequences would be dire if he didn't.

Death was the only thing that would keep him from Lindy. Unless… The thought was as crippling to him as the fear of him dying was to Lindy. "Then you'd better be waiting for me."

Her sturdy gaze held his and his hands slid from their grip on her shoulder to stroke her slim, swanlike neck.

"You still don't trust my love, do you?" she asked, looking sad and disappointed.

"Yes," he answered, nodding his head for emphasis. "I believe you." He wasn't sure he should—she was so young, so susceptible—but God help him, he needed everything Lindy was so generously offering him.

He took her hand and brushed his lips over her palm and then, because he couldn't resist and didn't give a tinker's damn who was watching, he kissed her mouth.

It was ten by the time the *Yakima* docked in Seattle. The hike to the apartment was a steep climb, but the night was so gorgeous that Lindy didn't want to hurry home. Every minute left was precious and wasting even a single one would be a crime.

"Let's go to the park," she suggested.

Rush looked bewildered for a moment, and asked, "What park?"

"The one here on the waterfront."

"Whatever for?"

Lindy laughed and slapped her hand noisily against her side. "So much for romance."

"Romance?"

"Come on, Rush. I'm finished crying. When you sail off into the sunset, I'll be there wearing a smile. All I ask is for you to humor me a little before you go. If that means taking a short detour to look at the stars from Waterfront Park, I think you should at least be willing."

"Lindy—" he said her name on the tail end of a sigh "—you've got to get up and go to work in the morning."

She thought for a moment he might refuse her, but he didn't. He slipped his arm around her waist and guided her in the direction of the park.

They climbed the stairs to the second level and stood at the railing, overlooking the quiet green water. The lights from Harbor Island and West Seattle flickered like moonbeams dancing in the distance.

Lindy folded her hands over the cold steel rail, Rush behind her, his chin resting on the crown of her head. "Remember the last time we were here?" Lindy asked, thinking of their wild race up the stairs and the joy she'd experienced in having bested him.

"Yes." Rush's low voice carried a frown.

Lindy twisted around and gazed up at him. "Why do you say it like that?"

"You called me Paul. Remember?"

It took her a second to recall that and all that had happened afterward. "Was that really such a short time ago?" It felt like years instead of just a few weeks.

"Yes." His brow pleated with a grim look.

"No wonder you think I can't possibly know my own heart," she whispered, a little desperately. "No wonder you've never told me how you feel."

His brows lowered even more, shadowing his face as though he'd realized he'd never said it. "I love you, Lindy."

She closed her eyes and let the words rain down over her heart like velvety smooth flower petals, relishing each one, holding them close so she would have them later when she needed them. "I know," she whispered, the tears back in her voice. "I just wanted to hear you say it one time before you left."

Nine

"Lindy?" Rush dropped his hands from her shoulders. His mind was buzzing, as active as any hive. He felt weak from her touch, weak from the effect of her tears, weak with a desperate need to hold her and make her his own. He'd loved unwisely before, and had given up the dream of ever finding happiness again. And then Lindy, his sweet beautiful Lindy, had slammed into his life, and Rush knew he would never be the same again. His heart felt as if it would burst as he pulled her closer, breathing in the perfumed scent that was hers alone.

"Yes?"

Rush couldn't believe the thoughts that were bouncing around in his mind like Mexican jumping beans. Nothing seemed to keep them still. He loved Lindy. He desired her in a way that went miles beyond the physical. Her courage, her honesty, her spirit—each had shattered every defense he'd managed to erect over the years. From the moment they'd met, she'd played havoc with his heart.

"Rush?" She was staring up at him with wide, inquiring eyes.

"I think we should get married." There. It was out. He watched as the surprise worked its way over her features, touching her eyes first, narrowing them as though she wasn't sure she'd heard him right. Then the excitement and happiness broke out and glowed from every part of her, followed almost immediately by swift tears that brimmed in her clear, brown eyes. When her teeth bit into her lower lip, Rush wasn't sure what to think. She tossed her arms around him, and Rush felt the shiver work through her despite the warmth of the June evening.

"Yes, I'll marry you." Her answer was issued in a small voice that pitched and faltered like a boat bobbing in a storm at sea. "When?"

"We'll buy the ring tomorrow."

She nodded, her eyes bright and eager. "I'll arrange to take off early enough so we can get to the courthouse before it closes."

"The courthouse?"

"For the license." She cast him a stern look that convinced him she would make a wonderful mother.

Once he understood the implication, Rush frowned, unsure how to proceed. "But I don't want to get married *now*."

The happiness that had been shining from her face faded, then vanished completely to be replaced by a stunned, hurt look.

"I see," she whispered, and took a step back, away from him. "You want us to wait six months until you return from this tour?"

It made a hell of a lot of sense to Rush, and when he spoke his voice was soft yet inexorable. "Of course."

"I see."

"Would you quit saying that like I'd just suggested we live in sin?"

Rush could tell that she was struggling to compose her thoughts. Confusion and another emotion he couldn't define tightened her brow, and she looked to be on the verge of breaking into tears—but these weren't tears of sudden happiness.

"I need to think," she announced, stiffly turning away from him and hurrying down the concrete stairs.

Rush, watching her run away from him like a frightened doe, held up his hands in a gesture of utter bewilderment. They couldn't get married so soon. For God's sake, they'd known each other less than three weeks.

Lindy walked as fast as her legs would carry her, and her heart was pounding so hard she could feel it all the way to her toes. She was a little embarrassed, because she'd assumed that Rush meant for them to marry right away, and she was troubled, too. She didn't want to wait, and she couldn't think of a way of explaining to Rush all the strong and conflicting emotions that were churning inside her.

Within a matter of seconds, Rush's quick-paced steps joined hers.

"For God's sake will you tell me what you find so damn insulting?" he demanded.

Lindy stopped and looked up at him, loving him so much her heart threatened to burst. His eyes seemed unusually dark and, as always, unreadable as he buried his thoughts and his pain deep within himself.

"Insulting? Oh Rush," she whispered contritely, "never that."

"Then why did you take off like a bat out of hell?"

She dropped her gaze to the sidewalk. "I don't want to wait… When you leave Saturday I want to be…"

"Lindy, that's crazy."

"…your wife," she finished.

Rush's jaw clamped shut, and Lindy saw the muscles in his lean cheek jerk as a hodgepodge of doubts clouded his mind. She didn't blame him, but if he was willing to make a commitment to her now, it seemed fruitless to wait six months.

"I've been through one long engagement," she whispered fiercely. "I have no desire for another. I'll marry you, Rush, and consider myself the luckiest woman alive. But when you place a ring on my finger there will be two, not one."

"Do you realize how ridiculous you sound?"

She watched him intently, her eyes riveted to his. "Yes, I suppose I do, from your point of view."

"In other words, it's all or nothing?"

"No," she answered softly. "I'd marry you tonight if I could, or six months from now if that's what you choose. But if you love me enough to want me as your wife then why should we wait? That's what I don't understand."

His eyes hardened. "But you might regret…"

"No," she cut in, shaking her head so hard her hair whipped across her face. "I swear to you I'm not going to regret it."

Rush inhaled and cast an imploring look to the dark sky as though seeking guidance, and if not that, then divine intervention.

"I don't even want to discuss it."

"Fine," Lindy said with a sigh.

The remainder of the walk was completed in silence. When Rush unlocked the apartment door, Lindy stepped inside, intent on going to her bedroom to give them both space and time to think matters through.

Rush's hand reached for hers, stopping her before she'd gone more than a few steps.

Surprised, she glanced up at him, the light so dim she could barely make out his features.

"It's not right to hurry this when we've only begun to know each other," he said in a tone that was low, husky and deliberately expressionless.

Gently Lindy brushed her fingertips across the taut line of his jaw. "I'm not going to repent at leisure, if that's what you're worrying about. You seem to find it so important that we wait, so we will. But I love you enough right now. I don't have a single doubt that our marrying is the right thing, and nothing is going to change my mind."

"Lindy, it's crazy."

"Marry me now, Rush."

He shook his head. "Six months is soon enough. You need…"

"Me? You're the one who seems to be having all the doubts."

"I'll marry you in six months, Lindy," he said sternly.

Maybe, her mind tossed back. Maybe he would.

Rush studied her for a full minute. "I want you to wear my engagement ring."

The ring finger on her left hand remained dented from the year in which she'd worn Paul's diamond. Unconsciously she rubbed her thumb back and forth over the groove now, reliving anew the desolation that engagement had brought her. The emotion rippled in her chest, each wave growing broader in its scope. She didn't want to be Rush's fiancée—she'd been Paul's for so long. She'd lost Paul and she could lose Rush, too, in a hundred different ways.

"Will you?" he asked, his voice as unemotional as if he were requesting the time.

Once more Lindy would be forced to face the truth. Rush loved her enough to want a commitment from her but not enough to make her his wife. She would be a fiancée. Again. But not a wife.

A strange light flared in his eyes that she faintly saw in the darkness. "It's important to me."

She sucked in a deep breath and felt all the resistance inside her collapse. Gone was her pride; gone was her conviction; gone was her stubbornness. He wanted to wait. She would. He wanted her to wear his ring. She would do that, too.

"Yes," she whispered brokenly. He needed that assurance. It was Lindy who required more.

Hours later something woke Lindy. Unsure what had stirred her from slumber, she rolled onto her side and rubbed the sleep from her eyes. Across the room a shadow moved and she noted Rush's profile outlined in the doorway of her bedroom. He was leaning against the frame of her door, his head dropped as if he were caught in the throes of some terrible quandary. Something about him, about the way his shoulders slouched and his head drooped, told her this was the last place in the world he wanted to be...or the first.

"Rush, what is it?" She raised herself up on one elbow.

Her words seemed to catch him unawares, and he jerked his head up and straightened. Moving to her side, he sank to the edge of the mattress. Tenderly he brushed

the unruly hair from her forehead, his face so intense
it seemed knotted. He didn't speak, and Lindy had no
way of knowing his thoughts. He groaned then, and his
mouth claimed hers in a fiery kiss that threatened to turn
her blood to steam. He lifted his mouth from hers and
tucked her head beneath his chin, rubbing his jaw back
and forth over her crown as if to soak in her softness.

Lindy dragged in a shuddering breath, her senses
fired to life by his touch. She'd assumed when she first
woke that he wanted to make love to her, but that wasn't
his intention. No lover would hold a look of such torment. His eyes were fierce, savage and yet unimagin-
ably tender.

He studied her, and his warm hands stroked her face
as though to memorize each loving feature. The smile
that touched the edge of his mouth was fleeting. And
still he didn't speak. His thumb lightly brushed over her
lips, and he closed his eyes briefly as if to compose his
troubled thoughts.

"I love you, Lindy," he whispered, in a voice that was
at once gruff and soft. "I love you so much it scares the
hell out of me."

His arms went around her, holding her as close as he
could with the blankets bunched between them. Inhaling
a deep breath, he buried his face in her neck.

Lindy's fingers riffled through his dark hair and she
lowered her lashes, cherishing this moment, although
she wasn't sure she understood it.

"Tomorrow," he told her. "I want you to take off early.
We have an appointment at the courthouse."

The longest—and shortest—days of Lindy's life were
the three they were required to wait before their wed-

ding. Rush made the arrangements with a navy chaplain, and Jeff and Susan Dwyer stood up for them. The ceremony itself lasted only a few short minutes. Rush stood close at Lindy's side, and she couldn't ever remember him looking more handsome than in full-dress uniform. When he repeated his vows, his voice was strong and confident. Lindy's own was much softer, but equally fervent.

Afterward they went to an expensive restaurant for dinner and were met by several other couples, all navy people, all friends of Rush's. Names and faces flew past Lindy, and after a while she gave up trying to keep track of who was who. She managed to smile at each one and made the effort to thank them for coming to share this day with her and Rush.

Once they were seated, Lindy placed the bouquet of baby's breath and pink rosebuds in her lap. Susan sat on her left and Rush on her right. Rush was talking to Jeff who sat on the opposite side from him. Rush's fingers closed around Lindy's and communicated his frustration at being trapped with all these people when he wanted to be alone with her. Lindy felt the same way. Rush was her husband and she was dying with the need to be his wife in every way. They had such little time left together. Three days and two nights to last them half a year.

"Do you think we're both crazy?" Lindy leaned over and whispered to Susan. There'd been so little time to talk before the ceremony.

"I think it's the most wildly romantic thing I've seen in years." Her new friend's eyes sparkled with shared joy. "A blind man could see how much Rush loves you."

"I honestly didn't think he'd do it," Lindy confessed.

"What? Marry you?"

"Yes, before he left anyway. He wanted to wait until he returned in December, and…then he didn't. I hardly had time to think once he made up his mind. The past three days have zoomed by. I feel as if I've been on a spaceship—everything's a blur. We've been up every night past midnight discussing the arrangements."

"Didn't you have to work?"

Lindy nodded and suppressed a yawn. "I didn't dare ask for any days off since I've been working such a short time. I regret that now, because I think my supervisor would have understood. But Rush didn't want me to jeopardize my job."

"You'll need it once he's gone," Susan said with a wisdom that must have come from her years as a navy wife. "It's important for you to keep busy. Rush knows that. Having a job to go to every day will help the time he's gone pass all the more quickly. The transition from being together almost constantly to being alone will be smoother, too."

"What about you?" Lindy knew that Susan didn't work outside the home. Her friend couldn't with Timmy and Tommy still so young.

"I manage to do some volunteer work with some of the other navy wives," Susan explained. "We help each other. Once everything settles down, I'll introduce you around."

Lindy smiled, more than willing to meet the others and make new friends. She wanted to do everything that was right to be a good wife to Rush. There was so much to learn, so much to remember. Susan was already a valuable friend, and now she was willing to show Lindy the ropes.

When they left the restaurant, several couples stood outside waiting, and Lindy and Rush were bombarded with flying rice.

Rush had chosen a hotel close to the restaurant for their wedding night. He'd checked in before the ceremony and had their luggage delivered to the suite.

"I didn't think I was ever going to get you alone, Mrs. Callaghan," he whispered to her in the elevator, wrapping his arms around her waist and looking very much as though he wanted to kiss her.

"And exactly what are you planning to do once you have me all to yourself?"

"Oh Lord, Lindy." He breathed in a giant whoosh of oxygen. "You have no idea how hard it's been to keep my hands off you these past few days."

"Yes, I do," she answered softly, blushing just a little. "Because it's been equally difficult for me."

The elevator came to a smooth halt and the door glided cheerfully open. With Rush's hand at her waist guiding her, they walked down the long narrow hallway to the honeymoon suite.

When they reached the room, Rush gently scooped her up and into his arms, managing to hold on to her, juggle the keys and unlock the door.

Rush carried her into the room, slammed the door closed with his foot and gently laid Lindy upon the huge king-size mattress.

Lindy's arms curled and locked around his neck and, unable to wait a minute longer, she smiled up at him, raised her head and kissed him. Rush groaned and pressed her deeper into the pillows, covering her upper body with his own. Her breasts felt the urgent pressure of his chest, her nipples already tingling with the need to experience his touch. The hammering rhythm of his heart echoed hers and seemed to thunder in her ears. Lindy had waited so long for this night.

Poised above her as he was, Rush's mouth dipped to capture hers.

"I can't believe we're finally here," he whispered, his mouth scant inches above hers.

"I can't believe we're actually married."

"Believe it, Lindy." The moist tip of his tongue outlined her bottom lip.

"I'm going to be a good wife to you," she whispered fervently, planting her hands on either side of his face and guiding his mouth to hers, taking his tongue in her mouth. "You won't regret marrying me... I promise."

"I have no regrets. Dear God, Lindy, how could I?" Again and again his mouth claimed her until she lost count.

"Lindy, Lindy," he whispered against her neck. "I don't think I can wait much longer... I wanted to do this slow and easy, but already I feel like I'm going to explode, I want you so much."

They kissed again tempestuously, their mouths grinding hard, their tongues meeting. The kissing sparked the coals of their desire with an urgency that left Lindy trembling in its wake.

Reluctantly, his breath coming in uneven gasps, Rush moved away from her enough to start unbuttoning his jacket. Lindy noted that his movements were abrupt, impatient.

With trembling, uncooperative fingers, she reached for the zipper at the back of her gown, letting the satin and lace knee-length dress fall to the floor.

She was about to slip the pale pink camisole over her head when Rush stopped her.

"Let me," he murmured, his eyes consuming her with a need he couldn't disguise.

She nodded and let her hands fall slack at her sides.

He stood before her—so tall, so solemn, so intent. Lindy could feel the spiraling desire wrap itself around them both, binding them to each other as effectively as any cord. His hands reached for the garment's hem and she raised her arms to better aid him. The silky material whispered against her skin as he drew it over her torso, and Lindy heard Rush's soft gasp as her breasts sprang free.

To her surprise, his hands came up to caress her neck and not her breasts. His touch was unbelievably light, as though he feared the slender thread of his control would snap. His hands gently stroked the sloping curve of her neck and then traveled down to her shoulders, his fingertips grazing her soft, smooth skin. Lindy's eyes grew heavy under the magic he wove around her and her body felt warm and restless. The fresh, clean scent of him filled her and her head rolled to one side. She was caught so completely in the spell he was weaving around her that she feared she might faint with her need for him.

With the softest of touches his hands found her breasts, fitting to their underswell, lifting them, weighing them as though on a delicate balance. The thumb on each hand grazed an already erect nipple. Lindy must have moaned or emitted some kind of sound, because he whispered, "I know, honey, I know."

Something like a flame began to warm the pit of her stomach—Lindy could think of no other way to describe it. The sensation grew more heated and more intense with every passing flick of his thumbs, until her nipples became throbbing velvet pebbles beneath his fingertips. When Lindy was convinced she could endure no more of this sweet torture, Rush lowered his mouth to hers. Gently, moistly, he kissed her lower lip, tugging at it with his teeth. Then he repeated the process and feasted feverishly on the upper.

Rush broke away from her long enough to finish undressing, then lowered himself to the mattress, propped beside her and slightly over her. The hand he slipped beneath her back felt cool and smooth against her heated flesh. He used it to arch her toward him, and she gasped when his hot mouth closed over a breast, feasting on one and then the other in turn.

The fire that had started in her stomach spread its flickering flames through her until Lindy felt she was about to be consumed by the heat Rush had generated.

If he didn't take her soon, she was convinced she'd melt with her need. Everything in her seemed to be pulsating. Her breasts throbbed and the apex of her womanhood beat its own pagan rhythm until Lindy tossed her head back and forth, trapped in a delirium of sexual tension.

Rush kissed and caressed her endlessly, his mouth exploring her breasts, her soft belly, her long legs until Lindy thought she'd go mad. Every nerve in her body was shouting with need. Once he had reduced her to quivering helplessness, Rush changed positions so that he was poised directly above her.

His knee parted her thighs and she willingly opened to him. Rush guided himself into position so that the tip of his engorged manhood was pressed against her moist opening.

"Lindy," he whispered hoarsely, "I...love...you." With each word his pulsating warmth plunged deeper and deeper into her, until he was so far inside her, so firmly locked within her, she was sure he had reached her soul.

Slowly, gradually he began to move, and his swollen heat created the most delicious, most pleasing friction against the most intimate of her surfaces.

Lindy's hands clutched at his broad back, wanting him closer, needing him. She was filled with a tautness, an indescribable demand that became more intolerable with every heart-stopping stroke until she was sure she would scream.

As she struggled to catch her breath, Rush's hands caressed her once more, finding her tingling breasts and then the flat of her stomach.

"Rush...oh Rush..." She tossed her head from side to side, completely lost in the pleasure.

"Kiss me," he pleaded. "Give me your tongue." He put a hand under her head, lifting her mouth to his. Gingerly she explored the hollow of his mouth, running her tongue over his smooth, even teeth. His lower lip was full and when she nipped at it the effect on him was electric. He drove into her again and again, gaining momentum with each thrust until there was only the insistent friction and the sweet, sweet pangs of an all-consuming pleasure. When he climaxed, Lindy felt him throbbing in the innermost recesses of her body and smiled, depleted and utterly content.

Panting, Rush rolled over and pulled her on top of him. He was as breathless as if he'd run for miles, and

Lindy's own breathing was as labored as his. Exhausted, she closed her eyes and pressed her flushed face to his heaving chest, allowed herself to be transported, floating in the warm aftermath of his love.

Lindy slept in his arms and Rush watched her, astonished at the woman who was now his wife. Even though he would do nothing to change the deed, he knew deep in his heart that they should have waited before marrying. But he'd wanted her so desperately, and the thought of losing her had been more than he could bear. So he had sealed their future. It was what Lindy wanted—it was what he wanted.

These past weeks with Lindy had begun to fill the emptiness in his soul. His heart had found a home with her. She had wiped away years of cynicism with her smile, erased the bitterness from his memory with her tenderness, healed him and given him a reason to live.

A thin ribbon of sunlight peeked through the crack in the drapes but Rush dared not raise his wrist to check the time for fear of disturbing Lindy's sleep. Lord, what a woman he'd found. Twice more during the night they had made love, and each time she had opened herself to him, holding back nothing. As their bodies had come together, their souls had merged as well. Their lovemaking was as Rush had always known it would be. He could hardly bear the thought of waiting six months to love her again. And they only had one night more.

"Rush." She tossed his name over her shoulder. "I've got to push your things aside if I'm going to get all my stuff into your closet."

"Then do it," he said, delivering another armful of dresses and blouses to her.

They'd decided to transport her personal things into Rush's bedroom; she could sleep in his room when he was away, which only made sense.

"I can't believe you hauled all this to Seattle in that dinky Rabbit you drive."

"I did."

She was so intent on her task that she didn't notice that Rush had moved behind her. He slipped his arms around her waist and hugged her, resting his chin on her shoulder, kissing her neck. Lindy finished pushing the hangers to one side before twisting around and shyly kissing him back.

"Is that everything?" she questioned, looping her arms around his neck.

"Just about. You know, there are better ways to spend a honeymoon."

Her lashes fluttered down. "Yes, I know, but…but I thought you'd be exhausted by now. I mean…well, you know."

Rush started unfastening the buttons of her blouse. "I find that you bring out the animal side of my nature."

Already Lindy could feel her body starting to respond. "You seem to be doing the same thing to me."

"We've got a million and one things to do," he muttered, but his fingers were intent on only one task.

"I know," Lindy returned, pulling his shirt free from his waistband.

He stripped the blouse from her shoulders and removed her bra. Her breasts stood out firm and round.

He fondled each one, then kissed them in turn. "Did I ever tell you about the morning I walked in on you in the bathroom?"

"Yes," she whispered hoarsely.

"I thought at the time your nipples were begging to be kissed."

"They are now, too."

Rush groaned. "Oh God, Lindy, I'm never going to get enough of you before I leave."

"But not for any lack of trying," she whispered back, threading her fingers through his hair. Tossing back her head, she whimpered softly as he sucked her breast with the hunger of a starving man. Already his hands were at the snap of her jeans, working that open and then tugging at the zipper. Lindy's fingers were equally busy.

They could hardly make it to the bed fast enough. Wordlessly Rush spread her legs and lowered his body into hers. At his first thrust, Lindy felt an electric charge shoot through her and she cried out.

Their lovemaking was a hungry, wild mating that was both tender and fierce and left them so exhausted they fell into a deep, drained sleep.

A sharp sound broke into Lindy's consciousness, but she resisted waking, not wanting to tear herself away from the warm, lethargic feeling of being held in Rush's arms.

"What the hell?"

Lindy's eyes shot open to discover her brother standing in the doorway of Rush's bedroom. Before she could move or speak, Steve had tossed his seabag on the floor and stormed into the room. With one sweeping motion, he hauled Rush out of bed and slammed him against the wall.

"Just what the hell are you doing in bed with my sister?" he demanded, his fist poised in front of Rush's face.

Ten

"Steve!" Lindy screamed. "We're married." She bolted upright and clenched the blankets to her naked breasts with her right hand while holding out her left in proof.

"Married!" Steve exclaimed on a long, slow breath. Gradually he released his grip on Rush's neck. "What the hell! But you hardly know each other. You can't possibly... You wouldn't."

"It happens that way sometimes," Rush explained, and reached for his pants.

"I don't believe this." Steve shook his head as though the action would dissolve the image before him, then turned and stalked out of the room. He paused at the doorway and looked back. "We need to talk."

Lindy wasn't sure which of them Steve wanted to speak with. What was clear was that Lindy hardly recognized her own brother. His solid, sturdy good looks hadn't changed in the time since she'd last seen him. He was still lean and handsome, the way she'd always remembered him, but his eyes had been so hard, so cruel, as though he would have relished an excuse to fight, even if it was with his best friend.

Rush sat on the edge of the mattress and Lindy moved behind him, looping her arms around his neck. "Are you all right?"

"It's not exactly the way I cherish being woken."

"Me, either." Her teeth nibbled his earlobe, and she rubbed her bare breasts against his back, loving the tingly feeling the action provoked. She grinned with satisfaction as she felt Rush's shoulders tighten and knew he'd experienced the same kind of delicious pleasure.

"Lindy, for God's sake, stop. I've got to go out there and talk to your brother."

The regret in his voice was enough to raise her blood pressure and she sighed, wishing her brother had chosen another time and day to make his appearance.

"I'm coming with you," Lindy said when Rush had finished buttoning his shirt.

"Honey, listen," Rush said, his voice low and thoughtful. "I think it might be better if Steve and I had a few minutes alone first."

"Why?"

"I want to tell Steve how things went between us," Rush explained. "If he's going to be angry, then I'd rather he was upset with me."

"Hey, Rush, come on. We're in this together." She reached for her clothes and was dressing as quickly as her fingers would allow. "It isn't as if you seduced me, you know. In fact it was more the other way around. You've been a perfect gentleman from the minute we met... Well, other than that first night—but that's understandable when you think about it... I think we should both talk to Steve. He is my brother and..."

Rush moved around to her side of the bed and stood in front of her.

Lindy was prepared to argue with her husband if he was determined to be obstinate, but when she glanced up his eyes were filled with such love and tenderness that all her determination to stand at his side and face her brother evaporated.

"Ten minutes," he said, taking her by the shoulders. "That's all I ask."

Denying Rush anything in that moment would have been impossible, and she nodded.

Her husband-of-a-day rewarded her with a quick but infinitely thorough kiss, his tongue darting into her mouth and shooting ripples of pleasure down the full length of her body. When he released her Lindy sank back onto the corner of the bed, her legs too weak to support her.

Rush left the bedroom and closed the door. Lindy stared at it helplessly, unable to move. Almost immediately the raised, angry voice of her brother followed as he demanded to know what the hell Rush thought he was doing marrying his little sister. Lindy didn't hear her husband's reply, but whatever he said apparently didn't appease Steve, because shortly afterward Steve started in again. Lindy grimaced at some of the language, impatient to speak to her brother herself. She was an adult and certainly capable of choosing her own husband.

She gave Rush the ten minutes she'd promised, but it was difficult. As the endless seconds ticked past, Lindy tried to remember the last time she'd seen Steve. Before he'd divorced Carol, Lindy realized. That was what?— one and a half years ago now. Steve had been happy then, excited, full of life. Could it really have been only eighteen months ago? She hardly recognized Steve as the same man. He looked so much older than his thirty-three years, and she wondered if the divorce was responsible for the changes in him. From what her parents had told her, Steve and Carol had broken up shortly after their visit to Minneapolis, and the divorce had been final for over a year. No one knew any of the details. Steve hadn't explained a thing, and Lindy hadn't asked. What went on between her brother and Carol was their business, not hers.

When Lindy couldn't stand it any longer, she stood and walked out of the bedroom. Both men stopped and turned around to face her. Anger flashed from their eyes, and it looked as if they were about to resort to physical violence. Lindy knew she'd timed her entrance perfectly.

"It's good to see you again, Steve," she said with a soft smile, walking to her husband's side and slipping her arm around his waist.

Her brother grumbled something in reply.

"Aren't you going to congratulate Rush and me?"

Steve's eyes hardened as they clashed with Rush's. "I'm not sure."

"Why not?" Lindy feigned a calmness she was far from feeling and smiled up at Rush, letting her warm gaze speak for her.

"Lindy, just what in the hell do you think you're doing?" Steve demanded, looking more upset by the minute. "You've been in Seattle how long? Three, four weeks?"

"Are you saying Rush will make me a terrible husband and that I've made a dreadful mistake? Obviously you know something about him that I don't."

"That's not what I mean and you know it," Steve shouted. He paused long enough to rake his fingers through his hair, mussing the well-groomed effect. "What about Paul Abrams?"

Lindy met her brother's gaze without emotion. "What about him?"

"You loved him…or so you said. Hell, the last time I heard from you, your heart was broken and you didn't know if you wanted to go on living. Remember?"

"Of course I remember."

"And that's all changed?" His voice carried a harsh sound of reprimand. "It didn't take you very long to forget him, did it? So much for undying love and devotion. Well, little sister, did you ever stop to think what could follow next? If your affections can change overnight, what's going to happen when Rush has sea duty? Are you going to divorce him once he's out of sight because you find yourself attracted to another man?"

Lindy felt her husband tense at her side. She wasn't pleased with Steve's insinuation, either, but she was willing to let it pass. "As you recall, Paul was the one who conveniently forgot about me. Thank God he did, otherwise I would never have met Rush."

"You're saying that now. God, what a mess." Steve abruptly turned away and marched to the other side of the room. Just as sharply, he turned back to face them. "Of all the people in the world, I thought you were the one I could trust the most."

His comment was directed at Rush.

"She's just a kid." The look Steve tossed his friend suggested Rush had resorted to robbing a day-care center.

"I'm twenty-two," Lindy cried, piqued.

"Damn it, Lindy. You don't know a thing about marriage."

"She knows enough about being a wife to satisfy me," Rush answered calmly.

"She's too young for you," Steve shouted, and started in again with hardly a breath. "Any fool could see she married you on the rebound. I thought you were smarter than this, Callaghan. You took advantage of her."

"If he'd taken advantage of me," Lindy cut in, growing more impatient with her sibling by the moment, "he wouldn't have married me."

"Of course he married you. He knew I'd beat the hell out of him if he didn't."

From the tight expression her brother wore, Lindy could see that he'd relish the opportunity to fight with Rush.

"Steve, stop it," she pleaded, holding out her hands. "I'm married, and although you seem to think it's some great tragedy, I don't. I plan on being a good wife to Rush. This isn't an overnight fling. We're committed to each other."

"I don't give this so-called marriage three months."

Rush's hands knotted into tight fists, but when he went to step forward, Lindy stopped him. Her husband had done an admirable job of keeping his cool, but Steve's accusations were beginning to wear on them both, and Lindy could tell Rush wouldn't put up with much more.

"Have you told Mom and Dad?"

"Of course. I'm not ashamed of what we've done." But she'd waited until after the ceremony to announce she was married for fear her mother would try to talk her out of it. When she did phone her parents, Grace Kyle hadn't been able to disguise her shock and had started to weep. When her father had come on the line, he'd been equally stunned, almost embarrassed, stumbling over his words, clearly not knowing what to say. It wasn't until Rush had talked to both her parents that Lindy's family had made an effort to offer their congratulations.

Steve's eyes narrowed. "I should kick your teeth down your throat for this, Callaghan."

Rush's mouth quirked into a half smile. "I'd like to see you try."

"Stop it, both of you!" Lindy cried, shocked at both men. "I don't know what's the matter with you, Steve, but this is my honeymoon. I have only one night left to spend with my husband, and I don't intend to waste it arguing with you."

"The *Mitchell* is leaving in the morning?"

Once more Steve's question was directed to Rush as he chose to ignore Lindy.

Rush nodded.

The two men stood not more than ten feet apart and glared heatedly at each other, issuing silent challenges. Steve broke away first, picked up his seabag and headed toward the door.

"I'll leave you two alone."

"It would be appreciated," Rush answered.

Steve turned back to face his friend and Lindy couldn't remember when his dark eyes had been more intense. "You hurt her, Callaghan, and you'll answer to me personally."

The tension in the room was so electric it was a miracle lightning didn't flash from the ceiling. It seemed to arc and flow between the two men, ready to ignite at any moment.

"I thought you knew me better than that," Rush answered through clenched teeth.

"I don't trust anyone. Not anymore. Just remember what I said. If Lindy's ever unhappy, I'm going to hold you responsible."

A throbbing, wounded silence filled the room after the front door slammed. Lindy sat on the davenport and forcefully expelled her breath. "What is his problem?"

"When was the last time you saw your brother?" Rush wanted to know, taking the seat beside her and reaching for her hand.

"About a year and a half ago. Steve and Carol drove to Minneapolis when Steve was on shore leave. They were so much in love and so happy, we were all stunned when a few months later we got a letter that said he'd filed for divorce. We never knew why. I think he would have told me had I asked, but I never did. What happened between him and Carol is their business."

"The divorce changed him," Rush explained softly.

"You're telling me. But his letters were never like this. He was always so encouraging, so upbeat. When he heard what happened with Paul, his letter helped me so much. He understood so well what I was going through, but now I feel like I hardly know him."

"He's upset," Rush answered after a moment. "He'll come around once he has time to think things through. He knows us both, probably better than anyone else."

Lindy nodded. "I'm not fickle and my brother knows that. I didn't marry you on the rebound. I swear that, Rush. I love you."

Rush's face broke into a slow, relaxed grin and he draped his arm over her shoulders. "And I love you, wife."

Lindy tucked her head beneath his chin and snuggled into his warm embrace, cherishing the closeness they shared. She didn't expect anyone else to understand something she couldn't explain herself. Finding Rush was like stumbling upon her other half. With him she was whole.

"What went wrong with Steve and Carol?" Lindy asked quietly as her thoughts drifted back to her brother. She was concerned about the changes she saw in him.

Rush was silent for a long moment. "I'm not sure. Like you, I felt it was his and Carol's business, but I'm almost certain she was unfaithful."

"No way." If Lindy knew anything about her ex-sister-in-law it was that gentle, sweet Carol would never cheat on Steve. "She just isn't the type."

"Then I haven't any idea what went wrong."

"How sad," Lindy murmured. It was obvious to her that Steve had changed drastically since his divorce. Although she couldn't believe Carol had been unfaithful to her brother, that would explain Steve's statement about not trusting anyone anymore.

"I think we could both learn a valuable lesson from what happened with your brother's marriage," Rush said, his voice tightening.

"What?" Lindy asked, and raised her head to study her husband's face. His eyes had darkened slightly and she wasn't able to read his thoughts, but she had a good idea what he was thinking. And she didn't like it. Not one damn bit. "Are you going to start lecturing me, Rush Callaghan?"

"Lecturing you?"

"Yes. I have a fair idea of what you're going to say."

The muscles of his face relaxed into a half smile as he leaned against the back of the davenport and crossed his arms. His knowing eyes came alive with mischief. "Oh, you do, do you?"

"You were about to give me some dopey line about what we're experiencing now being some kind of euphoric stage all lovers go through."

"I was?"

"Yes, you were. You were going to say we're experiencing a time when everything and everyone is perfect. There's no one else on the planet but us and nothing else but our newly discovered love."

Rush's brows arched, but if he was portraying anything other than amusement, Lindy couldn't tell.

"And…"

"There's more?" he asked, and laughed, his rich baritone sounding relaxed and amused.

"Oh, I'm just getting to the good part." She stood and rubbed the palms of her hands together, sorting through her thoughts.

"Well?" he pressed, having trouble disguising his amusement.

"You're about to tell me that the tension is gone. We've stepped over the line, entered the bedroom and now that territory has been charted."

"Not as much as I'd like, but we'll make up for lost time later." Rush's words were more promise than comment.

"Don't interrupt me."

"Sorry." He didn't look the least bit repentant.

"You're going to tell me we're about to step off cloud nine and should expect to be hit with a healthy dose of reality. We could be headed for trouble now. If we aren't careful, what happened to Steve and Carol could happen to us."

All traces of amusement faded from Rush's eyes and his face tightened. Lindy knew she was right. "By this time tomorrow, you'll be gone." She forced herself to offer him a brave smile. "And I'm going to be alone."

Rush stood. His eyebrows were pulled down into a heavy ledge of concern. "That's right, Lindy. Up until this point everything's gone smoothly for us. Our whole world has been telescoped into a two-part universe. After tomorrow everything will change, and I doubt that it'll ever be exactly the same again. In two weeks you could be wondering how you ever imagined yourself in love with me."

"That will never happen." She shook her head hard for emphasis.

"In two months, you'll have forgotten what I look like."

From his narrowed, tight expression, Lindy knew he wouldn't listen to any denials. She hadn't started this conversation to argue with him. The last thing she wanted was for them to spend their remaining hours fighting.

"You're married to a man you hardly know who's going to be leaving you for half a year. The next time I see you, it'll be close to Christmas."

She crossed her arms and cleared her throat loudly. "Have you finished?"

"Finished what?"

"Your lecture."

"Lindy, I'm serious. I—"

"You're not saying anything I haven't already thought about a hundred times. I love you, Rush, and I've never been more sure of anything in my life. My feelings aren't going to change in ten days or ten years."

Tenderly he wrapped her in his arms then, and held her close. If there was anything more he wanted to tell her, he left it unsaid.

Hours later Rush lay on his back in bed with Lindy nestled, sleeping, in his arms. He hadn't been able to sleep, dreading the thought of leaving her. Getting married the way they had was possibly the most irresponsible thing he'd done in his life. But he didn't care. Given the same set of circumstances he'd marry Lindy again. Gladly.

She astonished him. She was so sure, so absolutely confident they'd done the right thing. Her unwavering trust had been contagious. God knew, he'd wanted her badly enough. Steve seemed to think he'd taken advantage of her, and perhaps he had, but that couldn't be changed now. Lindy was his wife, and by all that he considered holy, he planned to be a good husband to her.

He closed his eyes and inhaled the fresh scent of jasmine and perfume that was Lindy's alone, knowing full well that within a few hours he would be walking away from her.

Rush thought his heart would burst with the love he felt for his wife. He softly kissed the crown of her head, cradled in the crook between his neck and shoulder.

Lindy Callaghan was some kind of woman. They'd made love together, their bodies moving in perfect synchronization, as though they'd been married for years. All afternoon and evening, they'd teased and played lovers' games, pretending they had forever. But it wasn't enough. Not nearly enough. Rush wanted her again. Now. But he had the feeling making love to her a thousand times wouldn't be enough to satisfy him.

* * *

Lindy woke from a sound sleep when Rush pushed the thin fabric of her nightgown aside, his fingers light and quick. She hardly felt his movements until his mouth closed greedily over her nipple. She sucked on her bottom lip to keep from whimpering as the hot stab of pleasure pierced her. Her head ground into the pillow with every moist stroke of his tongue. And when his teeth gently tugged at the raised peaks of her breasts, it felt as if he were pulling at a thread that was linked to the heart and heat of her womanhood. She moaned anew at a pleasure so intense it was akin to pain, and still Rush sucked at the pebbled hardness. Again and again, like a butterfly flitting from flower to flower, he sampled the sweetness of the nectar from her breasts until he was pleasurably sated.

When she was sure she was about to melt with liquifying, pulsating need, Rush lifted his head. He lay on his side and slid his hand down the smooth length of her stomach until his caressing fingers tangled in the nest of wispy hair. He paused.

Lindy stopped breathing as his fingers slowly delved deeper, charting fresh territory as they sought the opening to the moist warmth. With his probing finger inside her, Lindy lifted her bottom and rotated her hips, saying without words what she wanted. Rush's mouth returned to her nipple and the hot cord of pleasure joining her breasts and the core of her womanhood was drawn even tighter as he connected the two ends.

When he had nearly driven her to the limits of sanity, Rush moved his body over hers. In one unbroken action, he entered her.

They both gasped at the strength of the undiluted pleasure.

Their eyes met and locked in the darkness. He was buried as deeply inside her as he could go, and still he didn't move. Lindy felt his limbs tremble as he struggled to gain control of his raging desire. She moaned in protest and squirmed beneath him, grinding her hips against him until he cried out her name in an agonized plea.

"Honey...please...don't do that."

"I can't help it." Once more she raised her bottom enough to experience the intimate friction she craved so desperately.

"Lindy." He hissed her name again through clenched teeth. "For pity's sake, don't... Every time you do that... oh, Lindy..."

She gazed up at his tortured face and lifted her head to kiss him. He responded by thrusting his tongue in her mouth while all ten fingers tunneled through her hair.

He started to move then in a long, slow stroke that plunged him deep within her. She whimpered when he withdrew, but he quickly sank into her again and again and again, bringing them to a shared climax several moments later. Together they cried out, their hearts sailed and they soared into a new shining universe as their voices shouted in joyous celebration.

Still sheathed inside her, Rush whispered urgently, "You're mine, Lindy. Mine."

"Yours," she whispered in return. "Only yours."

Lindy had never seen so many people gathered in one place in her life. It seemed the entire navy had come to watch the tugboats tow the *Mitchell* out of Sinclair Inlet.

Susan Dwyer stood at Lindy's side on the long pier, looking at the huge aircraft carrier as it sliced through the dark green waters. Helicopters from the local television stations hovered overhead and small planes zoomed past to get pictures of the carrier as it was tugged away from the Bremerton shipyard.

"How do you feel?" Susan asked, shouting above the noise of the cheering crowd.

"I don't know." Lindy shook her head, feeling a little numb. A lump rose in her throat. When she'd kissed Rush goodbye, she'd felt the reluctance and tension in him, but no shrinking. As much as he wanted to stay with her, as much as he longed for them to be together, he longed for the sea more. He was going to leave her because it was his duty, his destiny. He belonged to the navy, and she had only been granted second rights.

"I'm not going to cry." That much Lindy knew.

"Good girl." Susan was dry-eyed herself. "You're going to do just fine. We both are. These six months will fly by. Just you wait and see, and before we know it they'll both be back, randy as hell and—" She stopped abruptly and heaved in a deep breath. "Who am I trying to kid? It's going to be the pits." Her gaze clouded and she bit into her trembling bottom lip. "I think I'm pregnant again."

Lindy didn't know what to say. "Does Jeff know?"

"Nope. I went off the Pill last month when they left the first time. There didn't seem to be any reason to keep taking them when Jeff was going away for all those months. I forgot to take the stupid things half the time anyway. Then Jeff was home and I didn't even think about it until yesterday morning."

"Why then?"

"I threw up."

"Oh, Susan. Are you going to be all right?"

"If I said yes, would you believe me?"

"Probably."

Her friend sighed. "Well, don't. I have miserable pregnancies. And I don't think Jeff's going to be pleased, either. We'd agreed to wait at least another couple of years."

Lindy found a tissue in her purse and handed it to her friend, who quickly wiped the moisture from her pale cheeks.

"Tears are another sure sign with me."

"I'd better keep track of these symptoms," Lindy muttered absently.

Susan paused, blew her nose and turned to face Lindy. "What do you mean?"

"Rush and I weren't using any birth control, either... It wasn't the right time of the month for me to start the Pill, and well, to be honest, we didn't discuss it."

"Oh, Lindy, how do we let these things happen?"

Lindy didn't have an answer to that. Not once during the last two nights had she given any thought to the fact that she could become pregnant. It certainly wouldn't be any great tragedy, but she would have preferred to wait a year or two before they started a family. Rush hadn't said a word, either. It seemed improbable that he hadn't thought of the possibility.

"You want to come back to the house with me and share a hot fudge sundae and a jar of pickles?" Susan asked seriously.

Lindy shook her head. "My brother arrived yesterday. We haven't had much of a chance to talk."

"Keep in touch."

"I will," Lindy promised.

* * *

Steve was watching the newscast that showed the *Mitchell* pulling out of Puget Sound when Lindy entered the apartment. He didn't so much as look away from the television screen when she entered the living room, and Lindy paused, anticipating the worst.

"If you're going to yell at me, do it now and get it over with," she said, standing just inside the room. After saying farewell to Rush she didn't need anything more to dampen her already low spirits.

Her brother leaned forward and pressed the remote control, turning off the television set.

"Dear God, Lindy, what have you done?"

"I just said goodbye to my husband," she answered him, in a steady, controlled voice.

"Why'd you marry him?"

"For the usual reasons, I assure you."

Steve wiped a hand down his face. "I wish to hell I could say how happy I am for you, but I can't. I know you too well, Lindy. This marriage just isn't going to work. You're not the type of woman who's going to accept the life-style the navy demands. How can you possibly expect to know a man well enough to marry him in three weeks?"

"I know everything I need to."

"I suppose he told you about Cheryl?"

She squared her shoulders and stiffened her spine in a defiant gesture. She knew there'd been someone else, but Rush hadn't filled in the details. She hadn't told him everything about Paul, either.

"Did he?" Steve pressed.

"No," she flared.

"You're married to a man and you know nothing about his past."

"I love Rush and he loves me. That's all I need." Lindy was painfully conscious of her brother's adverse feelings toward her and Rush, but she was at a loss to understand his hostility. Unless his divorce had completely tainted his views on marriage.

Steve shook his head, his face pinched in a deep frown. "I'm afraid you've made the biggest mistake of your life, Lindy Kyle."

She stepped into the room and sat on the sofa arm. "The name's Lindy Callaghan, now."

Eleven

Susan Dwyer met Lindy at the front door. "Welcome," she said, bringing her inside the house. A group of women sat in the living room and smiled enthusiastically when Lindy entered the room. She recognized several of the faces from the restaurant where she and Rush had eaten their wedding dinner, but remembering all their names would have been impossible.

"Hello," Lindy said, cordially nodding her head toward the others. She took the only available chair and crossed her long legs, hoping she gave the appearance of being at ease. Susan had invited her over for a late lunch the week before, but her friend hadn't mentioned that anyone else would be present.

"I thought it was time you got to know some of the other wives," Susan said as a means of explanation.

"And if no one else is going to say it, I will," an attractive blonde with wide blue eyes piped up. "We're all anxious to get to know you better."

"We've all been crazy about Rush for years. I'm Mary, by the way."

"I'm Paula," the blonde who'd spoken first added.

"Hello, Mary and Paula." Lindy raised her hand.

Four of the others quickly introduced themselves. Sissy, Elly, Sandy and Joanna.

"Did you get the wives' packet?" Joanna wanted to know scooting to the edge of her seat.

Lindy's eyes shot to Susan. "I don't think so." The *Mitchell* had been gone almost a month now and because Lindy had been so busy with her job and worrying about her brother, she hadn't been able to get together with Susan as soon as she'd wanted.

"I'll take care of that right now." Joanna opened a briefcase and brought out a thick packet. She stood and delivered it to Lindy. "This is a little something the navy hands out to new wives so they aren't completely in the dark about what they've gotten themselves into having married a man in the military."

"A sort of finding-your-sea-legs-while-still-on-land idea," Susan explained.

Lindy opened the packet to find several brochures and booklets. There was one on the social customs and traditions of the navy—guidelines for the wives of commanding officers and executive officers, another on overseamanship, and several others, including one that gave the history of the U.S. Navy.

"An issue of *Wifeline* should be in there, too."

"Joanna's one of the ombudsmen for the *Mitchell*," Susan explained.

Lindy wasn't sure what that meant. "Oh," she said weakly, hoping she didn't sound completely stupid.

Joanna must have read the confusion in her eyes, because she added. "I act as a liaison between the command and the families. If you have a problem with something, come to me."

"Wonder Woman here will take care of it for you," Sissy commented and smiled at Joanna. "I know she's helped me often enough."

"I'm not completely sure I understand," Lindy admitted, with some reluctance. Although Steve had been in the service fifteen years, as long as Rush, Lindy had little technical understanding of the way the military worked.

"Let me give you an example," Joanna said and tapped her index finger against her lips while she thought. "Let's say you get sick and need to go to the hospital when Rush is on a cruise, and there's some kind of screwup there and they won't take you."

"Call Joanna." Seven voices chimed in unison.

"I see."

Joanna playfully cocked her head and slanted her mouth in a silly grin, which caused the others to laugh. "Mainly my job is to be sure that no one feels they need to face a problem alone. When you married Rush, you married his career, too. You belong to the navy now just as much as Rush does. If you've got a problem there will always be someone here to help."

"That's good to know." Lindy hadn't thought about it before, but what Joanna said made sense. The knowledge that someone was there to lend a helping hand gave her a comforting sense of belonging. Although she knew Susan was her friend, Jeff's wife had been her only contact with Rush's life.

"When the guys are around there aren't that many problems, but once they're deployed we have to stick together and help each other," Sissy added, and a couple of the others nodded their agreement.

"What do you mean there aren't that many problems

with the guys around?" Mary, a slim redhead, cried. "I don't suppose anyone happened to mention to Lindy the hassles of shifting responsibilities and…"

"Hey, the poor girl just got married. Let's not hit her over the head with everything just yet."

"No," Lindy interrupted. "I want to know."

"It's just that we—meaning we wives—are left to handle the domestic situations when the men are at sea. It's not as if we have a whole lot of choice in the matter. Someone's got to do it. But then once our husbands sail home we're supposed to return to the docile role of wife and mother and automatically let the men take over. Sometimes it doesn't work that well."

"I don't imagine it would," Lindy said thoughtfully, and sighed inwardly. Briefly she wondered what problems the years held in store for her and Rush. She'd never thought about the shifting roles they'd need to play in their family life. It was a little intimidating, but she'd only been a bride for a month and didn't want to anticipate trouble.

"Every time Chuck's due back home, I get sick," Mary confessed, looking disgusted with herself. "It's all part of the syndrome."

"The homecoming is wonderful, but Wade and I tiptoe around each other for days for fear of saying or doing something that will ruin our reunion," another wife explained.

"We choose to ignore the obvious problems and pass over strife until it's time for him to be deployed again."

"That's when it really hits the fan," Susan inserted.

"What do you mean?" Lindy was curious to know. She could understand what the others were saying, although she hadn't been married long enough to experi-

ence with Rush a lot of what the women were warning
her about. But the time would come when she was bound
to, and she was eager to recognize the signs.

"It seems we're all susceptible to arguing before our
husbands' leave," Joanna explained.

Lindy remembered how Rush had purposely picked
a fight with her the afternoon he'd learned the repairs
to the *Mitchell* had been completed.

"Rush jumped all over me for putting his book away,"
Lindy told the others. "I didn't understand it at the time.
It was so ridiculous, so unreasonable and not like him
at all."

The others nodded knowingly.

"I imagine it was about that time that Rush realized
he loved you," Susan added smoothly. "Jeff pulled the
same thing. He always does. The day he comes home
and suggests it's time I go on a diet, I know what's coming. He's just learned when he'll be deployed. Jeff loves
what he does, but he loves me and the kids, too. It's a
crazy kind of tug-of-war that goes on inside him. He
dreads leaving, hates the thought of all those months
apart, and at the same time he's eager to sail. He can
hardly wait to get out on the open seas."

"Try to make sense out of that if you can," Mary
grumbled. "But this is all part of being a navy wife."

"And then there's the constant knowledge that we
can be transferred at any time."

"Say, did anyone else hear the rumor that the *Mitchell* could be reassigned to Norfolk?"

"It's just gossip, Sissy," Joanna answered. "There's
no need to worry about it now."

"See what I mean," Susan told Lindy with a soft
laugh.

"You mean the *Mitchell* might transfer its home port to Norfolk?" Already Lindy was thinking about what would happen with her job if Rush was to be stationed in another state. She'd have to go with him and leave Seattle. Of course she could always find another job, but she didn't relish the thought. A growing knot of concern started to form in her stomach.

"The *Nimitz* was transferred from Norfolk to Bremerton," Sissy reminded the group.

"Two joys of navy life," Mary muttered disparagingly. "Deployment separation and cross-country moves."

"If worse comes to worst, we'll survive."

It was apparent to Lindy that Joanna was the cool voice of reason in this friendly group. Lindy still had trouble keeping track of who was who, but felt that she was going to fit in nicely. It was as though she were being welcomed into a sorority. The other navy wives' acceptance of her was automatic, their reception warm.

"We always survive," Susan added softly. "Now, as I said earlier, we're not going to knock poor Lindy over the head with everything in one afternoon."

"Yeah, we plan to give it to you in small doses."

"Has anyone else stopped to figure out how much time married couples are separated if the husband is in the navy?" Mary asked, holding a calculator in her hand. Her fingers were punching in a long list of numbers that she called out at regular intervals. "According to my figures, during a twenty-year enlistment—" her fingers flew over the keys "—the husband and wife will spend six years apart."

"Six years?" Lindy repeated while the numbers whirled around her head.

"It's not so bad," Susan said, and patted Lindy's hand to tell her she understood her friend's distress. "In small doses."

"While I've got everyone here," Joanna added, snapping her briefcase shut and setting it aside. "Remember you need to have your letters mailed by the fifteenth of each month."

The other women nodded, apparently already aware of the deadline. Susan had explained to Lindy earlier that because the *Mitchell* was deployed in unfriendly waters, the mail would be flown in with supplies only once a month.

"When are we going to eat?" Sissy asked, craning her neck to peek into the kitchen.

"Every time Bill's gone, Sissy gains ten pounds."

"I work it off once he's home, so quit teasing me."

"I could make a comment here, but I won't," Sandy muttered, and the others laughed.

"Well, if a certain someone doesn't feed me soon, I'm going to fade away before your very eyes." Dramatically Sissy placed the back of her hand against her forehead and released a long, expressive sigh.

"Okay, okay," Susan said with a laugh. "Lunch is served."

Everyone stood at once and moved into the kitchen. The table was arranged with a variety of salads, buffet style. Plates and napkins were arranged at one end and the forks fanned out attractively.

"I brought the recipe for the Cobb salad, in case anyone's interested," Paula commented.

"I wish you had said something," Lindy complained under her breath to Susan. "I could easily have brought something."

"You're our guest of honor."

"We're all dying to know how you met Rush," Sissy said and Joanna moved Lindy to the front of the line and handed her a plate.

"I think he's sexy as hell, and Doug told me he could hardly believe Rush would marry someone he only knew two weeks."

"Well, actually," Lindy murmured as an embarrassed flash of color entered her cheeks, "it was closer to three weeks."

The women laughed.

Sissy pressed her hand over her heart and sighed. "That's the most romantic thing I've heard in years and years."

Elly's shoulders moved up and down as well in an elongated sigh. "I always knew when the big man tumbled, he'd fall hard."

"He's so handsome," Mary interjected.

"So dedicated," Paula added.

"Until the night of your wedding dinner, he was always so...detached and distant. We all noticed the change in him."

"Thank you," Lindy answered softly.

"I bet he's a good lover."

"Sissy!"

Lindy laughed because although the others had been quick to chastise their friend they eagerly looked in her direction for a response. Not willing to disappoint them, she wiggled her eyebrows a few times and nodded.

"I knew it. I just knew it," Sissy cried.

"Are we going to eat, or are we going to talk about Lindy's love life all afternoon?" Joanna asked.

The women looked at each other, came to some sort of tacit agreement and set their plates aside.

"Are you all right?" Jeff asked Rush as he moved past his friend to the engine-order telegraph.

"Fine." The word was as sharp as a new razor. Rush wasn't willing to discuss his problems with anyone, not even Jeff.

"There's got to be some logical explanation why Lindy hasn't written."

"Right," Rush answered, but he avoided looking at his friend, doing his best to look busy. He didn't want to be rude, but he wasn't going to discuss his troubles either.

"Susan's letter says the wives' association had Lindy over for lunch recently."

"Is that supposed to reassure me?"

"I think it should." Jeff unfolded Susan's thick letter and scanned its contents. "Lindy's kept in close contact with Susan and the others."

"That doesn't mean a damn thing."

"Apparently they had a wedding shower for her."

That made him feel a whole lot better, Rush mused sarcastically. Lindy seemed to have forgotten she had a husband, but she was busy accepting wedding gifts.

Jeff paused and cleared his throat. "It seems the wives went together and got Lindy a long silk nightie."

Rush didn't respond. His jaw was clenched so tightly that he was convinced his back molars would crack. He'd been four interminable weeks without a single word from Lindy. A whole damn month. The knot in his stomach was tight enough to double him over. His nerves were shot. He found himself snapping at his men, behaving irrationally, becoming angry and taking it out on everyone else. And worse, he wasn't sleeping. For two nights now he hadn't been able to so much as close his eyes. Every time he did, the images that filled his mind were of Lindy with another man, presumably Paul. The hot surges of anger and adrenaline that shot through him were so strong that any chance of falling asleep was a lost cause. Lindy might as well have taken a knife and cut open a vein as not written.

Unwillingly Rush's mind leaped to a memory of how it had been with Cheryl. At first there'd been a flood of letters, filled with all the right phrases, everything a man longs to hear when he's separated from the woman he loves. Then Cheryl's letters had petered out to a handful in a month, and then just a sporadic few before his return.

But damn it all to hell, Lindy was his wife. He'd slipped a diamond ring on her finger and committed his life to her. He'd expected more of her than this. But apparently she took her vows lightly because she'd sure as hell forgotten him the minute he was out of sight.

It was a mistake to have married her. But he'd been so much in love with her that he'd refused to listen to the calm voice of reason. He'd lost one woman and feared losing another. He should have known standing before a preacher wasn't going to make any difference, but he would never have believed Lindy could do this. All her reassurances about knowing her own heart had fooled him. She'd been so positive they were doing the right thing. None of that confidence was worth a damn now. They'd both made a mistake. A bad one. At the rate things were progressing, this marriage could be the single worst disaster of his life.

"I'm going below," Rush announced, walking away from the gyrocompass repeater, which indicated the *Mitchell*'s course. The sight of Jeff holding a letter from home was more than Rush could take. He needed to escape before he said or did something he'd regret.

Jeff nodded, but his brow was creased with tight bands of concern.

Once in his compartment, Rush lay on his back with his hands cupped behind his head. Steve was right. Rush had known it the minute his friend had said as much. Lindy had married him on the rebound, and now that he was gone she'd realized what a terrible error in judgment she'd committed and wanted out.

They'd been living in a fairy tale, forced to share the apartment the way they were, and like a fool Rush had gotten sucked into the fantasy. Lindy had been wounded by love and Rush had been a convenient source of comfort to her damaged ego.

Now that he was gone, Lindy realized their mistake. The muscles of his stomach knotted when he realized how helpless he was in this situation. Lindy didn't love him.

Now all he had to worry about was if she was pregnant. Not using any protection had been a conscious decision on his part. They hadn't even talked about it the way couples should—hadn't discussed the possibility of starting a family so soon. It wasn't that Rush had been so eager for Lindy to get pregnant, he realized with a flash of insight. But he hadn't wanted a repeat of what had happened with Cheryl. If Lindy's stomach was swollen with a baby when he returned, he didn't want any question in his mind about who was the father.

Rush refused to believe he'd actually done anything

so stupid as to play that sort of silly mind game. Lindy wasn't going to cheat on him—he refused to even consider the possibility. But then he'd honestly assumed she loved him, too—the same way he loved her. It hadn't even taken her a month to forget him.

Lindy let herself into the apartment and stopped when she found her brother sitting in front of the television, watching a late afternoon talk show. Steve's behavior was really beginning to concern her. He'd been assigned shore duty, and when he wasn't working he sat around the apartment with a lost, tormented look that reminded her of how she'd felt when she'd first arrived in Seattle. His behavior wasn't the only thing that was getting on her nerves. He'd become so cynical and so sarcastic about life. His thinking seemed so negative that she didn't like to talk to him anymore. There'd been a time when she'd admired him for the way he'd handled the emotional trauma of the divorce, but his letters had been a convenient front. It became clearer every day that the healing process hadn't even started in Steve. He still loved Carol, and he needed to either patch things up between them or accept the divorce as final. Otherwise it was going to ruin his life.

"Hi," she said, and walked into the kitchen, setting down the grocery bag on the counter. "What's Oprah got to say today?"

"Who?"

"The woman whose program you're watching."

"Hell, I don't know. Something about nursing mothers."

"And that interests you?"

"It's better than staring at some stupid game show."

"It's a beautiful day. You should be outside."

"Doing what?"

Lindy sighed. "I don't know. Something. Anything."

Steve stood and came into the kitchen. "Do you want me to do something for dinner? Peel potatoes, that sort of thing?"

She thanked him for his offer with a smile. "I've got everything under control." Opening the refrigerator, she set the milk inside and decided now was as good a time as any to wade into shark-infested waters. "Is Carol still living in Seattle?" Lindy asked the question and then turned to face her brother.

"Carol who?"

His words may have been flippant, but he couldn't disguise the instant flash of pain in his eyes.

"Carol Kyle, your wife."

"Ex-wife," he corrected bitterly. "As far as I know she is."

"I think I'll give her a call."

A year seemed to pass before Steve answered. "Before you start meddling in someone else's troubles, you'd better take care of your own, little sister."

Lindy's heart flew upward and lodged in her throat. "What do you mean by that?"

Steve pointed toward the mail that was stacked on the kitchen table. "You must have put the wrong address on that long letter you've been writing all month to Rush, because it's been returned."

"Oh, no." A sickening feeling invaded her limbs and her eyes widened with dread. "Returned? But why?" She reached for the thick manila envelope and checked the address. "Oh, Steve, what will Rush think if he doesn't get any mail from me?"

"The only thing he can assume under these circumstances. That you married him on the rebound and regret it."

She raised her hands in a gesture of abject defeat. "But I don't feel that way, not at all."

"Lindy, sit down. You look like you're about to faint." Her brother pulled out a chair and carefully lowered her into it. He walked a couple of times around her, as though gathering his thoughts on how to handle the situation.

Tears of frustration were hovering just beneath the surface. She'd faithfully written Rush each night, pouring out her heart to her husband, reassuring him each day how much she loved him and how proud she was to be his wife. She'd written about meeting the other wives and told him about the social get-together they were planning to celebrate the halfway mark of the six-month cruise. She'd drawn a picture of the lacy silk nightie the girls had given her as a wedding gift and told him how eager she was to model it for him.

There were weeks when she'd scribbled long epistles as many as six and seven times. Since the mail was only going to reach him once a month, Lindy had written it in journal form, marking the days.

To her surprise, this long separation wasn't anything like he'd suggested it would be. Rush had warned her that two weeks after he was gone she'd start to wonder how she ever imagined herself in love with him. Two weeks from the day he left, Lindy had made a giant card to tell him exactly the opposite had happened. If anything she loved him more than ever.

Over and over she had read the thick letter she'd received from him, until she had set each precious line in her memory. Rush's letters had been her lifeline to sanity.

The realization that he had received only a short one from her early after he sailed out of Bremerton, if that, was almost more than she could bear thinking about.

"What are you doing?" Steve asked, when Lindy reached for the phone.

"Calling Susan."

"What good is that going to do?"

"I… I don't know." But Lindy had to talk to someone before she went loony. Susan would know what to do.

"Hello?" Susan answered on the third ring, and Lindy could hear the twins crying in the background.

"Susan, it's Lindy. Something terrible has happened, and I don't know what to do." She was speaking as fast as she could, her voice raised and shaky.

"Lindy? Slow down. I can't understand a word you're saying."

"My letter to Rush came back," Lindy explained, doing her best to keep her voice as even as possible, although it wobbled like a toy top winding down after a long spin.

"Did you have the right address?"

Lindy reached for the envelope and read off Joanna's street numbers.

"Lindy," Susan muttered, interrupting her. "That's not the mailing address for the *Mitchell*."

"I know… It's Joanna's. She said we were supposed to get all the mail to her by the fifteenth. Remember?"

"You weren't supposed to mail it to *her*," Susan cried. "It was supposed to be mailed, period."

"But I thought she was in charge of that."

"No, Lindy, Joanna doesn't have anything to do with the mail."

"Oh God, Susan, what will Rush think?"

Susan hesitated, then sighed. "It isn't that bad. I wouldn't worry about it, since it's only the one letter. He'll receive the others."

Lindy felt like weeping all the more. "But there was only the one letter. A long, long one... Oh Susan, Rush must believe... I hate to even think about it. He'll assume I don't love him."

The line was silent. "The important thing is not to panic."

"I think it's too late for that."

"Now calm down," Susan muttered, and Lindy could picture her friend chewing on her lower lip, trying to come up with something. "Jeff will tell him."

"Tell him what?"

"Everything. How you've gotten involved in the wives' association and that we're seeing each other regularly. Rush is a smart man, Lindy. Give him credit for some intelligence."

"Right," Lindy said, nodding her head once. "He'll figure it out... He knows I love him." Lindy gnawed on her lip, remembering how the women's group had told her if she had any problems, she should contact Joanna.

A long silence stretched over the wire before Susan spoke. "Should I call Joanna or do you want to?"

The phone rang just after midnight. Lindy rolled onto her stomach and checked the time. She hadn't been sleeping well and had only turned off the light fifteen minutes before. The call was probably some prankster and she wasn't eager to answer it, figuring Steve would.

By the third ring, Lindy gave up on her brother and reached for the telephone receiver.

"Hello." She tried to make her voice sound as gruff and unfriendly as possible.

"This is a ham-radio operator in Anchorage, Alaska," the male voice explained. "A call is about to be transmitted to you from aboard the USS *Mitchell*. Talk as you would normally, but each time you're finished speaking you must say *over*. Do you understand?"

"Yes…"

"Okay. Go ahead and hang up and I'll connect you in about fifteen minutes."

Lindy's hand was shaking so badly she could barely replace the receiver. Rush. Somehow, someway, Rush had found a means of contacting her. She scooted off the bed and paced barefoot across the carpet, waiting. Fifteen minutes had never seemed to drag by more slowly.

When the phone rang, she nearly tore it off the nightstand.

"Lindy? Over."

The line sounded as if it were coming from the moon. Static filled the air. Popping and hissing.

"Yes, this is Lindy. Over."

"I only want to know one thing. Are you pregnant? Over."

Twelve

"You want to know what? Over," Lindy asked incredulously.

"Are you pregnant or not? Over." Rush demanded a second time. The long distance wire popped and hissed, making it almost impossible to hear him clearly.

"Not. Stop yelling at me and let me explain."

Silence followed.

A third voice interrupted. "Over?"

"Over," Lindy repeated.

"I'm listening. Over." Some of the bitter anger was gone from Rush's voice, but his frustration and anxiety were evident even through the poor quality of the connection.

"There was a screwup with the letters. I'll explain it later. Over."

"Explain it now. Over."

"I mailed the letter to Joanna instead of the address you gave me. Over."

"Joanna who? Over."

"Joanna Boston. She's an ombudsman for the *Mitchell*. I thought she was handling all the correspondence.

I didn't realize it would go through the normal channels. Over."

"In an entire month you only wrote me one letter? Over." The words were shouted into her ear.

"It was sixty-two pages long. Over." Lindy returned at equal volume.

Silence crackled like a morning breakfast cereal, and when Rush spoke again, his voice was more subdued, but still tense. "Do you regret the fact that we're married? Over."

"No. Do you? Over."

Rush seemed to take his own sweet time answering, and when he did his voice was almost a whisper. "Not now. Over."

"I love you," Lindy whispered, "I… I told you before you left that I know my own heart, and I do. Over."

"When I didn't get any mail, I thought you'd decided to…hell, I don't know what I thought. Over."

"I'll write every day, I promise. I'm not going to make the same mistake twice with the mail business. Over."

"Damn good thing. I nearly went berserk. Over."

"I'm really sorry, Rush. I felt terrible when the letter was returned. Over."

"I understand. Over."

They were married and hadn't seen each other in two months and there didn't seem to be anything more they had to say.

"I have to go. Over," Rush said, after an awkward moment.

"I know. Goodbye, Rush. Don't worry about anything at this end. I'm doing okay. Your letters help… I'm really sorry about what happened with yours. It won't happen again. Over."

"Goodbye, Lindy. I need you. Over."

The line went dead then and she was left holding the receiver in her hand. A tingling, burning feeling worked its way from her fingers down her arm and through her torso to settle in her stomach. Rush had been so angry with her. She couldn't blame him for being upset, but once that matter had been cleared up their conversation had remained awkward and stilted. They didn't have a lot to say to each other. His life was so far removed from hers now that there was nothing to share. He was a naval officer; she worked for an airline manufacturer. Their lives had briefly crossed paths for a three-week span and, when it came time to separate, they'd resisted and held on to each other. For the first time since Rush had been deployed, Lindy wondered if she had done the right thing in marrying him. At that moment it didn't feel right. Not for her, and from the way it sounded, not for Rush, either.

Lindy leaned back against the headboard and released a slow, agonized sigh. The shaking started then, and she gripped her hands together in a futile effort to control the trembling. She had married a man she barely knew, on an impulse. Doubts whizzed through her mind like buzzards circling a crippled animal, waiting for it to die. The picture was all too graphic in Lindy's troubled mind. She was stumbling and her family, particularly her brother, were all waiting for her to fall so they could tell her what a fool she'd been.

Lindy shook her head to dissolve the nightmarish image. She was being ridiculous. She loved Rush, and he loved her. He'd just ended their conversation by telling her of his need for her. A man like Rush Callaghan didn't say those words lightly. The circumstances they were trapped in had led to this negative thinking. These doubts would be gone by morning and she'd feel as strongly as ever about her commitment to Rush.

Swallowing at the hard lump in the back of her throat, Lindy turned off the bedside lamp and lay back down, resting her head on the pillow that had once been her husband's. Everything was going to work out fine. She'd done the right thing by marrying Rush. They were deeply in love with each other and if there were a few rocky roads ahead, that was to be expected. They'd weather those just fine.

But Lindy didn't sleep that night.

The tall waiter handed Lindy the oblong menu with the gold tassel. "This is a pleasant surprise," she said, looking across the linen-covered table at her older brother. Her relationship with Steve had gone much better this past month. He rarely mentioned Rush, and she stayed away from the subject of Carol. It wasn't exactly solid ground they stood on, but stable enough for the two of them to coexist without too many personality problems. The gesture of dinner was a delightful one, and Lindy wasn't about to refuse. They both needed a break from the humdrum of daily life.

These last couple of days Steve had been almost like his old self—teasing, joking and laughing. If she hadn't known him better, Lindy might have been fooled. She toyed with the idea of talking to Steve about the doubts that had been haunting her since the ship-to-shore call from Rush. She was terribly frightened that she'd done the wrong thing in marrying him, and she was unsure what, if anything, she could do about it.

"I figure I owe you at least one evening out before I leave," Steve said as a means of explanation for the unexpected invitation.

"You didn't need to pick the most expensive restaurant in town."

Steve glanced over the top of his menu and shrugged. "What else have I got to do with my money?"

"You could start dating again." She offered the suggestion flippantly, not really meaning it. Like Rush, Lindy had recognized almost immediately that her brother was still in love with his ex-wife.

"I could," Steve answered thoughtfully. "But I won't."

"I know," Lindy said, understanding perfectly.

"What do you know?"

It was almost as if they were children again, Lindy mused—the way his eyes sparkled with mischief and his mouth quirked with a teasing half smile.

"Well?" he pressed.

"I know you won't date again."

Slowly Steve set the menu aside, his fingers lingering over the gold tassel. The humor drained out of his eyes. "The lobster sounds good, doesn't it?"

Lindy didn't want to introduce a subject that would embarrass or intimidate her older brother. Any mention of Carol was taboo and they both knew it. Sadly she recognized that talking over her fears about her marriage wasn't going to work, either. She didn't know what she'd tell Steve anyway. She was scared to death she'd married the wrong man, terrified that everything her brother had accused her of was true.

Her biggest concern was that she'd accepted Rush's

proposal on the rebound and her marriage was based on emotional insecurity. Two weeks wasn't sufficient time to know a man well enough to commit her life to him. Even the regrets Rush had prophesied were beginning to come true. There were days when she had to struggle to remember what her husband looked like. A thousand unknowns haunted her. His phone call had only served to remind her how arrogant he could be, and the letters from him that had followed were filled with his angry frustration at not hearing from her.

Although Steve seemed more open than he had been, Lindy didn't feel she could discuss her doubts. Her brother was struggling with his own problems.

"Then lobster it is," she said, forcing her voice to sound airy and bright.

Steve picked up his butter knife and slowly ran the blade down his long fingers. "I wanted to take you to dinner for another reason, too."

"I'm a rotten cook and another night of my special enchiladas with homemade salsa was more than your stomach could tolerate?"

"Close," Steve answered, and chuckled. But his eyes quickly sobered and he lowered his gaze. "Actually I owe you an apology, sis."

"Oh?" This was a major surprise.

"I was wrong to come down on you and Rush the way I did." He lay the butter knife down and reached for the salad fork, absently stroking the tines. Every mannerism revealed his regret at the way he'd chastised her earlier. "If I'd gone out and handpicked a husband for you, I couldn't have found a better man than Rush Callaghan."

Lindy's gaze rested on the delicate floral design of the place setting.

"You saw what you wanted," Steve continued, "and went after it. It takes a special kind of woman to do that, Lindy, and although I'll admit I had my fears, you've managed to calm every one of them."

"He is wonderful."

"You both are."

Lindy's nod was decidedly noncommittal. She could feel the emotion gathering in the back of her eyes. How could Steve sound so certain about her and Rush when she was struggling to believe in her own marriage? He made her happiness sound like a foregone conclusion when she was dog-paddling in a mire of self-doubts, struggling to stay afloat. A week before he would have taken her in his arms and comforted her. Tonight he made her sound like Joan of Arc for being so brave and true. There was no justice left in the world. None.

"Attribute my foul mood to the fact that I was shocked by your news. That and a strong brotherly instinct to protect my baby sister. I think the two of you are going to do exceptionally well together."

With trembling hands Lindy smoothed the pink linen napkin in her lap, hardly able to breathe normally, let alone find words to answer her brother. His original disdain for her and Rush's marriage had a lot more to do with his own unpleasant experience with nuptial bliss than anything else. Lindy's greatest fear was that she'd made the same mistake her brother had.

After an awkward moment, Lindy murmured, "I appreciate the apology, Steve, but it wasn't necessary."

Her brother shook his head, dismissing her words. "Rush will be good to you, and you're exactly the right kind of woman for him. I expect you'll both be very happy."

"We're going to try." The words were squeezed out of Lindy's throat. If he didn't stop soon, she was going to embarrass them both by bursting into tears.

"Give this marriage everything you've got, Lindy." He set down the fork and reached for the water glass. "Hold on to the happiness with both hands. Don't ever let anything stand between you."

His eyes were so full of pain that Lindy had to look away. She felt certain he must have read all the fear in her eyes. How sad it was that the two of them, who had once been so close, could sit across from each other and ignore what was in their hearts.

Reaching for the menu once more, Steve released his breath in a long sigh. "What do you say we start off dinner with a Caesar salad?"

"Sure," Lindy answered, forcing herself to smile.

My dearest Lindy,
I feel like a first-class idiot, shouting at you the way I did on the phone the other night. I jumped to conclusions, thinking the worst when I didn't get any mail from you. Lindy, I can't even begin to explain what was going on inside me. Jeff tried to tell me there was some logical explanation why you hadn't written, but I wouldn't listen. It was as though my greatest fears were hitting me in the face. I couldn't sleep; I couldn't eat. In my mind, I was absolutely certain Paul had come back and told you he'd made a mistake and you'd left with him. I know it sounds crazy now, but at the time, it made perfect sense.

From the day when the mail was handed out and I didn't get any, I've been acting like a real ass. Jeff must have gone to the chaplain because the next thing I knew I got called in to talk to him. He was the one who arranged the ship-to-shore call. Thank God he did.

After we talked, I was ready to free-fly. There's no way to explain how much better I felt. Has anyone ever told you what a sweet, sexy voice you have? And when you told me you still loved me, I nearly broke down and wept. I was so relieved. God, Lindy, I don't even know how to explain how good it felt to know everything's all right.

After the things I said to you in my last letter, I wouldn't blame you if you wanted to bag this whole marriage, but I'm hoping to God you don't. All I can say is, I'm sorry.

Honey, it's been less than three months and I'm already keeping track of how many days until I see you again. Try to arrange some additional time off in December, if you can, will you? I'm going to take you to bed and I swear it'll be a full week before we venture out of the bedroom. I guess that tells you how I'm feeling right now.

Before I met you I was this sane, ordinary man who was content with his life and sure of his goals. Two weeks after I meet you, and I'm a completely different person. There's a wedding band on my finger and I'm thinking about how nice it would be to become a father. I've even been toying with the idea of buying a house. What do you think? You can bet I do a lot of thinking about making love to my wife. Mostly I'm wondering what the hell I'm doing on the other side of the world.

I saw something yesterday that drove that point

straight through my gut. We got orders to lend assistance to a Saudi oil tanker that had been hit by a Harpoon-type missile. One of our frigates pulled up alongside to help control the fire, and we sent a couple of Sea Kings with fire-fighting equipment and took their injured aboard. It really hit home that there could be trouble here, and this part of the world isn't sitting around enjoying crumpets and tea. I'm not telling you this to worry you, Lindy. I needed to see that burning tanker to take care of some business matters I should have done a long time before now. If anything happens to me, I want you to know you'll be well taken care of financially.

I've got to close this letter for now, but I'll write more later. Lots more. I love you, Lindy. It frightens me how much.

Dearest Rush,

Reading your latest letter was the best thing that's happened to me since our wedding. I've been feeling so confused and blue lately. After your letter, I felt like singing and dancing. I love you, husband. I don't have a single lingering doubt.

Did you hear the shouts of glee all across America this morning? No, we haven't landed on the moon or captured a Caribbean island. School started and those cries were the happy voices of mothers all over the land. At least, that's what Sandy and Mary and several of the other navy wives told me today. I've gotten to be good friends with several of them. Did you know that Sissy Crawford's real name isn't Sissy? It's something

completely different, like Angela or Georgia.
The other wives started calling her that because
she hates it so much when Bill's at sea, and she's
so sure everything's going to go wrong that the
women started calling her Sissy in a friendly, teasing way. The name stuck. I don't know if I should
tell you what they've been calling me. Actually
it's kind of embarrassing, but by the same token
it's true. Randy. Don't worry. Susan made them
stop. Good grief, we could all call each other that.

As for taking time off in December, you've
got it, fellow!

It's been over three months since you sailed...
were deployed. Are you impressed with the navy
lingo I'm picking up? Three months since we
kissed; three months since we made love; three
months since I've slept in your arms.

And another three to go.

I've got good news. I got a raise, which was
a pleasant surprise. I'm working out well with
Boeing and they seem to appreciate my obvious
talents. I decided to put the extra money in a savings account so we'll have a little something to fall
back on when it's time for me to give up working
to stay home with the children. It's difficult for me
to imagine myself a mother when being a wife is
still so new. I don't think we need to rush into this
parenting business—do you? I wish we'd talked
about these matters before you left. I have no idea
how you feel about starting a family. When you
asked if I was pregnant, it didn't exactly sound
as if you'd have been pleased with the prospect
if I had been.

Anyway, we're halfway through the tour and we've both managed to survive thus far. Susan and I and a bunch of other navy wives are celebrating Halfway Night this weekend. I don't know if I'm supposed to tell you this, so keep it under your hat because the other husbands are going to get insanely jealous. You, on the other hand, are sure to be coolheaded, mature and reasonable about this sort of thing, and I'm confident it isn't going to bother you.

The nine of us are carpooling it to a Seattle nightclub to see some male strippers. Doesn't that sound like fun? Susan and I have been looking forward to this night for weeks. In fact we've had the reservations since the first week in August. As you've probably guessed, this is a popular club.

Believe me, Rush, you're not going to say anything that will frighten me anymore than I already am about what's happening in the Middle East. Reports are on the news every night. All I ask is that you take care of yourself.

Steve left Monday for a week of sea trials, so it's really been lonely around here. It's the first time I've been in the apartment completely alone since I arrived in Seattle. It gives me lots of time to write to you so I don't mind.

I suppose you know by now that Susan is pregnant. She's feeling surprisingly good, especially after the doctor confirmed that there's only one baby. Susan's hoping for a girl this time.

I'm going to mail this off since I don't want a repeat of what happened last month. Remember, I love you. Please don't take any crazy risks.

Lindy,

What the hell do you mean, you're going to see a male strip show! You're damn right I didn't tell the others. Good God, they'd stage a mutiny. As for me being mature and coolheaded, you couldn't be more wrong. I don't like it. Not one damn bit.

My dearest, darling Rush,

The male strippers were sexy as hell. What gorgeous bodies! What cute buns. What attractive… never mind. We had a fantastic time, but, quite honestly, it was too much for us men-starved navy wives. We talked it over and agreed this kind of entertainment would be better served later in the tour when we could count on our husbands being home soon. We decided to go back for a Final Fling the week before the Mitchell is scheduled to arrive home.

I love you, Rush Callaghan. Take care of yourself.

Love,

Lindy

P.S. Would you ever consider wearing spurs and a cute little cowboy hat to bed?

"Line 314," Lindy murmured absently, answering the phone at her desk.

"Lindy, it's Steve."

Something in the pitch of her brother's low-modulated voice, something in the way he said her name instantly alerted Lindy. Goose bumps shot up and down her spine. Not once in all the weeks that Lindy had worked for

Boeing had her brother telephoned the office. She didn't even know where he'd gotten her work number.

"What's wrong?"

Steve hesitated. "I just heard a news bulletin over the radio. There's been a report of an accident aboard the *Mitchell*."

"Oh, God." The words were wrenched from her heart. "Rush… Did they say anything about Rush?"

"No, but it's much too soon. Don't panic, Lindy. There are nearly four thousand men aboard the carrier. The chance of Rush being a fatality is minute."

Lindy closed her eyes and cupped her hand over her mouth as terror gripped her. Her heart roared in her chest so loudly that it nearly drowned out her brother's words.

"I think it would be a good idea if you left work and met me at the apartment."

She nodded, unable to find her voice.

"Lindy?"

"I'm on my way." Already she was clearing her computer terminal, doing only what was absolutely necessary so she could leave.

"Lindy, can you drive? Do you want me to come get you?"

"No… I'm fine. When did it happen? How?"

"They're not exactly sure, but the preliminary reports are mentioning a plane crash."

"How many are dead?"

"Sweetie, listen. The only reason I phoned was so you wouldn't hear the news yourself or from someone at the office and panic. I'm telling you everything I know. I called the base and they're setting up an information center for wives and family. Once you're home I'll take you there."

"I'll meet you as soon as I can." Worry had already clogged Lindy's throat by the time she replaced the receiver. Her supervisor was just walking into her office when Lindy scooted her chair back from the desk.

"You heard? Someone just told me there was something about the *Mitchell* on the radio. Take whatever time you need."

"Thanks." Lindy grabbed her purse, her legs so weak she could hardly walk.

The drive from Renton to the apartment normally took fifteen to twenty minutes. Lindy made it in ten and had little memory of the ride. She dared not turn on the radio for fear of what she'd learn. The entire time she was driving, she prayed, mumbling the same desperate plea over and over again. An aircraft carrier was a huge ship, a city unto itself, able to house as many as six thousand men. The possibility of Rush being a fatality was infinitesimal. He was the chief navigator. The bridge was possibly the safest place of all. He would be free from harm. At least that was what Lindy kept telling herself.

Steve was waiting for her when she burst in the front door. "Did you learn anything more?"

He looked terribly pale, and nodded. "Lindy, sit down."

"No!" she screamed, knotting her fists. "Tell me! Is he dead? Is he?"

Steve raked his hands through his hair. "I don't know. Apparently an Intruder was landing and a wing caught on the arresting gear. It cartwheeled on the flight deck, spewing wreckage," he hesitated. "They haven't released any names yet. Five are known dead."

"Dear God."

Her brother placed his hands on her shoulders and his eyes revealed his own personal torment. She knew in that minute that he would have given his soul not to be the one to tell her this.

"What is it?" she asked, in a voice that was as calm and as accepting as she could make it.

"The latest information reports that part of the plane careened into the bridge."

Lindy shut her eyes and it was the last thing she should have done. Instantly she felt her legs give out as her mind conjured up the worst possible scene of bodies being hurled through space and men screaming in agony. Fire seemed to have erupted everywhere. Lindy gasped and her hands shot out.

Steve managed to catch her, pressing her head against his shoulder. "Rush is going to be all right," he murmured, while his hand smoothed her hair.

"No," she said, in a whisperlike sound. "He isn't." If there was any action or any trouble, Rush would be there right in the middle of it.

Steve escorted Lindy to the naval base, where an information center had been set up. The first person Lindy saw was Susan. The two women looked at each other and started sobbing. Timmy and Tommy, not knowing what to make of everything, were soon crying, too. Lindy took Tommy and attempted to comfort him, but the youngster wanted his mother and squirmed in Lindy's arms.

"Jeff?" Lindy finally managed to ask.

"I don't know. What about Rush?"

Lindy heaved in a calming breath. "I haven't heard."

It seemed hours passed before any additional information was released, and then the names of the injured were read. Neither Jeff nor Rush were listed. Lindy didn't know whether to be happy or terrified. The only choices that remained were that both men had somehow magically escaped the explosion or were among those listed as dead.

Steve was at Lindy's side as much as possible, doing what he could. One look at her brother told Lindy he suspected the worst. As much as she could, Lindy tried to be positive. If Rush had died in the explosion, she reasoned, she would have felt it. Deep within her heart, she would have felt a part of herself die. She wouldn't be this calm, this accepting.

People milled around everywhere. Wives, children, parents. Rather than sit and worry, Lindy mingled with the others, talking, praying and crying—sometimes all three at once.

It was when she turned to find Steve at her side that she knew word had finally come through. She looked up to the brother she had always loved, the brother who had shielded her from whatever pain he could, and Lindy smiled. She realized at the time how odd that was.

Her brother slipped his arm around her shoulder and his jaw jutted out in a gesture of grief and pain.

"Rush is listed as missing."

Thirteen

"What do you mean missing?" Lindy asked. "Rush couldn't have just disappeared." It astonished her how calm she felt, how controlled, as though they were discussing something as mundane as the tide tables or what to fix for dinner.

"Lindy, I think you should prepare yourself for the worst."

"That would be silly," she said, turning back to the little boy she'd been talking to and purposely ignoring her brother. "Rush is fine. I know he is. There's been some screwup and he's going to be furious when he learns the way the navy has everyone so worried about him."

"Lindy…" Steve hesitated, and his brow creased in thick folds of concern and regret. "I hope to God you're right."

"Of course I am."

Steve left her then and Lindy sank into an empty chair. Her hands shook so badly that she clenched them together in her lap, her long nails cutting crescents of pain into her palms. Soon her arms were shaking, then her legs, until her whole body felt as if it were consumed by uncontrollable spasms.

Susan took the chair beside Lindy and wrapped her own sweater around Lindy's shoulders. Susan held it there until some of the intense cold she was experiencing seeped away and a steady warmth invaded her limbs.

Lindy tried to smile, failed, and whispered one word. "Jeff?"

"He's fine."

Lindy nodded once. "Good."

"They'll find him, Lindy," Susan said, her voice thick with conviction, although she was struggling with her own fears. "I know they will. Jeff won't let anyone rest until they do."

"I know." Lindy remembered how Susan had once told her that she didn't worry so much about Jeff at sea because she always knew Rush would be there to watch out for her husband. The truth of what Susan was telling her now was the only slender thread Lindy had to hang on to. Jeff would turn hell upside down until he learned what had happened to Rush.

Soon the other wives joined Lindy, scooting their chairs and forming a protective circle around her. No one did much talking. No one tried to build her up with false hopes. No one suggested she try to eat or get some sleep. Or leave.

That night cots were brought into the information center for those who wished to stay. Lindy insisted the other wives go back to their families, but each one in turn refused. They were special sisters, bonded together in ways that were thicker than blood.

"No one's leaving until we find out what happened to Rush," Susan said, speaking for them all.

The others managed to sleep that night in the cots provided. Lindy tried, but couldn't. Every time she closed her eyes that same terrible scene flashed through her mind, and she was convinced she could hear Rush cry out in torment. As the hours slowly, methodically ticked away, Lindy sat and stared into space. In the darkest part of the night, surrounded by silence, she tried to prepare herself to accept Rush's death, but every time she entertained the notion, such piercing pain stabbed through her that she shoved the thought from her mind. This interminable waiting was the worst nightmare of her life.

Food was brought in the following morning and the others ate, but Lindy knew it would be impossible for her to hold anything down.

Susan handed her a glass of orange juice. "You didn't eat anything yesterday. Try this," she said softly, insistently. "You're going to need your strength."

Lindy wanted to argue with her friend but hadn't the fortitude. "Okay."

Another eternity passed, a lifetime—hours that felt like years, minutes that dragged like weeks, seconds that could have been days. And still they waited.

"He's dead," Lindy sobbed to the others late that afternoon, although just saying the words aloud nearly crippled her. "I know it. I can feel it in my heart. He's gone."

"You don't know it," Susan argued, and her own eyes shone brightly with unshed tears. Her hands trembled and she laced her fingers together as though offering a silent prayer.

"Don't even say it," Sissy cried, her face streaked with moisture.

Joanna gripped Lindy's fingers with her own and knelt in front of her, her gaze holding Lindy's. "He's alive until we know otherwise. Hold tight to that, Lindy. It's all we've got."

Lindy nodded, her eyes so blurred with tears that when she looked up to find her brother standing over her, she couldn't read his expression. A powerful magnetic force drove her to her feet.

"Tell me," she whispered urgently. "Tell me."

"He's alive."

Lindy didn't hear anything more than that before she broke down and started to weep, covering her face with her hands, her shoulders heaving with the depth of her relief. But these tears were ones of joy. A sheer release from the endless unknown. She tossed her arms around her brother's neck and he gripped her waist and swung her around. Susan and the others were jumping up and down, hugging each other, laughing and crying as well.

When everyone had settled back down, Steve gave them the rest of the information. "They found Rush buried under a pile of rubble; he's lost a lot of blood and in addition to internal injuries, his arm has been severely cut. He's being flown to Tripler Army Hospital in Hawaii for microsurgery. Apparently the nerves in his left arm were severed. He's unconscious, but alive."

"I'm going to him," Lindy said with raw determination, as though she expected an argument. Nothing would stop her. She wouldn't believe Rush was going to live until she saw him herself. Touched him. Kissed him. Loved him.

Steve nodded. "I already made arrangements for you to fly out today."

A pumpkin and a picture of a witch decorating the wall across the room from him were the first things Rush noticed when he opened his eyes. His mouth was as dry as Arizona in August and his head throbbed unmercifully. A hospital, he determined, but he hadn't any idea where.

Carefully and with a great deal of effort, he rolled his head to one side and stared at the raised rail of the bed. He blinked, sure he was imagining the vision that was before him.

"Lindy?"

The apparition didn't move. Her fingers were gripping the steel railing and her forehead was pressed against the back of her hands. She looked as though she were sleeping.

Rush tried to reach out and touch her, gently wake her, but he couldn't lift his arm. Even the effort sent a sharp shooting pain through his shoulder. He must have groaned because Lindy jerked her head up, her eyes wide with concern. When she saw he was awake, she sighed and grinned. Rush swore he'd never seen a more beautiful smile in his life. The pain that stabbed through him with every breath was gone. The ache in his head vanished as the look in his wife's eyes immersed him in an unspeakable joy that transcended everything else.

"You're real," he murmured. He refused to believe that she was a figment of his imagination. His head remained fuzzy and his vision blurred, but Lindy was real. He'd stake his life on that.

She nodded and her hand brushed lightly over his face, lovingly caressing his jaw. "And you're alive. Oh, Rush, I nearly lost you."

She bit into her bottom lip and Rush knew she was struggling not to cry. He wished he could have spared her all worry and doubt.

"Where am I...? How long?"

"You're in a hospital in Hawaii. Two days now."

He frowned. "That long?" Now that his eyesight was clearing, he could see the dark smudges under Lindy's eyes. She was as pale as death, as though recovering from a bad bout of flu. And much thinner than he remembered. Too thin. "You look terrible."

She laughed, and the sweet, lilting sound wrapped itself around his heart, squeezing emotion from him. Dear God, he loved Lindy. So much of the accident remained clouded in his mind. All he could remember was hearing a horrendous noise and seeing a ball of fire come hurtling toward him. Everything had happened so fast that there had barely been time to do anything more than react. All he knew was that he didn't want to die. He wanted to go home to Lindy. His Lindy. His love.

The next thing he remembered was pain. Terrible pain. More acute than anything he'd ever experienced. He knew he was close to dying, knew he might not make it, and still all he could think about was Lindy. Dying would have stopped the agony; slipping into the dark swirling void of death would have been welcome if only it would end the torment, but Rush chose the pain because he knew it would lead him back to Lindy.

"Have you looked in a mirror lately?" she asked, her

lips twitching with a teasing smile. "You're not exactly ready to be cast as Prince Charming yourself."

"You've been sick?" he pressed, his tongue faltering over the words. It was a struggle to keep awake, the pull back to unconsciousness greater with each second.

"No, just worried. It took them nearly forty hours to find you after the accident and until then you were listed as missing."

"Oh God, Lindy, I'm…sorry."

"I'm fine now that I know you're going to be all right." Again her fingers touched his face, smoothing the hair from his brow, lingering as though she needed the reassurance that he was real.

"How many…dead?"

"Seven. Three on the flight deck and four on the bridge."

Rush's jaw tightened. "Who?"

Lindy recited the names and each one fell upon his chest like a boulder dropped from the ceiling. "…good men," he said after a moment, and was shocked at how fragile his voice sounded.

"More than twenty suffered serious injuries."

Rush felt himself drifting off; he resisted, but the pull of the tide was too powerful for him to fight. "How bad…"

"The burn victims are the worst."

He nodded and that was the last he remembered.

When he woke again the room was pitch-dark. He felt a straw at his mouth and he sucked greedily. "What time is it?"

"Two a.m."

"Lindy, is that you?"

"Do you need something for the pain?"

He shook his head. "No." Her fingers curled around his own and he held on to her, savoring her touch. He slept again.

Lindy sat in a chair at her husband's side. She'd tried to sleep countless times, but the rest her body craved continued to elude her. Just as she'd start to drift off, the horror of those two days of not knowing if Rush was dead or alive returned and snapped her awake. She'd come so close to losing him. Seven men had died. Honorable men. And Rush had come a hairsbreadth from making the count eight. The men who had died were husbands, fathers, lovers—and now they were gone.

Standing, she walked over to the window. Palm trees swayed in the late afternoon breeze. The sun shone and the ocean lapped relentlessly against the white, sandy beach. The flawless beauty of the scene should have soothed her troubled spirit, but it didn't. Instead she felt a cold hard feeling settle in her lungs. It spread out, making her breathing labored and causing her throat to ache. Those men had died, and for what? Lindy had no answers, and every time she closed her eyes the questions started to pound at her, demanding answers when she had none.

"Lindy?"

She took a minute to compose herself, pasted a smile on her face and turned around. "So Sleeping Ugly is finally awake. How are you feeling?"

"You don't want to know."

Concern moved her to his bedside. "Should I get the nurse? She said if you needed something for pain, I could…"

"I'm doing okay." His brows folded into a tight frown

as he looked up at her. "You're still looking like death warmed over."

She forced a cheery laugh and decided to put her makeup on with a heavier hand before her next visit. "That's a fine thing to say to me!"

"When was the last time you had a decent meal?"

She opened her mouth to tell him, but paused when she realized she didn't know herself. "I'm fine, Rush. You're the patient here, not me."

He looked for a minute as if he were going to argue with her, but he didn't. "If you're not hungry, I am."

"I'll see what I can scrounge up."

She returned a few minutes later, carrying a tray. But it was soon apparent that Rush had no appetite and had used the excuse of hunger as a ploy to get her to sample something.

Three days passed. Rush grew stronger with each one, and Lindy grew paler and thinner. She still couldn't sleep—not more than an hour at a stretch.

A week after Rush arrived in Hawaii, Lindy strolled into his hospital room to discover her husband sitting up for the first time. His left arm was in a cast and hung in a sling over his chest. The swelling in his face had gone down considerably, and he looked almost like his old handsome self once more. Lindy paused and smiled, perhaps her first genuine one since she'd arrived in this tropical paradise.

"You're looking fit."

"Come here, wife," he said holding out his one good arm to her. "I'm tired of those skimpy pecks on the cheek you've been giving me. I'm starved for you."

Lindy walked across the room like a woman who'd

been wandering in the desert and been offered a glass of water. Once Rush had his arm around her, his mouth claiming hers, she felt whole again. He smelled incredibly good and tasted of peppermint.

The fears and doubts that had been hounding her all week dissolved in the warmth of his hold. When he lifted his head and smiled, Lindy felt weak and breathless in his embrace.

"Lindy, dear God, I've nearly died, I've wanted to hold you so much."

Angry, selfish thoughts flooded her mind, and she clamped her mouth shut. He'd nearly died, yes, but it was from a terrible plane crash and explosion that didn't have anything to do with her. But when Rush directed her mouth to his, she was engulfed in his kiss, lost and drowning. Nothing else mattered. As his lips closed over hers, demanding and hungry, he reclaimed everything that had once been his: her heart, her body, her soul. There was nothing left inside her to protest. He owned her so completely, so unquestionably, that she hadn't the will to say or do anything. All she could do was submit.

She wrapped her arms around his neck and leaned into him, giving him her tongue when he sought it, taking his when it was offered. Their need for each other was urgent. Fierce. Savage, yet tender. Nothing else in the world made sense except this. Only the driving need Lindy felt to be a part of Rush.

Moisture appeared in the corners of her eyes and Rush sipped away her tears. He kissed her eyes, her forehead, her cheeks, her lips, and nuzzled tenderly at her neck while his fingers tunneled through her dark hair.

"Lindy," he breathed. "My love, my own sweet love." His long fingers brushed the wisps of bangs from her face and wiped away the last trace of tears, as though she was the most precious thing he had ever touched.

"I talked to the doctor this morning," he whispered. "I'm going to be released at the end of the week."

Lindy's tender heart swelled with unrestrained joy.

"We have one night, love, just one night before I fly back to the *Mitchell*."

For one frenzied moment, Lindy was sure she'd heard him incorrectly. Going back? He couldn't possibly be returning to the Persian Gulf after what had happened.

"No." She freed herself from his grip and took a step back. "You can't go back!"

"Honey, I have to. It's my job."

"But…"

"What did you expect me to do?"

Lindy wasn't sure what she'd assumed would happen. Anything but having him return to the same nightmare.

"Honey, listen. We've only got six weeks of the cruise left. Hell, for all I know we could even be headed back sooner than that, depending on the amount of damage we sustained. Six weeks isn't such a long time. I'll be home before you know it."

Somehow Lindy managed to nod. They had precious time left, and the thought of spending these last days together arguing was intolerable. After all, there wasn't much she could say. She'd thought—or at least hoped— he'd be coming home with her now. She needed him sleeping at her side to chase away the demons and dissolve the horror from her mind.

Rush may want to make love to her, Lindy realized, but he wanted to get back to his ship more. She'd noted that when he started talking about the *Mitchell* his eyes had seemed to spark with new life. He didn't like lying around the hospital; she would have been surprised if he had. Rush longed to go back to his ship, back to his men. He wanted to leave her behind, safely tucked away in a Seattle apartment while he was gallivanting all over the world, risking his life. Risking her peace of mind. Risking their happiness.

"I hope that hotel room of yours has a double bed," Rush said, smiling up at her.

"It does," she assured him, averting her gaze to the scene outside the window.

Something was wrong with Lindy. Rush knew it, felt it every time she walked in the room. She looked a little better—at least he knew she was eating regularly. Some color had returned to her pale cheeks when they'd walked in the sunshine.

Rush tried to draw her out, tried to get her to tell him what was troubling her, but she held it all inside and he didn't press her. He would be leaving the hospital early that afternoon and leaving Lindy first thing in the morning. She'd been through a great deal and so had he. If what was bothering her was important, she'd say something to him.

The petite blond nurse who had been assigned his room strolled in, holding a small white cup and a glass of water. She was young and pretty, the kind of woman who might have attracted his attention before he met Lindy. Now he only had eyes for his wife and barely gave the woman more than a second glance.

"Pill time," she announced cheerfully.

Rush grumbled and held out his hand. The blue-eyed nurse waited while he took the two capsules and swallowed down a glass of water.

"Where's your wife this afternoon?"

"She'll be by later," Rush explained. He was surprised Lindy wasn't there already. Lindy was as keen as he was to get out of this sterile environment, but he was far more eager to get his wife into bed. One damn night was all they had. He wished to hell it could be more. It seemed their entire married life had been crammed into three all-too-short nights.

"I hear you're leaving us."

He nodded. He didn't like the antiseptic smell here, and he swore the food must taste better in prison. It had been torture to be this close to the ocean, to smell the clean tangy scent of it and be prohibited from doing anything more than gaze at the blue waters. He was anxious to get back to the *Mitchell*. He felt a lot like someone who had fallen off a horse and needed to climb right back on again. He'd been mentally shaken by the accident, his courage tested. He needed to set foot on the bridge, look down on that flight deck and know he was in control once more.

"I don't know when I've seen a woman more in love with her husband. Or more worried," the pretty blond nurse went on to say. "When your wife first arrived, I thought we were going to have to admit her. I swear she was as pale as bleached flour. I suppose you know she wouldn't leave your side. For three days, she didn't move. The doctors tried repeatedly to assure her you were going to be all right, but she wouldn't believe it. Not until you woke, and even then she refused to go."

Rush rested his head against the thin pillow and held in a sigh until his chest ached with the effort. He'd known that every time he woke Lindy had been with him, but he hadn't realized she'd spent every minute at his side.

"I hope you appreciate that woman," the nurse continued.

"I do," Rush countered. Tonight he'd show Lindy just how much.

Lindy was determined that this one night with Rush would be as perfect as she could make it. She planned to blot out all her doubts and grab hold of what happiness she could before Rush returned to the Persian Gulf. She yearned to encapsulate these last hours together and hold them in her memory until he returned safely to her in December.

"How are you feeling?" she asked, once they were inside her hotel room.

"A little weak," Rush admitted reluctantly. "But I'm getting stronger every day."

She helped him into a chair. It was on the tip of her tongue to suggest he wait a few more days before flying across the world and rejoining his ship, but she knew it would be useless. She knew Rush. She'd seen that hard look of determination he wore more than once. He wouldn't listen to her.

"I thought we'd order dinner from room service," she said, standing awkwardly in the middle of the floor.

He nodded. "Good idea." He hesitated and gave her a look that was almost shy. "I have another good idea, too. Come to me, Lindy. I need you."

She couldn't have refused him had her life depended on it. He stood, reached for her hand and walked her to the bed. He kissed her once, hard, his tongue delving into her mouth, stroking hers. His right hand was fumbling with the buttons of her blouse, but the left one was incapable of giving much assistance. With their mouths still linked, Lindy brushed his hand aside and helped him. When she was finished with her own, she freed his uniform shirt from his waistband and unbuttoned it for him.

"Thanks," Rush breathed hoarsely, when she'd finished the task. Lindy paused, biting her lip as she ran her hand over the dark-furred chest. The muscles of his abdomen felt hard and sleek, the curling hairs wispy against the tips of her fingers.

"I want you like hell," he groaned.

Lindy let her eyes fall and released a short, delicate chuckle. "I can tell." His free hand cupped her breast and her nipple blossomed and grew incredibly hard. "I want you, too."

He flicked his thumb over the rose tip of her breast and she moaned.

"I can tell," he repeated thickly.

They finished undressing each other with trembling hands. Lindy helped Rush with the parts he couldn't manage, and he helped her the best he could. Soon they were lying on the mattress, their bodies on fire for each other.

When he moved on top of her, Lindy smiled up at him, craving the fiery release his body would give her. Still trembling, she closed her eyes and gave herself over to this experience. She allowed herself to be swallowed up in his tenderness, and when he entered her, her body answered in perfect counterpoint to his. Rush's touch, his lovemaking, was a balm, a healing potion for all they had suffered. Tears wet her face and his lips found them. Intuitively he knew she needed assurances and he gave them to her with the ebb and flow of his body into her own. No matter what the future held, he seemed to be telling her, no matter what happened in the next six weeks, they would have this night to hold on to and to remember.

They made love again after dinner, and he held and kissed her long after midnight. While Rush soundly slept, Lindy climbed out of bed and cuddled up in the chair across from him.

She'd tried so hard to put the fear behind her, but she couldn't. A hundred times in the past week, she'd hungered to tell him how she'd nearly gone crazy with worry, and she hadn't said a word. She wanted to explain how every time she closed her eyes the same freakish nightmare haunted her sleep. But again and again she'd held her tongue, gliding over what was important for fear of shattering the peace of these past days together.

In a few hours Rush would return to his ship and she would go back to Seattle. She'd been wrong not to tell Rush what she was feeling, wrong to allow him to assume she could go on playing this charade. Steve was right. He had been all along—she wouldn't make a good navy wife. It wasn't in her to bid her husband farewell time after time and handle whatever crisis befell them with calm acceptance.

Twice now Lindy had found herself deeply in love, convinced she knew her own heart each time. Confident enough to wear the rings each man had given her. Both times she'd been wrong. She wasn't the type of woman Rush needed. She wasn't strong enough to endure months of loneliness and deal with the knowledge that she would always take second place in her husband's life.

Hot tears scalded her eyes and when she could restrain them no longer, she let them flow freely down her face, no longer willing to hold them back.

Rush raised his head from the pillow, looking disoriented and groggy. He turned and stared at his sobbing wife.

"Lindy," he breathed her name into the night. "What's wrong?"

"Do you love me, Rush?"

"Of course I do." He threw back the sheet and sat on the edge of the bed. "You know I do."

"If you love me...if you really love me, you'll understand..." She paused.

Rush moved off the bed, knelt down in front of her and took her two hands in his one. "Understand what, honey?"

"I want you to get out of the navy."

He tossed his head back as if she'd slapped him. "Lindy, you don't know what you're asking."

"I do know. I know you love it. I know you've always loved being on the sea. But there are other jobs, other ways... I can't bear this, Rush, not knowing from one day to the next if you're going to be dead or alive. Let some other man put his life on the line. Someone without a wife. Anyone but you."

"Lindy—oh love." He pressed his forehead on her bent knee and seemed to be pulling his thoughts together. When he raised his head, his eyes were hard. "The navy is my life. It's where I belong. I can't walk away from a fifteen-year commitment because you're afraid I'm going to be injured again."

Lindy felt as though her heart were crumbling, the emotional agony was so intense. She pulled her hands free of his grasp and stiffened. "Then you leave me no choice."

Fourteen

"I don't leave you any choice? What do mean by that?" Rush demanded.

Lindy didn't know. All she did know was that everything the other wives had warned her about was happening. Rush and she had such little time together and, not wanting to say or do anything to disrupt these precious few days, Lindy had skimmed the surface of their relationship, ignoring the deep waters of unhappiness and strife. They'd avoided any chance of conflict in their marriage until everything was ready to burst inside her.

"Well?" he repeated.

"I don't know," she admitted reluctantly. "I want you to do something else with your life. Something outside of the navy that isn't dangerous. You've got me to think about now...and children later. Maybe you think I'm being selfish, but I want you to be a husband and father before anything else. The navy is first with you now and I'll always be a poor second. I hate it."

Rush rammed his fingers through his hair. "Honey, you can't change a man from what he already is. You don't have any idea what you're asking me to do—it'd be impossible."

"You don't seem to understand what you want of *me*," she countered sharply. "You claim you love me. You claim you want our marriage to work. But I'll always play second fiddle in your life, and I can't. I just can't deal with that. If playing hero is so important to you, then fine."

Rush's lips tightened and he stood and walked away from her.

"I love you, Rush." Her voice was taut, strangled. "All I'm asking is for you to love me as much as I do you."

"I do love you," he shouted.

"No." She shook her head with such force that her hair went swirling around her face. "You love the navy more."

"It's been my life for fifteen years."

"I want to be your life now."

"God, Lindy, you want me to give up everything that's ever been important to me." He threw back his head as a man in agony would, closed his eyes and then glared at the dark ceiling.

Lindy bounced her index finger against her chest. "I want to be the most important person in your life."

"You are!"

"No," she murmured sadly. "I'm not. Look at you. You nearly died on that stupid aircraft carrier and you can hardly wait to get back. I can feel the restlessness in you. It's like you've got to prove something."

Rush whirled around to face her then, his eyes wide, his body taut. "You knew what I was when we got married. You were perfectly aware how I felt about the navy then. You were willing to accept it as my career. What

happened to that unshakable confidence you had that
we were doing the right thing to rush into marriage?
Lord, I can't believe this."

"I was confident I loved you. I'm sure of it now."

"The navy is part of me, Lindy. A big part of who
and what I am. Don't you see that?"

"No." Her voice cracked, and she sobbed once.

The sight of her tears seemed to tear at him and Rush
knelt beside her and pulled her into one arm, holding
her tightly, as though he felt her pain and was desperate to do anything he could to alleviate it. Lindy wept
against his shoulder, her arms moving up and clinging
to his neck. His mouth sought and found hers and he
kissed her into submission while his hand worked its
magic on her body, destroying her will to argue.

Before Lindy knew what was happening, Rush had
her back in bed and his mouth was sucking on her
breast; he was tormenting her nipples with his tongue,
and she was being devoured by the licking flames of
desire.

"No…no," she sobbed, and pushed him away. She
jumped out of bed, her shoulders heaving with the effort it had cost her to leave his arms. "You aren't going
to use me this way!"

Rush rolled on his back and closed his eyes in angry
frustration. "Use you! Now it's a sin to make love to
you, too?"

"It is when you use lovemaking to bury an issue."

"Can you blame me?" he shouted, his patience obviously on a short fuse. "I'm flying out of here shortly. I
won't see you until the middle of December—if then,
from the way you're talking. I'd prefer that we spend

our last hours making love, not fighting. If that's such a terrible crime, then I'm guilty."

The alarm rang, and the tinny sound echoed around the room, startling them both. Lindy glared accusingly at the clock radio. Already it was time for Rush to leave her, and she hadn't said even half of what was in her heart.

Without a word her husband climbed out of bed and started dressing in his uniform. He had some difficulty, with his left arm in a cast, but he didn't seek her help, and she didn't offer.

Numb with pain and disbelief, Lindy watched him. Nothing she'd said had mattered to him. Not one word had seemed to reach him. He was so intent on getting back to the *Mitchell* that nothing, not her love, not her demands or her pleas, was important enough to delay him.

Once he finished buttoning his shirt, Rush picked up his things that littered the room, preparing to leave.

Lindy hated the way he ignored her so completely. For all the notice he gave her, she might as well have been an empty beer can. Savored for the moment of pleasure it brought, discarded once used.

She was kneeling in the middle of their bed, and the tears streaked her face. "It's either the navy or me," she said, and her voice wobbled as she struggled not to beg him.

Rush paused at the door, his hand on the knob, but he didn't turn around to look at her. "I love you, Lindy, but I can't change what I am because of your fears. I could leave the navy, but it wouldn't be the right decision for either of us. If you're going to force me to decide, then I have to go with what I am."

Lindy felt as though he'd struck her. She closed her eyes and covered her face with both hands. The door of the hotel room opened, and desperate now, she scooted off the bed. "Rush."

He paused.

"When the *Mitchell* returns, I won't be on that dock waiting for you!" She shouted the words at him, in a voice that was threatening as a shark's jaw. "I mean it. I won't be there."

His shoulders were stiff, his head held high and proud. "Then I won't expect you," he said, and walked away from her without looking back.

Steve was waiting for Lindy when she stepped out of the jetway that led into the interior of Sea-Tac Airport. He brushed a quick kiss over her cheek and took the carry-on bag from her hand. When he lifted his head and looked at her, he paused and frowned.

"How was the flight?"

Lindy shrugged, praying she didn't look as bad as she felt. "Fine."

"How's Rush?"

"He couldn't be better," she answered, unable to keep her voice from dipping with heavy sarcasm. "He's all navy—you know him. God, country, apple pie—the whole patriotic bit. He nearly lost his arm. He nearly bled to death, but he couldn't enjoy a few days in paradise because it was more important for him to get back to the *Mitchell*. He's got a job to do, you know. He alone is going to uphold world peace. You didn't tell me what a hero I married, Steve."

Looking stunned, her brother stopped and glared

at her, his eyes wide and filled with surprise. "Exactly what is your problem?"

"Nothing," she flared. "Everything," she amended.

"What happened?"

She didn't want Steve to be gentle and concerned. Not when she was being forced to admit her blunder. "You were right from the first. I made a mistake... A bad one. I'm not the kind of woman who will ever make a good navy wife... You knew that from the beginning."

Steve's frown deepened. "I've come to think differently in the past few weeks. Lindy, when we got the news there'd been an accident aboard the *Mitchell*, you were as solid as a rock. It was me who fell apart at the seams. Don't you remember how I kept telling you you should prepare yourself for the worst? Everything I said and did was wrong. You were like an anchor during that whole time. I was the one leaning on you for strength."

Lindy's smile was weak and gentle as she placed her hand on her brother's forearm. "You were wonderful. I thank God you were there."

"But you love Rush. Dear God, Lindy, you were so strong and brave when we learned he was missing, and yet I was afraid it would have killed you if the damage control party hadn't found Rush in time."

"Yes, I love him. But I'm not willing to take second place in his life. With Rush—" she paused and looked up at him, her gaze narrowing "—and with *you*, the navy will always come first."

"Did you tell Rush this?"

She nodded, and her eyes filled with an unspeakable sadness. "He knows exactly how I feel."

"What are you going to do now?"

"I... I don't know."

Steve placed his free arm around her shoulder and squeezed gently. "Don't decide anything yet. You're hurting and miserable. You've got several weeks to think matters through and then, once Rush is safely back in Seattle, you two can sort things out."

"I told Rush I wouldn't be there to meet him when the *Mitchell* sails home. I meant it, Steve. He put the navy first. He was the one who chose his career over me."

Steve's mouth and eyes thinned with frustration. "You sent Rush back to the *Mitchell* with that piece of good news? Come on, Lindy. It's time to grow up here. So you were worried about him. That's only natural. But don't try to suffocate him now because eventually it'll kill your marriage. Rush isn't the kind of man who's going to let someone else dictate his life. You knew that when you agreed to be his wife."

Lindy pulled herself free from her brother's hold. "I didn't expect you to understand."

"For God's sake, Lindy, you want to castrate a man because he's got a job to do and feels honor-bound to do it? What kind of logic is that?"

"I'm not going to talk about it anymore." Quick-paced, determined steps carried her down the concourse and away from her brother. She should have known better than to even try to talk to him. Steve Kyle was as much into patriot games as Rush.

"Lindy," her brother called, catching up with her. "I can't let you ruin your life like this—and Rush's in the process. Any idiot can see how much you two love each other."

"I don't want to hear this. It's none of your business, so keep your opinions to yourself."

"I can't!"

"Get your own house in order, big brother, and then you can start cleaning mine. Until then, stay out of my affairs." Lindy regretted the harsh words the minute they tumbled over her tongue. Steve looked at her as though she'd stabbed a knife into his chest. A muscle in his jaw leaped to life and she saw her brother mentally withdrawing from her, as if a mechanical door were slowly lowering, blocking her out.

His eyes narrowed and hardened as his angry gaze briefly met hers. "If that's the way you want it."

It wasn't, but she didn't know how to retract those cruel words. He didn't bother to wait for an answer and marched away from her. Lindy caught up with him in the baggage claim area and they rode into the city in a stilted, uneasy silence.

"I didn't mean what I said earlier," Lindy told him, once they were inside the apartment.

Her brother didn't look at her. "Yes, you did," he said after a moment, and walked away from her.

"I seem to be batting a thousand lately," Lindy confided to Susan. She'd been back from Hawaii almost three weeks now, but this was the first opportunity she'd had to visit her friend. "In one short week, I managed to alienate both my husband and my brother."

"Have you heard from Rush?" Susan asked, replenishing the coffee in both their cups.

"No. But then I didn't expect to."

"Have you written him?"

Lindy reached for her coffee cup, cradling it with both hands, letting the warmth burn her palms. "No."

Susan pulled out a chair and slumped down. She was nearly five months pregnant and just starting to wear maternity tops. She looked soft and fragile, but underneath she was as tough as leather. Lindy would have given everything she owned to possess the same grit and fortitude as her friend.

"From what I can tell, you've put yourself in a no-win situation," Susan said softly, sadly.

"My God, Rush was nearly killed. It was so close. The doctors said—" Lindy paused and bit into her bottom lip to control the emotion that rocked her every time she thought about the accident.

"He could have gotten hurt in a car accident driving to an office just as easily. Would you suggest he never sit in a car again?"

"No. Of course not." Her hands shook as she raised the mug to her lips and took a sip. "The accident taught me something more. Whatever it takes to be a good navy wife, I don't have it. I couldn't stand on that pier and smile the next time Rush gleefully sails off into the sunset. I can't take these long months of separation. I always thought married people were one, a unit, two people sculpting a life together. It's not that way with Rush. It won't ever be that way—not as long as he's in the navy. I can't be like you, Susan. I wish I could, but it's just not in me."

"You'd rather be separated for a lifetime?" Susan questioned, frowning.

"Yes. It would be easier than dying by inches. No. Oh God, Susan, I don't know what I want anymore."

Her friend didn't say anything for a long time, and when she did, her voice was gentle, understanding. "I stopped counting the times I've said goodbye to Jeff a long time ago. Every time I stand out on that pier and watch that huge carrier pull away,

I think I'll never be able to do it again. Letting Jeff go, and doing it with a smile, takes everything there is inside me. You've got it wrong, Lindy. You think I'm so brave and good, but I'm not."

"But you are."

"No. I'm just a woman who loves her man."

"I love Rush, too," Lindy returned defiantly.

"I know, and he loves you." The tip of Susan's finger circled the rim of her coffee cup as she averted her gaze, her look thoughtful. "I don't think I'll ever forget the night I first met you. We were in the kitchen chatting, and Rush and Jeff were fiddling around on the patio with the barbecue. Remember?"

Lindy nodded.

"You were holding one of the boys and I saw Rush look at you. Lindy, there's no way I can describe the longing that came into his eyes. Just watching him stare at you with such tenderness made me want to weep. It was as if you were the Madonna holding the baby Jesus. In that moment, I knew how much your love had changed Rush, and how important you had become to him in those short weeks.

"You might succeed in getting him to leave the navy, but in time you'll regret it. I know Rush will. Eventually it would cripple him, and in the process, you. If ever there was a man who was meant to lead others, meant to serve his country, it's Rush."

"Why is it always the woman who has to change?" Lindy cried. "It's not fair."

"You're right," Susan agreed, with a sad smile. "It isn't fair. All I can say is, if you try to change Rush and succeed, he won't be the same man you fell in love with, or the same man you married."

Lindy bowed her head, more confused than ever.

"Rush took your words to heart," Susan added, looking both disheartened and disappointed.

Lindy jerked her gaze up. "How do you know that?"

"He doesn't expect you to be waiting for him when the *Mitchell* docks next month. Jeff wrote that Rush has volunteered for the first watch."

"What does that mean?"

"It means he's going to remain on board as officer of the day the first twelve hours after the crew is dismissed. He told Jeff he didn't have any reason to hurry home since you weren't going to be there."

"But, I didn't mean I wouldn't be at the apartment!"

Susan shrugged. "How was Rush supposed to know that?"

The phone rang twice and Lindy glanced at her watch, calculating if she had enough time to answer it before meeting Susan and the other navy wives. She had no intention of being late for this last fling before the *Mitchell* docked. Taking a chance, she hurried into the kitchen.

"All right, all right," she grumbled, and reached for the receiver. "Hello?"

Her greeting was followed by a short silence, and then a soft female voice asked, "Is Steve Kyle available, please?"

"Carol? Is that you?" Lindy's heart started to pound with excitement. She'd been wanting to talk to her former sister-in-law for weeks.

"Who's this?"

Carol's voice was far from fragile and she could almost picture the petite, gentle blonde squaring her shoulders and bringing up her chin.

"It's Lindy."

"Lindy! I didn't know you were in Seattle."

"Six months now."

"You should have called. I'd love to see you again."

"I wanted to contact you," Lindy said, her spirits lifting as a Christmas song came over the radio, "but Steve wasn't in favor of the idea. How are you?"

"Good. Real good. Well, tell me—are you Mrs. Paul Abrams yet?" The question was followed by a light, infectious laugh. "The last time I saw you, Paul had just given you a diamond ring and you were floating on cloud nine."

It was difficult for Lindy to remember those days. She may have been fooled into thinking she was happy, but that contentment had been short-lived. She would never have been the right woman for Paul. Once again she thanked God he'd had enough foresight to have recognized as much.

"I married Rush Callaghan," Lindy told her.

A short, shocked silence followed. "You did? Why that's wonderful—congratulations. I've always had a soft spot in my heart for Rush."

The last person Lindy wanted to discuss was her husband, especially the way matters were between them now. "Steve isn't here at the moment, but he'll be back soon. I'll tell him you called." Lindy hesitated and then decided she couldn't hold her tongue any longer. "I don't know what happened between you two—Steve never told me—but whatever it is, I hope you can patch it up. He misses you dreadfully." Lindy knew her brother would have her hide if he knew she'd told Carol that.

Carol laughed, but the mirth couldn't disguise her pain. "He's gotten along fine without me, and I've learned to manage without him, too. Leave a message for him, will you?"

"Of course."

"But tell him—" Carol added quickly "—tell him it isn't overly important."

"Sure. I'll be happy to."

"It was nice talking to you again, Lindy. Really nice. I'm pleased for you and Rush. Be happy, you hear?"

Lindy nodded, although she knew Carol couldn't see the action. "I will," she mumbled. "I will."

Rush stood at the bridge ready to be relieved of duty. The sky was a deep shade of pearl gray and he expected it to start raining any minute. The foul weather suited his mood. The *Mitchell* was home, and his friends had hurried off the carrier and down the gangway to a happy reunion with their wives and families, eager to spend the holidays with their loved ones.

Rush had stood on the bridge, hungrily scanning the crowds through his binoculars, hoping with everything in him that he'd find Lindy there. He would have given his retirement pay to have found her among the well-wishers, waiting for him.

But Lindy hadn't been there, and a small part of Rush had died with the knowledge. Cheryl hadn't been there for him, either. Rush shouldn't have been surprised. Lindy had told him in Hawaii she had no intention of standing on the gangway, and she'd meant it. He was a fool to even have expected her.

His watchful gaze scanned the outline of the city of Bremerton and the Christmas decorations that hung from the streetlights. For the past six weeks of the cruise, he'd closed himself off from thoughts of Lindy, mentally chastising himself for exposing his heart a second time. Over and over again, he'd told himself women were too fickle to be trusted. But now that he was in port everything had changed and he knew he would eventually have to face her.

Marrying Lindy had been a gamble—he'd known it the day he slipped the wedding band on her finger. Her brother had had every reason to come down on him so hard. His friend was right. Rush had taken advantage of Lindy. He'd cashed in on her pain and insecurities, used her infatuation with him for his own purposes. It wasn't any wonder Lindy was confused and miserably unhappy now. Everything that had happened between them was his fault and he accepted full responsibility. Lindy wasn't ready to be a wife and she wanted out.

Rush didn't blame her.

His relief arrived and, after making the necessary notations in the log, Rush picked up his seabag and headed down the steep gangway. A stiff, cold breeze hit him and he paused to raise the collar of his thick wool jacket. There was no reason to hurry, and his steps were heavy.

His left arm was free of the cast now, but he still hadn't regained full use of it. His shoulder ached almost unbearably at times, but Rush had welcomed the pain. The physical throbbing somehow helped overshadow the mental agony of what had happened between him and Lindy.

Halfway down the gangway, something made him glance up. He stopped, his heart thundering against his rib cage, unable to believe his own eyes. There, alone at the end of the pier stood Lindy. The strong wind plastered her long coat to her torso and beat her thick dark hair roughly about her face. Her hands were buried in her coat pockets and she'd raised her chin, her loving eyes following his movements, patiently waiting.

Years of discipline, weeks of control, snapped within Rush as he dropped his seabag and started walking toward her. His chest felt as though he was on fire, he was fighting so hard to bury the emotion that pounded through him. His pulse started to beat in his temple. She'd come. His Lindy had come.

Rush quickened his pace and Lindy started running toward him, her arms outstretched. He caught her and pulled her into his embrace, burying his face in her soft hair, breathing in her delicate scent.

He tried to speak and found he couldn't. His tongue might as well have been attached to the roof of his mouth, and after a half second, he gave up trying to voice his thoughts. It came to him then how unnecessary words really were.

He sighed and reveled in the warm glow of Lindy's love at full strength. It worked on him like a healing potion, a relentless tide surging against him at full crest. It was as though they had exchanged their wedding vows there, at that moment on that pier, so strong was the love that flowed between them.

"Rush," she cried, tears in her voice. "I'm sorry, so sorry."

She held him so tightly that Rush could barely breathe. He closed his eyes, letting his heart and mind soak up her words. Each one tenderly removed the barbs of doubt that had tormented him, each one healed the pain and deep sense of loss these past weeks of separation had brought him. Each word confirmed what he'd always known but had been afraid to admit, fearing it would cripple him for life. He loved Lindy, loved her beyond anything else there could ever be in his world. He loved her more than the thrill of navigating the oceans, more than serving his country and commanding men. From the minute she'd given him her heart, Rush had only one mistress, only one wife, and that was Lindy.

"I love you," she said fiercely. "I've been such a fool." Lindy felt home at last in Rush's arms. This was where she belonged, where she planned to stay. It had taken these long weeks apart for her to realize what a fool she'd been to risk losing this wonderful man. Everything Susan had said was true, and Lindy had finally recognized the truth in her friend's words.

"You?" His voice was strained and husky with emotion. "If anyone was a fool, it was me. I should never have walked away from you in Hawaii."

The muscles in his lean jaw bunched and she kissed him, not able to wait a moment longer. Her hands lovingly stroked the sides of his face, relishing touching him so freely. Her mind groped for the words to explain.

"I was wrong, Rush, so wrong to try to force you to choose between me and the navy."

"Lindy, stop." He held a hand to her mouth to cut off her words. "Listen to me, my love. The reenlistment papers are in my pocket. I haven't signed them, and I won't."

She broke away, her face tight with disbelief. "You most certainly will sign those papers, Rush Callaghan."

From the look he gave her, Lindy knew she couldn't have shocked him more had she announced she was six months pregnant. His gaze narrowed as he studied her.

"The last time we talked, you were dead set against

the navy. You wanted to be first in my life. I'm telling you I'm willing to give you what you want."

"You came so close to dying," she reminded him softly, and her voice trembled slightly with remembered pain. "I don't know if you're even aware of how badly you were injured."

He shook his head.

Rush had changed in so many ways since Hawaii. His shoulders were broader and his eyes less clouded, letting her look into his heart and know his thoughts.

"I couldn't bear the thought of losing you, Rush. It terrified me. I decided that if I was going to be forced to give you up, I'd rather get it over with quickly instead of letting go of you a little at a time. That was why I asked you to give up the navy. That was why I told you I wouldn't be here when you returned. Believe me, I know how crazy that sounds now. But at the time I felt I was doing the right thing."

"That's the most twisted piece of reasoning I've ever heard."

"I know," she whispered, dropping her gaze.

"Lindy, I meant what I said about those reenlistment papers. If you want a civilian for a husband, I'll do my damnedest to adjust."

She met his intense gaze and smiled through her tears. "Sign the papers, Rush. I've done a lot of maturing these past six weeks. You wanted a navy wife and by God, you've got one."

He stared at her and a strange, unidentifiable light flared in his gaze, darkening and then lightening their cornflower blue.

"You mean it, don't you?"

She nodded vigorously. "You bet I do. I may make

Dear Debbie Macomber Fan,

IT'S A FACT: if you answer 4 quick questions, we'll send you 4 FREE REWARDS!

I'm not kidding you. As a leading publisher of women's fiction, we value your opinions… and your time. That's why we are prepared to **reward** you handsomely for completing our mini-survey. In fact, we have 4 Free Rewards for you, including 2 free books and 2 free gifts.

As you may have guessed, that's why our mini-survey is called **"4 for 4".** Answer 4 questions and get 4 Free Rewards. It's that simple!

Thank you for participating in our survey,

Pam Powers

To get your 4 FREE REWARDS:
Complete the survey below and return the insert today to receive 2 FREE BOOKS and 2 FREE GIFTS guaranteed!

"4 for 4" MINI-SURVEY

1 Is reading one of your favorite hobbies?
[ ] YES [ ] NO

2 Do you prefer to read instead of watch TV?
[ ] YES [ ] NO

3 Do you read newspapers and magazines?
[ ] YES [ ] NO

4 Do you enjoy trying new book series with FREE BOOKS?
[ ] YES [ ] NO

YES! I have completed the above Mini-Survey. Please send me my 4 FREE REWARDS (worth over $20 retail). I understand that I am under no obligation to buy anything, as explained on the back of this card.

194/394 MDL GMYQ

FIRST NAME	LAST NAME

ADDRESS

APT.#	CITY

STATE/PROV.	ZIP/POSTAL CODE

READER SERVICE—Here's how it works:

▲ If offer card is missing write to: Reader Service, P.O. Box 1341, Buffalo, NY 14240-8531 or visit www.ReaderService.com ▲

BUSINESS REPLY MAIL

FIRST-CLASS MAIL   PERMIT NO. 717   BUFFALO, NY

POSTAGE WILL BE PAID BY ADDRESSEE

READER SERVICE
PO BOX 1341
BUFFALO NY 14240-8571

NO POSTAGE
NECESSARY
IF MAILED
IN THE
UNITED STATES

mistakes along the way, but I'm willing to learn. I love you, Rush."

"I love you, wife."

"Navy wife," she amended.

Rush laughed and folded her in his arms, holding on to her as though he never planned to let her go. When they broke apart, Rush retrieved his seabag, and with their arms wrapped around each other's waists, they stepped forward toward tomorrow—a naval officer and his first mate.

* * * * *

NAVY BLUES

One

Seducing her ex-husband wasn't going to be easy, Carol Kyle decided, but she was determined. More than determined—resolute! Her mind was set, and no one knew better than Steve Kyle how stubborn she could be when she wanted something.

And Carol wanted a baby.

Naturally she had no intention of letting him in on her plans. What he didn't know wouldn't hurt him. Their marriage had lasted five good years, and six bad months. To Carol's way of thinking, which she admitted was a bit twisted at the moment, Steve owed her at least one pregnancy.

Turning thirty had convinced Carol that drastic measures were necessary. Her hormones were jumping up and down, screaming for a chance at motherhood. Her biological clock was ticking away, and Carol swore she could hear every beat of that blasted timepiece. Everywhere she turned, it seemed she was confronted with pregnant women, who served to remind her that her time was running out. If she picked up a magazine, there would be an article on some aspect of parenting.

Even her favorite characters on television sitcoms were pregnant. When she found herself wandering through the infant section of her favorite department store, Carol realized drastic measures needed to be taken.

Making the initial contact with Steve hadn't been easy, but she recognized that the first move had to come from her. Getting in touch with her ex-husband after more than a year of complete silence had required two weeks of nerve building. But she'd managed to swallow her considerable pride and do it. Having a woman answer his phone had thrown her for a loop, and Carol had visualized her plans swirling down the drain until she realized the woman was Steve's sister, Lindy.

Her former sister-in-law had sounded pleased to hear from her, and then Lindy had said something that had sent Carol's spirits soaring to the ceiling: Lindy had claimed that Steve missed her dreadfully. Lordy, she hoped that was true. If so, it probably meant he wasn't dating yet. There could be complications if Steve was involved with another woman. On the other hand, there could also be problems if he wasn't involved.

Carol only needed him for one tempestuous night, and then, if everything went according to schedule, Steve Kyle could fade out of her life once more. If she failed to get pregnant...well, she'd leap that hurdle when she came to it.

Carol had left a message for Steve a week earlier, and he hadn't returned her call. She wasn't overly concerned. She knew her ex-husband well; he would mull it over carefully before he'd get back to her. He would want her to stew awhile first. She'd carefully figured the time element into her schedule of events.

Her dinner was boiling on the stove, and Carol turned

down the burner after checking the sweet potatoes with a cooking fork. Glaring at the orange-colored root, she heaved a huge sigh and squelched her growing dislike for the vegetable. After she became pregnant, she swore she would never eat another sweet potato for as long as she lived. A recent news report stated that the starchy vegetable helped increase the level of estrogen in a woman's body. Armed with that information, Carol had been eating sweet potatoes every day for the last two weeks. There had to be enough of the hormone floating around in her body by now to produce triplets.

Noting the potatoes were soft, she drained the water and dumped the steaming roots into her blender. A smile crowded the edges of her mouth. Eating sweet potatoes was a small price to pay for a beautiful baby…for Steve's baby.

"Have you called Carol back yet?" Lindy Callaghan demanded of her brother as she walked into the small kitchen of the two-bedroom apartment she shared with her husband and Steve.

Steve Kyle ignored her until she pulled out the chair and plopped down across the table from him. "No," he admitted flatly. He could see no reason to hurry. He already knew what Carol was going to tell him. He'd known it from the minute they'd walked out of the King County Courthouse, the divorce papers clenched in her hot little hands. She was remarrying. Well, more power to her, but he wasn't going to sit back and blithely let her rub his nose in the fact.

"Steve," Lindy insisted, her face tight with impatience. "It could be something important."

"You told me it wasn't."

"Sure, that's what Carol said, but…oh, I don't know, I have the feeling that it really must be. It isn't going to do any harm to call her back."

Methodically Steve turned the page of the evening newspaper and carefully creased the edge before folding it in half and setting it aside. Lindy and Rush, her husband, couldn't be expected to understand his reluctance to phone his ex-wife. He hadn't told either of them the details that had led to his and Carol's divorce. He preferred to keep all thoughts of the disastrous relationship out of his mind. There were plenty of things he could have forgiven, but not what Carol had done—not infidelity.

As a Lieutenant Commander aboard the submarine USS *Atlantis*, Steve was at sea for as long as six months out of a year. From the first Carol hadn't seemed to mind sending him off on a three-to-four month cruise. She even used to joke about it, telling him all the projects she planned to complete when he was at sea, and how pleased she was that he would be out of her hair for a while. When he'd returned she'd always seemed happy that he was home, but not exuberant. If anything had gone wrong in his absence—a broken water pipe, car repairs, anything—she'd seen to it herself with barely more than a casual mention.

Steve had been so much in love with her that the little things hadn't added up until later—much later. He'd deceived himself by overlooking the obvious. The physical craving they had for each other had diluted his doubts. Making love with Carol had been so hot it was like a nuclear meltdown. Toward the end she'd been eager for him, but not quite as enthusiastic as in the past. He'd been trusting, blind and incredibly stupid when it came to his ex-wife.

Then by accident he'd learned why she'd become so blasé about his comings and goings. When he left their bed, his loveless, faithless wife had a built-in replacement—her employer, Todd Larson.

It was just short of amazing that Steve hadn't figured it out earlier, and yet when he thought about it, he could almost calculate to the day when she'd started her little affair.

"Steve?"

Lindy's voice cut into his musings, and he lifted his gaze to meet hers. Her eyes were round and dark with concern. Steve experienced a small twinge of guilt for the way he'd reacted to his sister and Rush's marriage. When he'd learned his best friend had married his only sister after a dating period of a mere two weeks, Steve had been furious. He'd made no bones about telling them both the way he felt about their hurry-up wedding. Now he realized his own bitter experience had tainted his reasoning, and he'd long since apologized. It was obvious they were crazy about each other, and Steve had allowed his own misery to bleed into his reaction to their news.

"Okay, okay. I'll return Carol's call," he answered in an effort to appease his younger sibling. He understood all too well how much Lindy wanted him to settle matters with Carol. Lindy was happy, truly happy, and it dismayed her that his life should be at such loose ends.

"When?"

"Soon," Steve promised.

The front door opened, and Rush let himself into the apartment; his arms were loaded with Christmas packages. He paused just inside the kitchen and exchanged a sensual look with his wife. Steve watched the heated gaze and it was like throwing burning acid on his half-healed wounds. He waited a moment for the pain to lessen.

"How'd the shopping go?" Lindy asked, her silky smooth voice eager and filled with pleasure at the sight of her husband.

"Good," Rush answered and faked a yawn, "but I'm afraid it wore me out."

Steve playfully rolled his eyes toward the ceiling and stood, preparing to leave the apartment. "Don't tell me you two are going to take another nap!"

Lindy's cheeks filled with crimson color and she looked away. In the past few days the two of them had taken more naps than a newborn babe. Even Rush looked a bit chagrined.

"All right, you two," Steve said good-naturedly, reaching for his leather jacket. "I'll give you some privacy."

One glance from Lindy told him she was grateful. Rush stopped Steve on his way out the door and his eyes revealed his appreciation. "We've decided to look for a place of our own right away, but it doesn't look like we'll be able to move until after the first of the year." He paused and lowered his gaze, looking almost embarrassed. "I know this is an inconvenience for you to keep leaving, but…"

"Don't worry about it," Steve countered with a light chuckle. He patted his friend on the back. "I was a newlywed once myself."

Steve tried to sound casual about the whole matter, but doubted if he'd succeeded. Being constantly exposed to the strong current of love flowing between his friend and his sister was damn difficult, because he understood their need for each other all too well. There'd been a time when a mere look was all that was required to spark flames between him and Carol. Their desire seemed to catch fire and leap to brilliance with a single touch, and they couldn't get to bed fast enough. Steve had been crazy in love with her. Carol had appealed to all his senses and he'd ached with the desire to possess her completely. The only time he felt he'd accomplished that was when he was making love to her. Then and only then was Carol utterly his. And those times were all too brief.

Outside the apartment, the sky was dark with thick gray clouds. Steve walked across the street and headed toward the department stores. He didn't have much Christmas shopping to do, but now appeared to be as good a time for the task as any.

He hesitated in front of a pay phone and released a long, slow breath. He might as well call Carol and be done with it. She wanted to gloat, and he would let her. After all, it was the season to be charitable.

The phone rang just as Carol was coming in the front door. She stopped, set her purse on the kitchen counter and glared at the telephone. Her heart rammed against her rib cage with such force that she had to stop and gather her thoughts. It was Steve. The phone might as well have been spelling out his name in Morse code, she was that sure.

"Hello?" she answered brightly, on the third ring.

"Lindy said you phoned." His words were low, flat and emotionless.

"Yes, I did," she murmured, her nerves clamoring.

"Do you want to tell me why, or are you going to make me guess? Trust me, Carol, I'm in no mood to play twenty questions with you."

Oh Lord, this wasn't going to be easy. Steve sounded so cold and uncaring. She'd anticipated it, but it didn't lessen the effect his tone had on her. "I… I thought we could talk."

A short, heavy silence followed.

"I'm listening."

"I'd rather we didn't do it over the phone, Steve," she said softly, but not because she'd planned to make her voice silky and smooth. Her vocal chords had tightened and it just came out sounding that way. Her nerves were stretched to their limit, and her heart was pounding in her ear like a charging locomotive.

"Okay," he answered, reluctance evident in every syllable.

"When?" Her gaze scanned the calendar—the timing of this entire venture was of primary importance.

"Tomorrow?" he suggested.

Carol's eyes drifted shut as the relief worked its way through her stiff limbs. Her biggest concern was that he would suggest after the Christmas holidays, and then it would be too late and she would have to reschedule everything for January.

"That would be fine," Carol managed. "Would you mind coming to the house?" The two bedroom brick rambler had been awarded to her as part of the divorce settlement.

Again she could feel his hesitation. "As a matter of fact, I would."

"All right," she answered, quickly gathering her wits.

His not wanting to come to the house shouldn't have surprised her. "How about coffee at Denny's tomorrow evening?"

"Seven?"

Carol swallowed before answering. "Fine. I'll see you then."

Her hand was still trembling a moment later when she replaced the telephone receiver in its cradle. All along she'd accepted that Steve wasn't going to fall into her bed without some subtle prompting, but from the brusque, impatient sound of his voice, the whole escapade could well be impossible...this month. That bothered her. The one pivotal point in her plan was that everything come together quickly. One blazing night of passion could easily be dismissed and forgotten. But if she were to continue to invite him back one night a month, several months running, then he just might catch on to what she was doing.

Still, when it had come to interpreting her actions in the past, Steve had shown a shocking lack of insight. Thankfully their troubles had never intruded in the bedroom. Their marriage relationship had been a jumbled mess of doubts and misunderstandings, accusations and regrets, but their love life had always been vigorous and lusty right up until the divorce, astonishing as it seemed now.

At precisely seven the following evening, Carol walked into Denny's Restaurant on Seattle's Capitol Hill. The first year she and Steve had been married, they'd had dinner there once a month. Money had been tight because they'd been saving for a down payment on the house, and an evening out, even if it was only Saturday night at Denny's, had been a real treat.

Two steps into the restaurant Carol spotted her former husband sitting in a booth by the window. She paused and experienced such a wealth of emotion that advancing even one step more would have been impossible. Steve had no right to look this good—far better than she remembered. In the thirteen months since she'd last seen him, he'd changed considerably. Matured. His features were sharper, clearer, more intense. His lean good looks were all the more prominent, his handsome masculine features vigorous and tanned even in December. A few strands of gray hair streaked his temple, adding a distinguished air.

His gaze caught hers and Carol sucked in a deep, calming breath, her steps nearly faltering as she advanced toward him. His eyes had changed the most, she decided. Where once they had been warm and caressing, now they were cool and calculating. They narrowed on her, his mistrust shining through as bright as any beacon.

Carol experienced a moment of panic as his gaze seemed to strip away the last shreds of her pride. It took all her willpower to force a smile to her lips.

"Thank you for coming," she said, and slipped into the red upholstered seat across from him.

The waitress came with a glass coffeepot, and Carol turned over her cup, which the woman promptly filled after placing menus on the table.

"It feels cold enough to snow," Carol said as a means of starting conversation. It was eerie that she could have been married to Steve all those years and feel as if he were little more than a stranger. He gave her that impression now. This hard, impassive man was one she didn't know nearly as well as the one who had once been her lover, her friend and her husband.

"You're looking fit," Steve said after a moment, a spark of admiration glinting in his gaze.

"Thank you." A weak smile hovered over her lips. "You, too. How's the Navy treating you?"

"Good."

"Are you still on the *Atlantis*?"

He nodded shortly.

Silence.

Carol groped for something more to say. "It was a surprise to discover that Lindy's living in Seattle."

"Did she tell you she married Rush?"

Carol noted the way his brows drew together and darkened his face momentarily when he mentioned the fact. "I didn't realize Lindy even knew Rush," Carol said, and took a sip of the coffee.

"They were married two weeks after they met. Lord, I can't believe it yet."

"Two weeks? That doesn't sound anything like Rush. I remember him as being so methodical about everything."

Steve's frown relaxed, but only a little. "Apparently they fell in love."

Carol knew Steve well enough to recognize the hint of sarcasm in his voice, as if he were telling her what a mockery that emotion was. In their instance it had certainly been wasted. Sadly wasted.

"Are they happy?" That was the important thing as far as Carol was concerned.

"They went through a rough period a while back, but

since the *Mitchell* docked they seem to have mended their fences."

Carol dropped her gaze to her cup as reality cut sharply into her heart. "That's more than we did."

"As you recall," he said harshly, under his breath, "there wasn't any fence left to repair. The night you started sleeping with Todd Larson, you destroyed our marriage."

Carol didn't rise to the challenge, although Steve had all but slapped her face with it. There was nothing she could say to exonerate herself, and she'd given up explaining the facts to him more than a year ago. Steve chose to believe what he wanted. She'd tried, God knew, to set the record straight. Todd had been her employer and her friend, but never anything more. Carol had pleaded with Steve until she was blue with exasperation, but it hadn't done her any good. Rehashing the same argument now wasn't going to help either of them.

Silence stretched between them and was broken by the waitress who had returned to their booth, pad and pen in hand. "Have you decided?"

Carol hadn't even glanced at the menu. "Do you have sweet-potato pie?"

"No, but pecan is the special this month."

Carol shook her head, ignoring the strange look Steve was giving her. "Just coffee then."

"Same here," Steve added.

The woman replenished both their cups and left.

"So how is good ol' Todd?"

His question lacked any real interest, and Carol had already decided her former boss was a subject they'd best avoid. "Fine," she lied. She had no idea how Todd was doing, since she hadn't worked for Larson Sporting Goods for over a year. She'd been offered a better job with Boeing and had been employed at the airplane company since before the divorce was final.

"I'm glad to hear it," Steve said with a soft snicker. "I suppose you called this little meeting to tell me the two of you are finally going to be married."

"No. Steve, please, I didn't call to talk about Todd."

He arched his brows in mock consternation. "I'm surprised. What's the matter, is wife number one still giving him problems? You mean to tell me their divorce hasn't gone through?"

A shattering feeling of hopelessness nearly choked Carol, and she struggled to meet his gaze without flinching. Steve was still so bitter, so intent on making her suffer.

"I really would prefer it if we didn't discuss Todd or Joyce."

"Fine. What do you want to talk about?" He checked his watch as if to announce he had plenty of other things he could be doing and didn't want to waste precious time with her.

Carol had carefully planned everything she was going to say. Each sentence had been rehearsed several times over in her mind, and now it seemed so trite and ridiculous, she couldn't manage a single word.

"Well?" he demanded. "Since you don't want to rub my nose in the fact that you're marrying Todd, what could you possibly have to tell me?"

Carol gestured with her hand, her fingers trembling. "It's Christmastime," she murmured.

"Congratulations, you've glanced at a calendar lately." He looked straight through her with eyes as hard as diamond bits.

"I thought...well, you know, that we could put our differences aside for a little while and at least be civil to each other."

His eyes narrowed. "What possible reason could there be for us to have anything to do with each other? You mean nothing to me, and I'm sure the feeling is mutual."

"You were my husband for five years."

"So?"

She rearranged the silverware several times, choosing not to look at Steve. He wore his anger like a tight pair of shoes and sitting across from him was almost too painful to bear.

"We loved each other once," she said after a drawn-out, strained moment.

"I loved my dog once, too," he came back. One corner of his mouth was pulled down, and his eyes had thinned to narrow slits. "What does having cared about each other have to do with anything now?"

Carol couldn't answer his question. She knew the divorce had made him bitter, but she'd counted on this long time apart to have healed some of his animosity.

"What did you do for the holidays last year?" she asked, refusing to argue with him. She wasn't going to allow him to rile her into losing her temper. He'd played that trick once too often, and she was wise to his game.

"What the hell difference does it make to you how I spent Christmas?"

This wasn't going well, Carol decided—not the least bit as she'd planned. Steve seemed to think she wanted him to admit he'd been miserable without her.

"I... I spent the day alone," she told him softly, reluctantly. Their divorce had been final three weeks before the holiday and Carol's emotions had been so raw she'd hardly been able to deal with the usual festivities connected with the holiday.

"I wasn't alone," Steve answered with a cocky half smile that suggested that whoever he was with had been pleasant company, and he hadn't missed her in the least.

Carol didn't know how anyone could look so damned insolent and sensuous at the same moment. It required effort to keep her chin up and meet his gaze, but she managed.

"So *you* were alone," he added. The news appeared to delight him. "That's what happens when you mess around with a married man, my dear. In case you haven't figured it out yet, Todd's wife and family will always come first. That's the other woman's sad lot in life."

Carol went still all over. She felt as though her entire body had turned to stone. She didn't breathe, didn't move, didn't so much as blink. The pain spread out in waves, circling first her throat and then her chest, working its way down to her abdomen, cinching her stomach so tightly that she thought she might be sick. The whole room seemed to fade away and the only thing she was sure about was that she had to get out of the restaurant. Fast.

Her fingers fumbled with the snap of her purse as she opened her wallet. Her hands weren't any more steady as she placed several coins by the coffee cup and scooted out of her seat.

Mutely Steve watched Carol walk out of the restaurant and called himself every foul name that he could come up with from his extensive Navy vocabulary. He hadn't meant to say those things. Hadn't intended to lash out at her. But he hadn't been able to stop himself.

He'd lied, too, in an effort to salvage his pride. Lied rather than give her the satisfaction of knowing he'd spent last Christmas Day miserable and alone. It had been the worst holiday of his life. The pain of the divorce had still ached like a lanced boil, while everyone around him had been celebrating and exchanging gifts, their happiness like a ball and chain shackling his heart. This year didn't hold much prospect for happiness, either. Lindy and Rush would prefer to spend the day alone, although they'd gone out of their way to convince him otherwise. But Steve wasn't stupid and had already made other plans. He'd volunteered for watch Christmas Day so that a fellow officer could spend time with his family.

Gathering his thoughts about Carol, Steve experienced a healthy dose of regret about the way he'd behaved toward his ex-wife.

She'd looked good, he admitted reluctantly—better than he'd wanted her to look for his own peace of mind. From the moment they'd met, he'd felt the vibrant energy that radiated from her. Thirteen months apart hadn't diminished that. He'd known the minute she walked into Denny's; he'd felt her presence the instant the door opened. She wore her thick blond hair shorter than he remembered so that it fell forward and hugged the sides of her face, the ends curling under slightly, giving her a Dutch-boy look. As always, her metallic blue eyes were magnetic, irrevocably drawing his gaze. She looked small and fragile, and the desire to protect and love her had come at him with all the force of a wrecking ball slamming against his chest. He knew differently, but it hadn't seemed to change the way he felt—Carol needed him about as much as the Navy needed more salt water.

Sliding out of the booth, Steve laid a bill on the table and left. Outside, the north wind sent a chill racing up his arms and he buried his hands into his pants pockets as he headed toward the parking lot.

Surprise halted his progress when he spied Carol leaning against the fender of her car. Her shoulders were slumped, her head hanging as though she were burdened by a terrible weight.

Once more Steve was swamped with regret. He had never learned the reason she'd phoned. He started walking toward her, not knowing what he intended to say or do.

She didn't glance up when he joined her.

"You never said why you phoned," he said in a wounded voice after a moment of silence.

"It isn't important… I told Lindy that."

"If it wasn't to let me know you're remarrying, then it's because you want something."

She looked up and tried to smile, and the feeble effort cut straight through Steve's resolve to forget he'd ever known or loved her. It was useless to try.

"I don't think it'll work," Carol said sadly.

"What?"

She shook her head.

"If you need something, just ask!" he shouted, using his anger as a defense mechanism. Carol had seldom wanted anything from him. It must be important for her to contact him now, especially after their divorce.

"Christmas Day," she whispered brokenly. "I don't want to spend it alone."

Two

Until Carol spoke, she hadn't known how much she wanted Steve to spend Christmas Day with her—and not for the reasons she'd been plotting. She sincerely missed Steve. He'd been both lover and friend, and now he was neither; the sense of loss was nearly overwhelming.

He continued to stare at her, and regret worked its way across his features. The success of her plan hinged on his response and she waited, almost afraid to breathe, for his answer.

"Carol, listen…" He paused and ran his hand along the back of his neck, his brow puckered with a condensed frown.

Carol knew him well enough to realize he was carefully composing his thoughts. She was also aware that he was going to refuse her! She knew it as clearly as if he'd spoken the words aloud. She swallowed the hurt, although she couldn't keep her eyes from widening with pain. When Steve had presented her with the divorce papers, Carol had promised herself she would never give him the power to hurt her again. Yet here she was, handing him the knife and exposing her soul.

She could feel her heart thumping wildly in her chest and fought to control the emotions that swamped her. "Is it so much to ask?" she whispered, and the words fell broken from her lips.

"I've got the watch."

"On Christmas…" She hadn't expected that, hadn't figured it into the scheme of things. In other words, the excuse of Christmas wasn't going to work. Ultimately her strategy would fail, and she would end up spending the holiday alone.

"I'd do it if I could," Steve told her in a straightforward manner that convinced her he was telling the truth. She felt somewhat less disappointed.

"Thank you for that," she said, and reached out to touch his hand, in a small gesture of appreciation. Amazingly he didn't draw away from her, which gave her renewed hope.

A reluctant silence stretched between them. There'd been a time when they couldn't say enough to each other, and now there was nothing.

"I suppose I'd better get back." Steve spoke first.

"Me, too," she answered brightly, perhaps a little too brightly. "It was good to see you again…you're looking well."

"You, too." He took a couple of steps backward, but still hadn't turned away. Swallowing down her disappointment, Carol retrieved the car keys from the bottom of her purse and turned to climb into her Honda. It dawned on her then, hit her square between the eyes. If not Christmas Day then…

"Steve," she whirled back around, her eyes flashing.

"Carol." He called her name at the same moment.

They laughed and the sound fell rusty and awkward between them.

"You first," he said, and gestured toward her. The corner of his mouth was curved upward in a half smile.

"What about Christmas Eve?"

He nodded. "I was just thinking the same thing."

Carol felt the excitement bubble up inside her like fizz in a club soda. A grin broke out across her face as she realized nothing had been lost and everything was yet to be gained. Somewhere in the distance, Carol was sure she could hear the soft, lilting strains of a Brahms lullaby. "Could you come early enough for dinner?"

Again, he nodded. "Six?"

"Perfect. I'll look forward to it."

"I will, too."

He turned and walked away from her then, and it was all Carol could do to keep from doing a war dance, jumping up and down around the car. Instead she rubbed her bare hands together as though the friction would ease some of the excitement she was feeling. Steve hadn't a clue how memorable this one night would be. Not a clue!

"Your mood has certainly improved lately," Lindy commented as Steve walked into the kitchen whistling a lively Christmas carol.

His sister's words stopped him. "My mood has?"

"You've been downright chipper all week."

He shrugged his shoulders, hoping the action would discount his cheerful attitude. "'Tis the season."

"I don't suppose your meeting with Carol has anything to do with it?"

His sister eyed him skeptically, seeking his confidence, but Steve wasn't going to give it. This dinner with his ex-wife was simply the meeting of two lonely people struggling to make it through the holidays. Nothing less and certainly nothing more. Although he'd been looking for Carol to deny that she was involved with Todd, she hadn't. Steve considered her refusal to talk about the other man as good as an admission of guilt. That bastard had left her alone for Christmas two years running.

If Lindy was right and his mood had improved, Steve decided, it was simply because he was going to be out of his sister's and Rush's hair for the evening; the newlyweds could spend their first Christmas Eve together without a third party butting in.

Steve reached for his coat, and Lindy turned around, her dark eyes wide with surprise. "You're leaving."

Steve nodded, buttoning the thick wool jacket.

"But…it's Christmas Eve."

"I know." He tucked the box of candy under his arm and lifted the bright red poinsettia he'd purchased on impulse earlier in the day.

"Where are you going?"

Steve would have liked to say a friend's house, but that wouldn't be true. He didn't know how to classify his relationship with Carol. Not a friend. Not a lover. More than an acquaintance, less than a wife.

"You're going to Carol's, aren't you?" Lindy prompted.

The last thing Steve wanted was his sister to get the wrong impression about this evening with Carol, because that's all there was going to be. "It's not what you think."

Lindy raised her hands in mock consternation. "I'm

not thinking a single thing, except that it's good to see you smile again."

Steve's frown was heavy with purpose. "Well, don't read more into it than there is."

"Are the two of you going to talk?" Lindy asked, and her dark eyes fairly danced with deviltry.

"We're going to eat, not talk," Steve explained with limited patience. "We don't have anything in common anymore. I'll probably be home before ten."

"Whatever you say," Lindy answered, but her lips twitched with the effort to suppress a knowing smile. "Have a good time."

Steve chose not to answer that comment and left the apartment, but as soon as he was outside, he discovered he was whistling again and stopped abruptly.

Carol slipped the compact disk into the player and set the volume knob so that the soft Christmas music swirled festively through the house. A small turkey was roasting in the oven, stuffed with Steve's favorite sage dressing. Two pies were cooling on the kitchen counter—pumpkin for Steve, mincemeat for her. To be on the safe side a sweet-potato-pecan pie was in the fridge.

Carol chose a red silk dress that whispered enticingly against her soft skin. Her makeup and perfume had been applied with a subtle hand. Everything was ready.

Well, almost everything.

She and Steve were two different people now, and there was no getting around the fact. Regretting the past was an exercise in futility, and yet Carol had been overwhelmed these past few days with the realization that the divorce had been wrong. Very wrong. All the emotion she'd managed to bury this past year had seeped to the surface since her meeting with Steve and she couldn't remember a time when she'd been more confused.

She wanted a child, and she was using her ex-husband. More than once in the past week, she'd been forced to deal with twinges of guilt. But there was no going back. It would be impossible to recapture what had been between them before the divorce. There could be no reconciliation. Even more difficult than the past, Carol had trouble dealing with the present. They couldn't come in contact with each other without the sparks igniting. It made everything more difficult. They were both too stubborn, too temperamental, too obstinate.

And it was ruining their lives.

Carol felt they couldn't go back and yet they couldn't step forward, either. The idea of seducing Steve and getting pregnant had, in the beginning, been entirely selfish. She wanted a baby and she considered Steve the best candidate...the only candidate. After their one short meeting at the restaurant, Carol knew her choice of the baby's father went far beyond the practical. A part of her continued to love Steve, and probably always would. She wanted his child because it was the only part of him she would ever be able to have.

Everything hinged on the outcome of this dinner. Carol pressed her hands over her flat stomach and issued a fervent prayer that she was fertile. Twice in the past hour she'd taken her temperature, praying her body would do its part in this master plan. Her temperature was slightly elevated, but that could be caused by the hot sensation that went through her at the thought of sharing a bed with Steve again. Or it could be sheer nerves.

All day she'd been feeling anxious and restless with anticipation. She was convinced Steve would take one look at her and instantly know she intended for him to spend the night. The crux of her scheme was for Steve to think their making love was *his* idea. Again and again, her plans for the evening circled her mind, slowly, like the churning blades of a windmill stirring the air.

The doorbell chimed, and inhaling a calming breath, Carol forced a smile, walked across the room and opened the door for her ex-husband. "Merry Christmas," she said softly.

Steve handed her the poinsettia as though he couldn't get rid of the flower fast enough. His gaze didn't quite meet hers. In fact, he seemed to be avoiding looking at her, which pleased Carol because it told her that the red dress was having exactly the effect she'd hoped for.

"Thank you for the flower," she said and set it in the middle of the coffee table. "You didn't need to do that."

"I remembered how you used to buy three and four of those silly things each year and figured one more couldn't hurt."

"It was thoughtful of you, and I appreciate it." She held out her hand to take his coat.

Steve placed a small package under the tree and gave her a shy look. "Frangos," he explained awkwardly. "I suppose they're still your favorite candy."

"Yes. I have a little something for you, too."

Steve peeled off his heavy jacket and handed it to her. "I'm not looking for any gifts from you. I brought the flowers and candy because I wanted to contribute something toward dinner."

"My gift isn't much, Steve."

"Save it for someone else. Okay?"

Her temper nearly slipped then, but Carol managed to keep it intact. Her smile was just a little more forced when she turned from hanging his jacket in the hall closet, but she hoped he hadn't noticed.

"Would you like a hot-buttered rum before we eat?" she offered.

"That sounds good."

He followed her into the kitchen and brought the bottle of rum down from the top cupboard while she put water on to boil.

"When did you cut your hair?" he asked unexpectedly.

Absently Carol's fingers touched the straight, thick strands that crowded the side of her head. "Several months ago now."

"I liked it better when you wore it longer."

Gritting her teeth, she managed to bite back the words to inform him that she styled her hair to suit herself these days, not him.

Steve saw the flash of irritation in his ex-wife's eyes and felt a little better. The comment about her hair wasn't what she'd wanted to hear; she'd been waiting for him to tell her how beautiful she looked. The problem was, he hadn't been able to take his eyes off her from the moment he entered the house. The wisecrack was a result of one flirtatious curl of blond hair that swayed when she moved. He hadn't been able to look past that single golden lock. Neither could he stop staring at the shape of her lips nor the curve of her chin, nor the appealing color of her china blue eyes. When he'd met her at Denny's the other night he'd been on the defensive, waiting for her to drop her bombshell. All his protective walls were lowered now. He would have liked to blame it on the Christmas holidays, but he realized it was more than that, and what he saw gave him cause to tremble. Carol was as sensuous and appealing to him as she'd always been. Perhaps more so.

Already he knew what was going to happen. They would spend half the evening verbally circling each other in an anxious search for common ground. But there wasn't one for them…not anymore. Tonight was an evening out of sequence, and when it had passed they would return to their respective lives.

When Carol finished mixing their drinks, they wandered into the living room and talked. The alcohol seemed to alleviate some of the tension. Steve filled the silence with details of what had been happening in Lindy's life and in his career.

"You've done well for yourself," Carol admitted, and there was a spark of pride in her eyes that warmed him.

Steve didn't inquire about her career because it would involve asking about Todd, and the man was a subject he'd sworn he would avoid at all costs. Carol didn't volunteer any information, either. She knew the unwritten ground rules.

A half hour later, Steve helped her carry their meal to the table.

"You must have been cooking all day."

She grinned and nodded. "It gave me something to do."

The table was loaded with sliced turkey, creamy potatoes, giblet gravy, stuffing, fresh broccoli, sweet potatoes and fruit salad.

Carol asked him to light the candles and when Steve had, they sat down to eat. Sitting directly across the table from her, Steve found he was mesmerized by her mouth as she ate. With all his might he tried to remember the reasons he'd divorced Carol. Good God, she was captivating—too damn good to look at for his own peace of mind. Her hands moved gracefully, raising the fork from her plate to her mouth in motions as elegant as those of a symphony director. He shouldn't be enjoying watching her this much, and he realized he would pay the price later when he returned to the apartment and the loneliness overtook him once more.

When he'd finished the meal, he leaned against the shield-back dining-room chair and placed his hands over his stomach. "I can't remember when I've had a better dinner."

"There's pie…"

"Not now," he countered quickly and shook his head. "I'm too full to down another bite. Maybe later."

"Coffee?"

"Please."

Carol carried their dishes to the sink, stuck the left-overs in the refrigerator, and returned with the glass coffeepot. She filled both their cups, returned it to the kitchen and then took her seat opposite him. She rested her elbows on the table, and smiled.

Despite his best intentions through a good portion of the meal, Steve hadn't been able to keep his eyes away from her. The way she was sitting—leaning forward, her elbows on the tabletop—caused her breasts to push together and more than amply fill the bodice of her dress. His breath faltered someplace between his lungs and his throat at the alluring sight she made. He could have sworn she wasn't wearing a bra. Carol had fantastic breasts and Steve watched, captivated, as their tips beaded against the shiny material. They seemed to be pointing directly at him, issuing a silent invitation that asked him to fondle and taste them. Against his will, his groin began to swell until he was throbbing with painful need. Disconcerted, he dropped his gaze to the steaming cup of coffee. With his hands shaking, he took a sip of his coffee and nearly scalded the tender skin inside his mouth.

"That was an excellent dinner," he repeated, after a moment of silence.

"You're not sorry you came, are you?" she asked unexpectedly, studying him. The intent look that crowded her face demanded all Steve's attention. Her skin was pale and creamy in the muted light, her eyes wide and inquiring, as though the answer to her question was of the utmost importance.

"No," he admitted reluctantly. "I'm glad I'm here."

His answer pleased her and she smiled, looking tender and trusting, and Steve wondered how he could ever have doubted her. He knew what she'd done—knew that she'd purposely destroyed their marriage—and in that moment, it didn't matter. He wanted her again. He wanted to hold her warm and willing body in his arms. He wanted to bury himself so deep inside her that she would never desire another man for as long as they both lived.

"I'll help you with the dishes," he said, and rose so abruptly that he nearly knocked over the chair.

"I'll do them later." She got to her feet as well. "But if you want to do something, I'd appreciate a little help with the tree."

"The tree?" The words sounded as foreign as an obscure language.

"Yes, it's only half decorated. I couldn't reach the tallest limbs. Will you help?"

He shrugged. "Sure." He could have sworn that Carol was relieved, and he couldn't imagine why. The Christmas tree looked fine to him. There were a few bare spots, but nothing too noticeable.

Carol dragged a dining-room chair into the living room and pulled a box of ornaments out from underneath the end table.

"You're knitting?" Steve asked, hiding a smile as his gaze fell on the strands of worsted yarn. Carol had to be the worst knitter in the world, yet she tackled one project after another, seeming oblivious of any lack of talent. There had been a time when he could tease her about it, but he wasn't sure his insight would be appreciated now.

She glanced away as though she feared his comment.

"Don't worry, I'm not going to tease you," he told her, remembering the time she'd proudly presented him with a sweater she'd made herself—the left sleeve had been five inches longer than the right. He'd tried it on and she'd taken one look at him and burst into tears. It was one of the few times he could ever remember Carol crying.

Carol dragged the chair next to the tree and raised her leg to stand on it.

Steve stopped her. "I thought you wanted me to do that?"

"No, I need you to hand me the ornaments and then stand back and tell me how they look."

"Carol…if I placed the ornaments on the tree, you wouldn't need the chair."

She looked at him and sighed. "I'd rather do it. You don't mind, do you?"

He didn't know why she was so determined to hang the decorations herself, but it didn't make much difference to him. "No, if you want to risk your fool neck, feel free."

She grinned and raised herself so that she was standing on the padded cushion of the chair. "Okay, hand me one," she said, tossing him a look over her shoulder.

Steve gave her a shiny glass bulb, and he noted how good she smelled. Roses and some other scent he couldn't define wrapped gently around him. Carol stretched out her arms and reached for the tallest branch. Her dress rose a solid five inches and exposed the back of her creamy smooth thighs and a fleeting glimpse of the sweet curve of her buttocks. Steve knotted his hands into fists at his sides to keep from touching her. It would be entirely plausible for him to grip her waist and claim he was frightened she would tumble from her perch. But if he allowed that to happen, his hands would slip and soon he would be cupping that cute rounded bottom. Once he touched her, Steve knew he would never be able to stop. He clenched his teeth and inhaled deeply through his nose. Having Carol standing there, exposing herself in this unconscious way, was more than a mere man could resist. At this point, he was willing to use any excuse to be close to her once more.

Carol lowered her arms, her dress fell back into place and Steve breathed normally again. He thought he was safe from further temptation until she twisted around. Her ripe, full breasts filled the front of her dress, their shape clearly defined against the thin fabric. If he'd been guessing about the bra before, he was now certain. She wasn't wearing one.

"I'm ready for another ornament," she said softly.

Like a blind man, Steve turned and fumbled for a second glass bulb. He handed it to her and did everything within his power to keep his gaze away from her breasts.

"How does that one look?" Carol asked.

"Fine," Steve answered gruffly.

"Steve?"

"Don't you think that's enough decorations, for God's sake?"

His harsh tone was as much a surprise to him as it obviously was to Carol.

"Yes, of course."

She sounded disappointed, but that couldn't be helped. Steve moved to her side once more and offered her his hand to help her down. His foot must have hit against one leg of the chair because it jerked forward. Perhaps it was something she did, Steve wasn't sure, but whatever happened caused the chair to teeter on the thick carpet.

With a small cry of alarm, Carol threw out her arms.

With reflexes born of years of military training, Steve's hands shot out like bullets to catch her. The chair fell sideways onto the floor, but Steve's grip on Carol's waist anchored her firmly against his torso. Their breathing was labored, and Steve sighed with relief that she hadn't fallen. It was on the tip of his tongue to berate her, call her a silly goose for not letting him place the glass bulbs on the tree, chastise her for being such a fool. She shouldn't put herself at risk over something as nonsensical as a Christmas tree. But none of the words made it to his lips.

Their gazes were even, her haunting eyes stared into his and said his name as clearly as if it were spoken. Carol's feet remained several inches off the floor, and still Steve held on to her, unable to release her. His heart was pounding frantically with wonder as he raised a finger and touched her soft throat. His gaze continued to delve into hers. He wanted to set her back on the carpet, to free them both from this invisible grip before it maimed them, but he couldn't seem to find the strength to let her go.

Slowly she slid down his front, between his braced feet, crimping the skirt of her dress between them. Once she was secure, he noted that her lower abdomen was tucked snugly in the joint between his thighs. The throbbing in his groin began again, and he held in a groan that threatened to emanate from deep within his chest.

He longed to kiss her more than he'd ever wanted anything in his life, and only the greatest strength of will kept him from claiming her sweet mouth with his own.

She'd betrayed him once, crippled him with her deceit. Steve had sworn he would never allow her to use him again, yet his arguments burned away like dry timber in a forest fire.

His thumb found her moist lips and brushed back and forth as though the action would be enough to satisfy either of them. It didn't. If anything, it created an agony even more powerful. His heart leaped into a hard, fast rhythm that made him feel breathless and weak. Before he could stop himself, his finger lifted her chin and his mouth glided over hers. Softly. Moistly. Satin against satin.

Carol sighed.

Steve groaned.

She weakened in his arms and closed her eyes. Steve kissed her a second time and thrust his tongue deep into her mouth, his need so strong it threatened to consume him. His hand was drawn to her breast, as if caught by a vise and carried there against his will. He cupped the rounded flesh, and his finger teased the nipple until it beaded and swelled against his palm. Carol whimpered.

He had to touch her breasts again. Had to know for himself their velvet smoothness. Releasing a ragged sigh, he reached behind her and peeled down her zipper. She was as eager as he when he lowered the top of her dress and exposed her naked front.

Her hands were around his neck, and she slanted her mouth over his, rising to her tiptoes as she leaned her weight into his. Steve's mouth quickly abandoned hers to explore the curve of her neck and then lower to the rosy tips of her firm, proud breasts. His moist tongue traced circles around the pebbled nipples until Carol shuddered and plowed her fingers through his hair.

"Steve…oh, I've missed you so much." She repeated the sentence over and over again, but the words didn't register in his clouded mind. When they did, he went cold. She may have missed him, may have hungered for his touch, but she hadn't been faithful. The thought crippled him, and he went utterly still.

Carol must have sensed his withdrawal, because she dropped her arms. Her shoulders were heaving as though she'd been running in a heated race. His own breathing wasn't any more regular.

Abruptly Steve released her and stumbled two paces back.

"That shouldn't have happened," he announced in a hoarse whisper.

Carol regarded him with a wounded look but said nothing.

"I've got to get out of here," he said, expelling the words on the tail end of a sigh.

Carol's gaze widened and she shook her head.

"Carol, we aren't married anymore. This shouldn't be happening."

"I know." She lowered her gaze to the carpet.

Steve walked to the hall closet and reached for his jacket. His actions felt as if they were in slow motion—as if every gravitational force in the universe was pulling at him.

He paused, his hand clenching the doorknob. "Thank you for dinner."

Carol nodded, and when he turned back, he saw that her eyes had filled with tears and she was biting her bottom lip to hold them back. One hand held the front of her dress across her bare breasts.

"Carol..."

She looked at him with soft, appealing eyes and held out her hand. "Don't go," she begged softly. "Please don't leave me. I need you so much."

Three

Carol could see the battle raging in Steve's tight features. She swallowed down the tears and refused to release his gaze, which remained locked with her own.

"We're not married anymore," he said in a voice that shook with indecision.

"I...don't care." Swallowing her pride, she took one small step toward him. If he wouldn't come to her, then she was going to him. Her knees felt incredibly weak, as though she were walking after being bedridden for a long while.

"Carol..."

She didn't stop until she was standing directly in front of him. Then slowly, with infinite care, she released her hold on the front of her dress and allowed it to fall free, baring her breasts. Steve rewarded her immediately with a swift intake of breath, and then it seemed as if he stopped breathing completely. Carol slipped her flattened hands up his chest and leaned her body into his. When she felt his rock-hard arousal pressing against her thigh, she closed her eyes to disguise the triumph that zoomed through her blood like a shot of adrenaline.

Steve held himself stiffly against her, refusing to yield to her softness; his arms hung motionless at his sides. He didn't push her away, but he didn't welcome her into his embrace, either.

Five years of marriage had taught Carol a good deal about her husband's body. She knew what pleasured him most, knew what would drive him to the edge of madness, knew how to make him want her until there was nothing else in their world.

Standing on the tips of her toes, she locked her arms tightly around his neck and raised her soft lips to gently brush her mouth over his. Her kiss was as moist and light as dew on a summer rose. Steve's lashes dropped and she could feel the torment of the battle that raged in his troubled mind.

Slightly elevating one foot, she allowed her shoe to slip off her toes. It fell almost silently to the floor. Carol nearly laughed aloud at the expression that came over Steve's contorted features. He knew what was coming, and against his will, Carol could see that he welcomed it. In a leisurely exercise, she raised her nylon-covered foot and slid it down the backside of his leg. Again and again her thigh and calf glided over his, each caressing stroke moved higher and higher on his leg, bringing her closer to her objective.

When Steve's hand closed, almost painfully, over her thigh, Carol knew she'd won. He held her there for a timeless moment, neither moving nor breathing.

"Kiss me," he ordered, and the words seemed to be ground out from between clenched teeth.

Although Carol had fully intended to comply with his demand, she apparently didn't do it fast enough to suit her ex-husband. He groaned and his free hand locked around the back of her head, compelling her mouth to his. Driven by urgency, his kiss was forceful and demanding, almost grinding, as if he sought to punish her for making him want her so much. Carol allowed him to ravage her mouth, giving him everything he wanted, everything he asked for, until finally she gasped for breath and broke away briefly. Steve brought her mouth back to his, and gradually his kisses softened until Carol thought she was sure her whole body would burst into flames. Sensing this, Steve moved his hand from the back of her head and began to massage her breast in a leisurely circular motion, his palm centering on her nipple. Her whole torso started to pulsate under his gentle touch.

Carol arched her spine to grant him easier access, and tossed back her head as his fingers worked their magic. Then his hand left her breast, and she wanted to protest until she felt his fingers slip around her other thigh and lift her completely off the carpet, raising her so that their mouths were level, their breath mingling, moist and excited.

They paused and gazed into each other's eyes. Steve's were filled with surprise and wonder. Carol met that look and smiled with a rediscovered joy that burst from deep within her. An inner happiness that had vanished from her life the moment Steve had walked away from her, returned. She leaned forward and very gently rubbed her mouth across his, creating a moist, delicious friction. Gently her tongue played over the seam of his lips, sliding back and forth, teasing him, testing him in a love game that had once been familiar between them.

Carol gently caught his lower lip between her teeth

and sucked on it, playing with it while darting the tip of her tongue in and out of his mouth.

The effect on Steve was electric. His mouth claimed hers in an urgent kiss that drove the oxygen from her lungs. Then, with a strength that astonished her, he lifted her even higher until his mouth closed over her left breast, rolling his tongue over her nipple, then sucking at it greedily, taking in more and more of her breast.

Carol thought she was going to go crazy with the tidal wave of sensation that flooded her being. She locked her legs around his waist and braced her hands against his shoulders. His mouth and tongue alternated from one breast to the other until she was convinced that if he didn't take her soon, she was going to faint in his arms.

Braced against the closet door, Steve used what leverage he could to inch his hand up the inside of her thigh. His exploring fingers reached higher and higher, then paused when he encountered a nylon barrier. He groaned his frustration.

Carol was so weak with longing that if he didn't carry her voluntarily into the bedroom soon, she was going to demand that he make love to her right there on the entryway floor.

"You weren't wearing a bra," he chastised her in a husky thwarted voice. "I was hoping…"

He didn't need to finish for Carol to know what he was talking about. When they were married, she'd often worn a garter belt with her nylons instead of panty hose so their lovemaking wouldn't be impeded.

"I want you," she whispered, her hands framing his face. "But if you think it would be best to leave…go now. The choice is yours."

His gaze locked with hers, Steve marched wordlessly across the living room and down the long hallway to the bedroom that had once been theirs.

"Not here," she told him. "I sleep there now," she explained, pointing to the room across the hall.

Steve switched directions and marched into the smaller bedroom, not stopping until he reached the queen-size bed. For one crazy second, Carol thought he meant to drop her on top of the mattress and storm right out of the house. Instead he continued to hold her, the look in his eyes wild and uncertain.

Carol's eyes met his. She was nearly choking on the sadness that threatened to overwhelm her. Tentatively she raised one hand and pressed it to the side of his face, her eyes wide, her heart pounding so hard she was sure the sound of it would soon bring down the walls.

To her surprise, Steve tenderly placed her on the bed, braced one knee against the edge of the mattress and leaned over her.

"We aren't married... Not a damn thing has been settled between us," he announced, as though this should be shocking news.

Carol said nothing, but she casually slipped her hand around the side of his neck, urging his mouth down to hers. She met with no resistance.

"Make love to me," she murmured.

Steve groaned, twisted around and dropped to sit on the side of the bed, granting her a full view of his solid back. The thread of disappointment that wrapped itself around Carol's heart was followed by a slow, lazy smile that spread over her mouth as she recognized his frantic movements.

Steve was undressing.

* * *

Feeling deliciously warm and content, Carol woke two hours later to the sound of Steve rummaging in the kitchen. No doubt he was looking for something to eat. Smiling, she jerked her arms high above her head and stretched. She yawned and arched her back, slightly elevating her hips with the action. She felt marvelous. Stupendous. Happy.

Her heart bursting with newfound joy, she reached for Steve's shirt and purposely buttoned it just enough to be provocative while looking as if she'd made some effort to cover herself.

Semiclothed, she moved toward the noise emanating from her kitchen. Barefoot, dressed only in his slacks, Steve was bent over, investigating the contents of her refrigerator.

Carol paused in the doorway. "Making love always did make you hungry," she said from behind him.

"There's hardly a damn thing in here except sweet potatoes. Good grief, woman, what are you doing with all these leftover yams?"

Carol felt sudden heat rise in her cheeks as hurried excuses crowded her mind. "They were on sale this week because of Christmas."

"They must have been at rock-bottom price. I counted six containers full of them. It looks like you've been eating them at every meal for an entire week."

"There's some pie if that'll interest you," she said, a little too quickly. "And plenty of turkey for a sandwich, if you want."

He straightened, closed the refrigerator and turned to face her. But whatever he'd intended to say apparently left him when he caught sight of her seductive pose.

She was leaning against the doorjamb, hands behind her back and one foot braced against the wall, smiling at him, certain he could read her thoughts.

"There's pumpkin, and the whipped topping is fresh."

"Pumpkin?" he repeated.

"The pie."

He blinked, and nodded. "That sounds good."

"Would you like me to make you a sandwich while I'm at it?"

"Sure." But he didn't sound sure of anything at the moment.

Moving with ease around her kitchen, Carol brought out the necessary ingredients and quickly put together a snack for both of them. When she'd finished, she carried their plates to the small table across from the stove.

"Would you like something to drink?" she asked, setting their plates down.

"I'll get it," Steve said, apparently eager to help. "What would you like?"

"Milk," she responded automatically. She'd never been overly fond of the beverage but had recently made a habit of drinking a glass or two each day in preparation for her pregnancy.

"I thought you didn't like milk."

"I... I've acquired new tastes in the past year."

Steve grinned. "There are certain things about you that haven't changed, and then there's something more, something completely unexpected. Good God, woman, you've turned into a little she-devil, haven't you?"

Carol lowered her gaze and felt the heated blush work its way up her neck and spill into her cheeks. It wasn't any wonder Steve was teasing her. She'd been as hot as a stick of dynamite. By the time he'd undressed, she'd behaved like a tigress, clawing at him, driven by mindless passion.

Chuckling, Steve delivered two glasses of milk to the table. "You surprised me," he said. "You used to be a tad more timid."

Doing her best to ignore him, Carol brought her feet up to the edge of the chair and pulled the shirt down over her legs. With feigned dignity, she reached for half of her sandwich. "An officer and a gentleman wouldn't remind me of my wicked ways."

Still grinning, Steve lounged against the back of the chair. "You used to be far more subtle."

"Steve," she cried, "stop talking about it. Can't you see you're embarrassing me?"

"I remember one time when we were on our way to an admiral's dinner party and you casually announced you'd been in such a rush that you'd forgotten to put on any underwear."

Carol closed her eyes and looked away, remembering the time as clearly as if it had been last week instead of several years ago. She remembered, too, how good the lovemaking had been later that same evening.

"There wasn't time for us to go back to the house, so all night while you strolled around, sipping champagne, chatting and looking sedately prim, only I knew differently. Every time you looked at me, I about went crazy."

"I wanted you to know how much I longed to make love. If you'll recall, you'd just returned from a three-month tour."

"Carol, if *you'll* recall, we'd spent the entire day in bed."

She took a sip of her milk, then slowly raised her gaze to meet his. "It wasn't enough."

Steve closed his eyes and shook his head before grudgingly admitting, "It wasn't enough for me, either."

As soon as it had been socially acceptable to do so, Steve had made their excuses to the admiral that night and they'd hurriedly left the party. The entire way home, he'd been furious with Carol, telling her he was certain someone must have known what little trick she was playing. Just as heatedly, Carol had told Steve she didn't care who knew. If some huffy admiral wanted to throw a dinner party he shouldn't do it so soon after his men return from deployment.

They'd ended up making love twice that evening.

"Steve," Carol whispered with ragged emotion.

"Yes?"

"Once wasn't enough tonight, either." She dared not look at him, dared not let him see the way her pulse was clamoring.

Abruptly he stopped eating, and when he swallowed, it looked as if he'd downed the sandwich whole. A full minute passed before he spoke.

"Not for me, either."

Their lovemaking was different this time. Unique. Unrepeatable. Earlier, it'd been like spontaneous combustion. This time was slow, easy, relaxed. Steve led her into the bedroom, unfastened the buttons of the shirt that she was wearing and let it drop unheeded to the floor.

Carol stood before him tall and proud, her taut nipples seeming to beg for his lips. Steve looked at her naked body as if seeing her for the first time. Tenderly he raised his hand to her face and brushed back a wisp of blond hair, his touch light, gentle. Then he lowered his hands and cupped the undersides of her breasts, as though weighing them in a delicate measure. The velvet stroke of his thumbs worked across her nipples until they pebbled to a throbbing hardness. From there he slid the tips of his fingers down her rib cage, grazing her heated flesh wherever he touched her.

All the while, his dark, mesmerizing gaze never left hers, as though he half expected her to protest or to stop him.

Carol felt as if her hands were being manipulated like a puppet's as she reached for his belt buckle. All she knew was that she wanted him to make love to her. Her fingers fumbled at first, unfamiliar with the workings of his belt, then managed to release the clasp.

Soon Steve was nude.

She studied him, awed by his strength and beauty. She wanted to tell him all that she was feeling, all the good things she sensed in him, but the words withered on her tongue as he reached out and touched her once more.

His hand continued downward from her rib cage, momentarily pausing over her flat, smooth stomach, then moving lower until it encountered her pelvis. Slowly, methodically, he braced the heel of his hand against the apex of her womanhood and started a circling, gyrating motion while his fingers explored between her parted thighs.

Hardly able to breathe, Carol opened herself more to him, and once she had, he delicately parted her and slipped one finger inside. Her eyes widened at the stab of pleasure that instantly sliced through her and she bit into her lower lip to keep from panting.

She must have made some kind of sound because Steve paused and asked, "Did I hurt you?"

Carol was incapable of any verbal response. Frantically she shook her head, and his finger continued its deft movements, quickly bringing her to an exploding release. Wave upon wave of seething spasms, each one stronger, each one more intense, overtook every part of her. Whimpering noises escaped from deep within her throat as she climaxed, and the sound propelled Steve into action.

He wrapped his arms around her and carried her to the bed, laying her on top of the rumpled sheets. Not allowing her time to alter her position or rearrange the sheets, Steve moved over her, parted her thighs and quickly impaled her.

His breathing was ragged, barely under control.

Carol's wasn't any more even.

He didn't move, torturing her with an intense longing she had never experienced. Her body was still tingling in the aftermath of one fulfillment and reaching, striving toward another. Her whole person seemed to be filled with anxious expectancy…waiting for something she couldn't define.

Taking her hands, Steve lifted them above her head and held them prisoner there. He leaned over her, bracing himself on his arms on either side of her head. The action thrust him deeper inside Carol. She moaned and thrashed her head against the mattress, then lifted her hips, jerking them a couple of times, seeking more.

"Not yet, love," he whispered and placed a hand under her head, lifting her mouth to his. Their kiss was wild and passionate, as though their mouths couldn't give or take enough to satisfy their throbbing need.

Steve shifted his position and completely withdrew his body from hers.

Carol felt as if she'd suddenly gone blind; the whole world seemed black and lifeless. She started to protest, started to cry out, but before the sound escaped her throat, Steve sank his manhood back inside her. A shaft of pure light filled her senses once more and she sighed audibly, relieved. She was whole again, free.

"Now," Steve told her. "Now." He moved eagerly then, in deep, calculated strokes, plunging into her again and again, gifting her with the sun, revealing the heavens, exploring the universe. Soon all Carol knew was this insistent warm friction and the sweet, indescribable pangs of pleasure. Her body trembled as ripple after ripple of deep, pure sensation pulsed over her, driving her crazy as she remembered what had nightly been hers.

Breathless, Steve moved to lie beside her, bringing her into the circle of his arms. An hour passed, it seemed, before he spoke. "Was it always this good?"

The whispered question was so low Carol had to strain to hear him. "Yes," she answered after a long, timeless moment. "Always."

He pressed his forehead against the top of her head and moaned. "I was afraid of that."

The next thing Carol was aware of was a muffled curse and the unsettling sound of something heavy crashing to the floor.

"Steve?" she sat up in bed and reached for a sheet to cover her nakedness. The room was dark and still. Dread filled her—it couldn't be morning. Not yet, not so soon.

"I'm sorry. I didn't mean to wake you."

"You're leaving?" She sent her hand searching for the lamp on the nightstand. It clicked and a muted light filled the room.

"I've got the watch today," he reminded her.

"What time is it?"

"Carol, listen," he said gruffly, "I didn't mean for any of this to happen." All the while he was speaking, Steve's fingers were working the buttons of his shirt and having little success in getting it to fasten properly. "Call what happened last night what you will—the holiday spirit, a momentary slip in my better judgment… whatever. I'm sure you feel the same way." He paused and turned to study her.

She leaned forward, resting her chin on her raised knees. Her heart was in her throat, and she felt shaken and miserable. "Yes, of course."

His mouth thinned and he turned his back to her once more. "I thought as much. The best thing we can do is put the entire episode out of our minds."

"Right," she answered, forcing some enthusiasm into her voice. It was working out exactly as she'd planned it: they would both wake up in the morning, feel chagrined, make their apologies and go their separate ways once more.

Only it didn't feel the way she'd anticipated. It felt wrong. Very wrong.

Steve was in the living room before she moved from the bed. Grabbing a thin robe from her closet, she slipped into it as she rushed after him.

He seemed to be waiting for her, pacing the entryway. He combed his fingers through his hair a couple of times before turning to look at her.

"So you want to forget last night?" he asked.

"I…if you do," she answered.

"I do."

Carol's world toppled for a moment, then quickly righted itself. She understood—it was better this way.

"Thank you for the poinsettia and candy." It seemed inappropriate to mention the terrific lovemaking.

"Right." His answer was clipped, as though he was eager to be on his way. "Thanks for the dinner...and everything else."

"No problem." Stepping around him, Carol opened the door. "It was good to see you again, Steve."

"Yeah, you, too."

He walked out of the house and down the steps, and watching him go did crazy things to Carol's equilibrium. Suddenly she had to lean against the doorjamb just to remain upright. Something inside her, something strong and more powerful than her own will demanded that she stop him.

"Steve," she cried frantically. She stood on tiptoe. "Steve."

He turned around abruptly.

They stared at each other, each battle scarred and weary, each hurting. Each proud.

"Merry Christmas," she said softly.

"Merry Christmas."

Three days after Christmas, Carol was convinced her plan had worked perfectly. Thursday morning she woke feeling sluggish and sick to her stomach. A book she'd been reading on pregnancy and childbirth stated that the best way to relieve those early bouts of morning sickness was to nibble on soda crackers first thing— even before getting out of bed.

A burning sense of triumph led her into the bathroom, where she stared at herself in the mirror as though her reflection would proudly announce she was about to become a mother.

It had been so easy. Simple really. One tempestuous night of passion and the feat was accomplished. Her hand rested over her abdomen, and she patted it gently, feeling both proud and awed. A new life was being nurtured there.

A baby. Steve's child.

The wonder of it produced a ready flow of emotion and tears dampened her eyes.

Another symptom!

The book had explained that her emotions could be affected by the pregnancy—that she might be more susceptible to tears.

Wiping the moisture from the corners of her eyes, Carol strolled into the kitchen and searched the cupboard for saltines. She found a stale package and forced herself to eat two, but she didn't feel any better than she had earlier.

Not bothering to dress, she turned on the television and made herself a bed on the sofa. Boeing workers were given the week between Christmas and New Year's off as part of their employment package. Carol had planned to spend the free time painting the third bedroom—the one she planned to use for the baby. Unfortunately she didn't have any energy. In fact, she felt downright sick, as though she were coming down with a case of the flu.

A lazy smile turned up the edges of her mouth. She wasn't about to complain. Nine months from now, she would be holding a precious bundle in her arms.

Steve's and her child.

Four

With his hands cupped behind his head, Steve lay in bed and stared blindly at the dark ceiling. He couldn't sleep. For the past hour he hadn't even bothered to close his eyes. It wouldn't do any good; every time he did, the memory of Christmas Eve with Carol filled his mind.

Releasing a slow breath, he rubbed his hand down his face, hoping the action would dispel her image from his thoughts. It didn't work. Nothing did.

He had never intended to make love to her, and even now, ten days later, he wasn't sure how the hell it had happened. He continued to suffer from a low-grade form of shock. His thoughts had been in utter chaos since that night, and he wasn't sure how to respond to her or where their relationship was headed now.

What really distressed him, Steve realized, was that after everything that had happened between them, he could still want her so much. More than a week later and the memory of her leaning against the doorjamb in the kitchen, wearing his shirt—and nothing else— had the power to tighten his loins. Tighten his loins! He nearly laughed out loud; that had to be the understatement of the year.

When Carol had stood and held out her arms to him, he'd acted like a starving child offered candy, so eager he hadn't stopped to think about anything except the love she would give him. Any protest he'd made had been token. She'd volunteered, he'd accepted, and that should be the end of it.

But it wasn't.

Okay, so he wasn't a man of steel. Carol had always been his Achilles' heel, and he knew it. She knew it. In thinking over the events of that night, it was almost as though his ex-wife had planned everything. Her red dress with no bra, and that bit about placing decorations on the tree. She'd insisted on standing on the chair, stretching and exposing her thigh to him…his thoughts came to a skidding halt.

No.

He wasn't going to fall into that familiar trap of thinking Carol was using him, deceiving him. It did no good to wade into the muddy mire of anger, bitterness, regret and doubt.

He longed to repress the memory of Carol's warm and willing body in his arms. If only he could get on with his life. If only he could sleep.

He couldn't.

His sister, Lindy, had coffee brewed by the time Steve came out of his bedroom. She sat at the table, cradling a cup in one hand while holding a folded section of the *Post-Intelligencer* in the other.

"Morning." She glanced up and greeted him with a bright smile. Lately it seemed his sister was always smiling.

Steve mumbled something unintelligible as a means of reply. Her cheerfulness grated against him. He wasn't in the mood for good humor this morning. He wasn't in the mood for anything…with the possible exception of making love to Carol again, and that bit of insight didn't suit him in the least.

"It doesn't look like you had a good night's sleep, brother dearest."

Steve's frown deepened, and he gave his sister another noncommittal answer.

"I don't suppose this has anything to do with Carol?" She waited, and when he didn't answer, added, "Or the fact that you didn't come home Christmas Eve?"

"I came home."

"Sure, sometime the following morning."

Steve took down a mug from the cupboard and slapped it against the counter with unnecessary force. "Drop it, Lindy. I don't want to discuss Carol."

A weighted silence followed his comment.

"Rush and I've got almost everything ready to move into the new apartment," she offered finally, and the light tone of her voice suggested she was looking for a way to put their conversation back on an even keel. "We'll be out of here by Friday."

Hell, here he was snapping at Lindy. His sister didn't deserve to be the brunt of his foul mood. She hadn't done anything but mention the obvious. "Speaking of Rush, where is he?" Steve asked, forcing a lighter tone into his own voice.

"He had to catch an early ferry this morning," she said, and hesitated momentarily. "I'm happy, Steve, really happy. I was so afraid for a time that I'd made a dreadful mistake, but I know now that marrying Rush was the right thing to do."

Steve took a sip of coffee to avoid looking at his sister. What Lindy was actually saying was that she wanted him to find the same contentment she had. That wasn't possible for him now, and wouldn't be until he got Carol out of his blood.

And making love to her Christmas Eve hadn't helped.

"Well, I suppose I should think about getting dressed," Lindy said with a heavy dose of feigned enthusiasm. "I'm going to get some boxes so Rush and I can finish up the last of the packing."

"Where's your new apartment?" Steve had been so preoccupied with his own troubles that he hadn't thought to inquire until now.

As Lindy rattled off the address Steve's forehead furrowed into a brooding frown. His sister and Rush were moving less than a mile away from Carol's place. Great! That was the last thing he needed to hear.

Steve's day wasn't much better than his sleepless night had been. By noon he'd decided he could no longer avoid the inevitable. He didn't like it, but it was necessary.

He had to talk to Carol.

He was thankful the apartment was empty when he arrived home shortly after six. Not willing to test his good fortune, and half expecting Lindy or Rush to appear at any minute, he walked directly to the phone and punched out Carol's number as though punishing the telephone would help relieve some of his nervousness.

"Hello?" Carol's soft, lilting voice clawed at his abdomen.

"It's Steve."

A pregnant pause was followed by a slightly breathless "Hi."

"I was thinking we should talk."

"All right." She sounded surprised, pleased, uncertain. "When?"

Steve rotated his wrist and looked at the time. "What are you doing right now?"

She hesitated. "I…nothing."

Although slightly awkward, their conversation to this point had felt right to Steve. But the way she paused, as though searching for a delaying tactic, troubled him. Fiery arrows of doubt hit their mark and he said, "Listen, Carol, if you're 'entertaining' Todd, I'd prefer to stop by later."

The ensuing silence was more deafening than jungle drums pounding out a war chant.

It took her several seconds to answer him, and when she did, the soft voice that had greeted him was racked with pain. "You can come now."

Steve tightened his hold on the phone receiver in a punishing grip. He hated it when he talked to her like that. He didn't know who he was punishing: Carol or himself. "I'll be there in fifteen minutes."

Carol replaced the telephone in its cradle and battled down an attack of pain and tears. How dare Steve suggest Todd was there. Suddenly she was so furious with him that she could no longer stand in one place. She started pacing the living room floor like a raw recruit, taking five or six steps and then doing an abrupt aboutface. And yet she was excited—even elated.

Steve had taken the initiative to contact her, and it proved that he hadn't been able to stop thinking about her, either.

Nothing had been right for her since Christmas Eve. Oh, she'd reached her objective—exceeded it. Everything had gone according to plan. Only Carol hadn't counted on the doubts and bewilderment that had followed their night of loving. Their short hours together brought back the memory of how good their lives had once been, how much they'd loved each other and how happy those first years were.

Since Christmas Eve, Carol had been crippled with "if onlys" and "what ifs," tossing around those weak phrases as though she expected them to alter reality. Each day it became more difficult to remember that Steve had divorced her, that he believed her capable of the worst kind of deception. One night in his arms and she was fool enough to be willing to forget all the pain of the past thirteen months.

Almost willing, she amended.

It took vindictive, destructive comments like the one he'd just made to remind her that they had a rocky road to travel if they hoped to salvage their relationship.

Before Steve arrived, Carol had time to freshen her makeup and run a brush through her thick blond hair. She paused to study her reflection in the mirror and wondered if he would ever guess her secret. She doubted it. If he couldn't read the truth in her eyes about Todd, then he wasn't likely to recognize her joy, or guess the cause.

Thinking about the baby helped lighten the weight of Steve's bitterness. Briefly she closed her eyes and imagined holding that precious bundle in her arms. A little girl, she decided, with dark brown eyes like Steve's and soft blond curls.

The mental picture of her child made everything seem worthwhile.

When the doorbell chimed, Carol was ready. She held the door open for Steve and even managed to greet him with a smile.

"I made coffee."

"Good." His answer was gruff, as though he were speaking to one of his enlisted men.

He followed her into the kitchen and stood silently as she poured them each a cup of coffee. When she turned around, she saw Steve standing with his hands in his pockets, looking unsettled and ill at ease.

"If you're searching for traces of Todd, let me tell you right now, you won't find any."

He had the good grace to look mildly chagrined. "I suppose I should apologize for that remark."

"I suppose I should accept." She pulled out a chair and sat.

Steve claimed the one directly across from her.

Neither spoke, and it seemed to Carol that an eternity passed. "You wanted to talk to me," she said, after what felt like two lifetimes.

"I'm not exactly sure what I want to say."

She smiled a little at that, understanding. "I'm not sure what I want to hear, either."

A hint of a grin bounced from his dark eyes. "Forgiving you for what happened with Todd..."

Carol bolted to her feet with such force that her chair nearly fell backward. "Forgiving me!" she demanded, shaking with outrage.

"Carol, please, I didn't come here to fight."

"Then don't start one. Don't come into my home and

hurl insults at me. The one person in this room who should be seeking forgiveness is *you!*"

"Carol…"

"I should have known this wouldn't work, but like a lovesick fool I thought… I hoped you…" She paused, jerked her head around and rubbed the heels of her hands down her cheeks, erasing the telltale tears.

"Okay, I apologize. I won't mention Todd again."

She inhaled a wobbly breath and nodded, not trusting her voice, and sat back down.

Another awkward moment followed.

"I don't know what you've been thinking, or how you feel about…what happened," Steve said, "but for the past ten days, I've felt like a leaf caught in a windstorm. My emotions are in turmoil… I can't stop remembering how good it was between us, and how right it felt to have you in my arms again. My instincts tell me that night was a fluke, and best forgotten. I just wish to hell I could."

Carol bowed her head, avoiding eye contact. "I've been thinking the same thing. As you said when you left, we should chalk it up to the love and goodwill that's synonymous with the season. But the holidays are over and I can't stop thinking about it, either."

"The loving always was terrific, wasn't it?"

He didn't sound as though he wanted to admit even that much, as if he preferred to discount anything positive about their lives together. Carol understood the impulse. She'd done the same thing since their divorce; it helped ease the pain of the separation.

Grudgingly she nodded. "Unfortunately the love-making is only a small part of any marriage. I think Christmas Eve gave me hope that you and I might be able to work everything out. I'd like to resolve the past and find a way to heal the wounds." They'd been apart for over a year, but Carol's heart felt as bloodied and bruised as if their divorce had been decreed yesterday.

"God knows, I want to forget the past…"

Hope clamored in her breast and she raised her eyes to meet Steve's, but his gaze was as weary and doubtful as her own.

His eyes fell. "But I don't think I can. I don't know if I'll ever be able to get over finding Todd in our bedroom."

"He was in the shower," Carol corrected through clenched teeth. "And the only reason he was there was because the shower head in the other bathroom wasn't working properly."

"What the hell difference does it make?" Steve shouted. "He spent the night here. You've never bothered to deny that."

"But nothing happened…if you'd stayed long enough to ask Todd, he would have explained."

"If I'd stayed any longer, I would have killed him."

He said it with such conviction that Carol didn't doubt him. Long before, she'd promised herself she wouldn't defend her actions again. Todd had been her employer and her friend. She'd known Todd and his wife, Joyce, were having marital troubles. But she cared about them both and didn't want to get caught in the middle of their problems. Todd, however, had cast her there when he showed up on her doorstep, drunk out of his mind, wanting to talk. Alarmed, Carol had brought him inside and phoned Joyce, who suggested Todd sleep it off at Carol's house. It had seemed like a reasonable solution, although she wasn't keen on the idea. Steve was away and due back to Seattle in a couple of days.

But Steve had arrived home early—and assumed the worst.

The sadness that settled over her was profound, and when she spoke, her voice was little more than a whisper. "You tried and found me guilty on circumstantial evidence, Steve. For the first couple of weeks, I tried to put myself in your place... I could understand how you read the scene that morning, but you were wrong."

It looked for a moment as though he was going to argue with her. She could almost see the wheels spinning in his mind, stirring up the doubts, building skyscrapers on sand foundations.

"Other things started to add up," he admitted reluctantly, still not looking at her.

Carol could all but see him close his mind to common sense. It seemed that just when they were beginning to make headway, Steve would pull something else into their argument or make some completely ridiculous comment that made absolutely no sense to her. The last time they'd tried to discuss this in a reasonable, nonconfrontational manner, Steve had hinted that she'd been Todd's lover for months. He'd suggested that she hadn't been as eager to welcome him home from his last cruise, which was ridiculous. They may have had problems, but none had extended to the bedroom.

"What 'other things' do you mean now?" she asked, defeat coating her words.

He ignored her question. His mouth formed a cocky smile, devoid of amusement. "I will say one thing for ol' Todd—he taught you well."

She gasped at the unexpected pain his words inflicted.

Steve paled and looked away. "I shouldn't have said that—I didn't mean it."

"Todd did teach me," she countered, doing her best to keep her bottom lip from quivering. "He taught me that a marriage not based on mutual trust isn't worth the ink that prints the certificate. He taught me that it takes more than a few words murmured by a man of God to make a relationship work."

"That's not what I meant."

"I know what you meant. Your jealousy has you tied up in such tight knots that you're incapable of reasoning any of this out."

Steve ignored that comment. "I'm not jealous of Todd—he can have you if he wants."

Carol thought she was going to be sick to her stomach. Indignation filled her throat, choking off any possible reply.

Steve stood and walked across the kitchen, his hands knotted into fists at his sides. He closed his eyes briefly, and when he opened them, he looked like a stranger, his inner torment was so keen.

"I didn't mean that," he said unevenly. "I don't know why I say such ugly things to you."

Carol heard the throb of pain in her voice. "I don't know why you do, either. If you're trying to hurt me, then congratulations. You've succeeded beyond your expectations."

Steve stood silently a few moments, then delivered his untouched coffee to the sink. His hesitation surprised Carol. She'd assumed he would walk out—that was the way their arguments usually ended.

Instead he turned to face her and asked, "Are Todd and Joyce still married?"

She'd gotten a Christmas card from them a couple of weeks earlier. Until she'd seen both their names at the bottom of the greeting, she hadn't been sure if their marriage had weathered better than hers and Steve's. "They're still together."

Steve frowned and nodded. "I know that makes everything more difficult for you."

"Stop it, Steve!" This new list of questions irritated her almost as much as his tireless insinuations. "All the years we were married, not once did I accuse you of being unfaithful, even though you were gone half the time."

"It's difficult to find a woman willing to fool around 400 feet under water."

"That's not my point. I trusted you. I always did, and I assumed that you trusted me, too. That's all I've ever asked of you, all I ever wanted."

He was quiet for so long that Carol wondered if he'd chosen to ignore her rather than come up with an appropriate answer.

"You didn't discover another woman lounging around in a see-through nightie while I showered, either. You may be able to explain away some of what happened, but as far as I'm concerned there are gaping holes in your story."

Carol clenched her teeth so tightly that her jaw ached. She'd already broken a promise to herself by discussing Todd with Steve. When the divorce was final, Carol had determined then that no amount of justifying would ever satisfy her ex-husband. Discussing Todd had yet to settle a single problem, and in the end she only hurt herself.

"I don't think we're going to solve anything by rehashing this now," she told him calmly. "Unless our love is firmly grounded in a foundation of trust, there's no use even trying to work things out."

"It doesn't seem to be helping, does it? I wanted us—"

"I know," she interrupted softly, sadly. "I wanted it, too. The other night only served to remind us how much we'd loved each other."

They shared a discouraged smile, and Carol felt as though her heart was breaking in half.

He took a few steps toward the front door. "I'll be leaving in less than three weeks."

"How long will you be away?" For a long time she hadn't felt comfortable asking him this kind of question, but he seemed more open to discussion now.

"Three months." He buried his hands in his pockets and Carol got the impression that the action was to keep him from reaching for her and kissing her goodbye. He paused, turned toward her and said, "If you need anything…"

"I won't."

Her answer didn't appear to please him. "No, I don't suppose you will. You always could take care of yourself. I used to be proud of you for being so capable, but it intimidated me, too."

"What do you mean?"

He hedged, as if searching his reserve of memories to find the perfect example, then shook his head. "Never mind, it isn't important now."

Carol walked him to the front door, her heart heavy. "I wish it could be different for us."

"I do, too."

Steve stood, unmoving, in the entryway. Inches from him, Carol felt an inner yearning more potent than anything she'd ever experienced engulf her, filling her heart with regret. Once more she would have to watch the man she loved walk away from her. Once more she must freely allow him to go.

Steve must have sensed the intense longing, because he gently rested his hands on the curve of her shoulders. She smiled and tilted her chin toward him, silently offering him her mouth.

Slowly, without hurry, Steve lowered his face to hers, drawing out each second as though he were relaxing a hold on his considerable pride, admitting his need to kiss her. It was as if he had to prove, if only to himself, that he had control of the situation.

Then his mouth grazed hers. Lightly. Briefly. Coming back for more when it became apparent the teasing kisses weren't going to satisfy either of them.

What shocked Carol most was the gentleness of his kiss. He touched and held her as he would a delicate piece of porcelain, slipping his arms around her waist, drawing her close against him.

He broke off the kiss and Carol tucked her forehead against his chest. "Have a safe trip." Silently she prayed for his protection and that he would come back to her.

"If you want, I'll phone when I return. That is…if you think I should?"

Maybe she could tell him about the baby then, depending on how things went between them. "Yes, by all means, phone and let me know that you made it back in one piece."

His gaze centered on her mouth and again he bent his head toward her. This time his kiss was hungry, lingering, insistent. Carol whimpered when his tongue, like a soft flame, entered her mouth, sending hot sparks of desire shooting up her spine. Her knees weakened and she nearly collapsed when Steve abruptly released her.

"For once, maybe you could miss me," he said, with a sad note of bitterness.

The following morning, Carol woke feeling queasy. It'd been that way almost since Christmas morning. She reached for the two soda crackers on the nightstand and nibbled on them before climbing out of bed. Her hand rested lovingly on her flat stomach.

She'd wanted to schedule an appointment with the doctor, but the receptionist had told her to wait until her monthly cycle was a week late. She was only over-due by a day, but naturally she wouldn't be having her period. As far as Carol was concerned, another week was too long to wait, even if she was certain she bore the desired fruit from her night with Steve.

In an effort to confirm what she already knew, Carol had purchased a home-pregnancy test. Now she climbed out of bed, read the instructions through twice, did what the package told her and waited.

The waiting was the worst part. Thirty minutes had never seemed to take so long.

Humming a catchy tune, she dressed for work, poured herself a glass of milk, then went back to the bathroom to read the test results.

She felt so cocky, so sure of what the test would tell her that her heart was already pounding with excite-ment.

The negative reading claimed her breath. She blinked, certain she'd misread it.

Stunned, she sat on the edge of the bathtub and took several deep breaths. She started to tremble, and tears of disappointment filled her eyes. She must be preg-

nant—she had to be. All the symptoms were there—
everything she'd read had supported her belief.

Once more she examined the test results.

Negative.

After everything she'd gone through, after all the
sweet potatoes she'd forced down her throat, after the
weeks of planning, the plotting, the scheduling…

There wasn't going to be any baby. There never had
been. Her plan had failed.

There was only one thing left to do.

Try again.

Five

It took courage for Carol to drive to Steve's apartment. Someone should award medals for this brand of lion-heartedness, she murmured to herself—although she was more interested in playing the role of a tigress than a lion. If this second venture was anything like the first, Steve wouldn't know what hit him. At least, she hoped he wouldn't guess.

She straightened her shoulders, pinched some color into her cheeks and pasted on a smile. Then she rang the doorbell.

To say Steve looked surprised to see her when he opened the door would be an understatement, Carol acknowledged. His eyes rounded, his mouth relaxed and fell open, and for a moment he was utterly speechless. "Carol?"

"I suppose I should have phoned first..."

"No, come in." He stepped aside so that she could enter the apartment.

Beyond his obvious astonishment, Carol found it difficult to read Steve's reaction. She stepped inside gingerly, praying that her plastic smile wouldn't crack. The first thing she noticed was the large picture window in the living room, offering an unobstructed view of the Seattle waterfront. It made Elliott Bay seem close, so vivid that she could almost smell the seaweed and feel the salty spray in the air. A large green-and-white ferry boat plowed its way through the dark waters, enhancing the picture.

"Oh…this is nice." Carol turned around to face him. "Have you lived here long?"

He nodded. "Rush had the apartment first. I moved in after you and I split and sort of inherited it when Rush and Lindy moved into their own place recently."

The last thing Carol wanted to remind him of was their divorce, and she quickly steered the conversation to the reason for her visit. "I found something I thought might be yours," she said hurriedly, fumbling with the snap of her eel-skin purse to bring out the button. It was a weak excuse, but she was desperate. Retrieving the small gray button from inside her coin purse, she handed it over to him.

Steve's brow pleated into a frown and he stiffened. "No…this isn't mine. It must belong to another man," he said coldly.

A bad move, Carol realized, taking back the button. "There's only been one man at my house, and that's you," she said, trying to stay calm. "If it isn't yours, then it must have fallen off something of my own."

Hands in his pockets, Steve nodded.

An uneasy pause followed.

Steve didn't suggest she take off her coat, didn't offer her any refreshment or any excuse to linger. Feeling crestfallen and defeated, Carol knew there was nothing more to do but leave.

"Well, I suppose I should think about getting myself some dinner. There's a new Mexican restaurant close to here I thought I might try," she said with feigned enthusiasm, and glanced up at him through thick lashes. Steve loved enchiladas, and she prayed he would take the bait. God knew, she couldn't have been any more obvious had she issued the invitation straight out.

"I ate earlier," he announced starkly.

Steve rarely had dinner before six. He was either wise to her ways or lying.

"I see." She took a step toward the exit, wondering what else she could do to delay the inevitable. "When does the *Atlantis* leave?"

"Monday."

Three days. She had only three days to carry out her plan. Three days to get him into bed and convince him it was all his idea. Three miserable days. Her fingers curled into impotent fists of frustration inside her coat pocket.

"Have a safe trip, Steve," she said softly. "I'll... I'll be thinking of you."

It had been a mistake to come to his place, a mistake not to have plotted the evening more carefully. It was apparent from the stiff way Steve treated her, he couldn't wait to get her out of his apartment. Since it was Friday night, he might have a date. The thought of Steve with another woman produced a gut-wrenching pain that she did her best to ignore. Dropping by unexpectedly like this wasn't helping her cause.

She'd hoped they could make love tonight. Her temperature was elevated and she was as fertile as she was going to get this month.

Swallowing her considerable pride, she paused, her

hand on the door handle. "There's a new spy thriller showing at the Fifth Avenue Theater… You always used to like espionage films."

Steve's eyes narrowed as he studied her. It was difficult for Carol to meet his heated gaze and not wilt from sheer nerves. She was sure her cheeks were hot pink. Coming to his apartment was the most difficult thing she'd done in years. Her heart felt as if it was going to hammer its way right out of her chest, and her fingers were shaking so badly that she didn't dare remove them from her pockets.

"Why are you here?" His question was soft, suspicious, uncertain.

"I found the button." One glance told her he didn't believe her, as well he shouldn't. That excuse was so weak it wouldn't carry feathers.

"What is it you *really* want, Carol?"

"I… I…" Her voice trembled from her lips, and her heart, which had been pounding so furiously a second before, seemed to stop completely. She swallowed and forced her gaze to meet his before dropping it. When she finally managed to speak, her voice was low and meaningful. "I thought with you going away…" Good grief, woman, her mind shouted, quit playing games. Give him the truth.

She raised her chin, and her gaze locked with his. "I'm not wearing any underwear."

Steve went stock-still, holding his jaw tight and hard. The inner conflict that played over his face was as vivid as the picturesque scene she'd viewed from his living-room window. The few feet of distance between them seemed to stretch wider than a mile.

It felt as if an eternity passed as Carol waited for his

reaction, and she felt paralyzed with misgivings. She'd exposed her hand and left her pride completely vulnerable to him.

She saw it then—a flicker of his eyes, a movement in the line of his jaw, a softening in his tightly controlled facial features. He wanted her, too—wanted her with a desperation that made him as weak as she was. Her heart leaped wildly with joy.

Steve lifted his hand and held it out to her, and Carol thought she would collapse with relief as she hurried toward him. He crushed her in his arms and his mouth hungrily came down on hers. His eager lips smothered her cry of happiness. Equally greedy, Carol returned his kiss, reveling in his embrace. She twined her arms around his neck, her softness melding against the hardened contours of his body.

His hands tightened around her possessively, stroking her spine, then lowered over the rounded firmness of her buttocks. He gathered her pelvis as close to him as was humanly possible.

"Dear God, I've gone crazy."

Carol raised her hands to frame his face and gazed lovingly into his eyes. "Me, too," she whispered before spreading a circle of light kisses over his forehead, chin and mouth.

"I shouldn't be doing this."

"Yes, you should."

Steve groaned and clasped her tighter. He kissed her, plunging his tongue into the sweet softness of her mouth, exploring it with a desperate urgency. Carol met his tongue with her own in a silent duel that left them both exhausted.

While they were still kissing, Steve unfastened the

buttons of her coat, slipped it from her shoulders and dropped it to the floor. His hands clawed at the back of her skirt, lifting it away from her legs, then settled once again, cupping her bare bottom.

He moaned, his breath seemed to jam in his throat, and his eyes darkened with passion. "You weren't kidding."

Carol bit her lower lip as a wealth of sensation fired through her from the touch of his cool hands against her heated flesh. She rotated her lower body shamelessly against the rigid evidence of his desire.

His hands closed over her breasts and her nipples rose as though to greet him, to welcome him. His eager but uncooperative fingers fiddled with the fastenings of her blouse. Smiling, content but just as eager, Carol gently brushed his hands aside and completed the task for him. He pulled the silk material free of her waistline and disposed of it as effectively as he had her coat. Her breasts sprang to life in his hands and when he moaned, the sound of it excited her so much that it throbbed in her ears.

The moist heat of his mouth closed over her nipple and she gasped. The exquisite pleasure nearly caused her knees to buckle. Blood roared through her veins, and liquid fire scorched her until she was certain she would soon explode. She lifted one leg and wrapped it around his thigh, anchoring her weight against him.

Steve's fingers reached for her and instinctively she opened herself to him. He teased her womanhood, toyed with her, tormented her with delicate strokes that drove her over the brink. Within seconds, she tossed back her head and groaned as the pulsating climax rocked through her, sending out rippling waves of release.

By the time Steve carried her into his bedroom,

Carol was panting. He didn't waste any time, discarding his clothes with an urgency that thrilled her. When he moved to the bed, his features were keen with desire.

Carol lifted her arms to welcome him, loving him with a tenderness that came from the very marrow of her bones.

Steve shifted his weight over her and captured her mouth in a consuming kiss that sent Carol down into a whirlpool of the sweetest oblivion. Anxious and eager, she parted her thighs for him and couldn't hold back a small cry as he sheathed himself inside her, slipping the proud heat of his manhood into her moist softness.

He waited, as though to prolong the pleasure and soak in her love before he started to move. The feelings that wrapped themselves around her were so incredible that Carol had to struggle to hold back the tears. With each delicious stroke the tension mounted and slowly, methodically began to uncurl within her until she was thrashing her head against his pillow and arching her hips to meet each plunging thrust.

Steve groaned and threw back his head, struggling to regain control, but soon he, too, was over the edge. When he cried out his voice harmonized with hers in a song that was as ageless as mankind.

Breathless, he collapsed on top of her. Her arms slipped around his neck and she buried her face in the hollow of his throat, kissing him, hugging him, needing him desperately. Tears slipped silently from the corners of her eyes. They spoke the words that she couldn't, eloquently telling him of all the love buried in her heart—words Carol feared she would never be able to voice again.

When Steve moved to lift himself off of her, she

wouldn't let him. She held him tightly, her fingers gripping his shoulders.

"I'm too heavy," he protested.

"No…hold me."

With his arms wrapped around her, he rolled over, carrying her with him in one continuous motion until their positions were reversed.

Content for the moment, Carol pressed her ear over his chest, listening to the strong, steady beat of his heart.

Neither spoke.

His hand moved up and down her spine in a tender caress as though he had to keep touching her to know she was real. Her tears slid onto his shoulder, but neither mentioned it.

In her soul, Carol had to believe that something this beautiful would create a child. At this moment everything seemed perfect and healed between them, the way it had been two years before.

Gently Steve kissed her forehead, and she snuggled closer, flattening her hands over his chest.

He wrapped his arms around her and his thumb tenderly wiped the moisture from her cheek. Tucking his finger under her chin, he lifted it enough to find her mouth and kiss her. Sweetly.

"I tried, but I never could stop loving you," he whispered in a voice raw with emotion. "I hated myself for being so weak, but I don't anymore."

"I'll always love you," she answered. "I can't help myself. This year has been the worst of my entire life. I've felt as if I was trapped in a freezer, never able to get warm."

"No more," he said, his eyes trapping hers.

"No more," she agreed, and her heart leaped with unleashed joy.

They rested for a full hour, their legs entwined, their arms wrapped around each other. Every now and again, Steve would kiss her, his lips playing over hers. Then Carol would kiss him back, darting her tongue in and out of his mouth and doing all the things she knew he enjoyed. She raised herself up on her elbows and brushed a thick swatch of dark hair from his brow. It felt so good to be able to touch him this freely.

"What's the name of that Mexican restaurant you mentioned earlier?" Steve asked.

Carol smiled smugly. "You are so predictable."

"How's that?"

"Making love never fails to make you hungry!"

"True," he growled into her ear, "but often my appetite isn't for food." His index finger circled her nipple, teasing it to a rose-colored pebble. "I've got a year's worth of loving stored up for you, and the way you make me feel tonight, we may never leave this bedroom."

And they didn't.

Carol woke when Steve pressed a soft kiss on her lips.

"Hmm," she said, not opening her eyes. She smiled up at him, sated and unbelievably happy. She wore the look of a woman who loves wisely and who knows that her love is returned. "Is it morning yet?"

"It was morning the last time we made love." Steve laughed and leaned over to kiss her again, as if one sample wasn't nearly enough to satisfy him.

"It was?" she asked lazily. They'd slept intermittently, waking every few hours, holding and kissing each other. While asleep, Carol would roll over and forget Steve was at her side. Their discovery each time was worth far

more than a few semiprecious hours of sleep. And Steve
seemed equally excited about her being there with him.

"Currently," he said, dragging her back to reality,
"it's going on noon."

"Noon!" She bolted upright. She'd been in her teens
the last time she'd slept this late.

"I'm sorry to wake you, honey, but I've got to get
to the sub."

Carol was surprised to see that he was dressed and
prepared to leave. He handed her a fresh cup of coffee, which she readily took from him. "You'll be back,
won't you?"

"Not until tomorrow morning."

"Will you…could you stop off and see me one more
time, before you leave?"

His dark gaze caressed her. "Honest to God, Carol,
I don't think I could stay away."

As Steve walked away from his parked car at the
Navy base in Bangor, less than ten miles north of
Bremerton, he was convinced his strut would put a
rooster to shame. Lord, he felt good.

Carol had come to him, wanted him, loved him as
much as he'd always loved and wanted her. All the world
felt good to him.

For the first time since they'd divorced, he felt whole.
He'd been a crazed fool to harp on the subject of Todd
Larson to Carol. From this moment on, he vowed never
to mention the other man's name again. Obviously whatever had been between the two was over, and she hadn't
wanted Todd back. Okay, so she'd made a mistake. Lord
knew, he'd committed his share, and a lot of them had

to do with Carol. He'd been wrong to think he could flippantly cast her out of his life.

In his pain, he'd lashed out at her, acted like a heel, refused to have anything to do with her because of his foolish pride. But Carol had been woman enough to forgive him. He couldn't do anything less than be man enough to forget the past. The love they shared was too precious to muddy with doubts. They'd both made mistakes, and the time had come to rectify those and learn from them.

Dear God, he felt ready to soar. He shouldn't be on a nuclear submarine—a feeling this good was meant for rockets.

Carol found herself humming as she whipped the cream into a frothy topping for Steve's favorite dessert: French pudding. She licked her index finger, grinned lazily to herself and leaned her hip against the kitchen counter, feeling happier than she could remember being in a long time.

Friday night had been incredible. Steve had been incredible. The only cost had been her bruised pride when she'd arrived at his apartment with such a flimsy excuse. The price had been minor, the rewards major.

Not once during the entire evening had Steve mentioned Todd's name. Maybe, just maybe, he was ready to put that all behind them now.

If she was pregnant from their Friday night lovemaking, which she sincerely prayed she was, it would be best for the baby to know "her" father. Originally Carol had intended to raise the child without Steve. She wasn't sure she would ever have told him. Now the thought of suppressing the information seemed both childish and petty. But she wasn't going to use the baby as a convenient excuse for a reconciliation. They would settle matters first—then she would tell him.

Steve would make a good father; she'd watched him around children and had often been amazed by his patience. He'd wanted a family almost from the first. Carol had been the one who'd insisted on waiting, afraid she wouldn't be able to manage her job, a home and a baby with her husband away so much of the time, although she'd never admitted it to Steve. She knew how important it was for him to believe in her strength and independence. But this past year had matured her. Now she was ready for the responsibility.

Naturally hindsight was twenty-twenty, and she regretted having put off Steve's desire to start a family. The roots of their marriage might have been strong enough to withstand what had happened if there'd been children binding them together. But it did no good to second-guess fate.

Children. Carol hadn't dared think beyond one baby. But if she and Steve were to get back together—something that was beginning to look like a distinct possibility—then they could plan on having a houseful of kids!

It was early afternoon by the time Steve made it to Carol's house. A cold wind from the north whistled through the tops of the trees and the sky was darkening with a brewing storm.

Carol tossed aside her knitting and flew across the room the minute she heard a car door close, knowing it had to be Steve. By the time he was to the porch, she had the front door open for him.

He wore his uniform, which told her he hadn't

stopped off at his apartment to change. Obviously he was eager to see her again, Carol thought, immeasurably pleased.

"I'm glad to see you're waiting for me," he said, and his words formed a soft fog around his mouth. He took the steps two at a time and rubbed his bare hands together.

"I can't believe how cold it is." Carol pulled him inside the house and closed the door.

His gaze sought hers. "Warm me, then."

She didn't require a second invitation, and stood on the tips of her toes to kiss him, leaning her weight into his. Steve wrapped her in his embrace, kissing her back greedily, as if they had been apart six weeks instead of a single day. When he finished, they were both breathless.

"It feels like you missed me."

"I did," she assured him. "Give me your coat and I'll hang it up for you."

He gave her the thick wool jacket and strolled into the living room. "What's this?" he asked, looking at her knitting.

Carol's heart leaped to her throat. "A baby blanket."

"For who?"

"A...friend." She considered herself a friend, so that was at least a half-truth. She'd been working on the blanket in her spare time since before Christmas. It had helped her feel as if she was doing something constructive toward her goal.

Suddenly she felt as if she had a million things to tell him. "I got energetic and cleaned house. I don't know what's wrong with me lately, but I don't have the energy I used to have."

"Have you been sick?"

She loved him for the concern in his voice. "No, I'm in perfect health… I've just been tired lately…not getting enough vitamins, I suppose. But it doesn't matter now because I feel fantastic, full of ambition—I even made you French pudding."

"Carol, I think you should see a doctor."

"And if he advises bed rest, do you promise to, er… rest with me?"

"Good heavens, woman, you've become insatiable."

"I know." She laughed and slipped her arm around his waist. "I was always that way around you."

"Always?" he teased. "I don't seem to recall that."

"Then I'll just have to remind you." She steered him toward the bedroom, crawled onto the mattress and knelt there. "If you want French pudding, fellow, you're going to have to work for it."

The alarm went off at six. Carol blindly reached out and, after a couple of wide swipes, managed to hit the switch that would turn off the electronic beeping.

Steve stirred at her side. "It's time," she said in a small, sad voice. This would be their last morning together for three months.

"It's six already?" Steve moaned.

"I'm afraid so."

He reached for her and brought her close to his side. His hand found hers and he laced her fingers with his. "Carol, listen, we only have a little time left and there's so much I should have said, so much I wanted to tell you."

"I wanted to talk to you, too." In all the years they were married, no parting had been less welcome. Carol yearned to wrap her arms around him and beg him not to leave her. It was times like this that she wished Steve had chosen a career outside the Navy. In a few hours he would sail out of Hood Canal, and she wouldn't hear from him for the entire length of his deployment. Other than hearsay, Carol wasn't even to know where he would be sailing. For reasons of national security, all submarine deployments were regarded as top secret.

"When I return from this tour, Carol, I'd like us to have a serious talk about getting back together. I know I've been a jerk, and you deserve someone better, but I'd like you to think about it while I'm away. Will you do that for me?"

She couldn't believe how close she was to breaking into tears. "Yes," she whispered. "I'll think about it very seriously. I want everything to be right...the second time."

"I do, too." He raised her hand to his mouth and kissed her knuckles. "Another thing...make an appointment for a physical. I don't remember you being this thin."

"I lost fifteen pounds when we were divorced; I can't seem to gain it back." The tears broke through the surface and she sobbed out the words, ending in a hiccup. Embarrassed, she pressed her fingertips over her lips. "I've been a wreck without you, Steve Kyle... I suppose it makes you happy to know how miserable and lonely this past year has been."

"I was just as miserable and lonely," he admitted. "We can't allow anything to do this to us again. I love you too damn much to spend another year like the last one." His touch was so tender, so loving that she melted into his embrace.

"You have to trust me, Steve. I can't have you coming back and even suspecting I'd see another man."

"I know... I do trust you."

She closed her eyes at the relief his words gave her. "Thank you for that."

He kissed her then and, with a reluctance that tore at her heart, pulled away from her and started to dress.

She reached for her robe, not looking at him as she slipped her arms into the long sleeves. "If we do decide to make another go at marriage, I'd like to seriously think about starting a family right away. What would you say to that?"

Steve hesitated. Carol turned around to search out his gaze in the stirring light of early morning, and the tender look he wore melted any lingering doubts she harbored.

"Just picturing you with my child in your arms," he whispered hoarsely, "is enough to keep me going for the next three months."

Six

A week after Steve sailed, Carol began experiencing symptoms that again suggested she was pregnant. The early morning bouts of nausea returned. She found herself weeping over a rerun of *Magnum, P.I.* And she was continually tired, feeling worn-out at the end of the day. Everything she was going through seemed to point in one direction.

Self-diagnosis, however, had misled her a month earlier, and Carol feared her burning desire to bear a child was dictating her body's response a second time.

Each morning she pressed a hand over her stomach and whispered a fervent prayer that her weekend of lovemaking with Steve had found fertile ground. If she wasn't pregnant, then it would be April before they could try again, and that seemed like a thousand years away.

Carol was tempted to hurry out and buy another home pregnancy test. Then she would know almost immediately if her mind was playing tricks on her or if she really was pregnant. But she didn't. She couldn't explain—even to herself—why she was content to wait it out this time. If her monthly cycle was a week late, she decided, then and only then would she make an appointment with her doctor. But until that time she was determined to be strong—no matter what the test results said.

The one thing that astonished Carol the most was that in the time since Steve's deployment she missed him dreadfully. For months she'd done her utmost to drive every memory of that man from her mind, and sometimes she'd succeeded. Since Christmas, however, thoughts of Steve had dominated every waking minute. Until their weekend, Carol had assumed that was only natural. Steve Kyle did play a major role in her scheme to get pregnant. But she considered having a baby more of a bonus now. The possibility of rebuilding her marriage—which she had once considered impossible to do—claimed precedence.

Missing Steve wasn't a new experience. Carol had always felt at loose ends when he was aboard the *Atlantis*. But never had she felt quite like this. Nothing compared to the emotion that wrapped itself around her heart when she thought about Steve on this tour. She missed him so much that it frightened her. For more than a year she'd lived in the house alone; now it felt like an empty shell because he wasn't there. In bed at night her longing for him grew even more intense. She lay with her eyes closed, savoring the memory of their last two nights together. A chill washed over her at how close they'd come to destroying the love between them. The only thing that seemed to lessen this terrible longing she felt for her ex-husband was constructing dreams that involved him to help ease the loneliness as she drifted off to sleep.

Friday morning Carol woke feeling rotten and

couldn't seem to force herself out of bed. She pulled into the huge Boeing parking lot at the Renton plant ten minutes later than usual and hurriedly locked her car. She was walking toward her building, trying to find the energy to rush when she heard someone call out her name.

She turned, but didn't see anyone she recognized.

"Carol, is that you?"

"Lindy?" Carol could hardly believe her eyes. It was Steve's sister. "What are you doing here?"

"I was just about to ask you the same thing."

Lindy looked fantastic. It had been nearly two years since Carol had last seen her former sister-in-law. Lindy had been a senior in college at the time, girlish and fun loving that summer she and Steve had visited his family. Had that been only two summers ago? It felt as though a decade had passed. Lindy had always held a special place in Carol's heart, and she smiled and hugged her close. When she drew back, Carol was surprised at the new maturity Lindy's eyes revealed.

"I work here," Lindy said, squeezing Carol's fingers. "I have since this past summer."

"Me, too—for over a year now."

Lindy tossed the sky a chagrined look. "You mean to tell me we've been employed by the same company, working at the same plant, and we didn't even know it?"

Carol laughed. "It looks that way."

They started walking toward the main entrance, still bemused, laughing and joking like long-lost sisters... which they were of sorts.

"I'm going to kick Steve," Lindy muttered. "He didn't tell me you worked for Boeing."

"He doesn't know. I suppose he assumes I'm still at

Larson's Sporting Goods. I quit...long before the divorce was final. We haven't talked about my job, and I didn't think to mention it."

"How are you?" Lindy asked, but didn't give her more than a second to respond. "Steve growls at me every time I mention your name, which by the way, tells me he's still crazy about you."

Carol needed to hear that. She grinned, savoring the warm feeling Lindy's words gave her. "I'm still crazy about him, too."

"Oh, Carol," Lindy said with a giant sigh. "I can't tell you how glad I am to hear that. Steve never told any of us why the two of you divorced, but it nearly destroyed him. I can't tell you how happy I was when you phoned last Christmas. He hasn't been the same since."

"The divorce was wrong... We should never have gone through with it," Carol said softly. Steve had been the one who had insisted on ending their marriage, and Carol had been too hurt, too confused to fight him the way she should have. Not wanting to linger on the mistakes of the past, Carol added, "Steve told me about you and Rush. Congratulations."

"Thanks." Lindy's eyes softened at the mention of Rush's name, and translucent joy radiated from her smile. "You met Paul, didn't you?"

Carol nodded, recalling the time she had been introduced to Lindy's ex-fiance in Minneapolis. She hadn't been overly impressed by him and, as she recalled, neither had Steve.

"He married...someone else," Lindy explained. "I was devastated, convinced my life was over. That's how I ended up in Seattle. I'm so happy I moved here. Paul did me the biggest favor of my life when he dumped me; I found Rush and we were meant to be together—we both know it."

Hold on to that feeling, Carol mused, saddened that she'd been foolish enough to allow Steve to walk away from her. It had been a mistake, and one they'd both paid for dearly. "I'm really pleased for you, Lindy," she said sincerely.

"Thank you...oh, Carol, I can't tell you how good it is to see you again."

They paused once they passed the security gate, delaying their parting. "What area are you working in?" Carol asked, stopping. The others flooding through the entrance gate walked a wide circle around them.

"Section B."

"F for me." Which meant they were headed in opposite directions.

"Perhaps we could meet for lunch one day," Lindy suggested, anxiously glancing at her watch.

"I'd like that. How about next Tuesday? I can't until then, I'm involved with a special project."

"Great. Call me. I'm on extension 314."

"Will do."

Steve walked past the captain's quarters and through the narrow hallway to his stateroom. Tired, he sat on the edge of his berth and rubbed his hand across his eyes. This was his favorite time of day. His shift was complete, and he had about an hour to kill before he thought about catching some sleep. For the past several days, he'd been writing Carol. His letter had become a journal of his thoughts. Chances were that he would be home long before the letter arrived. Because submarines spent their deployment submerged, there were few opportunities for the pickup or delivery of mail. Any emergencies were handled by radio transmission. There were occasions when they could receive mail, but it wasn't likely to happen this trip.

Steve felt good. From the moment his and Carol's divorce had been declared final, he'd felt as if he'd steered his life off course. He'd experienced the first turbulent storm and, instead of riding it out as he should have, he'd jumped overboard. Ever since, he'd felt out of sync with his inner self.

In his letter, he'd tried to explain that to Carol, but putting it in words had been as difficult as admitting it had been.

He didn't know what had happened between Todd and Carol. Frankly he didn't want to know. Whatever had been between them was over and Steve could have her back. Lord knew he wanted her. He was destined to go to his grave loving that woman.

When he'd sailed out of Hood Canal and into the Pacific Ocean, Steve had felt such an indescribable pull to the land. He loved his job, loved being a part of the Navy, but at that moment he would have surrendered his commission to have been able to stay in Seattle another month.

Although he'd told Carol that they should use this time apart to consider a reconciliation, he didn't need two seconds to know his own mind: he wanted them to remarry.

But first they had to talk, really talk, and not about Todd. There were some deep-rooted insecurities he'd faced the past couple of weeks that needed to be discussed.

One thing that had always bothered Steve was the

fact that Carol had never seemed to need him. His peers continually related stories about how things fell apart at home while they were deployed. Upon their return, after the usual hugs and kisses, their wives handed them long lists of repairs needed around the house or relayed tales of horror they'd been left to deal with in their husband's absence.

Not Carol. She'd sent him off to sea, wearing a bright smile and greeted him with an identical one on his return. The impression she gave him was that it was great when he was home, but was equally pleasant if he wasn't.

Her easy acceptance of his life-style both pleased and irritated Steve. He appreciated the strength of her personality, and yet a small part of him wished she weren't quite so strong. He wasn't looking for a wife who was a clinging vine, but occasionally he wished for something less than Carol's sturdy oak-tree character. Just once he would have liked to hear her tell him how dreadful the weeks had been without him, or how she'd wished he'd been there to take care of the broken dryer or to change the oil in the car.

Instead she'd given him the impression that she'd been having a grand ol' time while he was at sea. She chatted about the classes she took, or how her herb garden was coming along. If he quizzed her about any problems, she brushed off his concern and assured him she'd already dealt with whatever turned up.

Steve knew Carol wasn't that involved in the navy-wife activities. He figured it was up to her whether or not she joined. He hadn't pressed her, but he had wished she would make the effort to form friendships with the wives of his close friends.

Carol's apparent strength wasn't the only thing that troubled Steve, but it was one thing he felt they needed to discuss. The idea of telling his ex-wife that the least she could do was shed a few tears when he sailed away from her made him feel ungrateful. But swallowing his pride would be a small price to pay to straighten matters between them.

What she'd said about wanting a baby right away made him feel soft inside every time he thought about it. He'd yearned for them to start a family long before now, but Carol had always wanted to wait. Now she appeared eager. He didn't question her motivation. He was too damned grateful.

A knock on his door jerked his attention across the room. "Yes?"

Seaman Layle stepped forward. "The Captain would like to see you, sir."

Steve nodded and said, "I'll be right there."

Carol sat at the end of the examination table, holding a thin piece of tissue over her lap. The doctor would be in any minute to give her the news she'd been waiting to hear for the past month. Okay, so her period was two weeks late. There could be any number of reasons. For one thing, she'd been under a good deal of stress lately. For another…

Her thoughts came to a grinding halt as Dr. Stewart stepped into the room. His glasses were perched on the end of his nose and his brow compressed as he read over her chart.

"Well?" she asked, unable to disguise the trembling eagerness in her voice.

"Congratulations, Carol," he said, looking up with a grandfatherly smile. "You're going to be a mother."

Seven

Carol was almost afraid to believe what Dr. Stewart was telling her; her hand flew to her heart. "You mean, I'm pregnant?"

The doctor looked up at her over the edge of his bifocals. "This is a surprise?"

"Oh, no... I knew—or at least I thought I knew." The joy that bubbled through her was unlike anything she had ever known. Ready tears blurred her vision and she bit her lower lip to hold back the tide that threatened to overwhelm her.

The doctor took her hand and gently patted it. "You're not sure how you feel—is that it?"

"Of course I do," she said, in a voice half an octave higher than usual. "I'm so happy I could just..."

"Cry?" he inserted.

"Dance," she amended. "This is the most wonderful thing that's ever happened to me since..."

"Your high-school prom?"

"Since I got married. I'm divorced now, but... Steve, he's my ex-husband, will marry me again...at least, I think he will. I'm not going to tell him about this right away. I don't want him to marry me again just because of the baby. I won't say a word about this. Or maybe I should? I don't know what to do, but thank you, Doctor, thank you so much."

A fresh smile began to form at the edges of his mouth. "You do whatever you think is best. Now, before we discuss anything else I want to go over some key points with you."

"Oh, of course, I'll do anything you say. I'll quit smoking and give up junk food, and take vitamins. If you really think it's necessary, I'll try to eat liver once a week."

His gaze reviewed her chart. "It says here you don't smoke."

"No, I don't, but I'd start just so I could quit if it would help the baby."

He chuckled. "I don't think that will be necessary, young lady."

Carol reached for his hand and pumped it several times. "I can't tell you how happy you've made me."

Still chuckling, the white-haired doctor said, "Tell me the same thing when you're in labor and I'll believe you."

Carol watched as Lindy entered the restaurant and paused to look around. Feeling a little self-conscious, she raised her hand. Lindy waved back and headed across the floor, weaving her way through the crowded tables.

"Hi. Sorry, I'm late."

"No problem." The extra time had given Carol a chance to study the menu. Her stomach had been so finicky lately that she had to be careful what she ate.

This being pregnant was serious business and already the baby had made it clear "she" wasn't keen on particular foods—especially anything with tomatoes.

"Everything has been so hectic lately," Lindy said, picking up the menu, glancing at it and setting it aside almost immediately.

"That was quick," Carol commented, nodding her head toward the menu.

"I'm a woman who knows my own mind."

"Good for you," Carol said, swallowing a laugh. "What are you having?"

"I don't know. What are you ordering?"

"Soup and a sandwich," Carol answered, not fooled. Lindy wasn't interested in eating, she wanted answers. Steve's sister had been bursting with questions from the moment they'd met in the Boeing parking lot.

"Soup and a sandwich sounds good to me," Lindy said, obviously not wanting to waste time with idle chit-chat.

Shaking her head, Carol studied Lindy. "Okay, go ahead and ask. I know you're dying to fire away."

Lindy unfolded the napkin and took pains spreading it over her lap. "Steve didn't come home Christmas Eve… Well, he did, but it was early in the morning, and ever since that night he's been whistling 'Dixie.'" She paused and grinned. "Yet every time I said your name, he barked at me to mind my own business."

"We've seen each other since Christmas, too."

"You have?" Lindy pinched her lips together and sadly shook her head. "That brother of mine is so tight-lipped, I can't believe the two of us are related!"

Carol laughed. Unwittingly Lindy had pinpointed the crux of Carol and Steve's marital problems. They were each private people who preferred to keep problems inside rather than talking things out the way they should.

"So you've seen Steve since Christmas," Lindy prompted. "He must have contacted you after Rush and I moved."

"Actually I was the one who went to him."

"You did? Great."

"Yes." Carol nodded, blushing a little at the memory of how they'd spent that weekend. "It *was* great."

"Well, don't keep me in suspense here. Are you two going to get back together or what?"

"I think it's the 'or what.'"

"Oh." Lindy's gaze dropped abruptly and she frowned. "I don't mind telling you, I'm disappointed to hear that. I'd hoped you two would be able to work things out."

"We're heading in that direction, so don't despair. Steve and I are going to talk about a reconciliation when he returns."

"Oh, Carol, that's wonderful!"

"I think so, too."

"You two always seemed so right together. The first time I saw Steve after you were divorced, I could hardly recognize him. He was so cynical and unhappy. He'd sit around the apartment and watch television for hours, or stare out the window."

"Steve did?" Carol couldn't imagine that. Steve always had so many things going—he'd never taken the time to relax when they were living together. Another problem had been that they didn't share enough of the same interests. Carol blamed herself for that, but she was willing to compromise now that her marriage was about to have new life breathed into it.

"I wasn't joking when I told you he's been miserable. I don't know what prompted you to contact him at Christmastime, but I thank God you did."

Carol smoothed her hand across her abdomen and smiled almost shyly. "I'm glad I did, too."

Steve's letter to Carol was nearly fifty pages in length now. The days, as they often did aboard a submarine, blended together. It felt as if they were six months into this cruise instead of two, but his eagerness to return to Carol explained a good deal of this interminable feeling.

Carol. His heart felt as though it would melt inside his chest every time he thought about her mentioning a baby. The first thing he was going to do after they'd talked was throw out her birth control pills. And then he was going to take her to bed and make slow, easy love to her.

Once he had her back, he wasn't going to risk losing her again.

In the past two months, Steve had made another decision. They needed to clear the air about Todd Larson. He'd promised her that he wouldn't mention the other man's name again, but he had to, just once, and then it would be finished. Laid to rest forever.

Finding Todd in their shower hadn't been the only thing that had led Steve to believe Carol and her employer were having an affair. There had been plenty of other clues. Steve just hadn't recognized them in the beginning.

For one, she'd been working a lot of overtime, and didn't seem to be getting paid for it. At first Steve hadn't given it much credence, although he'd been angry that

often she couldn't see him off to sea properly. At the
time, however, she'd seemed as sorry about it as he was.

His return home after a ten-week absence had been
the real turning point. Until that tour, Carol had always
been eager to make love after so many weeks apart.
Normally they weren't in the house ten minutes before
they found themselves in the bedroom. But not that
time. Carol had greeted him with open arms, but she'd
seemed reluctant to hurry to bed. He had gotten what he
wanted, but fifteen minutes later she'd made some silly
excuse about needing groceries and had left the house.

None of these events had made much sense at the
time. Steve had suspected something might be wrong,
but he hadn't known how to ask her, how to approach
her without sounding like an insecure schoolboy. Soon
afterward he'd flown east for a two-week communication class. It was when he'd arrived home unexpectedly
early that he'd found Carol and Todd together.

The acid building up in his stomach seemed to explode with pain and Steve took in several deep breaths
until the familiar ache passed. All these months he'd allowed Carol to believe he'd condemned her solely because he'd discovered another man in their home. It
was more than that, much more, and it was time he
freed his soul.

"Carol? Are you here?"

Carol remained sitting on the edge of the bathtub
and pressed her hand over her forehead. "I'm in here."
Her voice sounded weak and sick—which was exactly
how she felt. The doctor had given her a prescription
to help ease these dreadful bouts of morning sickness,
but it didn't seem to be doing much good.

"Carol?" Once more Lindy's voice vibrated down the hallway and Carol heard the sound of approaching footsteps. "Carol, what's wrong? Should I call a doctor?"

"No...no, I'll be fine in a minute. My stomach has been a little queasy lately, is all."

"You look awful."

"I can't look any worse than I feel." Her feeble attempt at humor apparently didn't impress Lindy.

"I take it the sale at the Tacoma Mall doesn't interest you?"

"I tried to call," Carol explained, "but you'd already left. You go ahead without me."

"I'll do no such thing," Lindy answered vehemently. "You need someone to take care of you. When was the last time you had a decent meal?"

Carol pressed her hand over her stomach. "Please, don't even mention food."

"Sorry."

Lindy helped her back into a standing position and led her down the hallway to her bedroom. Carol was ashamed to have Steve's sister see the house when it looked as if a cyclone had gone through it, but she'd had so little energy lately. Getting to work and home again drained her. She went to bed almost immediately after dinner and woke up exhausted the next morning.

No one had told her being pregnant could be so demanding on her health. She'd never felt more sickly in her life. Her appointment with Dr. Stewart wasn't for another two weeks, but something had to be done. She couldn't go on like this much longer.

The April sun seemed to smile down on Steve as he stepped off the *Atlantis*. He paused and breathed in the glorious warmth of afternoon in the Pacific Northwest. Carol wouldn't be waiting for him, he knew. She had no way of knowing when he docked.

But she needn't come to him. He was going to her. The minute he got home, showered and shaved, he was driving over to her house. He was so ready for this.

They were going to talk, make love and get married. Maybe not quite that simply, but close.

He picked up his mail and let himself into the apartment. Standing beside the phone, he listened to the messages on his answering machine. Three were from Lindy, who insisted he call first thing when he returned home.

He reached for the phone while he flipped through his assorted mail.

"You rang?" he asked cheerfully, when his sister answered.

"Steve? I'm so glad you called."

"What's wrong? Has Rush decided he's made a terrible mistake and decided to give you back to your dear, older brother to straighten out?" His sister didn't have an immediate comeback or a scathing reply, which surprised him.

"Steve, it's Carol."

His blood ran cold with fear. "What happened?"

"I don't know, but I wanted to talk to you before you went to see her," she said and hesitated. "You were planning on going there right away, weren't you?"

"Yes. Now tell me what's the matter with Carol."

"She's been sick."

"How sick?" His heart was thundering against his chest with worry.

"I...don't think it's anything...serious, but I thought I should warn you before you surprise her with a visit.

She's lost weight and looks terrible, and she'll never forgive you if you show up without warning her you're in town."

"Has she seen a doctor?"

"I...don't know," Lindy confessed. "She won't talk about it."

"What the hell could be wrong?"

The line seemed to vibrate with electricity. "If you want the truth, I suspect she's pregnant."

Eight

"**P**regnant?" Steve repeated and the word boomeranged against the walls of his mind with such force that the mail he'd been sorting slipped from his fingers and fell to the floor. He said it again. "Pregnant. But…but…"

"I probably shouldn't have said anything." Lindy's soft voice relayed her confusion. "But honestly, Steve, I've been so worried about her. She looks green around the gills and she's much too thin to be losing so much weight. I told her she should see a doctor, but she just smiles and says there's nothing to worry about."

The wheels in Steve's mind were spinning fast. "The best thing I can do is talk to her, and find out what's happening."

"Do that, but for heaven's sake be gentle with her. She's too fragile for you to come at her like Hulk Hogan."

"I wouldn't do that."

"Steve, I'm your sister. I know you!"

"Okay, okay. I'll talk to you later." He hung up the phone but kept his hand on the receiver while he mulled over his sister's news. Carol had said she wanted to have a baby, and she knew how he felt about the subject. He'd longed for a family since the first year they were together.

However, they weren't married now. No problem. Getting remarried was a minor detail. All he had to do was talk to the chaplain and make the arrangements. And if what Lindy said was true, the sooner he saw the chaplain, the better.

Without forethought he jerked the receiver off the hook and jabbed out Carol's number with his index finger. After two rings, he decided this kind of discussion was better done in person.

He showered, changed clothes and was halfway out the door when he remembered what Lindy had said about letting Carol know he was coming. Good idea.

He marched back over to the phone and dialed her number one more time.

No answer.

"Damn." He started pacing the floor, feeling restless, excited and nervous. He couldn't stay in the apartment; the walls felt as if they were closing in on him. He'd spent the last three months buried in the belly of a nuclear submarine and hadn't experienced a twinge of claustrophobia. Twenty minutes inside his apartment, knowing what he now did, and he was going ape.

He had to get out there even if it meant parking outside Carol's house and waiting for her to return.

He rushed out to his car and was grateful when it started right away after sitting for three months.

He was going to be a father! His heart swelled with joy and he experienced such a sense of elation that he wanted to throw back his head and shout loud enough to bring down brick walls.

A baby. His and Carol's baby. His throat thickened with emotion, and he had to swallow several times to keep from breaking down and weeping right there on the freeway. A new life. They were going to bring a tiny little being into this world and be accountable for every aspect of the infant's life. The responsibility seemed awesome. His hands gripped the steering wheel and he sucked in a huge breath as he battled down his excitement and fears.

He was going to be a good father. Always loving and patient. Everything would be right for his son…or daughter. Male chauvinist that he was, he yearned for a son. They could have a daughter the second time, but the thought of Carol giving him a boy felt right in his mind.

But he had so much to learn, so much to take care of. First things first. Steve tried to marshal his disjointed thoughts. He had to see to Carol's health. If this pregnancy was as hard on her as Lindy implied, then he wanted Carol to quit her job. He made good money; she should stay home and build up her strength.

The drive to Carol's house took less than fifteen minutes, and when Steve pulled up and parked he noticed her car in the driveway with the passenger door opened. His heart felt like it was doing jumping jacks, he was so eager to see her.

The front door opened and Carol stepped outside and to her car, grabbing a bag of groceries.

"Carol." She hadn't seen him.

She turned abruptly at the sound of her name. "Steve," she cried out brokenly and dropped the brown shopping bag. Without the least bit of hesitation, she came flying across the lawn.

He met her halfway, and wrapping his arms around

her waist, he closed his eyes to the welcome feel of her body against his. His happiness couldn't be contained and he swung her around. Her lips were all over his face, kissing him, loving him, welcoming him.

Steve drank in her love and it humbled him. He held her gently, fearing he would hurt her, and kissed her with an aching tenderness, his mouth playing over the dewy softness of hers.

His hands captured her face and her deep blue eyes filled with tears as she smiled tremulously at him. "I've missed you so much. These have been the longest three months of my life."

"Mine, too." His voice nearly choked, and he kissed her again in an effort to hide the tide of emotion he was experiencing.

Steve picked up the scattered groceries for her and they walked into the house together.

"Go ahead and put those in the kitchen. Are you hungry?"

She seemed nervous and flittered from one side of the room to the other.

"I could fix you something if you'd like," she suggested, her back braced against the kitchen counter.

Steve's eyes held hers, and the emotion that had rocked him earlier built with intensity every minute he was in her presence. "You know what I want," he whispered, hardly able to speak.

Carol relaxed, and blushed a little. "I want to make love with you so much."

He held his hands out to her and she walked toward him, locking her arms around his neck. She pressed her weight against him and Steve realized how slender she was, how fragile. Regret slammed into his chest with all the force of a wrecking ball against a concrete wall. She was nurturing his child within her womb, for God's sake, and all he could think about was getting her into bed. He hadn't even asked her how she was feeling. All he cared about was satisfying his own selfish lusts.

"Carol…" His breath was slow and labored. Gently he tried to break free, because he couldn't think straight when she was touching him.

"Hmm?" Her hands were already working at his belt buckle, and her mouth was equally busy.

He felt himself weakening. "Are you sure? I mean, if you'd rather not…"

She released his zipper and when her hands closed around his naked hardness, he thought he would faint. His eyes rolled toward the ceiling. "Don't…don't you think we should talk?" he managed to say.

"No."

"But—"

She broke away and looked up at him, her eyes hungry with demand. "Steven Kyle, what is your problem? Do you or do you not want to make love?"

"I think…we should probably talk first. Don't you?" He didn't know if she would take him seriously with his voice shaking the way it was.

She grinned, and when her gaze dropped to below his waistline, they rounded. "No. Because neither one of us is going to be able to say anything worth listening to until we take care of other things…"

It wasn't possible to love a woman any more than he did Carol at that moment, Steve thought. She reached for his hand and led him out of the kitchen and into the bedroom.

Like a lost sheep, he followed.

* * *

The newborn moon cast silvery shadows on the wall opposite the bed, and Steve sighed, feeling sated and utterly content. Carol slept at his side, her arm draped around his middle and her face nestled against his shoulder. Her tousled hair fell over his chest and he ran his fingers through it, letting the short, silky length slip through his hands.

Gently he brushed a blond curl off her cheek and twisted his head so that he could kiss her temple. She stirred and sighed in her sleep. He grinned. If he searched for a hundred years he would never find a woman who could satisfy him the way Carol did.

They hadn't talked, hadn't done anything but make love until they were both so exhausted that sleep dominated their minds. They may not have voiced the words, but the love between them was so secure it would take more than a bulldozer to rock it this time. Steve may not have had a chance to say the words, but his heart had been speaking them from the minute Carol had led him to bed.

Bringing the blanket more securely over her shoulders, he wrapped his arm around her and studied her profile in the fading moonlight. What Lindy told him was true. Carol had lost weight; she was as slender as a bamboo shoot, and much too pale. She needed someone to take care of her and, he vowed in his heart, he would be the one.

He almost wished she would roll over so that he could place his hand on her abdomen and feel for himself the life that was blossoming there. He felt weak with happiness every time he thought about their baby. He closed his eyes at the sudden longing that seared through his blood.

Carol hadn't yet told him that she was pregnant but he was sure she would in the morning. Until then, he would be content.

He closed his eyes and decided to sleep.

Steve woke first. Carol didn't so much as stir when he climbed out of bed and reached for his clothes. Silently he tiptoed out of the room and gently closed the door. She needed her sleep.

He made himself a pot of coffee and piddled around the kitchen, putting away the groceries that had been sitting on the counter all night. He pulled open the vegetable bin and carelessly tossed a head of lettuce in there. The drawer refused to close and he discovered the problem to be a huge shriveled up sweet potato. He took it out and, with an over the head loop shot Michael Jordan would have envied, tossed it into the garbage.

Carol and sweet potatoes. Honestly. The last time he'd looked inside her refrigerator, it had been filled with the stuff in every imaginable form.

He supposed he should get used to that kind of thing. It was a well-known fact that women often experienced weird food cravings when they were pregnant. Sweet potatoes were only one step above pickles and ice cream.

Just a minute! That had been last Christmas…before Christmas.

Steve's heart seemed to stop and slowly he straightened. Chewing on the inside of his lip, he closed the refrigerator door. Carol had been stuffing down the sweet potatoes long before he'd accepted her dinner invitation. Weeks before, from the look of it.

His thoughts in chaos, he stumbled into the living

room and slumped into the chair. An icy chill settled over him. No. He refused to believe it, refused to condemn her on anything so flimsy. Then his gaze fell on a pair of knitting needles. He reached for her pattern book and noted the many designs for infant wear.

His heart froze. The last time he'd been by the house, Carol had been knitting a baby blanket. When he'd asked her about it, she'd told him it was for a friend. His snort of laughter was mirthless. Sure, Carol! More lies, more deceit.

And come to think of it, on Christmas Eve she'd pushed her knitting aside so that he couldn't see it. She'd been knitting the *same* blanket for the *same* friend then, too.

He was still stewing when Carol appeared. She smiled at him so sweetly as she slipped her arms into her robe.

"Morning," she said with a yawn.

"Morning."

His gruffness must have stopped her. "Is something wrong?"

Such innocent eyes… She'd always been able to fool him with that look. No more.

"Steve?"

"You're pregnant, aren't you?"

She released her breath in a long, slow sigh. "I wondered if you'd guess. I suppose I should have told you right away, but…we got sidetracked, didn't we?"

He could hardly stand to look at her.

"You're not angry, are you?" she asked, her eyes suddenly reflecting uncertainty.

Again such innocence, such skill. "No, I suppose not."

"Oh, good," she said with a feeble smile, "you had me worried there for a minute."

"One question?"

"Sure."

"Just whose baby is it?"

Nine

"Whose baby is it?" Carol repeated, stunned. She couldn't believe Steve would dare to ask such a question when the answer was so obvious.

"That's what I want to know."

His face was drawn extremely tight—almost menacing. She moved into the room and sat across from him, her heart ready to explode with dread. She met his look squarely, asking no quarter, giving none. The prolonged moment magnified the silence.

"I'm three months pregnant. This child is yours," she said, struggling to keep her voice even.

"Don't lie to me, Carol. I'm not completely dense." The anger that seeped into his expression was fierce enough to frighten her. Steve vaulted to his feet and started pacing in military fashion, each step precise and clipped, as if the drill would put order to his thoughts and ultimately to his life.

Carol's fingernails dug into the fabric on the sides of the overstuffed chair and her pulse went crazy. Her expression, however, revealed none of the inner turmoil she was experiencing. When her throat felt as if it would cooperate with her tongue, she spoke. "How can you even think such a thing?"

Steve splayed his fingers and jerked them through his hair in an action that seemed savage enough to yank it out by the roots. "I should have known something was wrong when you first contacted me at Christmastime."

Carol felt some color flush into her cheeks; to her regret it probably convinced Steve she was as guilty as he believed.

"That excuse about not wanting to spend Christmas alone was damn convenient. And if that wasn't obvious enough, your little seduction scene should have been. God knows, I fell for it." He whirled around to face her. "You did plan that, didn't you?"

"I… I…"

"Didn't you?" he repeated, in harsh tones that demanded the truth.

Miserable and confused, Carol nodded. She had no choice but to admit to her scheme of seducing him.

One corner of his mouth curved up in a half smile, but there was no humor or amusement in the action. The love that had so recently shone from his eyes had been replaced by condemnation.

"If only you would let me explain." She tried again, shocked by this abrupt turn of events. Only a few hours before, they'd lain in each other's arms and spoken of a reconciliation. The promise that had sprung to life between them was wilting and she was powerless to stop it.

"What could you possibly say that would change the facts?" he demanded. "I was always a fool when it came to you. Even after a year apart I hadn't completely come to terms with the divorce and you, no doubt, knew that and used it to your advantage."

"Steve, I—"

"It's little wonder," he continued, not allowing her to finish speaking, "that you considered me that perfect patsy for this intrigue. You used my love for you against me."

"Okay, so I planned our lovemaking Christmas Eve. You're right about that. I suppose I was pretty obvious about the whole thing when you think about it. But I had a reason. A damn good one."

"Yes, I know."

Carol hadn't realized a man's eyes could be so cold. "What do you know?" she asked.

"That cake you're baking in your oven isn't mine."

"Oh, honestly, Steve. Your paranoia is beginning to wear a little thin. I'm doing my damnedest to keep my cool here, but you're crazy if you think anyone else could be the father."

He raised his index finger. "You're good. You know that? You're really very good. That fervent look about you, as though I'm going off the deep end to even suspect you of such a hideous deed. Just the right amount of indignation while keeping your anger in check. Good, very good."

"Stop that," she shouted. "You're being ridiculous. When you get in this mood, nothing appeases you. Everything I say becomes suspect."

His hand wiped his face free of expression. "If I didn't know better, I could almost believe you."

She hated it when Steve was like this. He was so convinced he was right that no amount of arguing would ever persuade him otherwise. "I'm going to tell you one last time, and then I won't say it again. Not ever. We—as in you and I, Steve—are going to have a baby."

Steve stared at her for so long that she wasn't sure what he was thinking. He longed to believe her—she could recognize that yearning in his eyes—and yet something held him back. His Adam's apple moved up and down, and he clenched his jaw so tightly that the sides of his face went white. Still the inner struggle continued while he glared at her, as if commanding the truth—as if to say he could deal with anything as long as it was true.

Carol met that look, holding her gaze as steady and sure as was humanly possible. He wanted the truth, and she'd already given it to him. Nothing she could say would alter the facts: he was her baby's father.

Steve then turned his back on her. "The problem is, I desperately want to believe you. I'd give everything I've managed to accumulate in this life to know that baby was mine."

Everything about Steve, the way he stood with his shoulders hunched, his feet braced as if he expected a blow, told Carol he didn't believe her. Her integrity was suspect.

"I...my birthday—I was thirty," she said, faltering as she scrambled to make him recognize the truth. "It hit me then that my childbearing years were numbered. Since the divorce I've been so lonely, so unhappy, and I thought a baby would help fill the void in my life."

He turned to look at her as she spoke, then closed his eyes and nodded.

Just looking at the anguish in his face was almost more than Carol could bear. "I know you never believed me about Todd, but there's only been one lover in my life, and that's you. I figured that you owed me a baby. I thought if I invited you to spend Christmas with me and you accepted, that I could probably steer us into the bedroom. None of the problems we had in our marriage had extended there."

"Carol, don't—this isn't necessary. I already know you were—"

"Yes, it is. Please, Steve, you've got to listen to me. You've got to understand."

He turned away from her again, but Carol continued talking because it was the only thing left for her to do. If she didn't tell him now, there might never be another chance.

"I didn't count on anything more happening between us. I'd convinced myself I was emotionally separated from you by that time and all I needed was the baby…"

"You must have been worried when I didn't fall into your scheme immediately."

"What do you mean?" Carol felt frantic and helpless.

"I didn't immediately suggest we get back together— that must have had you worried. After Christmas Eve we decided to leave things as they were." He walked away from her, but not before she saw the tilt of righteous indignation in his profile. "That visit to my apartment…what was your excuse? Ah yes, a button you'd found and thought might be mine. Come on, Carol, you should have been more original than that. As excuses go, that's about as flimsy as they get."

"All right, if you want me to admit I planned that seduction scene, too, then I will. I didn't get pregnant the way I planned in December… I had to try again. You had to know swallowing my pride and coming to you wasn't easy."

He nodded. "No, I don't suppose it was."

"Then you believe me?"

"No."

Carol hung her head in frustration.

"Naturally only one night of lovemaking wasn't enough," he said with a soft denunciation. "It made sense to plan more than one evening together in case I started questioning matters later. I'm pleased that you did credit me with some intelligence. Turning up pregnant after one time together would have seemed much too convenient. But twice… Well, that sounds far more likely."

Carol was speechless. Once more Steve had tried and found her guilty, choosing to believe the worst possible scenario.

"Fool that I am, I should have known something was up by how docile and loving you were. So willing to forget the past, forgive and go on with the future. Then there was all that talk about us starting a family. That sucked me right in, didn't it? You know, you've always known how much I want children."

"There's nothing I can say, is there?"

"No," he admitted bleakly. "I wonder what you would have told me next summer when you gave birth—although months premature, astonishingly the baby would weigh six or seven pounds and obviously be full term. Don't you think I would have questioned you then?"

She kept her mouth shut, refusing to be drawn into this kind of degrading verbal battle. From experience she knew nothing she could say would vindicate her.

"If you don't want to claim this child, Steve, that's fine, the loss is yours. My original intent was to raise her alone anyway. I'd thought… I'd hoped we could build a new life together, but it's obvious I was wrong."

"Dead wrong. I won't let you make a fool of me a second time."

A strained moment passed before Carol spoke, and when she did her voice was incredibly weak. "I think it would be best if you left now."

He answered her with an abrupt nod, turned away and went to her bedroom to retrieve his shirt and shoes.

Carol didn't follow him. She sat, feeling numb and growing more ill with each minute. The nausea swelled up inside her until she knew she was going to empty her stomach. Standing, she rushed into the bathroom and leaned over the toilet in a ritual that had become all too familiar.

When she'd finished, she discovered Steve waiting in the doorway, watching her. She didn't know how long he'd been there.

"Are you all right?"

She nodded, not looking at him, wanting him to leave so that she could curl into a tight ball and lick her wounds. No one could hurt her the way Steve did. No other man possessed the power.

He didn't seem to believe she was going to be fine, and slowly he came into the bathroom. He wet a washcloth and handed it to her, waiting while she wiped her face. Then, gently, he led her back into the bedroom and to the bed. Carol discovered that lying down did seem to ease the dizzy, sick feeling.

Steve took his own sweet time buttoning his shirt, apparently stalling so that he could stick by her in case she was sick a second time, although she knew he would never have admitted he cared. If she'd had the energy, Carol would have suggested he go, because for every minute he lingered it was more difficult for her to bear

seeing him. She didn't want him to care about her—
how could he when he believed the things he did? And
yet, every now and again she would find him watching
her guardedly, his eyes filled with worry.

"When do you see the doctor next?" He walked
around the foot of the bed and resumed an alleged search
for his socks.

"Two weeks." Her voice was faint and barely audible.

"Don't you think you should give him a call sooner?"

"No." She refused to look at him.

Steve apparently found what he wanted. He sat on
the edge of the mattress and slowly, methodically put
on his shoes. "How often does this sort of thing happen?" he asked next.

"It doesn't matter." Some of her energy returned, and
she tested her strength by sitting up. "Listen, Steve, I
appreciate your concern, but it just isn't necessary. My
baby and I are going to be just fine."

He didn't look convinced. His brooding gaze revealed his thoughts, and when he looked at her, his expression softened perceptibly. It took a moment for his
eyes to drop to her hand, which rested on her abdomen.

The change that came over him was a shock. His
face tightened and his mouth thinned. A surge of anger
shot through her. "You don't want to claim our daughter, then it's your loss."

"The baby isn't mine."

The anguish in his voice was nearly Carol's undoing.
She bit her lower lip and shook her head with mounting despair. "I can't believe you're actually saying that.
But you'll never know, will you, Steve? All your life
you're going to be left wondering. If she has dark eyes
like yours and dark hair, that will only complicate your

doubts. No doubt the Kyle nose will make you all the more suspicious. Someday you're going to have to face the fact that you've rejected your own child. If you can live with that, then so be it."

He twisted around and his fists were knotted into tight fists. "You were pregnant at Christmas and you're trying to pawn this pregnancy off on me."

"That is the most insulting thing you've ever said to me."

He didn't answer her for a long time. "You've insulted my intelligence. I may have loved you, but I'm not a blind fool."

"They don't come any blinder."

"Explain the milk?"

"What?" Carol hadn't a clue to what he was talking about.

"At Christmas, after we'd made love, we had a snack. Remember?"

Carol did.

"You poured yourself a glass of milk and I commented because you used to dislike it. We were married five years and the only time I can remember you having milk was with cold cereal. You could live your whole life without the stuff. All of a sudden you're drinking it by the glassful."

With deliberate calm Carol rolled her gaze toward the ceiling. "Talk about flimsy excuses. You honestly mean to say you're rejecting your own child because I drank a glass of milk an entire month before I was pregnant?"

"That isn't everything. I saw your knitting Christmas Eve, although you tried to hide it from me. Later, I asked you about it and you claimed it was a baby blanket. It was the same piece you were working on at Christmas, wasn't it?"

"Yes, but..."

"That blanket's for your baby isn't it, Carol? There never was any friend."

Frustration mounting in volcanic proportions, she yelled, "All right, it wasn't for any friend—that's what you want to hear."

"And then there were the sweet potatoes. Good God, you had six containers full of yams that night...pregnant women are said to experience silly cravings. And that's what it was, wasn't it—a craving?"

Standing, Carol felt the weight of defeat settle on her shoulders. No amount of arguing would change anything now. Steve had reasoned everything out in his own mind and found her answers lacking. There was no argument she could give him that would change what he'd already decided.

"Well?" he demanded. "Explain those things away, if you can."

She felt as if she were going to burst into helpless tears at any second. For six years she'd loved this man and given him the power to shatter her heart. "You're the only man I know who can put two and two together and come up with five, Steve," she said wearily.

"For God's sake, quit lying. Quit trying to make me doubt what's right before my eyes. You wanted to trick me into believing that baby is mine, and by God, it almost worked."

If he didn't leave soon, Carol was going to throw him out. "I think you should leave."

"Admit it!" he shouted.

Nothing less would satisfy him. She slapped her

hands against her thighs and feigned a sorrowful sigh. "I guess you're just too smart for me. I should have known better than to try to fool you."

Steve turned and marched to the front door, but stopped, his hand gripping the knob. "What's he going to do about it?"

"Who?"

"Todd."

It took every dictate of Carol's control not to scream that her former employer had nothing to do with her being pregnant. "I don't have anything more to say to you."

"Is he going to divorce Joyce and marry you?"

With one hand cradled around her middle, Carol pointed to the door with the other.

"I have a right to know," Steve argued. "If he isn't going to help you, something should be done."

"I don't need anything—especially from you."

"As much as I'd like to walk away from you, I can't. If you find yourself in trouble, call me. I'll always be there for you."

"If you want to help me, then get out of my life. This baby is mine and mine alone." There was no anger in her words; her voice was low and controlled...and sad, unbelievably sad.

Steve hesitated and his lingering seemed to imply that something would change. Carol knew otherwise.

"Goodbye, Steve."

He paused, then whispered, "Goodbye."

The pain in his voice would haunt her all her days, she thought, as Steve turned and walked out of her life.

The loud pounding noise disrupted Steve's restless slumber and he sat up and glared at the front door of his apartment.

"Who is it?" he shouted, and the sound of his own voice sent shooting pains through his temple. He moaned, tried to sit up and in the process nearly fell off the sofa.

"Steve, I know you're in there. Open up."

Lindy. Damn, he should have known it would be his meddling sister. He wished to hell she would just leave him alone. He'd managed to put her off for the past week, avoiding talking to her, inventing excuses not to see her. Obviously that hadn't been good enough because here she was!

"Go away," he said, his voice less loud this time. "I'm sick." That at least was the truth. His head felt like someone had used it for batting practice.

"I have my own key and I'll use it unless you open this door right now."

Muttering under his breath, Steve weaved across the floor until he reached the door. The carpet seemed to pitch and roll like a ship tossed about in a storm. He unbolted the lock and stepped aside so Lindy could let herself in. He knew she was about to parade into his apartment like an angel of mercy prepared to save him from hell and damnation.

He was right.

Lindy came into the room with the flourish of a suffragette marching for equality of the sexes. She stopped in the middle of the room, hands placed righteously on her hips, and studied him as though viewing the lowest form of human life. Then slowly she began to shake her head with obvious disdain.

"You look like hell," she announced.

Steve almost expected bugles to follow her decree. "Thank you, Mother Theresa."

"Sit down before you fall down."

Steve did as she ordered simply because he didn't have the energy to argue. "Would you mind not talking so loud?"

With one hand remaining on her hip, Lindy marched over to the window and pulled open the drapes.

Steve squinted under the force of the sunlight and shaded his eyes. "Was that really necessary?"

"Yes." She walked over to the coffee table and picked up an empty whiskey bottle, as though by touching it she was exposing herself to an incurable virus. With her nose pointed toward the ceiling, she walked into the kitchen and tossed it in the garbage. The bottle made a clanking sound as it hit against other bottles.

"How long do you intend to keep yourself holed up like this?" she demanded.

He shrugged. "As long as it takes."

"Steve, for heaven's sake be reasonable."

"Why?"

She couldn't seem to find an answer and that pleased him because he wasn't up to arguing with her. He knew there was a reason to get up, get dressed and eat, but he hadn't figured out what it was yet. He'd taken a week of leave in order to spend time with Carol. Now he would give anything to have to report to duty—anything to take his mind off his ex-wife.

His mouth felt like a sand dune had shifted there while he slept. He needed something cold and wet. With Lindy following him, he walked into the kitchen and got himself a beer.

To his utter amazement, his sister jerked it out of his hand and returned it to the refrigerator. "From the look of things, I'd say you've had enough to drink."

He was so stunned, he didn't know what to say.

She pointed her index finger toward a kitchen chair, silently ordering him to sit. From the determined look she wore, Steve decided not to test her.

Before he could object, she had a pot of coffee brewing and was rummaging through the refrigerator looking for God knew what. Eggs, he realized when she brought out a carton.

She insisted he eat, which he did, but he didn't like it. While he sat at the table like an obedient child, Lindy methodically started emptying his sink, which was piled faucet-high with dirty dishes.

"You don't need to do that," he objected.

"Yes, I know."

"Then don't… I can get by without any favors from you." Now that he had something in his stomach, he wasn't about to be led around like a bull with a ring through his nose.

"You need something," she countered. "I'm just not sure what. I suspect it's a swift kick in the seat of the pants."

"You and what army, little sister."

Lindy declined to answer. She poured herself a cup of coffee, replenished his and claimed the chair across the table from him. "Okay," she said, her shoulders rising with an elongated sigh. "What happened with Carol?"

At the mention of his former wife's name, Steve's stomach clenched in a painful knot. Just thinking about her carrying another man's child produced such an inner agony that the oxygen constricted his lungs and he couldn't breathe.

"Steve?"

"Nothing happened between us. Absolutely nothing."

"Don't give me that. The last time we talked, you

were as excited as a puppy about her being pregnant.
You could hardly wait to see her. What's happened since
then?"

"I already told you—nothing!"

Lindy slumped forward and braced her hand against
her forehead. "You've buried yourself in this apartment
for an entire week and you honestly expect me to believe that?"

"I don't care what you believe."

"I'm to blame, aren't I?"

"What?"

"I shouldn't have said a word about Carol and the
baby, but she'd been so sick and I've been so concerned
about her." Lindy paused and lightly shook her head.
"I still am."

Steve hated the way his heart reacted to the news
that Carol was still sickly. He didn't want to care about
her, didn't want to feel this instant surge of protective-
ness when it came to his ex-wife. For the past week, he'd
tried to erase every memory of her from his tortured
mind. Obviously it hadn't worked, and the only thing
he'd managed to develop was one hell of a hangover.

"I shouldn't have told you," Lindy repeated.

"It wouldn't have made one bit of difference; I would
have found out sooner or later."

Lindy's hands cupped the coffee mug. "What are you
going to do about it?"

Steve shrugged. "Nothing."

"Nothing? But Steve, that's your baby."

He let that pass, preferring not to correct his sister.
"What's between Carol and me isn't any of your business. Leave it at that."

She seemed to weigh his words carefully. "I wish I could."

"What do you mean by that?"

"Carol looks awful. I really think she needs to see her doctor. Something's wrong, Steve. She shouldn't be this sick."

He shrugged with feigned indifference. "That's her problem."

Lindy's jaw sagged open. "I can't believe you. Carol is carrying your child and you're acting like she got pregnant all by herself."

Steve diverted his gaze to the blue sky outside his living-room window and shrugged. "Maybe she did," he whispered.

Ten

Carol sat at her desk and tried to concentrate on her work. This past seven days had been impossible. Steve honestly believed she was carrying another man's child, and nothing she could ever say would convince him otherwise. It was like history repeating itself and all the agony of her divorce had come back to haunt her.

Only this time Carol was smarter.

If Steve chose to believe such nonsense, that was his problem. She wanted this baby and from the first had been prepared to raise her daughter alone. Now if only she could get over these bouts of nausea and the sickly feeling that was with her almost every day and night. Most of it she attributed to the emotional upheaval in her life. Within a couple of weeks it would pass and she would feel a thousand times better—at least, that was what she kept telling herself.

"Hi."

A familiar, friendly voice invaded Carol's thoughts. "Lindy!" she said, directing her attention to Steve's sister. "What are you doing here?"

"Risking my job and my neck. Can we meet later? I've got to talk to you. It's important."

As fond as Carol was of her former sister-in-law, she knew there was only one subject Lindy would want to discuss, and that was Steve. Her former husband was a topic Carol preferred to avoid. Nor was she willing to justify herself to his sister, if Lindy started questioning her about the baby's father. It would be better for everyone involved if she refused to meet her, but the desperate worry in Lindy's steady gaze frightened her.

"I suppose you want to ask me about Steve," Carol said slowly, thoughtfully. "I don't know that any amount of talking is going to change things. It'd be best just to leave things as they are."

"Not you, too."

"Too?"

"Steve's so closed mouthed you'd think your name was listed as classified information."

Carol picked up the clipboard and flipped over a page, in an effort to pretend she was exceptionally busy. "Maybe it's better this way," she murmured, but was unable to disguise the pain her words revealed.

"Listen, I've got to get back before someone important—like my supervisor—notices I'm missing," Lindy said, scribbling something on a pad and ripping off the sheet. "Here's the address to my apartment. Rush is on sea trials, so we'll be alone."

"Lindy…"

"If you care anything about my brother you'll come." Once more those piercing eyes spelled out his sister's concern.

Carol took the address, and frowned. "Let me tell you

right now that if you're trying to orchestrate a reconciliation, neither one of us will appreciate it."

"I..."

"Is Steve going to mysteriously arrive around the same time as I do?"

"No. I promise he won't. Good grief, Carol, he won't even talk to me anymore. He isn't talking to anyone. I'm not kidding when I say I'm worried about him."

Carol soaked in that information and frowned, growing concerned herself.

"You'll come?"

Against her better judgment, she nodded. Like her ex-husband, she didn't want to talk to anyone, and especially not to someone related to Steve. The pain of his accusations was still too raw to share with someone else.

Yet she knew she would be there to talk about whatever it was Lindy found so important, although she also knew that nothing Lindy could say would alter her relationship with Steve.

At five-thirty, Carol parked her car outside Lindy's apartment building. She regretted agreeing to the meeting, but couldn't see any way of escaping without going back on her word.

Lindy opened the door and greeted her with a weak smile. "Come in and sit down. Would you like something cold to drink? I just finished making a pitcher of iced tea."

"That sounds fine." Carol still wasn't feeling well and would be glad when she saw her doctor for her regular appointment. She took a seat in the living room while Lindy disappeared into the kitchen.

Lindy returned a couple of minutes later with tall glasses filled with iced tea.

"I wish I could say you're looking better," Lindy said, handing Carol a glass and a colorful napkin.

"I wish I could say I was, too."

Lindy sat across from her and automatically crossed her long legs. "I take it the medication the doctor gave you for the nausea didn't help?"

"It helped some."

"But generally you're feeling all right?"

Carol shrugged. She'd never been pregnant before and had nothing to compare this experience to. "I suppose."

Lindy's fingers wiped away the condensation on the outside of her glass. She hedged, and her gaze drifted around the room. "I think the best way to start is to apologize."

"But what could you have possibly done to offend me?"

Lindy's gaze moved to Carol's, and she released a slow breath. "I told Steve I suspected you were pregnant."

"It's true," Carol answered with a gentle smile. She would be a single mother, and although she would have preferred to be married, she was pleased and proud to be carrying this child.

"I know…but it would have been far better coming from you. I left a message for Steve to call me once he returned from his deployment. I was afraid he was going to come at you with his usual caveman tactics and you've been so ill lately… It's a weak excuse, I know."

"Lindy, for goodness' sake, don't worry about it. This baby isn't a deep, dark secret." Remembering the life she was nurturing in her womb was what had gotten her through the bleakest hours of this past week. Steve might choose to reject his daughter, but he could never take away this precious gift he had unknowingly given her.

"I don't know what's going on with my brother," Lindy muttered, dropping her gaze to her tea. "I wish Rush were here. If anyone could talk some sense into him, it's my husband."

"Get used to him being away when you need him most. It's the lot of a navy wife. The Navy blues doesn't always refer only to their dress uniform, you know."

Lindy nodded. "I'm learning that. I'm also learning I'm much stronger than I thought I was. Rush was involved in an accident last year in the Persian Gulf—you probably read about it in the papers—well, really that doesn't have anything to do with Steve, but he was with me the whole time when we didn't know if Rush was dead or alive. I can't even begin to tell you how good he was, how supportive. In a crisis, my brother can be a real trooper."

"Yes, I know." Carol paused and took a sip of her tea. On more than one occasion in their married life, she had come to admire Steve's levelheadedness in dealing with both major and minor emergencies. It was in other matters, like trust and confidence in her love, that he fell sadly short.

"I don't understand him anymore," Lindy admitted. "He was ecstatic when I mentioned my suspicions about you being pregnant… I thought he was going to go right through the ceiling he was so excited. He was bubbling over like a little kid. I know he drove over to your place right after that and then we didn't hear from him again. I phoned, but he just barked at me to leave him alone, and when I went to see him…well, that's another story entirely."

Carol stiffened. It was better to deal with Lindy honestly since it was apparent Steve hadn't told her. "He doesn't believe the baby is his."

Lindy's brow folded into a dark, brooding frown. "But that's ridiculous."

Carol found it somewhat amazing that her former sister-in-law would believe her without question and her ex-husband wouldn't.

"I...can't believe this." Lindy pressed her palm over her forehead, lifting her bangs, and her mouth sagged open. "But, sadly, it explains a good deal." As if she couldn't remain sitting any longer, Lindy got up and started walking around the room, moving from one side to the other without direction. "What is that man's problem? Good grief, someone should get him to face a few fundamental facts here."

Carol smiled. It felt good to have someone trust and believe her.

"What are you going to do? I mean, I assumed Steve was going to remarry you, but..."

"Obviously that's out of the question."

"But..."

"Single women give birth every day. It's rather commonplace now for a woman to choose to raise a child on her own. That was my original intention."

"But, Steve..."

"Steve is out of my life." Her hand moved to her stomach and a soft smile courted the edges of her mouth. "He gave me what I wanted. Someday he'll be smart enough to calculate dates, but when he does it'll be too late."

"Oh, Carol, don't say that. Steve loves you so much."

"He's hurt me for the last time. He can't love me

and accuse me of the things he has. It's over for us, and there's no going back."

"But he does love you." Lindy walked around a bit more and then plopped down across from Carol. "When he wouldn't talk to me on the phone, I went over to the apartment. I've never seen him like this. He frightened me."

"What's wrong?" Carol was angry with herself for caring, but she did.

"He'd been drinking heavily."

"That's not like Steve."

"I know," Lindy said heatedly. "I didn't know when he'd eaten last, so I fixed him something, which was a mistake because once he had something in his stomach he got feisty again and wanted me to leave."

"Did you?"

"No." Lindy started nibbling on the corner of her mouth. "I kept asking him questions about you, which only made him more angry. I soon learned you were a subject best avoided."

"I can imagine."

"After a while, he fell asleep on the sofa and I stayed around and cleaned up the apartment. It was a mess. Then... I heard Steve. I thought at first he was in the middle of a bad dream and I went to wake him, but when I came into the living room, I found him sitting on the end of the davenport with his hands over his face. He was weeping, Carol. As I've never seen a man weep before—heart-wrenching sobs that came from the deepest part of his soul. I can't even describe it to you."

Carol lowered her gaze to her hands, which had begun to tremble.

"This is the first time I've seen my brother cry, and his sobs tore straight through my heart. I couldn't stand by and do nothing. I wanted to comfort him and find out what had hurt him so badly. I'm his sister, for heaven's sake—he should be able to talk to me. But he didn't want me anywhere near him and ordered me out of the apartment. I left, but I haven't been able to stop thinking about it since."

A tear spilled out of the corner of Carol's eye and left a moist trail down the side of her face.

"By the time I got home I was crying, too. I don't know what to do anymore."

Carol's throat thickened. "There's nothing you can do. This is something Steve has to work out himself."

"Can't you talk to him?" Lindy pleaded. "He loves you so much and it's eating him alive."

"It won't do any good." Carol spoke from bitter experience.

"How can two people who obviously love each other let this happen?"

"I wish I knew." Carol's voice dropped to a whispered sob.

"What about Steve and the baby?"

"He doesn't want to have anything to do with this pregnancy. That's his decision, Lindy."

"But it's the wrong one! Surely you can get him to realize that."

She shook her head sadly. "Once Steve decides on something, his mind is set. He's too stubborn to listen to reason."

"But you love him."

"I wish I could deny that, but I do care about him,

with all my heart. Unfortunately that doesn't change a thing."

"How can you walk away from him like this?"

Carol's heart constricted with pain. "I've never left Steve. Not once. He's always been the one to walk away."

Eleven

"I'd do anything I could to make things right between me and Steve," Carol told Lindy, "but it isn't possible anymore."

"Why not?" Lindy pleaded. Carol knew it was hard for Lindy to understand when her own recent marriage was thriving. "You're both crazy in love with each other."

The truth in that statement was undeniable. Although Steve believed her capable of breaking her wedding vows and the worst kind of deceit, he continued to love her. For her part, Carol had little pride when it came to her ex-husband. She should have cut her losses the minute he'd accused her of having an affair, walked away from her and filed for the divorce. Instead she'd spent the next year of her life in limbo, licking her wounds, pretending the emotional scars had healed. It had taken Christmas Eve to show her how far she still had to go to get over loving Steve Kyle.

"You can't just walk away from him," Lindy pleaded. "What about the baby?"

"Steve doesn't want anything to do with my daughter."

"Give him time, Carol. You know Steve probably better than anyone. He can be such a stubborn fool sometimes. It just takes a while for him to come to his senses. He'll wake up one morning and recognize the truth about the baby."

"I have to forget him for my own sanity." Carol stood, delivered her empty iced-tea glass to the kitchen and prepared to leave. There wasn't anything Lindy could say that would change the facts. Yes, she did love Steve and probably always would, but that didn't alter what he believed.

Lindy followed her to the front door. "If you need something, anything at all, please call me."

Carol nodded. "I will."

"Promise?"

"Promise." Carol knew that Lindy realized how difficult it was for her to ask for help. Impulsively she hugged Steve's sister. From now on, Lindy would be her only link to Steve and Carol was grateful for the friendship they shared.

Steve had to get out of the apartment before he went crazy. He'd spent the past few days drowning his misery in a bottle and the only thing it had brought him was more pain.

He showered, shaved and dressed. Walking would help clear his mind.

With no real destination in mind, he headed toward the waterfront. He got as far as Pike Place Market and aimlessly wandered among the thick crowds there. The colorful sights of the vegetable and meat displays and the sounds of cheerful vendors helped lift his spirits.

He bought a crisp, red Delicious apple and ate it as he

ambled toward the booths that sold various craft items designed to attract the tourist trade. He paused and examined a sculpture made of volcanic ash from Mount Saint Helens. Another booth sold scenic photos of the Pacific Northwest, and another, thick, hand-knit Indian sweaters.

"Could I interest you in something?" a friendly older woman asked. Her long silver hair framed her face, and she offered him a wide smile.

"No, thanks, I'm just looking." Steve paused and glanced over the items on her table. Sterling silver jewelry dotted a black velvet cloth—necklaces, earrings and rings of all sizes and shapes.

"You can't buy silver anywhere for my prices," the woman said.

"It's very nice."

"If jewelry doesn't interest you, perhaps these will." She stood and pulled a box of silver objects from beneath the table, lifting it up for him to inspect.

The first thing Steve noticed was a sterling-silver piggy bank. He smiled, recalling how he and Carol had dumped their spare change in a piggy bank for months in an effort to save enough for a vacation to Hawaii. They'd spent it instead for the closing costs on the house.

"This is a popular item," the woman told him, bringing out a baby rattle. "Lots of jewelry stores sell these, but no one can beat my prices."

"How much?" Steve couldn't believe he'd asked. What the hell would he do with a baby rattle—especially one made of sterling silver.

The woman stated a reasonable price. "I'll take it," he said, astonished to hear the words come out of his mouth.

"Would you like one with blue ribbon or pink?"

Already Steve regretted the impulse. What was he planning to do? Give it to Carol? He'd decided the best thing for him to do as far as his ex-wife was concerned was to never see her again.

"Sir? Blue or pink?"

"Blue," he answered in a hoarse whisper. For the son he would probably never father. Blue for the color of Carol's eyes when she smiled at him.

By the time Steve walked back to the apartment, the sack containing the silver baby rattle felt like it weighed thirty pounds. By rights, he thought, he should toss the silly thing in the garbage. But he didn't.

He set it on the kitchen counter and opened the refrigerator, looking for something to eat, but nothing interested him. When he turned, the rattle seemed to draw his gaze. He stared at it for a long moment, yearning strongly to press it into the hand of his own child.

Blood thundered in his ears and his heart pounded so hard and fast that his chest ached. He would save the toy for Lindy and Rush whenever they had children, he decided.

Feeling only slightly better, he moved into the living room and turned on the television. He reached for the *TV Guide*, flipped through the pages, sighed and turned off the set. A second later, he rushed to his feet.

He didn't know who the hell he was trying to kid. That silver rattle with the pretty blue ribbon was for Carol and her baby, and it was going to torment him until he got rid of it.

He could mail her the toy and be done with the plaything. Or have Lindy give it to her without letting Carol know it had come from him. Or…or he could just set it on the porch and let her find it.

The last idea appealed to him. He would casually drive by her neighborhood, park his car around the block and wait until it was dark enough to sneak up and leave the rattle on the front step. He was the last person she would ever suspect would do something like that.

With his plan formulated, Steve drove to Carol's house. He was half a block away from her place when he noticed her car. She was leaving. This would work out even better. He could follow her and when she got where she was going, he could place the rattle inside her car. That way she would assume someone had mistaken her car for their own and inadvertently set the rattle inside. There wasn't anything she could do but take it home with her.

Carol headed north on Interstate 5, and her destination was a matter of simple deduction. She was going to the Northgate Mall. Lord, that woman loved to shop. The minute she steered onto the freeway on-ramp, Steve knew exactly where she was headed. They'd been married for five years, and their year apart hadn't changed her. The smug knowledge produced a smile.

But Carol exited before the mall.

Steve's heart started to pound. He was three cars behind her, but if she wasn't going shopping, he didn't know what she was planning. Maybe she was rendezvousing with Todd. Maybe all those times she'd told him she was shopping Carol had actually been meeting with her employer. The muscles in his stomach clenched into a knot so tight and painful that it stole his breath.

If there'd been any way to turn the car around, Steve

would have done it, but he was trapped in the center lane of traffic and forced to follow the heavy flow.

It wasn't until they'd gone several blocks that Steve noticed the back side of the mall. Perhaps she'd found a shortcut and had never bothered to tell him about it.

Carol turned onto a busy side street, and against his better judgment, he followed her. A few minutes later, when Carol turned into the large parking lot at Northgate Mall, Steve felt almost giddy with relief.

She parked close to the JCPenney store, and Steve eased his vehicle into a slot four spaces over. On a whim, he decided to follow her inside. He'd always wondered what women found so intriguing about shopping.

He was far enough behind her on the escalator to almost lose her. Standing at the top, he searched until he found her standing in women's fashions, sorting through a rack of dresses. It took him a minute to realize they were maternity dresses. Although she'd lost several pounds, she must be having difficulty finding things that fit her, he realized. According to his calculations, she was five months pregnant—probably closer to six.

He lounged around while she took a handful of bright spring dresses and moved into the changing room. Fifteen minutes passed before she returned, and to Steve it felt like a lifetime.

When she returned, she went back to the rack and replaced all but one of the dresses. She held up a pretty blue one with a wide sailor's collar and red tie and studied it carefully. Apparently she changed her mind because she hung it back up with the others. Still she lingered an extra minute, continuing to examine the outfit. She ran her fingers down the sleeve to catch the price tag, read it, shook her head and reluctantly walked away.

The minute she was out of sight, Steve was at the clothing rack. Obviously she wanted the dress, yet she hadn't bought it. He checked the price tag and frowned. It was moderately priced, certainly not exorbitant. If she wanted it, which she apparently did, then she should have it.

For the second time in the same day, Steve found himself making a purchase that was difficult to rationalize. It wasn't as if he had any use for a maternity dress. But why not? he asked himself. If he left the rattle in her car it shouldn't make any difference if he added a dress. It wasn't likely that she would tie him to either purchase. Let her think her fairy godmother was gifting her.

From his position at the cash register, Steve saw Carol walk through the infants' department. She ran her hand over the top rail of a white Jenny Lind crib and examined it with a look of such sweet anticipation that Steve felt guilty for invading her privacy.

"Would you like this dress on the hanger or in a sack?" the salesclerk asked him.

It took Steve a moment to realize she was talking to him. "A sack, please." He couldn't very well walk through the mall carrying a maternity dress.

Carol bought something, too, but Steve couldn't see what it was. Infant T-shirts or something like that, he guessed. His vantage point in the furniture department wasn't the best. Carol started to walk toward him, and he turned abruptly and pretended to be testing out a recliner.

Apparently she didn't see him, and he settled into the seat and expelled a sigh of relief.

"Can I help you?" a salesclerk asked.

"Ah, no, thanks," he said, getting to his feet.

Carol headed down the escalator, and Steve scooted around a couple of women pushing baby strollers in an effort not to lose sight of her.

Carol's steps were filled with purpose as she moved down the wide aisle to women's shoes. She picked up a red low-heeled dress shoe that was on display, but when the clerk approached, she smiled and shook her head. Within a couple of minutes she was on her way.

Feeling more like a fool with every minute, Steve followed her out of the store and into the heart of the mall. The place was packed, as it generally was on Saturday afternoon. Usually Steve avoided the mall on weekends, preferring to do his shopping during the day or at night.

He saw Carol stop at a flower stand and buy herself a red rosebud. She'd always been fond of flowers, and he was pleased that she treated herself to something special.

She'd gone only a few steps when he noticed that her steps had slowed.

Something was wrong. He could tell from the way she walked. He cut across to the other side, where the flow of shoppers was heading in the opposite direction. Feeling like a secret government agent, he pressed himself against the storefront in an effort to watch her more closely. She had pressed her hand to her abdomen and her face had gone deathly pale. She was in serious pain, he determined as a sense of alarm filled him. Steve could feel it as strongly as if he were the one suffering.

Although he was certain she had full view of him, Carol didn't notice. She cut across the streams of shoppers to the benches that lined the middle of the concourse and sat. Her shoulders moved up and down as though she were taking in deep breaths in an effort to control her reaction to whatever was happening. She closed her eyes and bit her lower lip.

The alarm turned to panic. He didn't know what to do. He couldn't rush up to her and demand to know what was wrong. Nor could he casually stroll by and pretend he just happened to be shopping and had stumbled upon her. But something needed to be done—someone had to help her.

Steve had never felt more helpless in his life. Not knowing what else he could do, he walked up and plopped himself down next to her.

"Hi," he said in a falsely cheerful voice.

"Steve." She looked at him, her eyes brimming with tears. She reached for his hand, gripping it so hard her nails cut into his flesh.

All pretense was gone, wiped away by the stampeding fear he sensed in her.

"What's wrong?"

She shook her head. "I… I don't know."

Her eyes widened and he was struck by how yellow her skin was. He took her hand in both of his. "You're in pain?"

She nodded. Her fear palatable. "I'm so afraid."

"What do you want me to do?" He debated on whether he should could call for an ambulance or contact her doctor and have him meet them at the hospital.

"I…don't know what's wrong. I've had this pain twice, but it's always gone away after a couple of minutes." She closed her eyes. "Oh, Steve, I'm so afraid I'm going to lose my baby."

Twelve

Restless, Steve paced the corridor of the maternity ward in Overlake Hospital, his hands stuffed inside his pants pockets. He felt as though he were carrying the world on his shoulders. Each passing minute tightened the knot in his stomach until he was consumed with worry and dread.

He wanted to see Carol—he longed to talk to her—but there wasn't anything more for him to say. He'd done what he could for her, and by rights he should leave. But he couldn't walk away from her. Not now. Not when she needed him.

Not knowing what else to do, he found a pay phone and contacted his sister.

"Lindy, it's Steve."

"Steve, how are you? I'm so glad you phoned. I haven't stopped thinking about you."

She sounded so pleased to hear from him, and he swallowed down his guilt for the way he'd treated her. He'd been rude and unreasonable when she'd only been showing concern for him.

"I'm fine," he said hurriedly. "Listen, I'm at Over-lake Hospital…"

"You're at the hospital? You're fine, but you're at Overlake? Good God, what happened? I knew it, I just knew something like this was going to happen. I felt it…"

"Lindy, shut up for a minute, would you?"

"No, I won't shut up—I'm family, Steve Kyle. Family. If you can't come to me when you're hurting, just who can you go to? You seem to think I'm too young to know anything about emotional pain, but you're wrong. When Paul dumped me it wasn't any Sunday-school picnic."

"I'm not the one in need of medical attention—it's Carol."

"Carol!" His blurted announcement seemed to sweep away all his sister's pent-up frustration. "What's wrong?" she asked quietly.

"I don't exactly know; the doctor's still with her. I think she might be losing the baby. She needs a woman—I'm the last person who should be here. I didn't know who else to call. Can you come?"

"Of course. I'll be there as fast as I can."

It seemed as though no more than a couple of minutes had passed before Lindy came rushing down the hall. He stood at the sight of her, immensely grateful. Relief washed over him and he wrapped his arms around her.

"The doctor hasn't come out yet," he explained before she could ask. He released her and checked his watch. "It's been over an hour now."

"What happened?"

"I'm not sure. Carol started having some kind of ab-dominal pains. I phoned her gynecologist, and after I explained what was happening, he suggested we meet him here."

"You said you thought Carol might be having a miscarriage?"

"Good Lord, I don't know anything about this woman stuff. All I can tell you is that she was in agony. I did the only thing I could—I got her here." The ten minutes it took to get Carol to the emergency room had been emotionally draining. She was terrified of losing the baby and had wept almost uncontrollably. Through her sobs she'd told him how much she wanted her baby and how this pregnancy would be her only opportunity. Little of what she'd said had made sense to Steve. He'd tried to find the words to assure her, but he hadn't really known what to say.

Just then Steve noticed Carol's physician, Dr. Stewart, push open the swinging door and walk toward the waiting area. He met him halfway.

"How is she?" he asked, his heart in his throat.

The gynecologist rubbed his hand down the side of his jaw and shook his head. His frown crowded his brows together. "She's as good as can be expected."

"The baby?"

"The pregnancy is progressing nicely...thus far."

Although the child wasn't his and Carol had tried to trick him into believing otherwise, Steve still felt greatly relieved knowing that her baby wasn't in any immediate danger.

"I'm sorry to keep you waiting so long, but quite frankly Carol's symptoms had me stumped. It's unusual for someone her age to suffer from this sort of problem."

"What problem?" Lindy blurted out.

"Gall bladder."

"Gall bladder," Steve repeated, frowning. He didn't know what he'd expected, but it certainly hadn't been that.

"She tells me she's been suffering from flulike symptoms, which she accepted as morning sickness. There wasn't any reason for either of us to assume otherwise. Some of her other discomforts can be easily misinterpreted as well.

"The most serious threat at the moment is that she's dangerously close to being dehydrated. Predictably that has prompted other health risks."

"What do you mean?" Lindy asked.

"Her sodium and potassium levels have dropped and her heart rate is erratic. I've started an IV and that problem should take care of itself within a matter of hours."

"What's going to happen?"

Once more, Dr. Stewart ran a hand down the side of his face and shook his head. His kind eyes revealed his concern. "I've called in a surgeon friend of mine, and we're going to do a few more preliminary tests. But from what I'm seeing at this point, I don't think we can put off operating. Her gall bladder appears to be acutely swollen and is causing an obstruction."

"If you do the surgery, what will happen to the baby?" For Carol's sake, Steve prayed for the tiny life she was carrying.

Dr. Stewart's sober expression turned grim. "There's always a risk to the pregnancy when anesthesia is involved. I'd like to delay this, but I doubt that we can. Under normal conditions gall-bladder surgery can be scheduled at a patient's convenience, but not in Carol's case, I fear. But I want you to know, we'll do everything I can to save the child."

"Please try." Carol had looked at him with such terror and helplessness that he couldn't help being affected. He would do everything humanly possible to see that she carried this child to full term.

"Please do what you can." Lindy added her own plea. "This child means a great deal to her."

Dr. Stewart nodded. "Carol's sleeping now, but you can see her for a couple of minutes, if you'd like. One at a time."

Steve looked to Lindy, who gestured for him to go in first. He smiled his appreciation and followed the grandfatherly doctor into Carol's room.

As Dr. Stewart had explained, she was sleeping soundly. She looked incredibly fragile with tubes stretching down from an IV pole to connect with the veins in her arm.

Steve stood beside her for several minutes, loving her completely. Emotion clogged his throat and he turned away. He loved her; he always would. No matter what had happened in the past, he couldn't imagine a future without Carol.

"How is she?" Lindy asked when he came out of the room.

He found he couldn't answer her with anything more than a short nod.

Lindy disappeared and returned five minutes later. By then Steve had had a chance to form a plan of action, and he felt better for it.

As Lindy stepped toward him, he held her gaze with newfound determination. He and Carol were both fools if they thought they could stay apart. It wasn't going to work. Without Carol he was only half-alive. And she'd admitted how miserable she'd been during their year's separation.

"I'm going to marry her," Steve informed his sister brusquely.

"What?" Lindy looked at him as though she'd misheard him.

"I'm going to get the chaplain to come to the hospital, and I'm going to marry Carol."

Lindy studied him for several moments. "Don't you think she should have some say in this?"

"Yes…no."

"But I thought… Carol told me you didn't believe the baby is yours."

"It isn't."

Lindy rolled her eyes, then shook her head, her features tight with impatience. "That is the most ridiculous thing you've ever said. Honestly, Steve, where do you come up with these crazy ideas?"

"What idea? That the baby isn't mine, or remarrying Carol?"

"Both!"

"Whether or not I'm the father doesn't make one bit of difference. I've decided it doesn't matter. From here on out, I'm claiming her child as mine."

"But…"

"I don't care. I love Carol and I'll learn to love her baby. That's the end of it." Once the decision had been made, it felt right. The two of them had played a fool's game for over a year, but no more—he wouldn't stand for it. "I'm not going to put up with any arguments from you or from Carol. I want her as my wife—we were wrong ever to have gone through with the divorce. All I'm doing now is correcting a mistake that should never have happened," he told his sister in a voice that men jumped to obey.

Lindy took a moment to digest his words. "Don't you think you should discuss this in a rational matter with Carol? Don't you think she should have some input into her own life?"

"I suppose. But she needs me—although she isn't likely to admit it."

"You've had just as difficult a time recognizing that fact yourself."

"Not anymore."

"When do you plan to tell her?"

Steve didn't know. He'd only reached this conclusion in the last five minutes, but already he felt in control of his life again.

"Well?" his sister pressed.

"I haven't figured out when... Before the surgery, I think, if it can be arranged."

"Steve, you're not thinking clearly. Carol isn't going to want to be married sitting in a hospital bed, looking all sickly and pale."

"The sooner we get this settled the better."

"For whom?" Lindy prompted.

"For both of us."

Lindy threw up her hands. "Sometimes the things you say utterly shock me."

"They do?" Steve didn't care—he felt as if he could float out of the hospital, he was so relieved. Carol would probably come through the surgery with flying colors and everything would fall into place the way it should have long ago. This had certainly been a crazy day. He'd bought a sterling silver rattle, followed Carol around a shopping mall like an FBI agent, driven her to the hospital, then made a decision that would go a long way toward assuring their happy future. Steve sighed deeply, feeling suddenly weary.

"Is there any other bombshell you'd care to hit me with?" Lindy asked teasingly.

Steve paused and then surprised her by nodding. Some of the happiness he'd experienced earlier vanished. There was one other decision he'd made—one not as pleasant but equally necessary.

"Should I sit down for this one?" Lindy asked, still grinning. She slipped her arm around his waist and looked up at him.

"I don't think so."

"Well, don't keep me in suspense, big brother."

Steve regarded her soberly. "I'm leaving the Navy."

Thirteen

Carol opened her eyes slowly. The room was dim, the blinds over the window closed. She frowned when her gaze fell on the IV stand, and she tried to raise herself.

"You're in the hospital." Steve's voice was warm and caressing.

She lowered her head back to the pillow and turned toward the sound. Steve stood at her bedside. From the ragged, tired look about him, she guessed he'd been standing there all night.

"How long have you been here?" she asked hoarsely, testing her tongue.

"Not very long."

She closed her eyes and grinned. "You never could tell a decent lie."

He brushed the hair from her cheek and his fingers lingered on her face as though he needed to touch her. She knew she should ask him to leave, but his presence comforted her. She needed him. She didn't know how he'd happened to be at Northgate Mall, but she would always be grateful he'd found her when he did.

Her hand moved to her stomach, and she flattened it there. "The baby's all right?"

Steve didn't answer her for a moment, and a sickening sense of dread filled her. Her eyes flew open. The doctor had repeatedly assured her that the baby was safe, but something might have happened while she had slept. She'd been out for hours and much of what had taken place after they arrived at the hospital remained foggy in her mind.

"Everything's fine with the pregnancy."

"Thank God," she whispered fervently.

"Dr. Stewart said you were near exhaustion." He reached for her hand and laced his fingers with hers. His thumb worked back and forth on the inside of her wrist.

"I think I could sleep for a week," Carol said, her voice starting to sound more sure. It seemed as though it had been years since she'd had a decent rest. Even before her pregnancy had been confirmed she'd felt physically and emotionally drained, as if she were running on a treadmill, working as fast as her legs would carry her and getting nowhere.

"How do you feel now?"

Carol had to think about it. "Different. I don't know how to describe it. I'm not exactly sick and I'm not in any pain, but something's not right, either."

"You should have recognized that weeks ago. According to Dr. Stewart, you've probably been feeling ill for months."

"They know what's causing the problem?" Her heart started to work doubly hard. Not until the severe attack of pain in the shopping mall had she been willing to admit something could be wrong with her.

"Dr. Stewart thinks it could be your gall bladder."

"My what?"

"Gall bladder," he repeated softly. "I'm sure he can explain it far better than I can, but from what I understand it's a pear-shaped pouch close to the liver."

Carol arched her brows at his attempt at humor and offered him a weak smile. "That explains it."

Steve grinned back at her, and for a moment everything went still. His eyes held such tenderness that she dared to hope again—dared to believe he'd discovered the truth about her and their baby. Dared to let the love that was stored in her heart shine through her eyes.

"I never thought I'd see you again," she said, and her voice quivered with emotion.

Steve lowered his gaze briefly. "I couldn't stay away. I love you too much."

"Oh, Steve, how could we do this to each other? You think such terrible things of me and I can't bear it anymore. I keep telling myself the baby and I would be better off without you, and then I feel only half alive. When we're separated, nothing feels right in my life— nothing is good."

"When I'm not with you, I'm only a shell." He raised her hand to his lips and kissed her knuckles.

Carol felt the tears gather in her eyes and she turned her head away, unwilling to have Steve witness her emotion. No man would ever be more right for her, and no man could ever be so wrong.

She heard the sound of a chair being pushed to the side of the bed. "I want us to remarry," he said firmly. "I've thought it over. In fact, I haven't thought of anything else in the past fifteen hours—and I'm convinced this is the right thing for us to do."

Carol knew it was right, too. "But what about the baby?" she whispered. "You think—"

"From this moment on, the child is mine in my heart and in my soul. He's a part of you and that's the only important thing."

"She," Carol corrected absently. "I'm having a girl."

"Okay…whatever you want as long as we're together."

Carol's mind flooded with arguments, but she hadn't the strength to fight him. The intervening months would convince Steve that this child was his far better than any eloquent speeches she could give him now. By the time the baby was born, his doubts would have vanished completely. In the meantime they would find a way to settle matters—that was essential because they were both so miserable apart.

"Will you marry me, Carol, a second time?"

"I want to say yes. Everything within me is telling me it's the right thing to do…for me and for the baby. But I'm frightened, too."

"I'm going to be a good husband and father, I promise you that."

"I know you will."

"I made another decision yesterday—one that will greatly affect both our lives." His hand pressed against the side of her face and gently brushed the hair from her temple. "I'm leaving the Navy."

Carol couldn't believe her ears. The military was Steve's life; it had been his goal from the time he was a teenager. His dream. He'd never wanted to be or do anything else.

"But you love your work."

"I love you more," he countered.

"It's not an either-or situation, Steve. I've lived all these years as a navy wife, I've adjusted."

A hint of a smile touched his face. "I won't be separated from you again."

For Steve's sake, Carol had always put on a happy face and seen him off with a cheerful wave, but she'd hated the life, dreading their months apart. Always had and always would. The promise of a more conventional marriage seemed too good to be true. Her head was swimming at the thought of him working a nine-to-five job. She wanted this—she wanted it badly.

"You're the most important person in my life. I'm getting out of the Navy so I can be the kind of husband and father I should be."

"Oh, Steve." The joy that cascaded through her at that moment brought tears to her eyes.

"I can't think of any other way to show you how serious I am."

Neither could Carol. Nevertheless his announcement worried her. Navy life was in Steve's blood, and she didn't know if he could find happiness outside the only career he'd ever known.

"Let's not make such a major decision now," she suggested reluctantly. "There'll be plenty of time to talk about this later."

Steve's eyes filled with tenderness. "Whatever you say."

Humming softly, a nurse wandered into the room and greeted them. "Good morning."

"Morning," Carol answered.

The room was bathed in the soft light of day as the middle-aged woman opened the blinds.

"I'm sorry, but there won't be any breakfast for you

this morning. Dr. Stewart will be in later, and I'm sure he'll schedule something for you to eat this afternoon."

Carol didn't feel the least bit hungry. Her appetite had been almost nonexistent for months.

"I'll check on you in an hour," the woman said on her way out the door.

Carol nodded. "Thank you." She was filled with nagging questions about what was going to happen. Naturally she hoped Dr. Stewart could give her a prescription and send her home, but she had the feeling she was being overly optimistic.

Steve must have read the doubt in her eyes because he said, "From what Dr. Stewart told me, he's going to have you complete a series of tests this morning. Following those, we'll be able to make a decision."

"What kind of tests? What kind of decision?"

"Honey, I don't know, but don't worry. I'm not leaving you—not for a minute."

Carol hated to be such a weakling, but she was frightened. "Whatever happens, whatever they have to do, I can take it," she said a little shakily.

"I know you can, love. I know you can."

As promised, for the next few hours Carol underwent several tests. She was pinched, poked and prodded and wheeled to several corners of the hospital. As Steve promised, he was with her each time they took her into another and waiting when she returned.

"Quit looking so worried," she told him, when she'd been wheeled back to her room once more. "I'm going to be fine."

"I know."

She slept after that and woke late in the afternoon.

Once more Steve was at her bedside, leaning forward, his face in his hands.

"Bad news?" she asked.

He smiled and Carol could tell by the stiff way his mouth moved that the action was forced.

"What's wrong?" she demanded.

He stood and came to stand beside her. She gave him her hand, her eyes wide with fear.

"Dr. Stewart assured me that under normal conditions, gall bladder surgery is optional. But not in your case. Your gall bladder is acutely swollen and is causing several complications to vital organs. It has to be removed, and the sooner the better."

Carol expelled her breath and nodded. She'd feared something like this, but she was young and healthy and strong; everything would be fine.

"He's called in a surgeon and they've scheduled the operating room for you first thing tomorrow morning."

Carol swallowed her worry. "I can handle that."

"This isn't minor surgery, Carol. I don't think you'd appreciate me minimizing the risks."

"No…no, I wouldn't."

"Dr. Stewart and his associate will be back later today to explain the details of what they'll be doing. It's major surgery, but you have several things in your favor."

She nodded, appreciating the fact that she would know precisely what the medical team would be doing to her body.

"What about the baby?"

Steve's expression tightened and he lifted his eyes from hers. "The pregnancy poses a problem."

"What kind of problem?"

"If the surgery could be delayed, Dr. Stewart would prefer to do that, but it can't be. Your life is at risk."

"What about the pregnancy?" Carol demanded. "I'm not agreeing to anything until I hear what will happen to my baby."

Steve's eyes revealed myriad emotions. Worry and fear dominated, but there was something else—something that took her an extended moment to analyze. Something that clouded his features and ravaged his face. Regret, she decided, then quickly changed her mind. It was more than that—a deep inner sorrow, even remorse.

When Steve spoke, it was as if each word had to be tugged from his mouth. "I'm not going to coat the truth. There's a chance the anesthesia will terminate the pregnancy."

"I won't do it," she cried automatically. "The whole thing's off. I'm not doing anything that will hurt my baby."

"Carol, listen to reason…"

"No." She twisted her head so that she wouldn't have to look at him. As long as she drew a single breath there was no way she would agree to do anything that would harm her daughter.

"Honey," he whispered. "We don't have any choice. If we delay the surgery, you could die."

"Then so be it."

"No." He almost shouted the word. "There's a risk to the baby, but one we're both going to have to take. There's no other choice."

She closed her eyes, unwilling to argue with him further. Her mind was made up.

"Carol, I don't like this any better than you do."

She refused to look at him and pinched her lips together, determined not to murmur a single word. Nothing he could say would change her mind.

The silence in the room was magnified to deafening proportions.

"I love you, Carol, and I can't allow you to chance your life for a baby. If the worst happens and the pregnancy is terminated, then we'll have to accept it. There'll be other children—lots more—and the next time there won't be any question about who the father is."

If Steve had driven a stake into her heart, he couldn't have hurt her more. No words had ever been more cruel. No wonder he was so willing to tell her he'd decided to accept this child as his own. She would likely lose the baby, and believing what he did, Steve no doubt felt that was for the best.

Carol jerked her head around so fast she nearly dislocated her neck. "The next time there won't be any questions?" she repeated in a small, still voice.

"I know this is painful for you, but—"

"I want *this* baby."

"Carol, please…"

"How long have you known about this danger?"

Steve looked stunned by her anger. "Dr. Stewart told me about the possibility after I brought you to the hospital yesterday."

Exactly what she'd expected. Everything Steve had done, everything he'd said from that point on was suddenly suspect. He wanted them to remarry and he was going to leave the Navy. His reasoning became as clear as water to her: he didn't really long for a change in their life-style, nor had his offer to leave the Navy been a decision based on his desire to build a strong marital relationship. He didn't dread their separations as she always had—he'd thrived on them. But if he wasn't in the military, then he could spend his days watching her. There would be no opportunity for her to have an affair. And when she became pregnant a second time, he would have the assurance that the baby was indeed his. His offer hadn't been made from love but from fear rooted in a lack of trust.

It amazed her, now that she thought about it, that he would be willing to give up such a promising career for her. He really did love her, in his own way, but not enough. Ultimately he would regret his decision, and so would she. But by then it would be too late.

"I'm probably doing a bad job of this," he said, and rammed his fingers through his hair. "I should have let Dr. Stewart explain everything to you."

"No," she said dispassionately. "What you've told me explains a good deal. You've been completely up-front with me and I appreciate what it cost you to tell me this. I... I think it's my turn to be honest with you now."

A dark frown contorted his features. "Carol..."

"No, it's time you finally learned the truth. I hesitated when you asked me to marry you and there's a reason. You don't need to worry about me, Steve. You never had to. My baby's father has promised to take care of me. When my plan to trick you didn't work, I contacted him and told him I was pregnant. He thought about it for a couple of days and has decided to marry me himself. I appreciate your offer, but it isn't necessary."

Steve looked as if she'd slipped a knife into his stomach. "You're lying."

"No, for once I'm telling you the truth. Go back to

your life and I'll go on with mine. We'll both be far happier this way."

He didn't move for several minutes. His hands curved around the raised railing at the side of the bed and she swore his grip was strong enough to permanently mark the bars. His eyes hardened to chips of glacial ice.

"Who is the father?" he demanded.

Carol closed her eyes, determined not to answer.

"Who is he?"

She looked away, but his fingers closed around her chin and forced her face back toward him.

"Todd?"

She was sick of hearing that name. "No."

"Who?"

"No one you know," she shouted.

"Is he married?"

"No."

A pounding, vibrating silence followed.

"Is this what you really want?"

"Yes," she told him. "Yes…"

A year seemed to pass before she heard him leave the room. When he did, each step he took away from her sounded like nails being pounded into a coffin.

It was finished. There was no going back now. Steve Kyle was out of her life and she'd made certain he would never come back.

Carol felt as if she were walking through a thick bog, every step was hindered, her progress painstakingly slow. A mist rose from the marsh, blocking her view, and she struggled to look into the distance, seeking the light, but she was met instead by more fog.

A soft cry—like that of a small animal—reverberated around her, and it took her a minute to realize she was the one who had made the sound.

She wasn't in any pain. Not physically anyway.

The agony she suffered came from deep inside—a weight of grief so heavy no human should ever be expected to carry it. Carol couldn't understand what had happened or why she felt this crippling sense of loss.

Then it came to her.

Her baby…they couldn't delay the surgery. The fog parted and a piece of her memory slipped into place. Steve had walked away from her, and soon after he'd gone she'd suffered another attack that had doubled her over with excruciating pain. The hospital staff had called for Dr. Stewart and surgery had been arranged immediately. The option of waiting for even one day had been taken out of her hands.

Now Steve was out of her life and she'd lost her baby, too.

Moisture ran down the side of her face, but when she tried to lift her hand, she found she hadn't the strength.

A sob came, wrenched from her soul. There would be no more children for her. She was destined to live alone for the rest of her life.

"Nurse, do something. She's in pain."

The words drifted from a great distance, and she tossed her head to and fro in an effort to discover the source. She saw no one in the fog. No one.

Once more the debilitating sense of loneliness overtook her and she was alone. Whoever had been there had left her to find her own way through the darkness.

More sobs came—her own, she realized—erupting in deafening sound all around her.

Then she felt something—a hand she thought—warm

and gentle, press over her abdomen. The weight of it was a comfort she couldn't describe.

"Your baby's alive," the voice told her. "Can you feel him? He's going to live and so are you!"

It was a voice of authority, a voice of a man who spoke with confidence; a voice few would question.

A familiar voice.

The dark fog started to close in again and Carol wanted to shout for it to stop. She stumbled toward the light, but it was shut off from her, and she found herself trapped in a black void, defenseless and lost. She didn't know if she would ever have the strength to escape it.

A persistent squeak interrupted Carol's sleep. A wheel far off in the distance was badly in need of oil. The irritating ruckus grew louder until Carol decided it would be useless to try to ignore it any longer.

She opened her eyes to discover Steve's sister standing over her.

"Lindy?"

"Carol, oh, Carol, you're awake."

"Shouldn't I be?" she asked. Her former sister-in-law looked as if she were about to burst into tears.

"I can't believe it. We've been so worried… No one thought you were going to make it." Lindy cupped her hands over her mouth and nose. "We nearly lost you, Carol Kyle!"

"You did?" This was news to her. She had little memory. The dreadful pain had returned—she remembered that. And then she'd been trapped in that marsh, lost and confused, but it hadn't felt so bad. She had been hot— so terribly hot—she recalled, but there were pleasant memories there, too. Someone had called out to her from there, assured her. She couldn't place what the voice had said, but she remembered how she'd struggled to walk toward the sound of it. The voice hadn't always been comforting. Carol recalled how one time it had shouted at her, harsh and demanding. She hadn't wanted to obey it then and had tried to escape, but the voice had followed her relentlessly, refusing to leave her alone.

"How do you feel?"

"Like I've been asleep for a week."

"Make that two."

"Two?" Carol echoed, shocked. "That long?"

"All right, *almost* two weeks. It's actually been ten days. You had emergency surgery and then everything that could go wrong did. Oh, Carol, you nearly died."

"My baby's okay, isn't she?" From somewhere deep inside her heart came the reassurance that whatever else had happened, the child had survived. Carol vividly remembered the voice telling her so.

"Your baby is one hell of a little fighter."

Carol smiled. "Good."

Lindy moved a chair closer to the bed and sat down. "The doctor said he felt you'd come out of it today. You made a turn for the better around midnight."

"What time is it now?"

Lindy checked her watch. "About 9:00 a.m."

Already her eyes felt incredibly heavy. "I think I could sleep some more."

"As well you should."

Carol tried to smile. "So my daughter is a fighter… Maybe I'll name her Sugar Ray Kyle."

"Go ahead and get some rest. I'll be here when you wake up."

Already Carol felt herself drifting off, but it was a

pleasant sensation. The warm black folds closed their arms around her in a welcoming embrace.

When she stirred a second time, she discovered Lindy was at her bedside reading.

"Is this a vigil or something?" she asked, grinning. "Every time I wake up, you're here."

"I wanted to be sure you were really coming out of it," Lindy told her.

"I feel much better."

"You *look* much better."

The inside of her mouth felt like a sewer. "Do you have any idea how long it'll be before I can go home?"

"You won't. You're coming to live with Rush and me for a couple of weeks until you regain your strength. And we won't take no for an answer."

"But—"

"No arguing!" Lindy's smile softened her brook-no-nonsense tone.

"I don't deserve a friend as good as you," Carol murmured, awed by Lindy's generosity.

"We should be sisters, and you know it."

Carol chose not to answer that. She preferred to push any thoughts of her ex-husband from her mind.

"This probably isn't the time to talk about Steve."

It wasn't, but Carol didn't stop her.

"I don't know what you said to him, but he doesn't seem to think you want to see him again. Carol, he's been worried sick over you. Won't you at least talk to him?"

A lump the size of a goose egg formed in her throat. "No," she whispered. "I don't want to have anything to do with Steve. We're better off divorced."

Fourteen

"I'm not an invalid," Carol insisted, frowning at her ex-sister-in-law as she carried her own breakfast dishes to the sink.

"But you've only been out of the hospital a week," Lindy argued, flittering around her like a mother hen protecting her smallest chick.

"For heaven's sake, sit down," Carol cried, "before you drive me crazy!"

"All right, all right."

Carol shared a knowing smile with Rush Callaghan, Lindy's husband. He was a different man than the Rush Carol had known before his marriage to Lindy. He smiled openly now. Laughed. Carol had been fond of Rush, but he'd always been so very serious—all Navy. The military wouldn't find a man more loyal than Rush, but loving Lindy had changed him—and for the better. Lindy had brought sunshine and laughter into his life and brightened his world in a wide spectrum of rainbow colors.

"Come on, Lindy," Rush said, "you can walk me to the door and kiss me goodbye."

With an eagerness that made Carol smile, her good friend escorted Rush to the front door and lingered there several minutes.

When she returned, Lindy walked blindly into the kitchen, wearing a dazed, contented grin. She plopped herself down in a chair, reached for her empty coffee cup and sighed. "He'll be gone for a couple of days."

"Are you going to suffer those Navy blues?"

"I suppose," Lindy said. She lifted her mug and rested her elbows on the table. "I'm a little giddy this morning because Rush and I reached a major decision last night." She smiled and the sun seemed to shine through her eyes. "We're going to start a family. Our first wedding anniversary is coming up soon, and we thought this would be a good way to celebrate."

"Sweet potatoes," Carol said, grinning from ear to ear. "They worked for me."

Lindy gave her a look that insinuated that perhaps Carol should return to the hospital for much-needed psychiatric treatment. "What was that?"

"Sweet potatoes. You know—yams. I heard a medical report over the news last year that reported the results of a study done on a tribe in Africa whose diet staple was sweet potatoes. The results revealed a higher estrogen level in the women and they attributed that fact to the yams."

"I see."

Lindy continued to study her closely. Carol giggled. "I'm not joking! They really work. I wanted to get pregnant and I couldn't count on anything more from Steve than Christmas Eve, so I ate enough sweet potatoes for my body to float in the hormone."

"One night did it?" Lindy's interest was piqued, although she struggled not to show it.

"Two actually—but who knows how long it would have taken otherwise. I ate that vegetable in every imaginable form—including some I wouldn't recommend. If you want, I'll loan you my collection of recipes."

A slow smile spread over Lindy's face, catching in her lovely brown eyes. "I want!"

Carol rinsed her plate and stuck it inside the dishwasher.

"Let me do that!" Lindy insisted, jumping to her feet. "Honest to goodness, Carol. You're so stubborn."

"No, please, I want to help. It makes me feel like I'm being useful." She never had been one to sit and do nothing. This period of convalescence had been troubling enough without Lindy babying her.

"You're recovering from major surgery, for heaven's sake!" Steve's sister insisted.

"I'm fine."

"Now, maybe, but a week ago…"

Even now Carol had a difficult time realizing how close she'd come to losing her life. It was the voice that had pulled her back, refusing to let her slip into the darkness, the voice that had urged her to live. Something deep within her subconscious had demanded she cling to life when it would have been so easy to surrender.

"Lindy, I need to ask you something." Unexpectedly Carol's mind was buzzing with doubts about the future.

"Sure, what is it?"

"If anything were to happen to me after the baby's born—"

"Nothing's going to happen to you," Lindy argued.

"Probably not." Carol pulled out the kitchen chair

and sat down. She didn't want to sound as though she had a death wish, but with the baby came a responsibility she hadn't thought of before her illness. "I don't have much in the way of family. My mother died several years ago—soon after Steve…soon after I was married. She and my father were divorced years before, and I hardly know him. He has another family and I rarely hear from him."

Lindy nodded. "Dr. Elgin, the surgeon, asked us to contact any close family members and Steve phoned your father. He…he couldn't come."

"He's a busy man," Carol said, willingly offering an excuse for her father, the way she had for most of her life. "But if I were to die," she persisted, "there'd be no one to raise my baby."

"Steve…"

Carol shook her head. "No. He'll probably marry again and have his own family someday. And if he doesn't, he'll be so involved in the Navy he won't be much good for raising a child." It was so much to ask of anyone, even a friend as near and dear as Lindy. "Would you and Rush consider being her guardians?"

"Of course, Carol," Lindy assured her warmly. "But nothing's going to happen to you."

Carol smiled. "I certainly plan on living a long, productive life, but something like this surgery hits close to home."

"I'll talk it over with Rush, but I'm sure he'll be more than willing for us to be your baby's guardians."

"Thank you," Carol said, and impulsively hugged Lindy. Steve's family had always been good to her.

"Okay, now that that's settled, how about a hot game of gin rummy? I feel lucky."

"Sure…" Carol paused and her eyes rounded. Her hand moved to the slight curve of her stomach as her heart filled with happiness.

"Are you all right?"

"I'm fine. The baby just moved—she does that quite a bit now—but never this strong."

"Does it hurt?"

Carol shook her head. "Not in the least. I don't know how to describe it, but every time she decides to explore her little world, I get excited. In four short months I'll be holding my daughter. Oh, Lindy, I can hardly believe it… I can hardly wait."

"Have you ever considered the possibility that *she* might be a *he*?"

"Nope. Not once. The moment I decided to get pregnant, I put my order in for a girl. The least Steve could do was get that right." His name slipped out unnoticed, but as soon as it left her lips, Carol stiffened. She was doing her utmost to disentangle him from her life, peeling away the threads that were so securely wrapped around her soul. There was no going back now, she realized. She'd confirmed every insulting thing he'd ever accused her of.

The mention of Steve seemed to subdue them both.

"Have you chosen a name for the baby?" Lindy asked a little too brightly in an all too apparent effort to change the subject.

Carol dropped her gaze. She'd originally intended to name the baby Stephanie, after Steve, but she'd since decided against that. There would be enough reminders that Steve was her baby's father without using his name. "Not yet," she answered.

"And you're feeling better?"

"Much." Although she was enjoying staying with Lindy and Rush, Carol longed to go back to her own home. Now that Steve was completely out of her life, living with his sister was flirting with misery. Twice Lindy had tried to casually bring Steve into their conversation. Carol had swiftly stopped her both times, but she didn't know who it was harder on—Lindy or herself. She didn't want to hear about Steve, didn't want to think about him.

Not anymore. Not again.

"So how are you feeling, young lady?" Dr. Stewart asked as he walked into the examination room. "I'll have you know you gave us all quite a scare."

"That's what I hear." This was her first appointment to see Dr. Stewart since she'd left the hospital. She'd been through a series of visits with the surgeon, Dr. Elgin, and everything was progressing as it should with the post-surgery healing.

"And how's that little fighter been treating you lately?" he asked with an affectionate chuckle, eyeing Carol's tummy. "Is the baby moving regularly now?"

She nodded eagerly. "All the time."

"Excellent."

"She seems determined to make herself felt."

"This is only the beginning," Dr. Stewart said chuckling. "Wait a few months and then tell me what you think."

The nurse came into the room and Carol lay back on the examination table while the doctor listened for the baby's heartbeat. He grinned and Carol smiled back. Her world might be crumbling around the edges, but the baby filled her with purpose and hope for a brighter future.

"You've returned to work?"

She nodded. "Part-time for the next couple of weeks, then full-time depending on how tired I get. Despite everything, I actually feel terrific."

He helped her into an upright position. "It's little wonder after what you went through—anything is bound to be an improvement." As he spoke he made several notations in her file. "You were one sick young lady. I don't mind telling you," Dr. Stewart added, looking up from her chart, "I was greatly impressed with that young man of yours."

Carol's smile was forced and her heart lurched at the reference to Steve. "Thank you."

"He wouldn't leave your side—not for a moment. Dr. Elgin commented on the fact just the other day. We both believe it was his love that got you through those darkest hours. He was determined that you live." He paused and chuckled softly. "I don't think God Himself would have dared to claim you."

Carol dropped her gaze, not knowing how to comment.

"He's a fine young man. Navy?"

"Yes."

"Give him my regards, will you?"

Carol nodded, her eyes avoiding his.

"Continue with the vitamins and make an appointment to see me in a couple of weeks." He gently patted Carol's hand and moved out of the room.

From the doctor's office, Carol returned to work. But when she pulled into the Boeing parking lot, she sat in her car for several moments, mulling over what Dr. Stewart had told her.

It was Steve's voice that called to her in the dark fog. Steve had been the one who'd comforted her. And when she'd felt the pull of the night, it was he who had demanded she return to the light. According to Dr. Stewart, he'd refused to leave her side.

Carol hadn't known.

She was stunned. She'd purposely lied to him, wanting to hurt him for being so insensitive about the possibility of the surgery claiming their baby's life. She'd been confused and angry because so much of what he wanted for her revealed his lack of faith in her integrity.

She'd sent him away and yet he'd refused to leave her to suffer through the ordeal alone.

Before she returned to her own job section, Carol stopped off to see Lindy.

"Hi," Lindy greeted, looking up from her desk. "What did the doctor have to say?"

"Take your vitamins and see me in two weeks."

"That sounds profound."

Carol scooted a chair toward Lindy's desk and clasped her purse tightly between her hands. The action produced a wide-eyed stare from her former sister-in-law.

"Something Dr. Stewart did say was profound," Carol stated in even tones, although the information Dr. Stewart had given her had shaken her soul.

"Oh? What?"

"He told me Steve was with me every minute after the surgery. He claimed it was Steve who got me through it alive."

"He was there, all right," Lindy confirmed readily.

"No one could get him to leave you. You know how stubborn he is. I think he was afraid that if he walked away, you'd die."

"You didn't tell me that."

"Of course I didn't! If you'll recall, I've been forbidden to even mention his name. You practically have a seizure if I so much as hint that there could be someone named Steve distantly related to either of us."

"But I'd told him the baby wasn't his... I sent him away."

"You told him what?" Lindy demanded, her eyes as round as dinner plates. "Why? Carol, how could you? Oh, good grief—it isn't any wonder you two have problems. It's like watching a boxing match. You seem to take turns throwing punches at each other."

"He...didn't say anything?"

"No. Steve never tells me what's going on in his life. No matter what's happened between you two, he won't say a word. I still don't know the reason you divorced in the first place. Even Rush isn't sure what happened. Steve's like that—he keeps everything to himself."

"And he stayed with me, even after I said I wouldn't remarry him," Carol murmured, feeling worse by the moment.

"There will never be anyone else for him but you, Carol," Lindy murmured. Some of the indignation had left her, but she still carried an affronted look, as if she wanted to stand up and defend her brother.

Carol didn't need Lindy's outrage in order to feel guilty. Lying had never set well with her, but Steve had hurt her so badly. She would like to think that she'd been delirious with pain at the time and not herself, but that wasn't the case. When she'd told Steve that she was going to accept another man's marriage proposal, she'd known exactly what she was doing.

"I owe him so much," Carol murmured absentmindedly.

"According to the surgeon and Dr. Stewart, you owe Steve your life."

Carol's gaze held Lindy's. "Why didn't you say something earlier?"

Lindy tossed her hands into the air. "You wouldn't let me. Remember?"

"I know… I'm sorry." Carol felt like weeping. Lindy was right, so very right. Her relationship with Steve was like a championship boxing match. Although they loved each other, they continued to strike out in a battle of words and deeds.

It wasn't until after she got home and had time to think matters through that Carol decided what she needed to do—what she had to do.

It wouldn't be easy.

Steve read the directions on the back of the frozen dinner entrée and turned the dial on the oven to the appropriate setting. He never had been much of a cook, choosing to eat most of his meals out. Lately, however, even that was more of an effort than he wanted to make. He'd been reduced to frozen TV dinners.

While they were married, Carol had—

Steve ground his thoughts to a screeching halt as he forced the name of his ex-wife from his mind. It astonished him how easily she slipped in where he desperately didn't want her. Yet he was doing everything he could to try to forget the portion of his life that they'd shared.

But that was more easily said than done.

He hadn't asked Lindy about Carol since she'd been released from the hospital. He wanted to know if Todd Larson was giving her the time she needed from work to heal properly. The amount of control it demanded to avoid the subject of Carol with his sister depleted his energy. He was like a man lost in the middle of a desert, dying of thirst. And water was well within sight, but he dared not drink.

Carol had her own life, and now that she and the baby were safe, she was free to seek her own happiness. As he could—only there would be little contentment in his life without her.

The sound of the doorbell caught him by surprise. He tossed the frozen dinner into the oven and headed to the front door, determined to get rid of whoever was there. He wasn't in any mood for company.

"Hello, Steve."

Carol stood on the other side of the threshold, and he was so shocked to see her that someone could have blown him over with the toot of a toy whistle.

"Carol…how are you?" he asked, his voice stiff, his body tense as though mentally preparing for pain.

"I'm doing much better."

She answered him with a gentle smile that spoke of reluctance and regret. Just looking at her tore through his middle.

"Would you like to come in?" he asked. Refusing her entry would be rude, and they'd done more than their share of hurting each other.

"Please."

He stepped aside, pressing himself against the door. She looked well, her coloring once more pink and healthy. Her eyes were soft and appealing when he dared to meet her gaze, which took effort to avoid.

Carol stood in the center of his living room, staring out the window at the panorama of the city. Steve had the impression, though, that she wasn't really looking at the view.

"Would you like something to drink?" he asked when she didn't speak immediately.

"No, thanks…this will only take a moment."

Now that he'd found his bearings, Steve forced himself to relax.

"I was in to see Dr. Stewart this afternoon," she said, and her voice pitched a little as if she were struggling to get everything out. "He…he told me how you were with me after the surgery."

"Listen, Carol, if you've come to thank me, it isn't necessary. If you'd told me who the baby's father is, I would have gone for him. He could have stayed with you, but—"

"I lied," Carol interrupted, squaring her shoulders.

He let her words soak into his mind before he responded. "About what?"

"Marrying the baby's father. I told you that because I was so hurt by what you'd said."

"What I'd said?" He couldn't recall doing or saying anything to anger her. The fact was, he'd done everything possible to show her how much he loved and cared about her.

"You suggested it would be better if I did lose this child," she murmured, and her voice trembled even more, "because next time you could be certain you were the father."

She seemed to want him to respond to that.

"I remember saying something along those lines."

Carol closed her eyes as if her patience was depleted and she was seeking another share. "I couldn't take any more of your insults, Steve."

Everything he said and did was wrong when it came to Carol. He wanted to explain, but doubted that it would do any good. "My concern was for you. Any husband would have felt the same way, pregnancy or no pregnancy."

"You aren't my husband."

"I wanted to be."

"That was another insult!" she cried, and a sheen of tears brightened her eyes.

"My marriage proposal was an insult?" he shouted, hurt and stunned.

"Yes…no. The offer to leave the Navy was what bothered me most."

"Then far be it from me to offend you again." There was no understanding this woman. He was willing to give up everything that had ever been important to him for her sake, and she threw the offer back in his face with some ridiculous claim. To hear her tell it, he'd scorned her by asking her to share his life.

The silence stretched interminably. They stood only a few feet apart, but the expanse of the Grand Canyon could have stretched between them for all the communicating they were doing.

The problem, Steve recognized, was that they were both so battle scarred that it was almost impossible for them to talk to each other. Every word they muttered became suspect. No subject was safe. They weren't capable of discussing the weather without finding something to fight about.

"I didn't come here to argue with you," Carol said in weary, reluctant tones. "I wanted to thank you for everything you did. I apologize for lying to you—it was a rotten thing to do."

It was on the tip of his tongue to suggest that he'd gotten accustomed to her lies, but he swallowed the cruel barb. He'd said and done enough to cause her pain in the last couple of years—there was no reason to hurt her more. He would only regret it later. She would look at him with those big blue eyes of hers and he would see all the way to her soul and know the agony he viewed there was of his making. Her look would haunt him for days afterward.

She turned and started to walk away, and Steve knew that if he let her go there would be no turning back. His heart and mind were racing. His heart with dread, his mind with an excuse to keep her. Any excuse.

"Carol—"

Already she was at the front door. "Yes?"

"I…have you eaten?"

Her brow creased, as if food was the last thing on her mind. Her gaze was weary as though she couldn't trust him. "Not yet."

"Would you like to go out with me? For dinner?"

She hesitated.

"The last time you were at the apartment, you said something about a restaurant you wanted to try close to here," he said, reminding her. She'd come to his place with a silly button in her hand and lovemaking on her mind. Things had been bad between them then, and had gone steadily downhill ever since.

She nodded. "The Mexican Lindo."

"Shall we?"

Still she didn't look convinced. "Are you sure this is what you want?"

Now it was his turn to nod. He wanted it so much he could have wept. "Yes, I want this," he admitted.

Some of the tiredness left her eyes and a gentle smile touched her lovely face. "I want it, too."

Steve felt like leaping in the air and clicking his heels. "I'll be just a minute," he said hurriedly. He walked into his kitchen and with a quick twist of his wrist, he turned off the oven. He would toss the aluminum meal later.

For now, he had a dinner date with the most beautiful woman in the world.

Fifteen

Elaborately decorated Mexican hats adorned the white stucco walls of the restaurant. A spicy, tangy scent wafted through the dining area as Carol and Steve read the plastic-coated menu.

Steve made his decision first.

"Cheese enchiladas," Carol guessed, her eyes linking with his.

"Right. What are you going to have?"

She set aside the menu. "The same thing—enchiladas sound good."

The air between them remained strained and awkward, but Carol could sense how desperately they were each trying to ignore it.

"How are you feeling?" Steve asked after a cumbersome moment of silence. His eyes were warm and tender and seemed to caress her every time he looked in her direction.

"A thousand times better."

He nodded. "I'm glad." He lifted the fork and absently ran his fingers down the tines.

"Dr. Stewart asked me to give you his regards," Carol

said in an effort to make conversation. There were so few safe topics for them.

"I like him. He's got a lot of common sense."

"The feeling's mutual—Dr. Stewart couldn't say enough good things about you."

Steve chuckled. "You sound surprised."

"No. I know the kind of man you are." Loving, loyal, determined, proud. Stubborn. She hadn't spent five years of her life married to a stranger.

The waitress came to take their order, and returned a couple of minutes later with a glass of milk for Carol and iced tea for Steve.

"I'm pleased we have this opportunity to talk before I'm deployed," he said, and his hand closed around the tall glass.

"When will you be leaving?"

"In a couple of weeks."

Carol nodded. She was nearly six months pregnant now and if Steve was at sea for the usual three, he might not be home when the baby was born. It all depended on when he sailed.

"I used to hate it when you went to sea." The words slipped from her lips without thought. She hadn't meant to make a comment one way or the other about his tour. It was a part of his life and one she had accepted when she agreed to marry him.

"You hated my leaving?" He repeated her words as though he was certain he'd heard her incorrectly. His gaze narrowed. "You used to see me off with the biggest smile this side of the Mississippi. I always thought you were happy to get me out of your hair."

"That was what I wanted you to think," she confessed with some reluctance. "I might have been smiling on the outside, but on the inside I was dreading every minute of the separation."

"You were?"

"Three months may not seem like a long time to you, but my life felt so empty when you were on the *Atlantis*." The first few years of their marriage, Carol had likened Steve's duty to his sub to a deep affection for another woman who whimsically demanded his attention whenever she wanted him. It wasn't until later that she realized how silly it was to be jealous of a nuclear submarine. She'd done everything possible to keep occupied when he was at sea.

"But you took all those community classes," he argued, breaking into her thoughts. "I swear you had something scheduled every night of the week."

"I had to do something to fill the time so I wouldn't go stir crazy."

"You honestly missed me?"

"Oh, Steve, how could you have doubted it?"

He flattened his hands on the table and slowly shook his head. "But I thought... I honestly believed you enjoyed it when I was away. You used to tell me it was the only time you could get anything accomplished." His voice remained low and incredulous. "My being underfoot seemed to be a detriment to all your plans."

"You had to know how I felt, or you wouldn't have suggested leaving the Navy."

Steve lowered his gaze and shrugged. "That offer was for me as much as you."

"So you could keep an eye on me—I figured that out on my own. If you held a regular nine-to-five job, then you could keep track of my every move and make sure there wasn't any opportunity for me to meet someone else."

"I imagine you found that insulting."

She nodded. "I don't know any woman who wouldn't."

A heavy silence followed, broken only by the waitress delivering their meals and reminding them that the plates were hot.

Steve studied the steaming food. "I suppose that was what you meant when you said my marriage proposal was an insult?"

Carol nodded, regretting those fiery words now. It wasn't the proposal, but what had followed that she'd taken offense to. "I could have put it a little more tactfully, but generally, yes."

Steve expelled his breath forcefully and reached for his fork. "I can't say I blame you. I guess I wasn't thinking straight. All I knew was that I loved…love you," he corrected. "And I wanted us to get married. Leaving the Navy seemed an obvious solution."

Carol let that knowledge soak into her thoughts as she ate. They were both quiet, contemplative, but the silence, for once, wasn't oppressive.

"I dreaded your coming home, too," Carol confessed partway through her meal.

Steve's narrowed gaze locked with hers, and his jaw clenched until she was sure he would damage his teeth, but he made no comment. It took her a moment to identify his anger. He'd misconstrued her comments and assumed the worst—the way he always did with her. He thought she was referring to the guilt she must have experienced upon his return. Hot frustration pooled in the pit of her stomach, but she forced herself to remain calm and explain.

"I could never tell what you were thinking when you returned from a deployment," she whispered, her voice choked and weak. "You never seemed overly pleased to be back."

"You're crazy. I couldn't wait to see you."

"It's true you couldn't get me in bed fast enough, but I meant in other ways."

"What ways?"

She shrugged. "For the first few days and sometimes even longer, it was like you were a different man. You would always be so quiet...so detached. There was so little emotion in your voice—or your actions."

"Honey, I'd just spent a good portion of that tour four hundred feet below sea level. We're trained to speak in subdued, monotone voices. If my voice inflections bothered you, why didn't you say something?"

She dropped her gaze and shrugged. "I was so pleased to have you back that I didn't want to say or do anything to cause an argument. It was such a small thing, and I would have felt like a fool for mentioning it."

Steve took a deep breath. "I know what you mean— I couldn't very well comment on how glad you were to see me leave without sounding like an insecure jerk— which I was. But that's neither here nor there."

"I wish I'd said something now, but I was trying so hard to be the kind of wife you wanted. Please know that I was always desperately lonely without you."

Steve took a couple more bites, but his interest in the food had obviously waned. "I can understand why you felt the need for...companionship."

Carol froze and a thread of righteous anger weaved its way down her spine. "I'm going to forget you said that," she murmured, having difficulty controlling her trembling voice.

Steve looked genuinely surprised. "Said what?"

Carol simply shook her head. They would only argue if she pressed the subject, and she didn't have the strength for it. "Never mind."

Her appetite gone, she pushed her plate aside. "You used to sit and stare at the wall."

"I beg your pardon?" Steve was finished with his meal, too, and scooted his plate aside.

"When you came home from a tour," she explained. "For days afterward, you hardly did a thing. You were so detached."

"I was?" Steve mulled over that bit of insight. "Yes, I guess you're right. It always takes me a few days to separate myself from my duties aboard the *Atlantis*. It's different aboard the sub, Carol. I'm different. When I'm home, especially after being at sea several weeks, it takes time to make the adjustment."

"You're so unfeeling... I don't know how to explain it. Nothing I'd say or do would get much reaction from you. If I proudly showed off some project I'd completed in your absence, you'd smile and nod your head or say something like 'That's nice, dear.'"

Steve grinned, but the action revealed little amusement. "Reaction is something stringently avoided aboard the sub, too. I'm an officer. If I panic, everyone panics. We're trained from the time we're cadets to perform our duties no matter what else is happening. There's no room for emotion."

Carol chewed on the corner of her lower lip.

"Can you understand that?"

She nodded. "I wish I'd asked you about all this years ago."

"I didn't realize I behaved any differently. It was always so good to get home to you that I didn't stop to analyze my behavior."

The waitress came and took away their plates.

"We should have been honest with each other instead of trying to be what we thought the other person wanted," Carol commented, feeling chagrined that they'd been married five years and had never really understood each other.

"Yes, we should have," he agreed. "I'm hoping it isn't too late for us to learn. We could start over right now, determined to be open and honest with each other."

"I think we should," Carol agreed, and smiled.

Steve's hand reached across the table for hers. "I'd like us to start over in other ways, too—get to know each other. We could start dating again the way we did in the beginning."

"I think that's a good idea."

"How about walking down to the waterfront for an ice-cream cone?" he suggested after he'd paid the tab.

Carol was stuffed from their dinner, but did not want their evening to end. Their love had been given a second chance, and she was grabbing hold of it with both hands. They were wiser this time, more mature and prepared to proceed cautiously.

"Are you insinuating that I need fattening up?" she teased, lacing her fingers with his.

"Yes," he admitted honestly.

"How can you say that?" she asked with a soft laugh. She may have lost weight with the surgery, but the baby was filling out her tummy nicely, and it was obvious that she was pregnant. "I eat all the time now. I didn't realize how sick I'd been and now everything tastes so good."

"Cherry vanilla?"

"Ooo, that sounds wonderful. Double-decker?"

"Triple," Steve answered and squeezed her hand.

Lacing their fingers like high-school sweethearts, they strolled down to the steep hill toward the waterfront like young lovers eager to explore the world.

As he promised, Steve bought them each huge ice-cream cones. They sat on one of the benches that lined the pier and watched the gulls circle overhead.

Carol took a long, slow lick of the cool dessert and smiled when she noted Steve watching her. "I told you I've really come to appreciate my food lately."

His gaze fell to the rounded swell of her stomach. "What did Dr. Stewart have to say about the baby?"

Carol flattened her hand over her abdomen and glowed with an inner happiness that came to her whenever she thought about her child. "This kid is going to be just fine."

He darted his gaze away as though he was uncomfortable even discussing the pregnancy. "I'm pleased for you both. You'll be a good mother, Carol."

Once more frustration settled on her shoulders like a dark shroud. Steve still didn't believe the baby was his. She wasn't going to argue with him. He was smart enough to figure it out.

"Do you need anything?" he surprised her by asking next. "I'd be happy to do what I can to help. I'm sure the medical expenses wreaked havoc with your budget, and you're probably counting on that income to buy things for the baby. I'd like to pitch in, if you'd let me."

His offer touched her heart and she took a minute

to swallow the tears that burned the back of her eyes at his generosity.

"Thank you, Steve, that means a lot to me, but I'm all right financially. It'll be tight for a couple of months, but nothing I can't handle. I've managed to save quite a bit over the past year."

He stood, buried his hands in his pockets and walked along the edge of the pier. Carol joined him, licking the last of the ice cream off her fingertips.

Steve looked down and smiled into her eyes. "Here," he said and used his index finger to wipe away a smudge near the corner of her mouth.

He paused and his gaze seemed to consume her face. His eyes, so dark and compelling, studied her as if she were some angelic being and he was forbidden to do anything more than gaze upon her. His brow compressed and his eyes shifted to her mouth. As if against his will, he ran his thumb along the seam of her lower lip and gasped softly when her tongue traced his handiwork. He tested the slickness with the tip of his finger, slowly sliding it back and forth, creating a delicate kind of friction.

Carol was filled with breathless anticipation. Everything around them, the sights, the sounds, the smells of the waterfront, seemed to dissolve with the feeling. He wanted to kiss her, she could feel it with every beat of her heart. But he held back.

Then, in a voice that was so low, so quiet, it could hardly be counted as sound, he said, "Can I?"

In response, Carol turned and slipped her arm around his neck. His eyes watched her, and a fire seemed to leap from them, a feral glow that excited her all the more.

She could feel the tension in him, his whole body seemed to vibrate with it.

His mouth came down on hers, open and eager. Carol groaned and instinctively swayed closer to him. His tongue plunged quickly and deeply into her mouth and she met it greedily. He tasted and teased and withdrew, then repeated the game until the savage hunger in them both had been pitched to a fevered level. Still his lips played over hers, and once the urgent need had been appeased, the kiss took on a new quality. His mouth played a slow, seductive rhythm over hers—a tune with which they were both achingly familiar.

He couldn't seem to get enough of her and even after the kiss had ended, he continued to take short, sweet samples of her lips, reluctant to part for even a minute. Finally he buried his head in the curve of her neck and took in short raspy breaths.

Carol surfaced in slow, reluctant degrees, her head buzzing. She clung to him as tightly as he held on to her.

"We have an audience," Steve whispered with no element of alarm apparent in his tone or action.

Carol opened her eyes to find a little girl about five years old staring up at them.

"My mom and dad do that sometimes," she said, her face wrinkled with displeasure, "but not where lots of people can see them."

"I think you have a smart mom and dad," Steve answered, his voice filled with chagrin. Gently he pulled away from Carol and wrapped his arm around her waist, keeping her close to his side. "'Bye," he told the preschooler.

"'Bye," she said with a friendly wave, and then ran

back to a boy who appeared to be an older brother who was shouting to gain her attention.

The sun was setting, casting a rose-red hue over the green water.

They walked back to where Steve had parked his car and he opened her door for her. "Can I see you again?" he asked, with an endearing shyness.

"Yes."

He looked almost surprised. "How about tomorrow night? We could go to a movie."

"I'd like that. Are you going to buy me popcorn?"

He smiled, and from the look in his eyes he would be willing to buy her the whole theater if he could.

Sixteen

Steve found himself whistling as he strolled up the walkway to Carol's house. He felt as carefree as a college senior about to graduate. Grand adventures awaited him. He had every detail of their evening planned. He would escort Carol to the movies, as they'd agreed, then afterward he would take her out for something to eat. She needed to gain a few pounds and it made him feel good to spend money on her.

When they arrived back at the house, she would invite him in for coffee and naturally he would agree. Once inside it would take him ten…fifteen minutes at the most to steer her into the bedroom. He was starved for her love, famished by his need for her.

The kiss they'd shared the night before had convinced him this was necessary. He was so crazy in love with this woman that he couldn't wait another night to take her to bed. She was right about them starting over—he was willing to do that. It was the going-nice-and-slow part he objected to. He understood exactly what she intended when she decided they could start over. It was waiting for the lovemaking that confused him. Good

Lord, they'd been married five years. It wasn't as if they were virgins anticipating their wedding night.

"Hi," Carol said and smiled, opening the door for him.

"Hi." Steve couldn't take his eyes off her. She was wearing the blue maternity dress he'd bought for her the day he'd followed her around like the KGB. "You look beautiful," he said in what had to be the understatement of the year. He'd heard about women having a special glow about them when they were pregnant—Carol had never been more lovely than she was at that moment.

"Do you like it?" she asked and slowly whirled around showing off the dress to full advantage. "Lindy bought it for me. She said she found it on sale and couldn't resist. It was the craziest thing because I'd tried on this very dress and loved it, but decided I really couldn't afford to be spending money on myself. She gave me a silver baby rattle, too. I have a feeling Aunt Lindy is going to spoil this baby."

"You look…marvelous."

"I'm getting so fat," she said, and chuckled. To prove her point, she scooped her hands under the soft swell of her abdomen and turned sideways to show him. She smiled, and her eyes sparkled as she jerked her head toward him and announced, "The baby just kicked."

"Can I feel?" Steve had done everything he could to convince himiself this child was his. Unfortunately he knew otherwise. But he loved Carol, and he'd love her baby. He would learn to—already he truly cared about her child. Without this pregnancy there was no way of knowing if they would ever have gotten back together.

"Here." She reached for his hand and placed it over the top of her stomach. "Feel anything?"

He shook his head. "Nothing."

"Naturally she's going to play a game of cat and mouse now."

Steve removed his hand and flexed his fingers. Some of the happiness he'd experienced earlier seeped out of him, replaced with a low-grade despondency. He wanted her baby to be his with a desperation that threatened to destroy him. But he couldn't change the facts.

"I checked the paper and the movie starts at seven," Carol said, interrupting his thoughts.

He glanced at his watch. "We'd better not waste any time then." While Carol opened the entryway closet and removed a light sweater and her purse, Steve noted the two gallons of paint sitting on the floor.

"What are you painting?" he asked.

"The baby's room. I thought I'd tackle that project this weekend. I suddenly realized how much I have to do yet to get ready."

"Do you want any help?" He made a halfhearted offer, and wished almost immediately that he hadn't. It wasn't the painting that dissuaded him. Every time Carol so much as mentioned anything that had to do with the baby, her eyes lit up like the Fourth of July. His reaction was just as automatic, too. He was jealous, and that was the last thing he wanted Carol to know.

She closed the closet door and studied him, searching his eyes. He boldly met her look, although it was difficult, and wasn't disappointed when she shook her head. "No, thanks, I've got everything under control."

"You're sure?"

"Very."

There was no fooling Carol. She might as well have read his thoughts, because she knew and her look told him as much.

"I'm trying," he said, striving for honesty. "I really am trying."

"I know," she murmured softly.

They barely spoke on the way to the theater and Carol hardly noticed what was happening with the movie. She'd witnessed that look on Steve's face before when she started talking about the baby. So many subjects were open to them except that one. She didn't know any man more blind than Steve Kyle. If she were to stand up in the middle of the show and shout out that she was having his child, he wouldn't hear her. He'd buried his head so deep in the sand when it came to her pregnancy that his brain was plugged.

Time would teach him, if only she could hold on to her patience until then.

Steve didn't seem to be enjoying the movie any more than she was. He shifted in his seat a couple of times, crossed and uncrossed his legs and munched on his popcorn as if he were chewing bullets.

Carol shifted, too. She was almost six months pregnant and felt eight. The theater seat was uncomfortable and the baby had decided to play baseball, using Carol's ribs for batting practice.

She braced her hands against her rib cage and leaned to one side and then scooted to the other.

"Are you all right?" Steve whispered halfway through the feature film.

Carol nodded. She wanted to explain that the baby was having a field day, exploring and kicking and struggling in the tight confines of her compact world, but she avoided any mention of the pregnancy.

"Do you want some more popcorn?"

Carol shook her head. "No, thanks."

Ten minutes passed in which Carol did her utmost to pay attention to the show. She'd missed so much of the plot already that it was difficult to understand what was happening.

Feeling Steve's stare, Carol diverted her attention to him. He was glaring at her abdomen, his eyes wide and curious. "I saw him move," he whispered, his voice filled with awe. "I couldn't believe it. He's so strong."

"She," Carol corrected automatically, smiling. She took his hand and pressed it where she'd last felt the baby kick. He didn't pull away but there was some reluctance in his look.

The baby moved again, and Carol nearly laughed aloud at the astonishment that played over Steve's handsome features.

"My goodness," he whispered. "I had no idea."

"Trust me," she answered, and grinned. "I didn't, either."

Irritated by the way they were disrupting the movie, the woman in the row in front of them turned around to press her finger over her lips. But when she saw Steve's hand on Carol's stomach, she grinned indulgently and whispered, "Never mind."

Steve didn't take his hand away. When the baby punched her fist on the other side of Carol's belly, she slid his hand over there. She loved the slow, lazy grin that curved up the edges of his mouth. The action caused her to smile too. She tucked her hand over his and soon they both went back to watching the action on the screen. But Steve kept his fingers where they were for the rest of the movie, gently caressing the rounded circle of her tummy.

By the time the film was over, Carol's head was resting on Steve's shoulder. Although the surgery had been weeks before, it continued to surprise her how quickly she tired. She'd worked that day and was exhausted. It irritated her that she could be so weak. Steve had mentioned getting something to eat after the movie, but she was having difficulty hiding her yawns from him.

"I think I'd better take you home," he commented once they were outside the theater.

"I'm sorry," she murmured, holding her hand to her mouth in a futile effort to hold in her tiredness. "I'm not used to being out so late two nights running."

Steve slipped his arm around her shoulders. "Me, either."

He steered her toward his car and opened the passenger door for her. Once she was inside, he gently placed a kiss on her cheek.

She nearly fell asleep on the short ride home.

"Do you want to come in for some coffee?" she offered when he pulled up to the curb in front of her house.

"You're sure you're up to this?" he asked, looking doubtful.

"I'm sure."

Carol thought she detected a bounce to his step as he came around to help her out of the car, but she couldn't be sure. Steve Kyle said and did the most unpredictable things at times.

Once inside he took her sweater, and while he was hanging it up for her, she went into the kitchen and got down the coffee from the cupboard. Steve moved behind her and slipped his arms around her waist.

"I don't really want coffee," he whispered and gently caught her earlobe between his teeth.

"You don't?"

"No," he murmured.

His hands explored her stomach in a loving caress and Carol felt herself go weak. "I... I wish you'd said something earlier."

"It was a pretense." His mouth blazed a moist trail down the side of her neck.

"Pretense," she repeated in a daze.

As if he were a puppet master directing her actions, Carol turned in his arms and raised her face to his, anticipating his kiss. Her whole body felt as if it were rocking with the force of her heartbeat, anticipating the touch of his mouth over hers.

Steve didn't keep her waiting long. His hands cradled her neck and his lips found hers, exploring them as though he wished to memorize their shape. She parted her mouth in welcome, and his tongue touched hers, then delicately probed deeper in a sweet, unhurried exploration that did incredible things to her. Desire created a churning, boiling pool deep in the center of her body.

His fingers slipped from her nape to tangle with her hair. Again and again, he ran his mouth back and forth over hers, pausing now and again to tease her with a fleck of his tongue against the seam of her lips. "I thought about doing this all day," he confessed.

"Oh, Steve."

His hands searched her back, grasping at the material of her dress as he claimed her mouth in a kiss that threatened to burst them both into searing flames. With a frustrated groan, he drew his arms around her front, searching. His breath came in ragged, thwarted gasps.

Carol could feel the heavy pounding of his heart and she pressed her open mouth to the hollow at the base of his throat, loving the way she could feel his pulse hammer there.

"Damn," he muttered, exasperated. "Where's the opening to this dress?"

It took Carol a moment to understand his question. "There is none."

"What?"

"I slip it on over my head…there aren't any buttons."

"No zipper?"

"None."

He muffled a groan against her neck and Carol felt the soft puffs of warm air as he chuckled. "This serves me right," he protested.

"What does?"

He didn't answer her. Instead, he cradled her breasts in his palms, bunching the material of her dress in the process. Slowly he rotated his thumb over her swollen, sensitive nipples until she gasped, first with shock and surprise, then with the sweet sigh of pleasure.

"Is it good, honey?" he asked, then kissed her, teasing her with his tongue until she was ready to collapse in his arms.

"It's very good," she told him when she could manage to speak, although her voice was incredibly low.

"I want you." He took her hand and pressed it down over his zipper so that she could feel for herself his bulging hardness.

"Oh, Steve." She ran her long fingernails over him.

Exquisitely aroused, he made small hungry sounds and whispered in a voice that shook with desire. "Come on, honey, I want to make love in a bed."

She made a weak sound of protest. "No." It demanded

every ounce of fortitude she possessed to murmur the small word.

"No?" he repeated stunned.

"No." There was more conviction in her voice this time. "So many of our discussions end up in the bedroom."

"Carol, dear God, talking was the last thing I had in mind."

"I know what you want," she whispered. "I think we should wait…it's too soon."

"Wait," he murmured, dragging in a deep breath. "Wait," he said again. "All right, if that's what you honestly want—then fine, anything you say." Reluctantly he released her. "I'm going to have to get out of here while I still can, though. Walk me to the door, will you?"

Carol escorted him to her front door and his hungry kiss revealed all his pent-up frustration.

"You're sure?" he asked one last time, giving her a round-eyed look that would put a puppy to shame.

"No… I'm not the least bit sure," she admitted, and when his eyes widened even more, she laughed aloud at the excitement that flared to life so readily. "I don't like this any better than you do," she told him, "but I honestly think it's necessary. When the time's right we'll know it."

He shut his eyes and nodded. "I was afraid of that."

Seventeen

Carol woke before seven Saturday morning, determined to get an early start on painting the baby's bedroom. She dressed in a old pair of summer shorts with a wide elastic band and a Seahawks T-shirt that had once been Steve's. A western bandana knotted at the base of her skull covered her blond hair. She looked like something out of the movie *Aliens*, she decided, smiling.

Oh, well, she wouldn't be seeing Steve. She regretted turning down his offer of help now, but it was too late for second thoughts. She hadn't seen him since the night they'd gone to the movies, nor had he phoned. That concerned her a little, but she tried not to let it bother her.

He was probably angry about her not letting him spend the night. Well, for his information, she'd been just as frustrated as he was. She'd honestly wanted him to stay—in fact, she'd tossed and turned in bed for a good hour after he'd left her, mulling over her decision. It may have been the right one, but it didn't take away this ache of loneliness, or ease her own sexual frustration.

For six years the only real communication between

them had been on a mattress. It was long past time they started building a solid foundation of love and trust. Those qualities were basic to a lifetime relationship, and they'd both suffered for not cultivating them.

By nine, Carol had the bedroom floor carpeted with a layer of newspapers. The windows were taped and she was prepared to do the cutting in around the corners and ceiling.

She carried the stepladder to the far side of the room and, humming softly, started brushing on the pale pink paint.

"What are you doing on that ladder?"

The voice startled her so much that she nearly toppled from her precarious perch. "Steve Kyle," she cried, violently expelling her breath. "You scared me half out of my mind."

"Sorry," he mumbled, frowning.

"What are you doing here?"

"I... I thought you could use some help." He held up a white sack. "Knowing you, you probably forgot to eat breakfast. I brought you something."

Now that she thought about it, Carol realized she hadn't had anything to eat.

"Thanks," she said grinning, grateful to see him. "I'm starved."

Climbing down the stepladder, she set aside the paint and brush and reached for the sack. "Milk," she said taking out a small carton, "and a muffin with egg and cheese." She smiled up at him and brushed her mouth over his cheek. "Thanks."

"Sit," he ordered, turning over a cardboard box as a mock table for her.

"What about you?"

"I had orange juice and coffee on the way over here." Hands on his hips, he surveyed her efforts. "Good grief, woman, you must have been at this for hours."

"Since seven," she said between bites. "It's going to be a scorcher today, and I wanted to get an early start."

He nodded absently, then turned the cap he was wearing around so that the brim pointed toward his back. Next, he picked up the paintbrush and coffee can she'd been using to hold paint. "I don't want you on that ladder, understand?"

"Aye, aye, Captain."

He responded to her light sarcasm with a soft chuckle. "Have you missed me?" he asked, turning momentarily to face her.

Carol dropped her gaze and nodded. "I thought you might be angry about the other night when you wanted to stay and—"

"Carol, no," he objected immediately. "I understood and you were right. I couldn't call—I've had twenty-four-hour duty."

Almost immediately Carol's spirits lifted and she placed the wrapper from her breakfast inside the paper sack. "Did you miss *me*?" she asked, loving the way his eyes brightened at her question.

"Come here and I'll show you how much."

Laughing, she shook her head. "No way, fellow. I'd like my baby's bedroom painted before she makes her debut." Carol noted the way Steve's face still tightened at the mention of her pregnancy and some of the happiness she'd experienced by his unexpected visit evaporated. He'd told her he was trying to accept her child and she believed him, but her patience was wearing perilously thin. After all, this child was his, too, and it was time he acknowledged the fact.

Pride drove her chin so high that the back of her neck ached. She reached for another paintbrush, her shoulders stiff with frustration. "I can do this myself, you know."

"I know," he returned.

"It isn't like I'm helpless."

"I know that, too."

Her voice trembled a little. "It isn't like you really want this baby."

An electric silence vibrated between them, arcing and spitting tension. Steve reacted to it first by lowering his brush.

"Carol, I'm sorry. I didn't mean to say or do anything to upset you. My offer to help is sincere—I'd like to do what I can, if you'll let me."

She bit into her lower lip and nodded. "I… I was being oversensitive, I guess."

"No," he hurried to correct her, "the problem is mine, but I'm dealing with it the best way I know how. I need time, that's all."

His gaze dropped to her protruding stomach and Carol saw a look of anguish flitter through his eyes, one so fleeting, so transient that for a second she was sure she was mistaken.

"Well," she said, drawing in a deep breath. "Are we going to paint or are we going to sit here and grumble at each other all day?"

"Paint," Steve answered, swiping the air with his brush, as if he were warding off pirates.

Carol smiled, then placed the back of her hand over her forehead and sighed. "My hero," she said teasingly.

By noon the last of the walls were covered and the white trim complete around the window and door.

Carol stepped back to survey their work. "Oh, Steve," she said with an elongated sigh. She slipped her arm around his waist. "It's lovely."

"I sincerely hope you get the girl you want so much, because a boy could take offense at all this pink."

"I am having a girl."

"You're sure?" He cocked his eyebrows with the question, his expression dubious.

"No-o-o, but my odds are fifty-fifty, and I'm choosing to think positive."

His arm tightened around her waist. "You've got paint in your hair," he said, looking down at her.

Wrinkling her nose, she riffled her fingers through her bangs. Steve's hand stopped her. His eyes lovingly stroked her face as if he meant to study each feature and commit it to memory. His gaze filled with such longing, such adoration that Carol felt as if she were some heavenly creature he'd been forbidden to touch. He raised his hand to her mouth and she stopped breathing for a moment.

His touch was unbelievably delicate as he rubbed the back of his knuckles over her moist lips. He released her and backed away, his breath audible.

Carol lifted her hand to the side of his face and he closed his eyes when the tips of her fingers grazed his cheek.

"Thank you for being here," she whispered. "Thank you for helping."

"I always want to be with you." He placed his hand over hers, intertwining their fingers. Tenderly, almost against his will, he lowered his knuckles to her breast, dragging them across the rigid, sensitive tip. Slowly. Gently. Back and forth. Again and again.

Carol sucked in her breath at the wild sensation that galloped through her blood. Her control was slipping. Fast. She felt weak, as though she would drop to the floor, and yet she didn't let go of his hand, pinning it against her throbbing nipple.

"How does that feel?" he asked, and he rotated his thumb around and around, intensifying the pleasure.

"...so good," she told him, her voice husky and barely audible.

"It's good for me, too."

His eyes were closed. As Carol watched his face harden with desire she knew her features were equally sharp.

He kissed her then, and the taste of him was so sweet, so incredibly good. His lips teased hers, his tongue probing her mouth, tracing first her upper and then her lower lip in a leisurely exercise. The kiss grew sweeter yet, and deeper.

Steve broke away and pressed his forehead against hers while taking in huge, ragged puffs of air. "There's something you should know."

"What?" She wrapped her hands around his middle, craving the feel of his body against her own.

"The orders for the *Atlantis* came in. I have to leave tomorrow."

Carol went stock-still. "Tomorrow?"

"I'm sorry, honey. I'd do anything I could to get out of this, but I can't."

"I...know."

"I got some Family-grams so you can let me know when the baby's born."

Carol remembered completing the short telegramlike messages while they were married. She was allowed to send a handful during the course of a tour, but under strict conditions. She wasn't allowed to use any codes, and she was prohibited from relaying any unpleasant news. She had forty-six words to tell him everything that was happening in her life. Forty-six words to tell him when his daughter was born, forty-six words to convince him this baby was his.

His hand slipped inside the waistband of her summer shorts and flattened over the baby. "I'll be waiting to hear."

Carol didn't know what to tell him. The baby could very well be born while he was away. It all depended on his schedule.

"I'd like to be here for you."

"I'll be fine… Both of us will." Carol felt as if she was going to dissolve into tears, her anguish was so keen. Her hand reached for his face and she traced his eyebrows, the arch of his cheek, his nose and his mouth with fingers that trembled with the strength of her love.

His hands slid behind her and cupped her buttocks, lifting her so that the junction between her thighs was nestled against the strong evidence of his desire.

"I want to make love," she whispered into his mouth, and then kissed him.

He shut his eyes. "Carol, no—you were right, we should wait. We've done this too often before…we…"

She hooked her left leg around his thigh and felt a surge of triumph at the shudder that went through him.

"Carol…"

Before he could think or move, she jerked the T-shirt off her head and quickly disposed of her bra. Her mouth worked frantically over his, darting her tongue in and out of his mouth, kissing him with a hunger that had been building within her for months. Her fingers worked feverishly at the buttons of his shirt. Once it was unfastened, she pulled his shirttails free of his waistband and bared his chest. Having achieved her objective, she leaned toward him just enough so that her bare breasts grazed his chest.

The low rumbling sound in Steve's throat made her smile. Slowly then, with unhurried ease, she swayed her torso, taking her pleasure by rubbing her distended nipples over the tense muscles of his upper body.

Steve's breathing came in short, rasping gasps as he spoke. "Maybe I was a bit hasty..."

Carol locked her hands behind his head. "How long will you be gone?" she asked, knowing full well the answer.

"Three months."

"You were too hasty."

"Does this mean...you're willing?"

"I was willing the other night."

"Oh, dear God, Carol, I want you so much."

She rubbed her thigh over his engorged manhood and he groaned. "I know what you want." She kissed him with all the pent-up longings of her heart. "I want you, too. Do you have any idea how much?"

He darted his tongue over one rigid nipple, feasting and sucking at her until she gave a small cry.

He lifted his head and chuckled. "Good, then the feeling's mutual."

With that, he swung her into his arms and carried her into the bedroom. Very gently he laid her atop the mattress and leaned over her, his upper body pinning her to the bed.

He stared down at her and his eyes darkened, but not with passion. It was something more, an emotion she couldn't readily identify.

"Will I...is there any chance I'll hurt the baby?" He whispered the question, his gaze narrowed and filled with concern.

"None."

He sighed his relief. "Oh, Carol, I love you so much."

She closed her eyes and directed his mouth to hers. She loved him, too, and she was about to prove how much.

Carol woke an hour before the alarm was set to ring. Steve slept soundly at her side, cuddling her spoon-fashion, his hand cupping the warm underside of her breast.

They'd spent the lazy afternoon making slow, leisurely love. Then they'd showered, eaten and made love again, with the desperation that comes of knowing it would be three months before they saw each other again.

It was morning. Soon he would be leaving her again. A lump of pain began to unflower inside her. It was always this way when Steve left. For years she'd hid her sorrow behind a cheerful smile, but she couldn't do that anymore. She couldn't disguise how weak and vulnerable she was without him.

Not again.

When it became impossible to hold back the tears, she silently slipped from the bed, donned her robe and moved into the kitchen. Once there, she put on a pot of coffee just so she'd be doing something.

Steve found her sitting at the table with a large pile of

tissues stacked next to her coffee cup. She looked up at him, and sobbed once, and reached for another Kleenex.

"G-g-good m-morning," she blubbered. "D-did you sleep well?"

Obviously bewildered, Steve nodded. "You didn't?"

"I s-slept okay."

Watching her closely, he walked over to the table. "You're crying."

"I know that," she managed between sobs.

"But why?"

If he wasn't smart enough to figure that out then he didn't deserve to know.

"Carol, are you upset because I'm leaving?"

She nodded vigorously. "Bingo—give the man a Kewpie doll."

He knelt down beside her, took her free hand and kissed the back of it. He rubbed his thumb over her knuckles and waited until she swallowed and found her voice.

"I hate it when you have to leave me," she confessed when she could talk. "Every time I think we're getting somewhere you sail off into the sunset."

"I'm coming back."

"Not for three months." She jerked the tissue down both sides of her face. "I always c-cry when you go. You just never see me. This t-time I can't...h-hold it in a minute longer."

Steve knelt in front of her and wrapped his arms around her middle. With his head pressed over her breast, one hand rested on top of her rounded stomach.

"I'll be back, Carol."

"I...know."

"But this time when I return, it'll be special."

She nodded because speaking had become impossible.

"We'll have a family."

She sucked in her breath and nodded.

"Dammit, Carol, don't you know that I hate leaving you, too?"

She shrugged.

"And worse, every time I go, I regret that we aren't married. Don't you think we should take care of that next time?"

She hiccuped. "Maybe we should."

Eighteen

"This works out great," Lindy said, standing in line for coffee aboard the ferry *Yakima* as it eased away from the Seattle wharf, heading toward Bremerton. "You can drop me off at Susan's and I can ride home with Rush. I couldn't have planned this any better myself."

"Glad to help," Steve answered, but his thoughts weren't on his sister. Carol continued to dominate his mind. He'd left her only a couple of hours earlier and it felt as if years had passed—years or simply minutes, he couldn't decide which.

She'd stood on the front porch as he walked across the lawn to his car. The morning sunlight had silhouetted her figure against the house. Tears had brightened her eyes and a shaky smile wobbled over her mouth. When he'd opened the car door and looked back, she'd raised a hand in silent farewell and done her best to send him off with a proud smile.

Steve had stood there paralyzed, not wanting to leave her, loving her more than he thought it was possible to care about anyone. His gaze centered on her abdomen and the child she carried and his heart lurched with such pain that he nearly dropped to his knees. There stood Carol, the woman he loved and would always love, and she carried another man's child. The anguish built up inside him like steam ready to explode out of a teakettle. But as quickly as the emotion came, it left him. The baby was Carol's, a part of her, an innocent. This child deserved his love. It shouldn't matter who the father was. If Steve was going to marry Carol—which he fully intended to do—she came as part of a package deal. Carol and the baby. He sucked in his breath, determined to do his best for them both.

Now, hours later, the picture of her standing there on the porch continued to scorch his mind.

"Lindy," he said, as they reached a table, "I need you to do something for me."

"Sure. Anything."

Steve pulled out his checkbook and set it on the table. "I want you to go to the JCPenney store and buy a crib, and a few other things."

"Steve, listen…"

"The crib's called the Jenny Lind—at least I think it was." The picture of Carol running her hand over the railing that day he'd followed her came to his mind. "It's white, I remember that much. I don't think you'll have any trouble knowing which one I mean once you see their selection."

"I take it you want the crib for Carol?"

"Of course. And while you're there, pick out a high chair and stroller and whatever else you can find that you think she could use."

"Steve, no."

"No!" He couldn't believe his sister. "Why the hell not?"

"When I agreed to do you a favor, I thought you

wanted me to pick up your cleaning or check on the apartment—that sort of thing. If you want to buy things for Carol, I'm refusing you point-blank. I won't have anything to do with it."

"Why?" Lindy and Carol were the best of friends. His sister couldn't have shocked him more if she'd suggested he leap off the ferry.

"Remember the dress?" Lindy asked, and her chest heaved with undisguised resentment. "I felt like a real heel giving her that, and worse, lying about it." Her face bunched into a tight frown. "Carol was as excited as a kid at Christmas over that maternity dress, and I had to tell her I'd seen it on sale and thought of her and how I hoped against hope that it would fit." She paused and glared at him accusingly. "You know I'm not the least bit good at lying. It's a wonder Carol didn't figure it out. And if I didn't feel bad enough about the dress, the rattle really did it."

Steve frowned, too. He'd asked Lindy to make up some story about the dress and the toy so that Carol wouldn't know he'd been following her that afternoon. Those had been dark days for him—and for Carol.

"Did you know," Lindy demanded, cutting into his thoughts and waving her finger under his nose, "Carol got all misty over that silver rattle?" The look she gave Steve accused him of being a coward. "*I* nearly started crying by the time she finished."

Steve's hand cupped the Styrofoam container of coffee. "I'm glad she liked it."

"It was the first thing anyone had given her for the baby, and she was so pleased that she could barely talk." Lindy paused and slowly shook her head. "I felt like the biggest idiot alive to take credit for that."

"If you'll recall, sister dearest, Carol didn't want to have anything to do with me at the time."

Lindy's eyes rounded with outrage. "And little wonder. You are so dense sometimes, Steve Kyle."

Steve ignored his sister's sarcasm and wrote out a check, doubling the amount he'd originally intended. "Buy her a bunch of baby clothes while you're at it… and send her a huge bouquet of roses when she's in the hospital, too."

"Steve… I don't know."

He refused to argue with her. Instead, he tore off the check, and slipped it across the table.

Lindy took it and studied the amount. She arched her eyebrows and released a soft, low whistle. "I'm not hiding this. I'm going to tell Carol all these gifts are from you. I refuse to lie this time."

"Fine…do what you think is best."

Steve watched as she folded the check in half and stuck it inside a huge bag she called her purse.

"Actually you may be sorry you trusted me with this task later," Lindy announced, looking inordinately pleased about something.

She said this with a soft smile, and her eyes sparkled with mischief.

"Why's that?"

Lindy rested her elbows on the tabletop and sighed. "Rush and I are planning to start our family."

The thought of his little sister pregnant did funny things to Steve. She was ten years younger than he was and he'd always thought of her as a baby herself. An equally strange image flittered into this mind—one of his friend Rush holding an infant in his arms. The thought brought a warm smile with it. When it came to the Navy, Rush knew everything there was to know. Every rule, every regulation—he loved military life. Rush was destined to command ships and men. But when it came to babies—why, Rush Callaghan wouldn't know one end from the other. One thing Steve did know about his friend, though—he knew Rush would love his children with the same intensity that he loved Lindy. Any brother and uncle-to-be couldn't ask for anything more.

"Rush will be a good father," Steve murmured, still smiling.

"So will you," Lindy countered.

Blood drained from his heart and brain at his sister's comment. "Yes," Steve admitted, and the word felt as if it had been ripped from his soul. He was going to love Carol's child; he accepted the baby then as surely as he knew the moon circled the earth. When the little one was born, he was going to be as proud and as pleased as if she were his own seed.

"Yes," he repeated, stronger this time, his heart throbbing with a newly discovered joy. "I plan on taking this parenting business seriously."

"Good," Lindy said, and opened her purse once more. She drew out a plastic dish and spoon. "I take it you and Carol are talking to each other now."

Smiling, Steve took a sip of his coffee and nodded, thinking about how well they'd "communicated" the day before. "You could say that," he answered, leaning back in his chair, content in the knowledge that once he returned they would remarry.

"There were times when I was ready to give up on you both," Lindy said, shaking her head. "I don't know anyone more stubborn than you. And Carol's so damn proud; there's no reasoning with her, either."

They'd both learned lessons in those areas. Painful ones.

"Take care of her for me, Lindy," he said, his eyes appealing to his sister. "I'm worried about her. She's so fragile now, delicate in body and spirit."

"I don't think she'll be working much longer, but I'll make a point of stopping in and seeing her as often as I can without being obvious about it."

Her job had been an area they'd both avoided discussing, because ultimately it involved Todd. As much as possible, Steve avoided all thoughts of the sporting goods store where Carol was employed.

"I'd appreciate that," he murmured.

"If you think it's necessary, I could suggest picking her up and driving her to work with me."

"That's miles out of your way."

"No, it isn't," she returned, giving him an odd look. "Rush's and my apartment is less than a mile from Carol's place. In fact, I drive right past her street on my way to work anyway. It wouldn't be any trouble to swing by and pick her up."

"True, but Larson's is the opposite direction from the Boeing plant."

"Larson's? What's Larson's?"

"Larson's Sporting Goods, where Carol works." Even saying it brought an unreasonable surge of anger. It had always bothered him to think of Carol having anything to do with the store.

"Carol doesn't work at a sporting goods store. She works for Boeing," Lindy informed him crisply, looking at him as though he'd recently landed from Mars. "She's been there over a year now."

"Boeing?" Steve repeated. "She works for Boeing? I... I didn't know that."

"Is Larson's the place she used to work?"

Steve nodded, wondering how much his sister knew about Carol's relationship with the owner.

"I think she mentioned it once. As I recall, they were having lots of financial troubles. She was putting in all kinds of extra hours and not getting paid. Not that it mattered, she told me. The couple who owned the place were friends and she was doing what she could to help out. I understand they're still in business. Carol never told me why she decided to change jobs."

Steve chewed on that information. Apparently for all their talk about honest communication they'd done a poor job of it. Again.

Lindy removed the lid from the Tupperware dish and started stirring some orange concoction that faintly resembled mashed carrots.

"Good Lord, that looks awful."

"This?" She pointed the spoon at the container. "Trust me, it's dreadful stuff."

"What is it?"

Lindy's gaze linked with his. "You mean you don't know?"

"If I did, do you think I'd be asking?"

"It's sweet potatoes."

"Sweet potatoes?" he echoed, wrinkling his nose. "What are you doing eating them at this time of year? I thought they were a holiday food."

"I just told you."

"No, you didn't." He didn't know what kind of guessing game Lindy was playing now, but apparently he'd missed some important clues.

"Rush and I are trying to get me pregnant."

"Congratulations, you already told me that."

"That's why I'm eating the sweet potatoes," Lindy went on to explain in a voice that was slow and clear, as though she were explaining this to a preschooler.

Steve scratched the area behind his left ear. "Obviously I'm missing something here."

"Obviously!"

"Well, don't keep me in suspense. You want to have a baby so you're eating sweet potatoes."

Lindy nodded. "Three times a day. At least, that was what Carol recommended."

"Why would she do that?"

Lindy offered him another one of those looks usually reserved for errant children or unusually dense adults. "Because she told me how well eating this little vegetable worked for her."

Steve's brow folded into a wary frown.

"Apparently she heard this report on the radio about yams raising a woman's estrogen level and she ate them by the bowlful getting ready for Christmas Eve with you." Lindy reached inside her purse and pulled out several index cards. "She was generous enough to copy down some recipes for me. How does sweet potato and ham casserole sound?" she asked, and rolled her eyes. "I don't think I'll be sampling that."

"Sweet potatoes," he repeated.

Lindy's gaze narrowed to thin slits. "That's what I just got done saying."

If she'd slammed a hammer over his head, the effect would have been less dramatic. Steve's heart felt as if it was about to explode. His mind whirled at the speed of a thousand exploding stars. A supernova—his own. Everything made sense then. All the pieces to the bizarre and intricate puzzle slipped neatly into place.

Slowly he rose to his feet, while bracing his hands against the edge of the table. His gaze stretched toward Seattle and the outline of the city as it faded from view.

"Steve?" Lindy asked, concern coating her voice. "Is something wrong?"

He shook his head. "Lindy," he said reaching for her hand and pumping it several times. "Lindy. Oh, Lindy," he cried, his voice trembling with emotion. "I'm about to become a father."

Nineteen

An overwhelming sense of frustration swamped Steve as the *Atlantis* sailed out of Hood Canal. As he sat at his station, prepared to serve his country for another tour, two key facts were prominent in his mind. The first was that he was soon to become a father and the second, that it would be three interminable months before he could talk to Carol.

He'd been a blind fool. He'd taken a series of circumstantial evidence about Carol's pregnancy and based his assumption solely on a series of events he'd misinterpreted. He remembered so clearly the morning he'd made his less-than-brilliant discovery. He'd gone into Carol's living room and sat there, his heart and mind rebelling at what he'd discovered…what he thought he'd learned.

Carol had come to him warm from bed, her eyes filled with love and laughter. He'd barely been able to tolerate the sight of her. He recalled the stunned look she'd given him when he first spoke to her. The shock of his anger had made her head reel back as though he'd slapped her. Then she'd stood before him, her body

braced, her shoulders rigid, the proud tilt of her chin un-
yielding while he'd blasted his accusations at her like
fiery balls from a hot cannon.

He'd been so confident. The sweet potatoes were only
the beginning. There was the knitting and the milk and
a hundred little things she'd said and done that pointed
to one thing.

His heart ached at the memory of how she'd swallowed her self-respect and tried to reason with him. Her
hand had reached out to him, implored him to listen.
The memory of the look in her eyes was like the mer-
ciless sting of a whip as he relived that horrible scene.

Dear God, the horrible things he'd said to her.

He hadn't been able to stop taunting her until she'd
told him what he wanted to hear. Repeatedly he'd
shouted at her to confirm what he believed until she'd
finally admitted he was too smart for her.

Steve closed his eyes to the agony that scene produced in his mind. She'd silently stood there until her
voice had come in desperate, throat-burning rasps that
sounded like sobs. That scene had been shockingly simi-
lar to another in which he'd set his mind based on a set
of circumstances and refused to believe her.

Steve rubbed a hand wearily across his face. Carol
had never had an affair with Todd. She'd tried to tell
him, begged him to believe her, and he'd refused.

"Oh, God," he whispered aloud, tormented by the
memory. He buried his face in his hands. Carol had en-
dured all that from him and more.

So much more.

Carol was miserable. She had six weeks of this pregnancy left to endure and each day that passed seemed

like a year. Next time she decided to have a baby, she was going to plan the event so that she wouldn't spend the hottest days of the summer with her belly under her nose.

She no longer walked—she waddled. Getting in and out of a chair was a major production. Rolling over in bed was like trying to flip hotcakes with a toothpick. By the time she made it from one position to another, she was panting and exhausted.

It was a good thing Steve wasn't around. She was tired and irritable and ugly. So ugly. If he saw her like this he would take one look and be glad they were divorced.

The doorbell chimed and Carol expelled her breath, determined to find a way to come to a standing position from the sofa in a ladylike manner.

"Don't bother to get up," Lindy said, letting herself in the front door. "It's only me."

"Hi," Carol said, doing her best to smile, and failing. "How do you feel?"

She planted her hands on her beach-ball-size stomach. "Let me put it this way—I have a much greater appreciation of what my mother went through. I can also understand why I'm an only child!"

Lindy giggled and plopped down on the chair. "I can't believe this heat," she said, waving her hand in front of her face.

"*You* can't! I can't see my feet anymore, but I swear my ankles look like tree trunks." She held one out for Lindy's inspection.

"Yup—oak trees!"

"Thanks," Carol groaned. "I needed that."

"I have something that may brighten your day. A preordered surprise."

With an energy Carol envied, Steve's sister leaped out of the chair and held open the front door.

"Okay, boys," she cried. "Follow me."

Two men marched through the house carrying a huge box.

"What's that?" Carol asked, struggling to get out of her chair, forgetting her earlier determination to be a lady about it.

"This is the first part of your surprise," Lindy called from the hallway.

Carol found the trio in the baby's bedroom. The oblong shaped box was propped against the wall. "A Jenny Lind crib," she murmured, reading the writing on the outside of the package. For months, every time she was in the JCPenney store she'd looked at the Jenny Lind crib. It was priced far beyond anything she could afford, but she hadn't seen any harm in dreaming.

"Excuse me," the delivery man said, scooting past Carol.

She hadn't been able to afford a new crib and had borrowed one from a friend, who'd promised to deliver it the following weekend.

"Lindy, I can't allow you to do this," Carol protested, although her voice vibrated with excitement.

"I didn't." She looked past Carol and pointed to the other side of the bedroom. "Go ahead and put the dresser there."

"Dresser!" Carol whirled around to find the same two men carrying in another huge box. "This is way too much."

"This, my dear, is only the beginning," Lindy told her, and her smile was that of a Cheshire cat.

"The beginning?"

One delivery man was back, this time with a mattress and several sacks.

Rush followed on the man's heels, carrying a toolbox in his hand. "Have screwdriver, will travel," he explained, grinning.

"The stroller, high chair and car seat can go over in that corner," Lindy instructed with all the authority of a company foreman.

Carol stood in the middle of the bedroom with her hand pressed over her heart. She was so overcome she couldn't speak.

"Are you surprised?" Lindy asked, once the delivery men had completed their task.

Carol nodded. "This isn't from you?"

"Nope. My darling brother gave me specific instructions on what he wanted me to buy for you—right down to the model and color. Before the *Atlantis* sailed he wrote out a check and listed the items he wanted me to purchase. Rush and I had a heyday in that store."

"Steve had you do this?" Carol pressed her lips tightly together and exhaled slowly through her nose in an effort to hold in the emotion. She missed him so much; each day was worse than the one before. The morning he'd left, she'd cried until her eyes burned. He probably wouldn't be back in time for the baby's birth. But even if he was, it really wouldn't matter because Steve Kyle was such an idiot, he still hadn't figured out this child was his own.

"And while we're on the subject of my dim-witted brother," Lindy said, turning serious, "I think you should know he was the one who bought you the maternity dress and the rattle, too."

"Steve did?"

Lindy nodded. "You two were going through a rough period and he didn't think you'd accept them if you knew he was the one who bought them."

"We're always going through a rough period," Carol reported sadly.

"I wouldn't say that Steve is so dim-witted," Rush broke in, holding up the instructions for assembling the crib. "Otherwise, he'd be the one trying to make sense out of this instead of me."

"Consider this practice, Rush Callaghan, since you'll be assembling another one in a few months."

The screwdriver hit the floor with a loud clink. "Lindy," Rush breathed in a burst of excitement. "Does this mean what I think it does?"

Steve wrote a journal addressed to Carol every day. It was the only thing that kept him sane. He poured out his heart and begged her forgiveness for being so stupid and so blind. It was his insecurities and doubts that had kept him from realizing the truth. Now that he'd accepted what had always been right before his eyes, he was astonished. No man had ever been so obtuse.

Every time Steve thought about Carol and the baby, which was continually, he would go all soft inside and get weak in the knees. Steve didn't know what his men thought. He wasn't himself. His mood swung from high highs to lower lows and back again. All the training he'd received paid off because he did his job without pause, but his mind was several thousand miles away in Seattle, with Carol and his baby.

His baby.

He repeated that phrase several times each night, letting the sound of it roll around in his mind, comforting him so he could sleep.

Somehow, someway, Steve was going to make this up to Carol. One thing he did know—the minute he was back home, he was grabbing a wedding license and a chaplain. They were getting married.

The last day that Carol was scheduled to work, the girls in the office held a baby shower in her honor. She was astonished by their generosity and humbled by what good friends she had.

Because she couldn't afford anything more than a three-month leave of absence, she was scheduled to return. A temporary had been hired to fill her position and Carol had spent the week training her.

"The shower surprised you, didn't it?" Lindy commented on the way out to the parking lot.

"I don't think I realized I had so many friends."

"This baby is special."

Carol flattened her hands over her abdomen. "Two weeks, Lindy. Can you believe in just two short weeks, I'll be holding my own baby?"

"Steve's due home around that time."

Carol didn't dare to hope that Steve could be with her when her time came. Her feelings on the subject were equally divided. She wanted him, needed him, but she would rather endure labor alone than have Steve with her, believing she was delivering another man's child.

"He'll be here," Lindy said with an unshakable confidence.

Carol bit into her lower lip and shook her head. "No, he won't. Steve Kyle's got the worst timing of any man I've ever known."

Carol let herself into the house and set her purse down. She ambled across the living room and caught a glimpse of herself in the hallway mirror as she walked toward the baby's bedroom. She stopped, astonished at the image that flashed back at her.

She looked as wide as a battleship. Everyone had been so concerned about the weight she lost when she'd been so sick. Well, she'd gained all that back and more. She'd become a walking, breathing Goodyear blimp.

Her hair needed washing and hung in limp blond strands, and her maternity top was spotted with dressing from the salad she'd eaten at lunch. She looked and felt like a slob. And she felt weird. She didn't know how to explain it. Her back ached and her feet throbbed.

Tired, hungry and depressed, she tried to lift her spirits by strolling around the baby's room, gliding her hand over the crib railing and restacking the neatly folded diapers.

According to Lindy and Rush, the *Atlantis* was due into port any day. Carol was so anxious to see Steve. She needed him so much. For the past two years, she'd been trying to convince herself she could live a good life without him. It took days like this one—when the sky had been dark with thunderclouds all afternoon, she'd gained two pounds that she didn't deserve and she felt so…so pregnant—to remind her how much she did need her ex-husband.

The doorbell chimed once, but before Carol could

make it halfway across the living room, the front door flew open.

"Carol." Steve burst into the room and slowly dropped his sea bag to the floor when he saw her. His eyes rounded with shock.

Carol knew she looked dreadful.

"Honey," he said, taking one step toward her. "I'm home."

"Steve Kyle, how could you do this to me?" she cried and unceremoniously burst into tears.

Twenty

Steve was so bewildered by Carol's tears that he stood where he was, not moving, barely thinking, unsure how to proceed. Handling a pregnant woman was not something listed in the Navy operational manual.

"Go away," she bellowed.

"You want me to leave?" he asked, his voice tight and strained with disbelief. This couldn't be happening—he was prepared to fall at her knees, and she was tossing him out on his ear!

With hands held protectively over her face, Carol nodded vigorously.

For three months he'd fantasized about this moment, dreamed of holding her in his arms and kissing her. He'd envisioned placing his hands over her extended belly and begging her and the baby's forgiveness. The last thing he'd ever imagined was that she wouldn't even listen to him. He couldn't let her do it.

Cautiously, as though approaching a lost and frightened kitten, Steve advanced a couple of steps.

Carol must have noticed because she whirled around, refusing to face him.

"I… I know the baby's mine," he said softly, hoping to entice her with what he'd learned before sailing.

In response, she gave a strangled cry of rage. "Just go. Get out of my house."

"Carol, please, I love you… I love the baby."

That didn't appease her, either. She turned sideways and jerked her index finger toward the door.

"All right, all right." Angry now, he stormed out of the house and slammed the door, but he didn't feel any better for having vented his irritation. Fine. If she wanted to treat him this way, she could do without the man who loved her. Their baby could do without a father!

He made it all the way to his car, which was parked in the driveway. He opened the door on the driver's side and paused, his gaze centered on the house. The frustration nearly drowned him.

Hell, he didn't know what he'd done that was so terrible. Well, he did…but he was willing to make it up to her. In fact, he was dying to do just that.

He slammed the car door and headed back to the house, getting as far as the front steps. He stood there a couple of minutes, jerked his hand through his hair hard enough to bruise his scalp, then returned to his car. It was obvious his presence wasn't sought or appreciated.

Not knowing where else to go, Steve drove to Lindy's.

Rush opened the door and Steve burst past him without a word of greeting. If anyone understood Carol it was his sister, and Steve needed to know what he'd done that was so wrong, before he went crazy.

"What the hell's the matter with Carol?" he demanded of Lindy, who was in the kitchen. "I was just there and she kicked me out."

Lindy's gaze sought her husband's, then her eyes widened with a righteousness that was barely contained. "All right, Steve, what did you say to her this time?"

"Terrible things like I loved her and the baby. She wouldn't even look at me. All she could do was cover her face and weep." He started pacing in a kitchen that was much too small to hold three people, one of whom refused to stand still.

"You're sure you didn't say anything to insult her?"

"I'm sure, dammit." He splayed his fingers through his hair, nearly uprooting a handful.

Once more Lindy looked to Rush. "I think I better go over and talk to her."

Rush nodded. "Whatever you think."

Lindy reached for her purse and left the apartment.

"Women," Steve muttered. "I can't understand them."

"Carol's pregnant," Rush responded, as though that explained everything.

"She's been pregnant for nine months, for God's sake. What's so different now?"

Rush shrugged. "Don't ask me." He walked across the kitchen, opened the fridge and took out a beer, silently offering it to Steve.

Steve shook his head. He wasn't interested in drinking anything. All he wanted was for this situation to be squared away with Carol.

Rush helped himself to a beer and moved into the living room, claiming the recliner. A slow smile spread across his face. "In case you haven't heard, Lindy's pregnant."

Steve stopped pacing long enough to share a grin with his friend. "Congratulations."

"Thanks. I'm surprised you didn't notice."

"Good grief, man, she could only be a few months along."

"Not her," Rush teased. "Me. The guys on the *Mitchell* claim I've got that certain glow about me."

Despite his own troubles, Steve chuckled. He paused, standing in the middle of the room, and checked his watch. "What could be taking Lindy so long? She should have phoned long before now."

Rush studied his own timepiece. "She's only been gone a few minutes. Relax, will you?"

Steve honestly tried. He sat on the edge of the sofa and draped his hands over his bent knees. "I suppose I'm only getting what I deserve." His fingers went through his hair once more. If this continued he would be bald before morning.

The national news came on and Rush commented on a recent senate vote. Hell, Steve didn't even know what his friend was talking about. Didn't care, either.

The phone rang and Steve bounced off the sofa as if the telephone had an electronic device that sent a shot of electricity straight through him.

"Answer that," Rush said, chuckling. "It might be a phone call."

Steve didn't take time to say something sarcastic. "Lindy?" he demanded.

"Oh, hi, Steve. Yes, it's Lindy."

"What's wrong with Carol?"

"Well, for one thing she's having a baby."

"Everyone keeps telling me that. It isn't any deep, dark secret, you know. Of course she's having a baby. My baby!"

"I mean she's having the baby *now*."

"Now?" Steve suddenly felt so weak, he sat back

down. "Well, for God's sake she should be at the hospital. Have you phoned the doctor? How far apart are the contractions? What does she plan to do about this?"

"Which question do you want me to answer first?"

"Hell, I don't know." His voice sounded like a rusty door hinge. His knees were shaking, his hands were trembling and he'd never felt so unsure about anything in his life.

"I did phone Dr. Stewart," Lindy went on to say, "if that makes you feel any better."

It did. "What did he say?"

"Not much, but he said Carol could leave for the hospital anytime."

"Okay…okay," Steve said, pushing down the panic that threatened to consume him. "But I want to be the one to drive her there. This is my baby—I should have the right."

"Oh, that won't be any problem, but take your time getting here. Carol wants to wash her hair first."

"What?" Steve shouted, bolting to his feet.

"There's no need to scream in my ear, Steven Kyle," Lindy informed him primly.

Steve's breath came in short, uneven rasps. "I'm on my way…don't leave without me."

"Don't worry. Now, before you hang up on me, put Rush on the line."

Whatever Lindy said flew out his other ear. Carol was in labor—their baby was going to be born anytime, and she was styling her hair! Steve dropped the phone to the carpet and headed toward the front door.

"What's happening?" Rush asked, standing.

Steve paused. "Lindy's with Carol. Carol's hair is in labor and the baby's getting washed."

"That explains everything," Rush said, and picked up the phone.

By the time Steve arrived at the house, his heart was pounding so violently, his rib cage was in danger of being damaged. He leaped out of the car, left the door open and sprinted toward the house.

"Where is she?" he demanded of Lindy. He'd nearly taken the front door off its hinges, he'd come into the house so fast.

His sister pointed in the direction of the bedroom.

"Carol," he called. He'd repeated her name four more times before he walked into the bedroom. She was sitting on the edge of the mattress, her hands resting on her abdomen, taking in slow, even breaths.

Steve fell to his knees in front of her. "Are you all right?"

She gave him a weak smile. "I'm fine. How about you?"

He placed his hands over hers, closed his eyes and expelled his breath. "I think I'm going to be all right now."

Carol brushed a hand over his face, gently caressing his jawline. "I'm sorry about earlier... I felt so ugly and I didn't want you to see me until I'd had a chance to clean up."

The frenzy and panic left him and he reached up a hand and hooked it around her neck. Gently he lowered her mouth to his and kissed her in a leisurely exploration. "I love you, Carol Kyle." He released her and lifted her maternity top enough to kiss her swollen stomach. "And I love you, Baby Kyle."

Carol's eyes filled with tears.

"Come on," he said, helping her into an upright position. "We've got a new life to bring into the world and we're going to do it together."

Sometime around noon the following day, Carol woke in the hospital to discover Steve sleeping across the room from her, sprawled in the most uncomfortable position imaginable. His head was tossed back, his mouth open. His leg was hooked over the side of the chair and his arms dangled like cooked noodles at his side, the knuckles of his left hand brushing the floor.

"Steve," she whispered, hating to wake him. But if he stayed in that position much longer, he wouldn't be able to move his neck for a week.

Steve jerked himself awake. His leg dropped to the floor with a loud thud. He looked around him as though he couldn't remember where he was or even who he was.

"Hi," Carol said, feeling marvelous.

"Hi." He wiped a hand over his face, then apparently remembered what he was doing in her hospital room. A slow, satisfied smile crept over his features. "Are you feeling all right?"

"I feel fantastic."

He moved to her side and claimed her hand with both of his. "We have a daughter," he said, and his voice was raw with remembered emotion. "I've never seen a more beautiful little girl in my life."

"Stephanie Anne Kyle," she told him. "Stephanie for her father and Anne for my mother."

"Stephanie," Steve repeated slowly, then nodded. "She's incredible. You're incredible."

"You cried," Carol whispered, remembering the tears that had run down the side of Steve's face when Dr. Stewart handed him their daughter.

"I never felt any emotion more powerful in my life," he answered. "I can't even begin to explain it." He raised her hand to his lips and briefly closed his eyes. "You'd worked so hard and so long and then Stephanie was born and squalling like crazy. I'd been so concerned about you that I'd hardly noticed her and then Dr. Stewart wrapped her in a blanket and gave her to me. Carol, the minute I touched her something happened in my heart. I felt so humble, so awed, that I'd been entrusted with this tiny life." He placed his hand over his heart as if it were marked by their daughter's birth and she would notice the change in him. "Stephanie is such a beautiful baby. We'd been up most of the night and you were exhausted. But I felt like I could fly, I was so excited. Poor Rush and Lindy, I think I talked their heads off."

"I was surprised you slept here."

He ran the tips of his fingers over her cheek. "I had to be with you. I kept thinking about everything I'd put you through. I was so wrong, so very wrong about everything, and yet you loved me through it all. I should have known from the first that you were innocent of everything bad I've ever believed. I was such a fool... such an idiot. I nearly ruined both our lives."

"It's in the past and forgotten."

"We're getting married." He said it as if he expected an argument.

"I think we should," Carol agreed, "seeing that we have a daughter."

"I never felt unmarried," Steve admitted. "There's only one woman in my life, and that's the way it'll always be."

"We may have divorce papers, but I never stopped being your wife."

The nurse walked into the room, tenderly cradling a soft pink bundle. "Are you ready for your daughter, Mrs. Kyle?"

"Oh, yes." Carol reached for the button that would raise the hospital bed to an upright position. As soon as she was settled, the nurse placed Stephanie Anne Kyle in her mother's arms.

Following the nurse's instructions, Carol bared her breast and gasped softly as Stephanie accepted her mother's nipple and sucked greedily.

"She's more beautiful every time I see her," Steve said, his voice filled with wonder. The rugged lines of his face softened as he gazed down on his daughter. Gently he drew one finger over her velvet-smooth cheek. "But she'll never be as beautiful as her mother is to me right this minute."

Love and joy flooded Carol's soul and she gently kissed the top of her daughter's head.

"We're going to be all right," Steve whispered.

"Yes, we are," Carol agreed. "We're going to be just fine—all three of us."

* * * * *